Praise for *It's Always the Husband*

"Readers will be left in an adrenaline-inducing 'whodunit' game, until the completely unpredictable conclusion. This book is perfect for fans of Liane Moriarty's *Big Little Lies*."
—*Redbook* magazine
(20 Must-Read Books for Spring)

"Demonstrating diabolical plotting chops and an ability to convincingly conjure settings, Campbell crafts a twisty page-turner."
—*Publishers Weekly*

"*It's Always the Husband* has great character development, allowing readers to really get inside the minds of the characters until the very end, where a shocking twist leaves readers stunned."
—*RT Book Reviews* (Top Pick)

"Campbell's debut novel is an intriguing whodunit that examines the explosive potential of secrets to destroy friendships, marriages, and lives. . . . A page-turner."
—*Kirkus Reviews*

"Riveting . . . keeps the tension high."
—Associated Press

"If you loved Liane Moriarty's *Big Little Lies*, put this thriller on the top of your list . . . you won't be sure 'whodunit' until the very (shocking) end."
—Today.com (Summer Beach Reads You Won't Want to Put Down)

"In the tradition of *Big Little Lies* comes the excellently titled *It's Always the Husband*, a thriller about three friends—frenemies, really—who met as college roommates. Twenty years later, one of them is standing on a bridge, with someone urging her to jump."
—*New York Post* (Recommended Reads)

"There's no shortage of drama and suspense in this novel about three college frenemies whose lives become inextricably linked after witnessing a mutual friend's death." —*InStyle* (7 Books You Won't Be Able to Put Down This Month)

"It's a whodunit suspense novel that will keep you guessing with every page." —Elle.com (6 Books to Cure Your *Big Little Lies* Withdrawals)

"A shocking page-turner from the first page to the addictive last, the whodunit that is *It's Always the Husband* will leave every suspense-loving mama stumped." —*POPSUGAR*

"The new page-turning thriller by Michele Campbell, *It's Always the Husband*, leaves readers guessing until the very last page." —*HuffPost*

"Jumping across time between three best friends' lives during college and adulthood, Campbell paints complicated relationships full of love and hate." —*Coastal Living* magazine (50 Best Books of Summer)

"A flawlessly spun whodunit tale that explores the delicate complexities of love-hate friendships, societal quickness to blame the husband, and the ghastly consequences of envy, [*It's Always the Husband*'s] readers will be in a delicious guessing game until the bombshell conclusion." —*SheKnows*

"A suspense that will not end as you expect! Seriously . . . it'll leave you hanging off a cliff!" —*FreshFiction*

"Michele Campbell's debut is a skillfully executed whodunit where virtually everyone is a viable suspect. . . . The twists and red herrings keep the pages turning. In the end, the truth comes out, but justice is a trickier question when everyone, victim included, ends up seeming a little bit guilty." —*Bookreporter*

"It's always the husband . . . or is it? This is the puzzling question readers will ask themselves as they devour this literary race of suspense, drama, and unpredictable twists. Don't miss this spectacular summer read that serves as a cautionary tale about the surprising depths of envy among friends." —*Working Mother*

"This suspenseful and captivating read takes on one of the most anticipated adventures of summer reading." —*Bookstr*

"Bubbling with drama and suspense, Campbell's debut novel tells a twisted tale of the complicated friendship of three women."
—*Metropolitan Luxe* magazine

"Secrets and scandals in an Ivy League setting. What could be more riveting? Michele Campbell's novel is a page-turning *Peyton Place*."
—Tess Gerritsen

"A brilliant, twisting read that kept me guessing until the final page. A roller-coaster friendship among three college roommates ends in murder years later—unless the husband did it. I read my eyes out!"
—Janet Evanovich

"A gripping, tangled web of a novel—it pulls you in and doesn't let you go. I loved it!" —Shari Lapena

"A skillful and addictive story of friendship, betrayal, and ultimately love, *It's Always the Husband* will keep you turning the pages until its dramatic end." —B. A. Paris

"A compelling and twisting story of friendship, buried secrets, and revenge, *It's Always the Husband* gets deep beneath the surface of the ties that bind. Intricately plotted and driven by an undeniable momentum, Michele Campbell's riveting story grabs on, holds tight, and haunts even after the book is closed. Don't miss it!" —Lisa Unger

it’s always the husband

it's always the husband

MICHELE CAMPBELL

St. Martin's Griffin
New York

This is a work of fiction. All of the characters, organizations, and events portrayed in this novel are either products of the author's imagination or are used fictitiously.

www.stmartins.com

The Library of Congress has cataloged the hardcover edition as follows:

Names: Martinez, Michele, 1962– author.
Title: It's always the husband / Michele Campbell.
Description: First edition. | New York : St. Martin's Press, 2017.
Identifiers: LCCN 2016050222 | ISBN 9781250081803 (hardcover) | ISBN 9781250081827 (ebook)
Subjects: | BISAC: FICTION / Suspense. | FICTION / Contemporary Women. | GSAFD: Suspense fiction.
Classification: LCC PS3613.A78648 I87 2017 | DDC 813/.6—dc23
LC record available at https://lccn.loc.gov/2016050222

ISBN 978-1-250-08181-0 (trade paperback)

Our books may be purchased in bulk for promotional, educational, or business use. Please contact your local bookseller or the Macmillan Corporate and Premium Sales Department at 1-800-221-7945, extension 5442, or by email at MacmillanSpecialMarkets@macmillan.com.

First St. Martin's Griffin Edition: May 2018

10

For my husband,
who has never tried to kill me . . .
as far as I know

I no doubt deserved my enemies
but I don't believe I deserved my friends.

—WALT WHITMAN

part one

1

Present Day
The Night of Her Fortieth Birthday

She stumbled through the dark woods, the trees dripping raindrops onto her hair and her party dress. Her shoes were covered in mud, and she trembled from the cold.

"Hey," she called out. "This is crazy. My shoes are soaked."

"Just a little farther."

She was out of breath, and her feet were killing her. It wouldn't be good for the baby if she tripped and fell. Then they rounded a bend. She got an open view ahead, and knew finally where they were. When she saw the ghostly shape looming in the distance, she stopped dead.

"*Why?*"

"You know why."

In a matter of minutes, they reached the foot of the bridge. A frigid wind blew in her face, carrying the scent of decaying leaves and ice-cold water. There were barriers across the bridge now, blocking access, and a profusion of warning signs. *Danger. Private Property. No Trespassing.* The signs were there for liability reasons, but from what she understood, the local kids still loved to make the breathless leap into the river. The more people who died here, the bigger the dare. Kids had no fear; they were young, and didn't know better. She could have told them. Somebody dies, and it changes the lives of those left behind, forever.

"I don't know what kind of point you're trying to make, bringing me here," she said, her voice shaking with tears. But she didn't turn back.

They walked forward a few paces, stepped over an old, tumbled-down metal fence and kept walking until they got to where the center of the bridge used to be. There it was, the abyss that he'd fallen through, the night he disappeared forever. She looked down and saw the water roiling against the rocks. The town had done a crappy job of boarding it over. They'd "fixed" it many times in the intervening years, but they were too cheap for the one fix that would work, which would've been to tear the evil thing down once and for all. Below, the water swirled and foamed. She could hear the roar from up here, over the pounding of her heart.

"No," she said, backing away from the edge.

"Go ahead."

"Go . . . *ahead?*"

"Go ahead and jump. You know you want to."

2

Twenty-Two Years Earlier

Aubrey Miller lugged her heavy duffel bag through ivy-covered Briggs Gate and let it drop to the ground, stopped in her tracks by her first real-life glimpse of Carlisle College's world-famous Quad. It was a gorgeous late-summer day, and she twirled around three hundred and sixty degrees, drinking in the sights and smells of the place. Green grass, old brick, towering trees. The promised land. Aubrey had been dreaming of this moment ever since she'd picked up a Carlisle brochure in her high school guidance office back in Las Vegas three years before. Now, against all the odds, after three years of nonstop studying and scheming, here she was. Carlisle was more beautiful than she'd dreamed. Pictures didn't capture the place. The sense of peace that flowed from the mellow brick, the cheery shouts of the students as they greeted each other. Everywhere she looked, she saw students with their families—the Carlisle student identifiable by the expensive backpack, the well-heeled dad toting cardboard boxes, the pretty mom with a designer handbag, the gaggle of younger siblings. Aubrey was here alone. Her financial aid didn't cover her mother flying across the country to the East Coast just for the frivolity of unpacking her clothes for her and tearing up when they hugged good-bye. She told herself that was just as well. Her mother, who'd dropped out of high school when she had Aubrey's sister at seventeen, would never fit in. She couldn't imagine a place like Carlisle, let alone know how to behave here.

Aubrey settled the duffel bag back onto her shoulder and got her bearings from the campus map that she'd tucked in the back pocket of her jeans. Her dorm was called Whipple Hall, and it was located somewhere along this exquisite quadrangle. At one end of the Quad was Founders' Hall, with the famous statue of Elias Carlisle holding up the lantern of knowledge. Once she spotted the statue, Aubrey knew where she was, and within moments she was gazing in wonder at the graceful brick façade of Whipple, her new home. She couldn't believe she'd get to live here, after spending her childhood in a succession of crappy apartments with leaky sinks and dank hallways. It was a miracle.

The entry foyer was dim after the bright sunshine. Aubrey followed signs to Registration and ended up in the dorm common room, where she handed her driver's license to the cheerful lady behind the desk. As the woman paged through boxes of envelopes searching for Aubrey's registration materials, Aubrey took in her surroundings. Dark wood paneling, a fireplace with an elegant marble mantel, a sparkling brass chandelier. The common room furniture was cozy and well used; the bookshelves full of old yearbooks and board games. She'd never been in a place with this much history in her life, not where she came from. Tons of famous people had graduated from Carlisle over the centuries. Scientists, writers—presidents, even. She could visualize them lounging here in this very room, engaged in dazzling conversation. She imagined studying here herself, on a cold winter night in front of a roaring fire, talking about ideas, or just drinking cocoa with her roommates.

Roommates.

The thought of her roommates made Aubrey's stomach sink. At the beginning of the summer, the Housing Office sent her their names, addresses, and pictures, and invited her to get in touch. The purpose seemed to be to encourage cooperation about setting up the room—who'd bring the mini-fridge, who'd bring the speakers, that sort of thing. Aubrey had nothing more to contribute than the clothes on her back, but she wrote anyway, because she longed to know these girls immediately. From the pictures and the limited biographical information provided in the mailing, Aubrey had spent hours daydreaming about them already. The blonde with the perfect turned-up little nose, who lived on Park Avenue and went to a fancy private boarding school, was a debutante, Aubrey imagined, who owned a horse and played tennis. The brunette with the glasses and gold-cross necklace was quiet, studious, and religious. But maybe she was wrong, and anyway, she was dying to know more, so she wrote two long, chatty letters asking each roommate all about herself—about her family, her high school, her likes and dislikes, what she planned to study, anything Aubrey could think of, really. She'd mailed the letters two months ago now, and checked the mail every day for their replies. She'd never heard back, not a word.

Aubrey had been so focused for so long on getting into Carlisle, then on the financial aid, the plane ticket, and making money to help her mother get her bills straightened out before she left, that she hadn't thought much about how life would be once she got here. Whenever she did, the debacle of the roommate letters loomed, and made her feel sick to her stomach. It was surely her own fault that they never replied. Aubrey wasn't good at friendship. Back home, she'd been in the advanced placement classes, studying constantly whenever she wasn't working at whatever part-time job she could find. She didn't think of herself as ambitious, just as somebody who really needed to get out. Her mother worked back-to-back shifts as a waitress, her father was out of the picture, her older sister slept where she wanted to and didn't come home for days at a time. Aubrey became a reader early so she wouldn't feel alone in her apartment at night. Books kept her company and became her friends; they were more welcoming than people, and less threatening. In her school, there were kids who wouldn't come near her because her family was so-called white trash, and other kids who would give her the time of day but were into drugs, and sex and partying, and would only drag her down. Then there were the nerds like her, who would rather study than hang out. The end result was no friends, and no social life. She didn't regret it. Look at the results. Here she was, eighteen years old, on the brink of realizing her dreams. But she didn't have a clue how to be a cool girl. No wonder the roommates hadn't written back.

All that was about to change. Her real life was starting. Whatever she'd done wrong before, she'd fix. If she'd been shy, she'd become the life of the party. If she'd been a nerd, she'd be the It Girl now. If she was skinny and gawky, she'd become thin like a model. No transformation was beyond her, not at this place. She'd make her roommates love her, no matter what it took.

The woman behind the desk handed her a packet.

"Key's inside, hon, suite 402," she said.

Aubrey thanked her and hauled her duffel bag out to the hall and up four flights of stairs. She stood outside the door to 402 for a minute, catching her breath and gathering her courage. As she rummaged in the envelope for her key, the door flew open, and a middle-aged woman rushed out, chattering in Spanish as she looked back over her shoulder.

"Ma, watch where you're going!" said a dark-haired girl, grabbing the woman's sleeve to stop her from plowing into Aubrey. "And speak English."

It was the roommate with the glasses, except she didn't have glasses anymore. Her pretty dark eyes and confident smile came as a surprise. She was intensely well groomed—perfect hair and makeup, cute capri pants and a starched white shirt—which immediately made Aubrey self-conscious about her crumpled traveling clothes and stringy hair.

"Jennifer?" Aubrey asked.

"It's Jenny, Jenny Vega. My mother was just leaving," she said.

The mother swept Aubrey into a bosomy embrace.

"*M'ija, cómo estás?* So happy to meet you. You come for supper Sunday, okay? I'm gonna make *pasteles.*"

"She doesn't want to come for supper, Ma."

Aubrey actually did want to—the hug had brought tears to her eyes, which she blinked back as she untangled herself—but she suspected it would be better for her future relationship with the cool and uber-well-groomed Jenny not to say so.

"Why you so mean?" Mrs. Vega said to her daughter.

"I'm not mean. It's time for you to go, that's all. See you Sunday. Love you." Jenny kissed her mother dismissively and gave her a little shove.

Mrs. Vega marched away, grumbling, and Jenny held the door open for Aubrey.

"I'm Aubrey, by the way."

"I figured. No parents? Lucky you," Jenny said, looking up and down at the hall.

"I came all the way from Nevada, so—"

"Oh, right. You said that in the letter."

"You got my letter? Why didn't you—?"

"I just got it a week ago. I was away all summer at this outdoor leadership camp thing in the Adirondacks."

"Wow. Cool."

"It was pretty lame actually. Looks good on the résumé though. C'mon in, I'll give you the tour. You're the last to show up, so you get the dregs, I'm afraid, but still, it's nice. For a dorm room, anyway."

Aubrey picked up her duffel and stepped into an adorable living room. The suite was on the top floor, under the eaves, with hardwood floors and quaint dormered windows. She spun around, wide-eyed, taking it in.

"Cute, right? The sofa smells though," Jenny said, wrinkling her nose. Jenny herself smelled of some fresh, springlike perfume. "I can probably get us something better from my parents' store. I'm a townie, if you haven't figured that out by now."

"A—townie?"

"You know, town and gown? I grew up right here in good old Belle River, New Hampshire, which would be the armpit of the universe if not for Carlisle. Born in the shadow of the college, as they say. But my parents aren't connected to the college, far from it. They own the hardware store in town."

"That's awesome. I'm jealous."

"Jealous of growing up here? Hah, don't be. The college looks down on the townies, you know. Carlisle is a head trip. You'll see. The *people*—I'm telling you," Jenny said, rolling her eyes.

"What do you mean?"

"*Kate,* for example. She showed up first and grabbed the single, even though the housing letter says to wait and decide together who gets which room. So you and I are stuck sharing the double whether we like it or not. There's a lot of that around here. You know, people all full of themselves, stepping on each other."

"Maybe she thought we wouldn't mind sharing the double."

"Why wouldn't we mind? Of course we mind."

"Well, maybe she didn't think about it."

"Yeah, that's the point."

"I'm sure if we talked to Kate . . ."

"Oh, I tried. She just acted all vague and sweet, like she didn't understand what my problem was. Bullshit. She knew exactly what she was doing. She thinks the rules don't apply to her, and the fact is, they don't. She's Kate *Eastman,* you know, like Eastman Commons? Like *President* Eastman?"

"President—who?"

"Her grandfather or something, or maybe great-grandfather, was president of the college. Her father's a trustee. Their name is on *buildings,* you catch my drift?"

"She isn't here now, is she?" Aubrey glanced around in alarm, worried about being overheard, and getting off on the wrong foot with this exalted personage.

"Don't worry," Jenny said. "She ran off when I got in her face about the room assignment. But I'll shut up about that now. You must want to unpack."

"I don't mind, really. I'm just excited to finally meet you."

"Aw, sweet," Jenny said, and Aubrey heard a note of condescension in her voice. But she was probably being paranoid.

The double turned out to be a bright, spacious room with dormered windows and a skylight. Aubrey loved it but didn't say so, lest she appear uncool. Jenny was being so welcoming, and a misstep from Aubrey might turn her off. The double had two of everything—matching twin beds, two wooden desks with chairs, two bookshelves, two modular wardrobes. Jenny had taken the side of the room with the nook for the bed and slightly more space. (Aubrey almost said something about that; by her own logic, shouldn't Jenny have waited? But she held her tongue. Don't rock the boat.) Jenny's bed was made up with a lavender and white polka-dot comforter and piles of pillows in varying shades of lavender and purple. A bulletin board hung over the bed, crammed with colorful photos of Jenny with her friends and family. Over the desk, there was a second bulletin board, this one meticulously laid out with the orientation schedule and class list, all neatly highlighted in pink. The desk lamp had a shade that exactly matched the comforter cover, and under the bed and on top of the armoire, there were a bunch of cute plastic storage units—also lavender—that looked like they'd been hand-selected by an expensive decorator.

"Your stuff is so pretty," Aubrey said, taken aback.

It had never occurred to her how rich people would be here. Even the townie girl was rich. Every dollar of Aubrey's work-study money was earmarked for tuition. She'd better get a second job ASAP, if she wanted to keep up with these people.

Jenny's glance flickered over Aubrey's ratty jeans and old Chuck Taylors, and the army surplus duffel on the floor.

"Hey, you know, if there's anything you forgot to bring, you should let me know, because we have a lot of extra stuff at the store," Jenny said.

She wasn't trying to be unkind, but the pity in her voice was palpable. Despite herself, Aubrey entertained Jenny's offer for a second. The frayed sheets crumpled up in the bottom of her duffel were pretty awful. She'd love some new ones, and a few cute plastic storage units, too. But she wasn't a charity case.

"No thanks, I'm good," Aubrey said.

"Oh, hey, I meant as a loan. Seriously, you'd be doing my parents a favor. The room décor items sit around gathering dust and taking up space. Customers don't come in for them because it's mainly a hardware store."

"Thank you, that's nice of you, but I'm fine. I'm not into material things."

That was a lie, and a pretty obvious one, but Jenny had the sense to let it go. She helped Aubrey unpack her stuff, which didn't take long. Orientation festivities officially kicked off in a couple of hours with a band and a barbecue on the Quad. In the meantime they walked around campus checking people out, went to the bookstore (where Jenny bought a Carlisle sleepshirt with their class year on it that she charged to her account, the concept of the bookstore charge account coming as a revelation to Aubrey), and got iced coffees at a perfect, grungy café on College Street called Hemingway's that looked and smelled exactly how Aubrey imagined a café should. They headed back to the Quad just as the barbecue was starting. The scent of charcoal and burgers floated on the velvety late-summer air, along with an occasional whiff of pot. A band played a cover of "Peace, Love and Understanding." Kids danced, and laughed, and hugged, and lounged on the grass. A bunch of cute guys with no shirts tossed a Frisbee, egging on a goofy yellow Lab that kept jumping up and trying to snatch the thing in midair.

Every freshman dorm had staked out its own patch of ground, where it set up blankets and camp chairs. Jenny and Aubrey made a beeline for the Whipple banner.

"There's Kate," Jenny said, pointing.

A bunch of guys had gathered around a petite girl in sky-high platform heels standing under the Whipple sign. Aubrey only semi-recognized Kate from the picture. The image she'd carried in her mind all summer was of a snooty country-club brat, but Kate in the flesh was more hippie princess, with long flaxen hair and a ruby in her belly button. She had a wide smile and a throaty rich-girl voice that caught Aubrey's ear as they approached. When she saw Jenny and Aubrey, she immediately turned her back on her admirers and walked straight toward them.

"The roomies return!" Kate screamed joyously, holding out her arms. "I've been looking *everywhere* for you two! Gimme some sugar, my sisters!"

Kate stumbled over her platforms, practically falling into Aubrey's embrace. She was tiny, with delicate bones, and she smelled of herbal shampoo, and reefer. Aubrey put her back on her feet.

"C'mere, you," Kate said, and hugged Jenny, too.

"My God, you're wasted," Jenny said, and giggled.

"Too true," Kate said with a laugh, righting herself. Her face was flushed and her eyes were bright. "It's college! I am out from under the watchful eye of my keepers, and ready to party with my bestest girlfriends. They say your freshman roommates become your best friends for life. So—shall we?"

Kate crooked her arms. Jenny took one, though only after a noticeable hesitation; but Aubrey laughed out loud with sheer happiness as she grabbed the other. In that moment, Carlisle opened up to her like a flower. Kate gave off waves of light and energy. Colors seemed brighter and the air felt softer in her company. Most of all, arm in arm with Kate, Aubrey felt like she belonged, like she was free to live the life she'd imagined. No wonder she'd been such a loner in high school. She'd known somehow that this amazing girl was out there, waiting for her, and she hadn't settled for less. Kate was the friend she'd been waiting for her whole life.

3

Jenny, you are *literally* a buzz kill," Kate said, over the whir of an electric fan. She paused with the match an inch away from the tip of the joint.

It was Saturday night, and classes started Monday morning. The three of them were draped across the new furniture that overflowed the cramped living room of suite 402. Jenny's father and brother had taken away the smelly couch and moved in a matching love seat and armchair upholstered in hot-pink suede. Kate immediately pronounced the new stuff "bourgeois," yet proceeded to lounge on it all afternoon in her cami-pajamas, with a cappuccino in a cardboard cup from Hemingway's perched on her bare stomach, talking on their shared room phone with some boy she knew from boarding school who was at USC now. (God, the phone bills the girl was racking up, that they'd probably have to chase her to pay, but it was impossible to stay mad at her.) The three of them were supposed to be getting ready to go out, but instead Aubrey felt marooned. They all did—weighed down by the heat, bathed in orangey-pink sunset that filtered through the skylight.

"Have it your way, then," Kate said.

She sighed and blew out the match. Aubrey admired Kate's delicate hands. Her chipped fingernails sparkled with sky-blue polish, and a spray of stars was tattooed on the inside of one wrist.

"I got all the way through high school without getting in trouble, and I don't plan to start now," Jenny said.

But there was no animosity in her voice. They were all lethargic, content to loll and idly chat. They'd been forecasting a thunderstorm, but it hadn't come yet, and the air coming in through the open windows was heavy and wet.

"Just for argument's sake, how exactly do you imagine we're going to get caught?" Kate asked.

"That fan does nothing to cover the smell. It blows it out into the hallway. I'm not judging you. Smoke if you want to, but if you do it here and the RA smells it, I'll get in trouble, too."

"That Asian girl? She would never rat us out."

"What does the fact that she's Asian have to do with it?"

"Nothing. She's some lowly biochem grad student. I could have her grant money pulled for looking at me the wrong way. Don't you understand what kind of protection you get by rooming with me?" Kate said.

"Well, I don't want that kind of protection. I don't agree with it."

"My, my, such an idealist," Kate drawled.

"Hey, it's after eight o'clock," Aubrey said. "Shouldn't we head out?"

They'd been through four deadly days of required orientation activities—team-building hikes, sexual harassment lectures, IT sessions where they learned to use Carly, the library's research database. Every night there had been pizza feeds, and bands, and open houses sponsored by some dorm or club. But tonight the true debauchery began. The first fraternity parties. Frat Row would be lit up like Times Square, and packed with hunky upperclassmen cruising for the tender flesh of freshman girls.

"If Miss Priss here is even coming," Kate said, but there was a note of affection in her voice.

"I'm thinking about it," Jenny said.

Aubrey sat up and reached for her sneakers.

"No you don't," Kate said. "Only geeks show up this early. And you're not going sober either. Not if you want to walk in with *me*. Where I come from, we pregame. Hold on a minute."

Kate got up and flounced off to her room.

"Have you registered for classes yet?" Jenny asked idly, considering her manicure.

"I thought we had until the end of next week," Aubrey said, sinking back down onto the sofa.

"Not if you want to take anything popular," Jenny said. "Popular classes fill up early. Tell me which courses you're thinking of, and I'll tell you if you should worry."

"I don't know. Maybe Renaissance Painting. Or Literature of the Outsider—I heard the prof for that is really amazing. Oh, and French New Wave Cinema, or Eastern Religions. There are so many."

Jenny frowned. "What do you do with courses like those?"

Kate came back, carrying a bottle of tequila and three paper cups.

"Courses like what?" she asked.

"Aubrey's thinking about taking Renaissance Painting and a bunch of other floofy stuff," Jenny said, smiling.

"*Floofy*?" Kate said, and laughed. "You're too much."

"You're saying those courses aren't practical," Aubrey said. "I get it, but why come to Carlisle if not to study things that inspire me?"

"Um, to get a job after?" Jenny said.

"What a bore," Kate said.

"Spoken like a girl with a trust fund," Jenny said.

"I swear, you are prejudiced against me, Jenny Vega, but I forgive you. Hey, I have an idea. I'll take Renaissance Painting, too, Aubrey. Then you can come to New York over break and we'll go to the Met and look at the paintings in the flesh," Kate said.

"Do paintings have flesh?" Aubrey said.

"Nudes do."

They laughed, pleased with their own cleverness. Kate sloshed a generous amount of tequila into each cup, releasing a bracing sting of alcohol into the steamy living room. Jenny made a face, which was a reaction to the smell of the alcohol, but Kate took it as a comment on her invitation.

"Don't be jealous, you can come to New York, too," Kate said, thrusting a cup at Jenny. "It's my personal mission to loosen you up. Once you're properly blotto, we'll go out and get you laid."

Jenny gave a snort of laughter and rolled her eyes, but she took the cup. Heavy drops spattered the skylight, and Jenny got up to lower the window sash. They spent the next hour drinking tequila and doing each other's makeup. Or rather, Jenny and Kate did Aubrey's makeup. Aubrey was missing the girly gene. She'd never been interested in the mall, or the cosmetics counter, never learned the tricks that made a girl attractive to boys. She was blessed with a tall, willowy figure and symmetrical features, but she was plain and rabbity-looking to her own eyes. Brows and lashes pale to the point of disappearing, lank hair, a shy manner. Her roomies transformed her. At their direction, she opened her eyes wide, sucked in her cheeks, puckered up. The tickly feel of the brushes on her face, the smell of alcohol on their warm breath, made the whole experience seem surreal, or maybe that was the effect of the tequila. When she looked in the mirror, Aubrey didn't recognize herself. They'd made her beautiful, with dramatic eyes and lovely cheekbones.

By the time they stumbled out of Whipple onto the Quad, the rain had stopped, and it had cooled off considerably. The sky was indigo, the air smelled sweet, and Aubrey felt like a new person. She also felt a raging headache coming on, but she didn't care. She'd borrowed a cute pair of cutoffs and a sexy top. Her new look made her brave, and what better thing to do with that feeling than go flirt with some frat boys?

Kate had a list of parties ranked in order of prestige. It was important to be seen at the right ones.

"The frats control social life on campus," Kate explained as they picked their way between puddles. "When you rush a sorority this spring, what the frats think of you will be made known, and it matters. Not for me, I can get in wherever I want. But for girls like you with no connections, having the guys think you're a cool girl, fun at parties, that can make all the difference."

"Oh please, what year is this, 1954?" Jenny said.

"In 1954, there were no women at Carlisle," Kate said.

"Exactly. You're a throwback, Kate. *If* I rush a sorority, which I haven't decided, it's because I want to network. Not 'cause I give a crap what some mentally deficient frat boy thinks of me."

"Don't listen to her. She'll spoil your fun," Kate said.

"Such fun," Jenny said. "These are the sort of places girls go into and they come out covered in bodily fluids."

"Sounds like a good time to me," Kate said.

They'd reached the far end of the Quad, and cut through Eastman Commons, which still smelled of the sauerkraut that had been served with dinner. On the other side of Eastman lay Dunsmore Avenue, a wide street that ran between the Main Quad and the Science Quad, and was open to vehicle traffic. The sidewalks on both sides of Dunsmore were lined with rowdy, drunken students heading to Frat Row. At the corner of Livingston Street—the official name for Frat Row—the crowd spilled over. Students were ignoring the red light and walking between cars to get to the parties faster. Drivers who honked were answered with cheerful fingers and strings of expletives. Kate stepped off the curb, pulling Jenny with her.

"C'mon, don't be a dweeb." They ran across the intersection, dodging cars and laughing.

"It's like you think I never jaywalked before," Jenny said, on the other side. They were all breathless.

"That's exactly what I think," Kate said.

"You prob'ly think I'm a virgin, too."

"Aren't you?"

"*No,*" Jenny said. "Not that it's any business of yours."

"I'm your roommate, it *is* my business," Kate said. "Anyway, *you* brought it up. Let me guess, some socially conscious Mormon boy from your leadership camp, tall, skinny, glasses?"

"Mormons don't do premarital sex," Aubrey piped in. "I know because there are a lot of Mormons in Nevada."

"It was a guy from my high school," Jenny said. "A hockey player," she added, to get a reaction out of Kate.

"A hockey player, seriously? No way! You never mentioned him."

"I've hardly told you my life story."

"Where are you hiding him? I want to see a picture. Spill, this instant."

"We agreed to cool it after graduation. You know, give each other space."

"That's big of you. No guy moves on from me, not if I can help it. They die first, of grief."

Aubrey was relieved when the crowd got so thick that they had to drop the conversation to concentrate on maneuvering. Kate would have interrogated her next, and she didn't want to admit to being the only virgin in the suite. Everything she did and said was wrong enough already.

Kate steered them toward the Sigma Sigma Kappa house, which supposedly had the hottest parties on Frat Row. A wedding-cake white mansion with a porticoed entrance and graceful balconies, ΣΣK was the grandest and most beautiful of all the grand and beautiful frat houses lining Livingston Street. It was known as the elite frat, with the richest boys, who had the best cars and clothes and connections, and were by far the most likely to end up at investment banks after Carlisle, with everything that entailed for their potential husband status. They were also considered the handsomest, although Delta Kappa Gamma, the jock frat, gave them a run for their money. Really, it depended on your taste, Kate said; they were all screwable, just in different ways.

The EEK front lawn teemed with girls dressed to the nines waiting behind a red-velvet rope to get into the party. Guys in colorful shorts and shirts walked up and down the line handing out red plastic cups. Occasionally they'd pull girls out of the line, leading to a chorus of "Pick me!" from those not chosen.

"This is disgusting," Jenny said.

"Would you chill? Hold on, I see a guy I know from Odell. Let me see if I can get us in," Kate said. She strode off toward a short, athletic-looking guy with a head of perfectly styled blond hair. He wore pink shorts and a navy blazer and looked straight off the yacht.

Odell Academy was the fancy boarding school Kate had graduated from. In the few days they'd been here so far, Aubrey had learned more than she imagined possible about the world of East Coast prep schools, whose alums ruled the tables in Eastman Commons. The prep school kids were all beautiful, with clear skin and the right clothes, good hair and boisterous, confident manners. There was an established pecking order. The boarding schools were on top, places like Exeter and St. Paul's, Andover, and Odell. The list went on; Aubrey didn't know all the names yet, but she would. Then came the prestige day schools from New York and D.C., Philly and Boston. All the prepster kids knew each other, or at least, they knew of each other. Or maybe it was just that they all *seemed* to know one another, because they dressed and behaved according to the same mysterious rules, rules Aubrey was only beginning to realize existed. Oh, there were public school kids, too—but they didn't matter. The kids from Stuyvesant and Bronx Science formed their own pale New York clique that people seemed to leave alone, even be slightly afraid of, but they didn't get asked to parties. Then there were strivers like Jenny, who had everything figured out for themselves and pretended not to care. But Aubrey knew better, she saw through that pose, and she didn't put on such airs herself. Kate and her friends represented the true Carlisle, and Aubrey would rather be a desperate tagalong scavenging their crumbs than be left out in the cold.

Kate hugged and kissed the guy in the pink shorts. After a minute, she turned and beckoned Aubrey and Jenny to come over.

"Smile," Aubrey said, standing up straighter. She'd never met a boy like that one before—rich and preppy and handsome—and she wanted to make a good impression.

"You're brainwashed," Jenny said, but she went along eagerly enough.

Kate introduced them to her friend.

"Griffin Rothenberg. Call me Griff," he said in a smooth baritone, taking Aubrey's hand and smiling into her eyes. His warm touch gave her a jolt, but then he turned and did the same thing with Jenny. He had nice manners, that was all. Anyway, you only had to look at him to see how dazzled he was by Kate.

With a glance and nod at another frat boy, Griff led them around the velvet rope. Inside, they got caught in a bottleneck at the top of the stairs that led down to the basement, where from the sound of it, the party was in full swing. Aubrey laughed nervously as the crowd crushed against them from behind. There was no air-conditioning, and the air was a hot funk of perfume and sweat and alcohol, with an undertone of vomit. Aubrey grabbed Jenny, feeling unsteady on her feet.

"Crazy," Jenny said.

The crowd surged forward and suddenly they were at the front. Aubrey saw what the holdup had been. A skinny guy wearing an orange bow tie—Carlisle's color—sat behind a desk that blocked the stairs down to the basement, wielding an ink pad and stamper. Griff pushed them forward.

"Yo, Rothenberg. You gonna pledge ΣΣK? We'd love to have you, dude," the bow-tied guy said.

"Planning on it."

"I'm supposedly checking IDs, but you're good. I know you."

Bow Tie marked Griff's hand with a stamp shaped like a beer bottle; then they bumped fists.

"Thanks, bro, and while you're at it, stamp my girl Kate Eastman from Odell, no ID necessary," Griff said.

"Kate Eastman. Remember me?" Bow Tie asked, looking starstruck.

"Uh—" Kate said.

"Duncan Treadwell. I roomed with your cousin Trevor at Milton, until he got kicked out. We met at a tailgate your freshman year at Odell."

"Ri-ight," Kate said, though it was obvious she didn't remember.

"Trev, what a wild man. I was sure he'd get into Carlisle, but I guess that little mishap with the DUI nixed it."

"Dead bodies are never a good thing on a college application," Kate said drolly. She held out her hand for a stamp, clearly uninterested in continuing the conversation.

"I assume you are of drinking age?" Duncan asked.

"Since I was twelve."

He laughed, and stamped her hand.

"My friends, too," she said.

Aubrey and Jenny got their hands stamped, and the foursome made its way slowly down the stairs. The basement was low-ceilinged and dimly lit. Hip-hop music blasted from speakers as people crowded around a keg.

"This way!"

Griff led them through a warren of rooms, all jam-packed with students standing around, or dancing, or making out on the ratty old couches. The floors were slick with spilled beer. The smell of it reminded her of her childhood: her father had been a drinker. Aubrey picked her way carefully to avoid slipping. Finally they reached a room that ran the length of the back of the house with French doors that opened out onto a stone patio. It was packed, too, but the air was less putrid. A card table in the corner held several large bowls of bright orange punch. Griff ladled drinks into plastic cups and handed them to the girls. The punch was sickeningly sweet, but had the virtue of being cold. Aubrey's raging headache disappeared with the first gulp, and she drained her cup quickly. A guy stepped up and refilled it for her.

"Thanks!" she said, glancing wistfully after Kate and Griff as they moved toward the French doors.

"You a frosh? Or as we prefer to say, fresh meat?"

"Yeah, I live in Whipple," she shouted. And just like that, she was talking to a cute boy. Not Griff-level cute, but cute enough.

She didn't quite catch his name—Brian? Ryan? He was a junior, from Tennessee, majoring in business administration, and played lacrosse. He had a nice body, a boyish grin, and reddish-brown hair. They shouted questions back and forth for a while, and by the time she looked up, Aubrey realized that her cozy little group was nowhere in sight.

"I should probably find my friends," she shouted over the music.

"Forget them."

"They'll be worried."

"They're too drunk to remember your name."

"No, really." The punch on top of the tequila was going to her head. The room had started to spin some time ago, but she was just noticing it.

"Fine, they're over this way," Brian/Ryan yelled, and took her hand. She let him pull her along even though she suspected he didn't actually know where they were, or even which friends she was talking about.

He led her into the darkest of the rooms. The couches and floor and pool table were covered with writhing bodies. Brian/Ryan shoved a couple of people aside and pushed Aubrey down into the corner of a creaky old sofa. Then he straddled her, pinning her to the sofa, and took her face in his hands.

"You're not half-bad-looking, you know," he said.

She couldn't help laughing. "Thanks."

He leaned down and pushed his tongue into her mouth. Aubrey thought about resisting, but at that same instant she was overcome with a wave of nausea, and had to concentrate completely to stop herself from hurling all over him. Unleashing a stream of vomit onto a frat boy would render her a social pariah from the start of her Carlisle career, so better to not make any sudden moves. The room went momentarily black, and Aubrey's head lolled back, which Brian/Ryan took as an invitation to yank her tank top aside and squeeze her boobs. The sharp pinch brought her to her senses, and she sat up fast, smashing her forehead into his nose. He yelped in pain. Aubrey seized the moment and shoved him off her, running for the patio with her hand over her mouth. The next thing she knew, she was on her knees in the dirt, spewing orange Kool-Aid vomit into a bush, hunkering down behind its branches to hide herself from view. Out of the corner of her eye, she saw a figure detach from the crowd on the patio. Aubrey's vision went blurry, and when it cleared a moment later, Jenny stood over her, holding her hair back.

"It's okay, let it out," Jenny said. "You'll feel better."

"Everybody saw," she said, her face wet with tears and snot.

"Nobody saw, I promise."

"There must be fifty people standing there."

"Every one of them's blind drunk."

"You're not."

"I'm the exception. Don't worry. Nobody cares." She stroked Aubrey's hair.

"I must smell like puke."

"It's a frat party. Everyone smells like puke. Here."

Jenny handed her a Kleenex, and Aubrey wiped her mouth.

"Still, it wouldn't be a bad idea to be more careful in the future," Jenny said. "Didn't your mom ever tell you, don't drink anything a boy gives you in a red plastic cup?"

Aubrey laughed weakly. "My mom isn't much for giving advice."

"Well, you have me now," Jenny said.

It was true. Aubrey couldn't believe her luck. Through a stroke of good fortune, she'd found the perfect roommate combination—Kate to get her into trouble, and Jenny to get her out.

4

That fall, Kate frequently mentioned the idea that the other two girls should visit her in New York. Whenever Jenny tried to follow up and set a specific date (she liked to keep an orderly calendar), Kate would get all vague and wave her off. Vagueness—a Kate specialty when confronted with anything she didn't feel like dealing with at that moment. After a while, Jenny figured the invitation was BS, like a lot of stuff Kate said, and let the subject drop. She was busy with classes, and chorus, and had been elected freshman rep to the student council from Whipple. She worked at the hardware store every Saturday, and had taken a second part-time job, typing and filing in the provost's office, because she wanted to learn how the college ran. (She was the first freshman ever hired by the provost, in fact.) It would have been a struggle to fit a trip to New York into her crazy schedule anyway.

Late one night a couple of weeks before Thanksgiving break, Jenny switched off her desk lamp and got into bed. The lavender comforter cover was freshly laundered, and she snuggled down under it, curling and uncurling her toes and trying to unwind from the difficult econ problem set she'd been working on. Aubrey had gone to bed an hour earlier, and Jenny assumed she was long asleep.

After a few minutes in the dark, however, Jenny became aware of quiet sniffling emanating from Aubrey's bed.

"Aubrey?" she whispered.

The sniffling stopped.

"Aubrey, are you crying? What's wrong?"

Aubrey broke into muffled sobs. Jenny sighed, threw the covers back, and climbed in next to Aubrey in the other bed. As usual, she was torn between feelings of tenderness and irritation for her roommate, who'd been having trouble getting her footing at Carlisle, and seemed to lurch from one crisis to the next. The only time Aubrey ever looked happy was tagging along with Kate to parties.

"What is it, sweetie? Tell me," Jenny said, stroking Aubrey's shaking back. "Is it about a boy?"

"No."

"Then what?"

"I . . . can't . . . go . . . home," Aubrey forced out between sobbing breaths.

"Home? You mean home for break, to Nevada?"

Aubrey nodded miserably, dissolving into sobs again. Jenny hopped out of bed, grabbed a box of Kleenex from her desk, and switched on the lamp.

"Here, sit up," she said, resuming her place next to Aubrey.

Aubrey sat up and blew her nose. "I can't afford the plane ticket. The dorms are closed for a week."

"Why didn't you say something? You'll come home with me. You know you're always welcome. Problem solved."

"Thank you. I'll take you up on that. But it's not the only problem."

"What, then?"

"I don't know where my mother is," Aubrey said, bursting into tears again.

"I don't understand. Did she go somewhere?" Jenny handed her another Kleenex, and Aubrey mopped her face.

"Her phone is disconnected. That happens sometimes. She waitresses, she doesn't always have enough to cover her bills. And even when she does, she isn't always organized enough to pay them. I used to handle that. I probably still should, it's just, with everything . . ."

"Of course. I'm so sorry, that's awful."

Jenny genuinely felt terrible for Aubrey. She couldn't imagine what it would be like, not only to have such money problems, but to be uncertain where your own mother was. Jenny's mother phoned her twice a day, and if Jenny didn't call back right away, she worried there was something wrong and called again. To not hear from your own mother was beyond her comprehension. Surely there was somebody back home who could help Aubrey get in touch. Jenny knew surprisingly little about Aubrey's home life, because Aubrey rarely chimed in when they talked about their families. Jenny had noticed this silence and tried to be sensitive to it, but now she felt compelled to ask.

"Is your father in the picture, or are your parents divorced? I'm sorry, I hope you don't mind if I ask."

"Ugh, I can't talk about this," Aubrey said, flopping down and pulling the pillow over her head. Jenny tugged it aside.

"Hey. Come on, divorce is nothing to be ashamed of in this day and age."

Aubrey looked at her with watery eyes. "If you want to know the truth, it's a lot worse than divorce. My parents never got married. My dad drove a long-haul truck, and my mom was like, his road girlfriend. She says he had another family somewhere, and one night he drove away and never came back. I'm so ashamed. Don't tell anyone? Please?"

"Of course not. I would never. This is not your fault. You're the victim. It must have been terrible for you. How old were you when it happened?"

"I was three. It's not like I missed him or anything. All I remember about him is the smell of beer. But after he left, things were rough financially. My mom couldn't catch a break. Vegas is a tough town for a woman. She was pretty when she was younger, and she made decent money waitressing. But she got old fast. And she didn't have the gumption to make a move. You know, take a GED course, learn to type. She never got her act together, and she lost one job after another. Once I was old enough to work, I did my best to help out. But then I left."

"Well of course you did, and I'm sure she wanted you to. Who'd want their kid to pass up a Carlisle scholarship? But wait, don't you have an older sister? Amanda, right? Why can't she check on your mom and help her get her phone turned back on?"

Aubrey's sister was in her early twenties, and worked as a cocktail waitress in one of the big hotels on the Strip in Las Vegas. She'd been in and out of trouble. Jenny knew the two of them weren't close.

"I tried, believe me, but Amanda doesn't return my calls," Aubrey said.

"Give me her number. I'll call her."

Jenny was relentless when it came to solving problems. Over the next couple of days, she left a series of increasingly urgent messages for Aubrey's sister. When she didn't hear back, she got the number of the hotel where Amanda worked and called the manager four times in a single afternoon demanding to talk to Amanda regarding a family emergency. That finally resulted in an expletive-laden return message from Amanda, left on the answering machine on the room phone. Buried among the swear words was the revelation that Mrs. Miller was fine, just temporarily without a telephone, so Jenny should back the hell off and tell that whiny idiot Aubrey to get bent.

Jenny played the message for Aubrey, who hugged her, with tears in her eyes, and whispered, "Thank you, thank you, thank you," over and over again.

"Don't mention it," Jenny said, basking in the gratitude as she rubbed her roommate's back. She loved helping someone in need, and Aubrey provided ample opportunity to do that.

Despite what seemed to Jenny to be an extremely satisfactory resolution to Aubrey's quandary, as Thanksgiving approached, Aubrey seemed increasingly depressed. In fact, Jenny noticed, she was growing paler and sadder—and also thinner, since she'd nearly stopped eating—with each passing day. This disappointed Jenny, who liked to see more concrete results from her efforts. It also alarmed her.

Jenny reviewed the protocols in her dorm rep handbook for what to do if you suspected that a student suffered from untreated or undiagnosed depression, anorexia, or any other of a long list of mental or emotional challenges. The first step was alerting the dorm RA, but Jenny dismissed that out of hand. Whipple's RA—a biochem grad student named Chen Mei—was rarely around, and when she was, she made it very clear that she'd taken the position for the free housing, and wasn't interested in being bothered with actual student problems. The handbook next counseled reporting Aubrey to Student Health Services or the dean of students' office, which could force Aubrey into a mental health evaluation, or even make her take a leave of absence to seek treatment. The thought of taking such drastic measures horrified Jenny. She was a friend, not a rat. She had to help Aubrey on her own, without getting the administration involved and possibly getting Aubrey in trouble.

But maybe not entirely on her own.

Aubrey idolized Kate, and tagged along with her everywhere. To meals, to parties, anywhere Kate would allow. She'd even bought some Nice'n Easy from the drugstore, in a shade called Palest Blonde, and dyed her mouse-brown hair a color practically identical to Kate's. Nobody but Jenny seemed to find this odd; everyone just said how great Aubrey looked. If Jenny weren't too busy to care, she might even feel hurt over how much Aubrey obviously preferred Kate's company, especially given that Kate was a snobbish bitch, and made Aubrey do menial things for her, like running out to Hemingway's for a cappuccino, or going to early lectures and taking notes when Kate didn't feel like getting out of bed—even for classes Aubrey wasn't enrolled in. (She claimed to enjoy it, but come on.) Jenny wasn't petty. She wanted Aubrey to be happy, and it was time for Kate to start pulling her weight as a friend to make that happen. Jenny just needed to make Kate step up.

On the Tuesday evening before Thanksgiving break, the Quad felt silent and melancholy. A lot of kids had already left for home, and a chill rain had been falling for days. The cobblestone paths were slick with wet leaves that stuck to Jenny's waterproof boots. She wished it would snow—at least that would be pretty. Near Whipple, the air smelled of woodsmoke, and she poked her head into the common room before heading upstairs, hoping to find a fire roaring in the fireplace, but the room was empty and the grate cold. Up in 402, the suite was dark except for a strip of light under Kate's door. Jenny hurried to put away her coat and backpack, the quick trip to the double confirming that Aubrey was out, and that it would be the perfect time to speak to Kate about helping out their roommate.

As she knocked on Kate's door, Jenny heard giggling.

"Come in," Kate called.

"Sorry, I didn't realize you had company," Jenny said, pushing the door open.

"It's cool. We're not naked. *Yet,*" Kate said, with a naughty laugh.

Kate was on her bed, tangled up with a dark-haired guy whose back was to Jenny. Kate's shirt and the guy's sweatshirt and jeans were on the floor at Jenny's feet. The guy turned around, a goofy grin on his face. When Jenny saw who it was, she froze.

"This is Lucas," Kate said.

"I—we know each other," she managed to say.

"*Jenny,*" the guy said, his grin disappearing fast. Jenny glanced down instinctively at his briefs, and saw something deflating there, too.

"Jesus," Lucas said, and grabbed his pants, hopping as he shoved his feet into the legs.

"What's the rush, Luke?" Kate said, amused. "Jenny's seen guys pantsless in my bed before. Nothing shocks her."

But Jenny was shocked.

"Sorry, gotta run," Lucas said. He stuck his feet into his sneakers and grabbed his shirt and backpack. A second later, the girls heard the front door slam.

"What was that about?" Kate asked.

"I'm sorry, what?"

"He hightailed it out of here like he saw a ghost."

Jenny shook her head. "I wouldn't know."

Kate wore nothing but jeans and a black push-up bra. Her mouth was raw from making out. The sight of it had Jenny flashing on what it felt like to kiss Lucas when he hadn't shaved, and how she'd savor the irritated feeling the next day—that proof that they'd been together. Jenny watched in sick fascination as Kate picked up a tube of lip balm from her nightstand and slicked shiny goo over her reddened lips. Everything about

Kate radiated sex. The ruby glinting dully in her belly button, the jeans that fit just so. Yet Kate never appeared trashy. Even when she acted like a slut, there was a classiness about her. She was playing with her golden hair now, twisting it into a messy braid at the nape of her neck without the benefit of a hair elastic. Jenny kept a basket on her desk filled with scrunchies and headbands and hair clips to match every outfit, yet with all the work that went into her hair, it never looked half as good as Kate's unwashed, unstyled locks did. Kate made it all seem effortless, like she didn't care, and didn't have to work for anything. No wonder Lucas was into her. Guys loved girls who didn't give a shit. Jenny's problem was that she cared too much.

"You look upset," Kate said suspiciously. "Is something wrong?"

"I'm sorry if I interrupted," Jenny said.

"Don't give it another thought. I have to pack tonight so I wasn't up for a hookup anyway. How do you know Luke?" Kate asked, standing up to pull on her shirt.

Lucas, Jenny thought, annoyed to no end to hear Kate call him something different than anybody else did, as if he belonged to her. Then Jenny noticed the fresh hickey on Kate's neck, and had a momentary vision of slamming Kate's head against the wall.

"We went to high school together," Jenny said, bracing for the obvious follow-up question. *Is he that hockey player you say you lost your virginity to?* But the question didn't come. Kate had probably forgotten the whole conversation they had the night they went to that first frat party. They were drunk enough—thankfully. She hoped Kate would never make the connection.

"No kidding, Luke's a townie?" Kate said. "He's so different from those pimply boys who work in the dining hall, I never would have guessed."

Jenny normally would've jumped all over that comment, but she had no interest in talking about Lucas with Kate for a moment longer than necessary.

"I thought you were dating Griff," Jenny said, to change the subject, and because it was the first thing that popped into her head. Griff from the frat party was one guy Jenny had definitely seen naked in Kate's bed, on several occasions.

"What are you, the dating police?" Kate said.

"You're right. It's not my business."

Griff was none of her business. Lucas, on the other hand—

Kate grabbed a pack of Marlboro Lights from her desk, and looked at it, hesitating. "Hmm, should I smoke a cig if we didn't bang? Oh, what the hell. Want one?"

Jenny had never smoked in her life. But she needed a distraction to help her deal with the bombshell, so she took a cigarette, and accepted Kate's light. When she inhaled, she willed herself not to cough, so Kate wouldn't notice that it was her first time and rib her about it. Though Kate was so obtuse when it came to other people's feelings that Jenny probably didn't need to worry.

Not this time, however.

"So were you close with Luke in high school?" Kate began.

"Forget Lucas, we need to talk about Aubrey," Jenny blurted. "It's really important. I'm worried about her."

"About how skinny she's getting?" Kate said, falling for Jenny's change of subject.

"You noticed."

"How could I not? I've been worrying about her, too. Do you think she's anorexic?"

"Maybe. Or maybe just depressed. She has problems at home."

"Poor thing. Money troubles?"

The cigarette made Jenny's head hurt, so she stubbed it out in the Carlisle mug that Kate used as an ashtray, and proceeded to explain the situation with Aubrey's mom.

"She never told me any of that," Kate said, which gave Jenny some satisfaction.

"She's worried you won't like her if you know she's poor," Jenny said.

"You can't really think I'm that shallow. Besides, obviously I know she's poor. Look at how she dresses. The same four skanky T-shirts in endless rotation."

"The thing is, she confides in me, and yet she doesn't always take my advice. I was thinking we should join forces. You know, sit her down and have a heart-to-heart. Sort of like an intervention. She would listen to you."

"I have a better idea," Kate said.

It annoyed Jenny that Kate dismissed her proposal so glibly. Just then, the front door opened, and they heard Aubrey bustling around in the living room.

"In here, Aubrey!" Kate called.

Aubrey walked in, bringing a scent of fresh, cold air. Snowflakes melted in her hair and on her eyelashes.

"It's snowing!" she announced, scooping snow off her thrift-store peacoat and holding her wet fingers out for them to inspect. "Isn't it wonderful? I've never seen snow before."

"How fabulous," Jenny said indulgently.

Kate dragged on her cigarette. "Enjoy it tonight, because tomorrow it'll be covered in dog pee."

Jenny took a deep breath, thinking about how best to broach this difficult subject with Aubrey.

"Guess what?" Kate said, before Jenny could get a word out.

"What?"

"Jenny and I were just saying how you seem a little blue lately, like maybe you could use a pick-me-up. So both of you are going to come to New York with me over Thanksgiving break!"

Jenny opened her mouth to protest. Aubrey was coming home with *her* for Thanksgiving. Her mom had already made up the guest room and planned the menu.

"Oh my God, really?" Aubrey shrieked, jumping up and down and throwing her arms around Kate. "That is the best thing I have ever heard! I'm so happy."

When Kate met Jenny's eyes over Aubrey's shoulder, Jenny could've sworn she saw a look of triumph there.

5

Jenny fell asleep on the train to New York and dreamed of Lucas. Nothing surreal, just an incredibly vivid experience of being with him, complete with sounds and smells and tastes. It was the worst type of dream she could have had at that moment. The two of them were alone together in the yearbook office late at night, talking and making out. The yearbook office was the one place they could spend time together without raising eyebrows. He was a jock and she was a brain, and in their school, those cliques didn't mix, so they were keeping their relationship on the down low for the time being. And that's where it stayed: they never ended up going public. If a tree falls in the forest and nobody hears, was Lucas really her boyfriend?

In the dream, she asked to see the photographs he'd taken that day, and he showed her one of them kissing. (This couldn't happen in real life. No photograph existed of them kissing, which made her sad to think about.) Jenny laughed and looked up into Lucas's eyes. You would call his eyes brown like hers, yet the word hardly captured them. They had flecks of gold and hazel that sparkled in the light. In the dream, Lucas wore his old blue Cape Cod T-shirt. She put her hands on his shoulders, feeling the hard muscles underneath the soft fabric, and moved her hands down to caress his bare arms. His skin was smooth and velvety. He took her hands, turning them over and kissing the underside of her wrists, then kissing her palms, and her heart went crazy. She felt the familiar heat in the pit of her stomach as he leaned in to kiss her. And then his kiss—soft and slow, his tongue exploring her mouth, yet hard at the same time, his chin bristly, his mouth aggressive.

The train jerked, and Jenny woke to the awful knowledge that it was only a dream. They weren't together anymore. Officially, they never had been. She had tried to banish him from her thoughts, but since she'd seen him in Kate's bed, he'd come back with a vengeance. When she looked out the window, the world seemed ugly. New England in November, viewed from the train tracks in the waning light, was a wasteland of sagging clapboard houses coated in a dirty snow that looked like ash. Some of the houses were three-families like the one her family lived in in Belle River, though her parents' house was in much better condition—perfectly kept, in fact. Her parents lived on the top floor, where Jenny's bedroom always awaited her return. Her older brother, Chris, occupied the apartment on the second floor. He'd come back from the army not quite the same, and her parents treated him like a conquering hero even though he'd never seen combat. Jenny suspected a substance abuse problem, but her snooping around his apartment had turned up nothing, so maybe she was wrong about that. Chris played video games and worked at the store, where he handled deliveries and moved boxes. The idea that Chris had the chops to take over the business someday was a fantasy, but it wasn't her problem, so long as her parents didn't start looking to her. She planned to get out of Dodge the second she had a diploma in her hand. She'd told them so, many times. Her mother kept saying that Jenny would change her mind. The first-floor apartment, currently rented out, had Jenny's name on it as far as her mother was concerned, no matter how often or how loudly she said she didn't want it. That reckoning could wait, however. At present Jenny was busy dealing with the fallout of abandoning her family to go to New York for Thanksgiving. Her mother actually cried when Jenny told her about the change of plans over the phone. Jenny had to make a special trip home before departing, where she sat at the kitchen table for half an hour explaining Aubrey's problems in gory detail, and how going to New York would cheer her up, before her mother grudgingly consented.

"Oh, you're awake," Aubrey said.

Jenny looked around. "Where's Kate?"

"She saw some girls from Omega Chi, and they said for her to go up to first class and sit with them. They want her to rush in the spring."

"Can you do that? Sit in first class if you didn't pay for it?"

Aubrey shrugged and smiled, as if to say, *Kate can.*

"Isn't it great?" Aubrey said, gesturing at the cold scene outside the window.

You're delusional, Jenny thought, but she said nothing, pulling her psychology textbook out of her backpack and pretending to do homework so Aubrey would leave her alone.

On its final approach to Penn Station, the train entered a pitch-dark tunnel and began to buck and wheeze, like it was having second thoughts about the trip to the city. Aubrey looked at Jenny wide-eyed.

"Is this normal?" she asked.

"Yeah, it's fine. Don't worry," Jenny said, trying to sound jaded.

Jenny had been to New York City several times at Christmas, to see the Radio City Christmas show with her mom, and she felt like an old pro, like the place belonged to her as much as it did to Kate. Her confidence was put to the test as the train pulled into the station, and Kate was nowhere to be seen. It would be just like Kate to forget all about them. What would they do if they lost track of her? Jenny hadn't brought along Kate's address or home phone number, since they expected to sit with her on the train. She thought she remembered Eightieth and Park, but was that enough information for them to find their way?

People began collecting their belongings from the overhead rack.

"Hurry up, get your things," she said to Aubrey. "We need to find Kate."

Out on the platform, that old New York City subway smell hit Jenny in the face, and she felt excited about the trip for the first time. She could handle Manhattan. The place was a grid. If you could count, you could navigate. She imagined living here—less than four years from now—going to work in a shiny office tower, in a suit and heels, carrying a briefcase.

They spotted Kate's bright hair in the distance, heading up the escalator, and hurried to catch up with her. Outside in the cold, Kate beckoned to them from the open door of a yellow cab. The driver popped the trunk. They heaved their luggage in and piled into the backseat of the taxi laughing breathlessly. On the ride uptown, Jenny craned her neck and drank in the tall buildings. She really should put Lucas—and Kate in bed with Lucas—out of her mind, and enjoy this trip, or she'd be wasting an opportunity, and Jenny hated waste. On Park Avenue, Christmas trees lined the medians. Their white lights twinkled against the blue of the evening sky, making her happy, until Kate killed the mood by warning them about what to expect.

"Beware the stepmonster," she said.

Kate's mother had died of cancer when she was ten, and she was on her second stepmother.

"Victoria hates me. She'll be all sorts of nasty when she sees you because she'll hate you by association. Ignore her. Dad will run interference, since you're from Carlisle, and anything Carlisle is cool with him."

"Wait a minute. They know we're coming, right?" Jenny said.

Kate waved her hand airily, and Jenny's stomach fell.

"Relax. It's fine," Kate said.

The cab came to a stop in front of a stately brick building. A uniformed doorman rushed over and open the door. He was jolly, with a silver mustache and a big smile, and wore a jaunty cap with earflaps.

"Welcome home, Katie," the doorman said, in a nasal New York accent, then knocked on the driver's window. "Open the trunk, my friend."

"Hey," Kate said, waving at the doorman perfunctorily as she jumped out and hurried into the lobby.

The sidewalk was wide here, and spanking clean. Well-dressed people glided by in both directions, some in furs, others walking fussy little dogs. Jenny stepped hesitantly from the cab. Kate was inside already, and the doorman was pulling bags from the trunk of the taxi and loading them onto a shiny brass luggage cart. Apparently their bags would be taken care of, but what about the cab fare? Jenny reached for her wallet, trying not to feel resentful. She was getting free lodging in New York, after all, and she knew Aubrey couldn't afford to cover the meter. Hopefully they wouldn't be taking too many cabs, or she'd end up with no money to buy Christmas presents this year.

The lobby sparkled in the light of a tall Christmas tree and an enormous crystal chandelier. Kate stood inside the open elevator, practically bristling with anxiety and impatience. It had never occurred to Jenny before that Kate might be nervous to come home.

"Let's *go*," Kate said.

"Our bags," Jenny said.

"Gus'll bring 'em up in the service elevator."

A second doorman lurked in the corner of the elevator, operating the old-fashioned controls. He slid the door closed noisily with a brass handle, and they started to climb. The elevator was dark and smelled of lemon furniture polish. A moment later, it deposited them directly into the Eastman apartment. The girls stepped into a grand entry gallery with a black-and-white checkerboard marble floor. There was no obvious place to put their boots and coats, only a carved table with a claw-foot base that held a tall vase of lilies, and impressive oil paintings on the walls. Three tow-headed boys, who all looked to be under the age of eight, came running into the foyer, shouting Kate's name.

"My favorite monsters!" she cried, patting them like puppies as they hugged her legs. Over their heads, she rolled her eyes at Jenny and Aubrey. "Every time Victoria pops out a little Eastman, my inheritance shrinks. Plus there's my stepsister Louise. She's not here, she lives in Switzerland with her mother. They spend money like it's water."

Money must be the source of the conflict, then. Certainly when Victoria came out to greet them a moment later, she didn't seem remotely like a monster. To the contrary, she was young and pretty, with expensively highlighted hair, and did her best to be gracious in receiving her stepdaughter's unexpected guests.

"A crowd at Thanksgiving, how jolly," she said, smiling tightly. "Plenty of food, and we'll make room at the table. I'll have Gus bring up some caterer's chairs from the storage room."

Kate hugged her stepmother hello and they exchanged pleasantries. Every word out of Kate's mouth dripped with contempt, no matter how innocuous the literal meaning. Comments as seemingly agreeable as "Don't you look fab" and "What gorgeous earrings. Are they new?" carried a poisonous undertone that was as apparent to Jenny as it surely was to Victoria.

Victoria showed them to a hall closet where they could stow their things, and said she would get to work finding sleeping bags for the floor of the library.

"You can duke it out for the couch," Victoria added.

"Can't we sleep in the maid's room so we can have some privacy? Rosalba's off for the holiday, isn't she?" Kate whined.

"She'd kill me if she found out. I don't need her moping over it," Victoria said, and strode off.

"See? She cares more about her housekeeper than she does about me," Kate said, loudly enough that Victoria surely heard.

Kate led them to the library, which was basically a large, lavishly appointed, misnamed den. The walnut shelves held no books, but were filled instead with expensive-looking knickknacks and silver-framed photographs of the little stepmonsters. Kate dumped her bag on the floor, and only then did Jenny realize that it wouldn't be just her and Aubrey camping on the gorgeous leather sofa. Kate didn't have her own bedroom in her father's apartment. This was Kate's only home away from Carlisle, and it didn't belong to her.

"Come on, this is better than the digs I usually rate," Kate said, seeing Jenny's dismayed expression.

"It's fine. I didn't say a word," Jenny said. "What do you usually rate?"

"Normally I sleep on a cot in the monsters' room so I'm not in Victoria's way. I got upgraded to the library because of you two, I guess. The room doesn't matter. We'll only be here to sleep," Kate said.

Kate set about making good on that promise. They changed out of their travel clothes and did their makeup in the hall bathroom, then hailed another cab. When they reached their destination, Jenny was careful to hop out first, and Kate opened her wallet without batting an eye. They cut a long line, and a bouncer looked them up and down and nodded, removing the velvet rope to let them into the nightclub of the moment, not bothering to check their IDs.

"Your new hair got us in!" Kate shouted to Aubrey over the din as they entered the dark club. Jenny thought that was generous. Kate got them in—something in her looks, her outfit, her attitude. Anybody who believed otherwise wasn't paying attention.

"Blondes have more fun," Aubrey said, smiling broadly.

They threaded through the packed crowd, looking for the friends Kate had arranged to meet up with. Music pulsated. Young, fabulous-looking people, dressed in the hottest fashions, danced and swayed and made out under flashing colored lights. Everywhere she looked, Jenny saw waiters carrying trays weighed down with lavish cocktails and oversize bottles of champagne.

"How much do the drinks cost?" Jenny worried aloud, but neither of them heard her.

Kate's friends were already ensconced in a large elevated booth overlooking the dance floor. Kate's on-again-off-again boyfriend Griff Rothenberg sat next to a glamorous brunette, who leaned toward him and giggled suggestively while he ignored her, his eyes searching the dance floor restlessly. He spotted Kate, and his face lit up with wild desperation.

As the girls mounted the steps to the booth, a security guard stepped in front of them.

Griff sprang to his feet. "She's with us," he said.

The guard turned. "Which one?" he asked.

"Oh. All of them," Griff replied, and Jenny realized he hadn't even noticed her, or Aubrey either, so preoccupied was he with Kate.

Griff sat down and slid over to make room, and the three girls crammed into the booth, thigh-to-thigh. Kate's friends were the most uniformly beautiful people Jenny had ever seen, from Griff with his fine profile and head of sun-streaked hair, to the glamorous brunette, to a waif with mile-long eyelashes who looked like Edie Sedgwick and turned out to be the daughter of a famous billionaire. (The bodyguard who'd stopped them belonged to her.) Jenny recognized a few people from Carlisle, from the frat parties Kate took them to, but most were strangers—Kate's friends from Odell, or kids from her set who went to other schools but hung out whenever they were back in New York at the same time. Every single one of them was thrilled to see Kate, and completely uninterested in Aubrey and Jenny after saying a cold hello when Kate introduced them. Jenny wondered why she was there, and thought about leaving. The music was too loud, plus she was worried they'd get arrested for underage drinking, which would put her scholarship money at risk. She tapped Kate on the shoulder and said she might leave. Kate snorted and handed her a Cosmopolitan—the first of many—which was tart and delicious and extremely strong, then shouted, "Lighten up and come dance!" She pulled Jenny down the steps into the middle of a gyrating mob. Disco lights flickered over them, and the bass line of the music throbbed deep in Jenny's head. Kate twirled and flipped her hair wildly, then did an Egyptian dance that made Jenny laugh.

Nobody alive could resist Kate in party mode. Why even try?

Jenny swayed to the music and grabbed another drink from a passing tray. As the alcohol hit her bloodstream, she thought, *Lucas who?* Kate was right: Jenny should lighten up and enjoy life. Jenny was the one who'd broken things off with *him,* though she'd regretted it terribly the second she did it. She wanted to experience college without the pressure of a—let's face it—precarious relationship. Well, *this* was experiencing college. Kate was her entrée into the high life, and she should appreciate that, not get mad at Kate for being Kate, for attracting boys, which was something she couldn't help doing. Maybe if Jenny stopped sulking and started paying attention, Kate's magic would rub off on her.

Hours passed in a drunken fog. Kate got into a loud argument with

Griff, who left in a huff, though to Jenny's great relief, not before making a big show of picking up the tab. The sun was rising as the three girls raced back up Park Avenue in a cab, the green lights falling into place one after the other, hypnotically. Kate had passed out, drooling, her head lolling back against the slimy vinyl seat. The world swam around Jenny in a wonderful way. She'd never been so drunk before, and she finally got why people liked it. Letting yourself lose control, allowing yourself to forget painful things and just have some mindless fun—people did that for a reason. Kate did that all the time, and she didn't suffer for it.

Not everybody was as good at avoiding consequences, however. Jenny's eyes focused on Aubrey, sitting in the middle looking pale and wasted. The deep purple shadows ringing her roommate's eyes worried Jenny.

"Hey," Jenny said, clutching Aubrey's hand as the taxi hit a bump. "Are you okay?"

"Super drunk, but yeah," Aubrey said.

"You had fun?" Jenny asked. Her voice was hoarse from all the shouting she'd done in the club. She sounded like Kate, with that throaty-sexy thing that was part of Kate's mystique.

"Yeah, totally," Aubrey said with a sloshed-looking grin. "This guy Elliot, who's a friend of Griff's from—somewhere? He was into me. He asked me to have sex in the bathroom."

Jenny laughed. "Was he into you, or did he just want to get laid?"

"No, he was *into* me. I mean, there were other girls who would've done it with him. But even after I said no, he kept talking to me. Kate was right. It's the blond hair. That and I lost a few pounds."

"Aubrey, you don't need to lose weight," Jenny said, but Aubrey didn't reply. "I'm glad you didn't do it with him. Not that I thought you would."

"I was worried he'd kiss and tell. I don't want Griff to think I'm a slut."

"Who cares what Griff thinks?"

"I don't want to get talked about."

"Right, that makes sense. You don't want to get a disease, either."

"Oh, Elliot's friends with Griff and Kate, I'm sure he doesn't have a *disease*. Anyway, Kate thinks I need to sleep with someone and get the whole virginity thing out of the way, you know? She thinks it's holding me back."

"Holding you back how?"

"Like, socially. I see her point, I just haven't found the right situation yet."

"I'll say. Losing your virginity in a nightclub bathroom? You can do better than that. Wait for a guy who treats you right."

"Well, Elliot did show me a picture of his dog."

Jenny burst out laughing. Aubrey laughed, too, and snuggled up against her, laying her head down on Jenny's shoulder.

"I feel like you guys are my good angel and my bad angel, sitting on my shoulder, whispering in my ear what I should do," Aubrey said, slurring her words adorably.

"Which one of us are you going to listen to, sweetie?" Jenny asked. She stroked Aubrey's hair, which was like a silver cloud, doubled by Jenny's drink-blurred vision.

"I can't decide. I love you both."

"Be careful. Kate can be a bad influence."

But Jenny couldn't muster much conviction to back up her words. Kate's head bounced against the seat as the taxi sped along, and she looked so vulnerable in her openmouthed stupor that Jenny felt guilty, and reached across Aubrey to shift Kate's head to a more secure position. How ungrateful was she to accept the free drinks and the hospitality, then say snarky things about Kate while she was passed out drunk in the seat next to them? Kate hadn't been under any obligation to include them tonight. She'd taken them out on the town, shown them a fabulous time, and asked nothing in return. She did that at school, too, a lot. Kate had proven herself to be a generous friend. Jenny shouldn't let jealousy over a guy poison their friendship, especially not a guy that she'd chosen to break up with of her own free will. The problem was, as often as she told herself that she'd been ready to leave Lucas behind, so they could focus on college and date other people, deep down, she knew that was a lie. She'd been afraid of getting hurt. She was determined to break up first, to stop Lucas from dumping her for someone more sophisticated, someone more beautiful, the second he got to Carlisle. Dumping her for someone like Kate. And now look.

6

They woke up around one, incredibly hungover, to the sound of a racket in the kitchen, and emerged with their eyes shut against the light, like newborn kittens. Victoria took one look at them, gave them mugs of coffee and a bottle of Tylenol, and told them to get lost until dinnertime. She made noises about the caterers needing space to work, but Jenny doubted that was the real reason. Jenny wouldn't want girls like them around her adorable towheaded children either.

They bundled up and went out into Central Park. The leaves were off the trees, and the bitter wind cut through their jackets, but still, Jenny felt grand walking around the city. She breathed in diesel-scented air and admired the wintry sunlight glinting off the magnificent apartment buildings visible over the treetops. Kate dragged them all the way across the park with the promise of Thanksgiving floats. When they reached the West Side, they found that the parade had ended hours ago. All that remained were hot dog vendors and piles of confetti, so they ate hot dogs for breakfast, and walked back across the park, all the way to Madison Avenue. The shops were closed. They linked arms and wandered up and down the deserted avenue, ogling the exquisite clothes in the windows, feeling like the city was theirs alone.

Back at Kate's building, they chattered all the way up in the elevator, and peeked into the overheated kitchen, which bustled with catering staff and smelled deliciously of roast turkey. They were ridiculously happy, right up until the minute Victoria cornered Kate outside the door to the library.

"I'm warning you, your father's here now, so you better clean up your act," Victoria hissed, in a tone that made Jenny look up from unpacking her dinner clothes.

Victoria and Kate stood in the doorway, glaring at each other. Kate made a sour face and turned away. Victoria grabbed Kate's arm. Kate yanked her arm away and slammed the door to the library, blocking Jenny and Aubrey's view of the confrontation. But their raised voices were still perfectly audible.

"You could show a little gratitude," Victoria said. "I'm trying to help you out. He's not too happy about the uninvited guests."

Jenny and Aubrey exchanged alarmed glances.

"How many guests do *you* have tonight, Victoria?" Kate demanded. "Let's count. Your low-class mother and her fat boyfriend who chews with his mouth open. The three bratty cousins from Bedford. Lauren from your tennis club with her fake boobs and her husband who tries to feel me up. Any others? You don't have any problem spending Dad's money feeding *your* people. If I bring a few of mine, I would think you would have the manners not to complain."

"Don't talk to me about manners. Not when you stumble in semiconscious at five o'clock in the morning and wake up my children. Honestly, Kate, I think I've been pretty indulgent. My life would improve considerably if your father cut you off, and yet, whenever he contemplates doing that, which I can assure you happens more and more often lately, I foolishly talk him out of it."

"You're lying."

"You know I'm not. I overheard your telephone conversation with him the other day. It's obvious why you brought these girls home. Looking at them, I don't even believe they're your friends. You're using their presence here to avoid your moment of reckoning. Well, it won't work."

"Victoria, nothing you say affects me, because I don't believe a word of it. You see me as a threat to your extremely lucrative relationship with my father, and you'll do anything to poison his feelings for me. So get out of my face. I have to dress for dinner. Thank you."

Kate stepped into the library and slammed the door. She looked like she'd been punched in the stomach.

"Is everything all right?" Aubrey asked.

"Should we leave?" Jenny said.

"Screw her. Get dressed," Kate said. Her face was bright red, and she was obviously trying not to cry.

Jenny rummaged in her suitcase. They pretended to be absorbed in getting dressed, and avoided each other's eyes. Aubrey pulled off her T-shirt and pulled on the sparkly top she'd worn to the club last night.

"My God, you cannot wear that," Kate said in horror. "This is a family dinner. It's completely inappropriate."

Aubrey blanched. "I'm sorry, I didn't really think—"

"How much thinking does it take? Only a trashy person would wear that."

Aubrey was on the verge of tears.

"Stop it," Jenny said. "Don't take it out on her."

"You shut up."

Jenny grabbed Kate by the shoulders. "Listen to me. Stop being a bitch, and tell us what's going on, because we're your friends. Honestly, Kate, we're the best friends you've got. We don't care about your parents or your apartment or your clothes. We actually care about *you*. Let us help."

"I don't need help," Kate declared, but her face said differently.

"Yes, you do," Jenny said. "And we *want* to help you, which is probably more than you can say for those people at the club last night."

"Is your dad really going to cut you off?" Aubrey asked, looking shell-shocked.

Kate sat down on the leather couch, buried her face in her hands, and burst into tears. Jenny and Aubrey both rushed to comfort her.

"He might," Kate said, sobbing.

"Your stepmother turned him against you?" Jenny asked.

"It's not that simple. He hated me ever since my mother died. He blames me."

Kate buried her face in Jenny's neck, her shoulders heaving with sobs. It was thrilling for Jenny, feeling the hot tears against her skin, realizing that the great Kate Eastman needed *her.*

"I'm sure that's not true," Jenny said soothingly.

"It is, you don't know us," Kate wailed.

"Your mother died of cancer. It wasn't your fault, and your father doesn't blame you. You're imagining things."

"No, he's right. I was a bad daughter."

"When you were *ten*?"

"I refused to visit her in the hospital because the tubes scared me. She got really upset, and that made her worse. My dad blamed me. He thinks I'm a terrible person."

"Hey, listen to me," Jenny said, pulling away and looking Kate in the eye. "You're talking crazy, okay? People die of cancer. I know that's hard to accept when it's your own mother. Nothing you did as a child made your mother die, and your father doesn't think that. Do you hear me?"

Kate nodded miserably.

"But it sounds like he's mad at you now. Do you know why?"

"Ugh, the usual. My bills, the clubbing, the drinking. I mean, what does he expect? It's college! I haven't killed anybody, for Christ's sake."

"It sounds like your stepmother is making things worse."

"That's what I've been telling you. What can I do? She has her hooks in him."

"You have to tough it out. We get dressed up, go out there and charm your dad. You said he loves Carlisle, right? Let's Carlisle him to death. Make him remember how proud he is to have a beautiful daughter at his beloved alma mater, with bright, responsible roommates who'll keep her on the straight and narrow. We'll make him forget he's mad. What do you say?"

Kate swiped her arm across her face. "You think that could work?"

"It's worth a shot. C'mon, let's find something for Aubrey to wear. You and I both packed for a week, we can come up with something."

The living room buzzed with conversation as they arrived for cocktail hour. A uniformed waiter passed hors d'oeuvres on a tray to the well-dressed guests.

"I'll introduce you to my father," Kate said, under her breath. "Ignore the others. They're Victoria's riffraff."

Kate went up to her father and kissed his cheek, which he received with notable coolness. Keniston Eastman was very much what Jenny had expected—tall, imposing, scary-looking even. His aquiline nose and heavy black brows reminded her of the grim-faced portrait of President Samuel Eastman hanging in Founders' Hall. He wore a perfectly tailored jacket and an orange-striped Carlisle rep tie, and peered at Jenny and Aubrey disapprovingly as they approached. As Kate introduced them, Aubrey shrank back. Jenny took Aubrey's elbow and propelled her forward, so Mr. Eastman could shake both their hands.

"Enjoying the college, are you?" he asked, in a perfunctory manner, grabbing a glass of champagne off a passing tray and taking a sip, as if he needed to fortify himself against *them*.

Aubrey went pale at his question and seemed unlikely to open her mouth, so Jenny jumped in with a chipper smile.

"We're very fortunate to be at Carlisle, Mr. Eastman, and we know it. I was elected Whipple rep to the student council last month, and I also work in Provost Meyers' office, so I have a lot of insight into how things stand at Carlisle at the moment. It's a wonderful time be a student."

"The provost's office? You don't say. Gloria Meyers is a good friend." He relaxed to the point that Jenny caught a hint of a smile in his eyes. "Tell me, what are the hot-button issues on campus these days?"

After that, they talked for fifteen minutes straight, Mr. Eastman quizzing Jenny on the latest campaign to clean up Greek life and progress on building the new athletic facility. Kate and Aubrey looked bored, and after a few minutes, wandered away, leaving Mr. Eastman in Jenny's capable hands. Jenny watched them edge toward the table where a handsome bartender stood mixing drinks. Out of the corner of her eye, Jenny saw Kate flirting with the bartender as he shook up a martini. Was Kate really stupid enough to start drinking at her father's party?

Jenny wondered. If so, she was beyond help. A nasty look and a whispered word from Victoria took care of the problem before Keniston spotted it, however. Kate and Aubrey stepped away from the bar. A moment later, Victoria announced that dinner was served, and Jenny turned toward the dining room with relief.

"You're saving my ass. Dad loved you," Kate said, catching up with Jenny as they moved into the dining room.

"Don't drink," Jenny whispered urgently.

"Huh?"

"Just don't drink anything alcoholic, not a drop, not for the whole night."

"But I'm hungover. Hair of the dog."

"I can't believe I have to tell you this. The plan is working. Don't ruin it."

In the dining room, the chandelier sparkled, casting a warm glow over the crystal stemware, fine china, and lavish flower arrangements. Each setting had a place card, and Jenny was disappointed to see that the three of them were seated next to the little Eastmans at the far end of the table, presumably to act as impromptu babysitters if the need arose. Jenny had hoped to be closer to the seat of power at the head, the better to continue her conversation with Mr. Eastman. She hadn't had time yet to make clear to him that she planned a future on Wall Street herself. The questions had been on the tip of her tongue when dinner was announced—did his firm hire interns, and could she forward a résumé?—but she hadn't gotten them out. It was a lesson. Never hesitate; never put somebody else's interests (especially Kate's; she had enough advantages already) ahead of your own career advancement, or the moment would pass you by.

The upside was that, sitting in Siberia, Jenny could relax and enjoy the spectacular food and setting. The second she lifted the silver spoon to her lips and tasted the lobster bisque, she forgot to be disappointed. It was Popsicle orange and silky-smooth, tasting of cream and sherry and the sea. She savored every drop, remembering to tilt the bowl away from her to catch the last bit rather than toward her, as the etiquette manual she had pored over in preparation for this trip instructed. She was sad when the soup was done, but then the main course arrived. Back home in Jenny's house, they had roast turkey with all the sides, American and Puerto Rican both. Every Thanksgiving, there were sweet potatoes with marshmallows on top, stuffing that came from a box but tasted delicious, green bean casserole doused in onion soup with lots of cheese and fried onions, and then *tostones,* rice and beans, because they all loved that food, so why not? She felt a twinge of homesickness as the waiter set a plate of rarefied tidbits before her, but it vanished with her first bite. The turkey had been prepared *en croûte,* a tender breast wrapped in puff pastry and delicately seasoned. It was accompanied by spicy cranberry compote and two fluffy vegetable purees, one of sweet potato, the other of asparagus, both heavenly. Jenny knew what the dishes were only because of the dainty calligraphic menu that sat before her in a silver holder. She loved looking at this menu, and wondered if they would mind if she took it home. This must be what it was like to be the queen of England, or damn close anyway. She'd put up with grief from a scary dad and a jealous stepmother, in exchange for a life like this. But of course, if Keniston Eastman were Jenny's father, he wouldn't be angry with her. She would never give him reason to be.

As she ate, Jenny feasted her eyes on the beautifully appointed dining room. The windows were tall and elegant, framed by blue silk drapes with elaborate tassels. By far the most impressive feature of the room was a hand-painted mural that covered all four walls, depicting New York City in an earlier time, complete with sailing ships, and a family in eighteenth-century garb picnicking beneath a tree. Looking closer, Jenny saw that the family bore an uncanny resemblance to the Eastmans. It was them, she was certain—Keniston, Victoria, and their three towheaded monsters, enjoying a lovely spring day in the eighteenth century. But Kate and her half sister Louise were nowhere in sight. The artist had omitted them. They didn't live in this house, and apparently they weren't worthy of preserving in paint. Officially, they weren't part of the family.

At the end of the meal, the other guests departed, and Jenny went up to Victoria and Keniston, thanked them profusely, and offered her services to help clean up.

"That's not necessary," Victoria said.

"But it's a lovely offer," Mr. Eastman said. "I'm glad you're rooming with my daughter. If only some of your attitude would rub off on her."

Jenny blushed. Kate, who had been moving toward them, smiled.

"Isn't she awesome, Dad? I told you, I'm on the right track now. Look who I'm hanging out with."

The heavy black eyebrows drew together. "It's not so easy, Katherine. Come into the study. We need to talk."

Kate's face fell. As her father led her away, she glanced back over her shoulder at Jenny with a sick look.

It was an hour later when Kate found them in the library. They'd changed into their pajamas, and were hanging out on the sofa with the door half closed, looking at fashion magazines, afraid to make a sound.

"We have to go," Kate said, her makeup streaked from crying. "I'm not sleeping under his goddamn roof tonight."

"What happened?" Jenny said.

"That bastard," Kate said, her jaw set.

"Did he cut you off?" Jenny asked.

"God, no. Leave me destitute? People would know, and it would reflect badly on him. But you should've heard the way he talked to me. I can't stay here after that."

"Kate," Aubrey protested, "it's after eleven o'clock."

"I don't give a shit what time it is," Kate said.

Jenny saw that Kate was beyond consoling. "If we hurry, we can make the midnight train," she said. "It's a local, it gets into Belle River at six thirty tomorrow morning."

"The dorms are closed till Sunday," Aubrey said.

"I'll call my parents," Jenny said. "They can meet us at the station. You can both stay with me."

"Thank you," Kate whispered, drawing Jenny into a deep hug. "You always know what to do. You're the best. Just absolutely the very best friend, *ever.* Aubrey, you too, my little lamb, I love you to pieces. Get over here. What would I do without you guys?"

Aubrey joined in the hug. The three of them stayed there holding each other like that for a long time, and Jenny thought that even if sometimes she hated Kate, and sometimes she got incredibly frustrated with Aubrey, she also loved them more than she'd thought it was possible to love friends, ever.

"Promise me," Kate said, and Jenny realized that Kate was still crying.

"What?"

"We'll never let anything come between us. Not a guy, nothing. We won't hurt each other. We won't screw up this amazing friendship."

"Of course we won't, silly. We love each other too much for that," Aubrey said, tears standing out in her eyes.

"Do you promise?" Kate said.

"I promise," Aubrey replied.

Kate turned to Jenny. "You, too. Say it."

"I promise I won't let anything come between us," Jenny said.

She meant it, and yet Kate's urgency left her uneasy. You didn't demand a promise like that unless you had a premonition of bad things to come.

7

Present Day

In June, Kate moved back to Belle River after twenty-two years away. It was unseasonably hot for early summer, and the afternoon was as oppressive as her mood, with airless streets, black skies, and wilted flowers under dusty maple trees. The clouds opened just as Kate pulled up in front of the ugly brown house on Faculty Row. She sat in the BMW with music blasting and rain battering the windshield, her head on the steering wheel. It was all around her again. Carlisle, the past, her so-called friends. All the things she'd been running from for years now. Throw a rock from the front porch of this dump and you'd hit Briggs Gate. After a minute, Kate took her sandals off and tossed them onto the floor in the back, and lowered her seat into a reclining position. She'd take a nap. Who gave a crap what the neighbors thought? She didn't know them, and didn't care to. She refused to get out of her air-conditioned car and venture into this deluge in order to enter a place she was distraught to live in. She'd rather stay in her car all afternoon, or at least until the rain stopped, enjoying the plush leather seats. She had no job to go to, no prospects, and she couldn't stand her husband. If she had more gumption—or more money—she would drive away and never come back.

Jenny pulled up beside the BMW in her minivan, leaned over, and lowered the passenger window. Kate saw Jenny's lips moving. Sighing with exasperation, she turned down the music and lowered her window.

"What?"

"I said, what are you doing in there?" Jenny shouted over the pounding rain.

"What does it look like? Thinking about blowing my brains out."

"Come on, enough of that. I brought you some cupcakes from that new place in Riverside."

Riverside was a formerly industrial neighborhood in Belle River, full of warehouses and factories that were being redeveloped into lofts and restaurants. Belle River trying pathetically to be *chic* was what it was.

"I don't eat sugar," Kate said.

"I brought wine, too. You can't tell me you don't drink."

Jenny held up a bottle, which got Kate's attention. Damn, she could stand an ice-cold vodka right about now, but chardonnay would do in a pinch.

"Is Aubrey coming?" she asked. Jenny without Aubrey was too much to take.

"Of course. She'll be here any minute."

"All right, but do me a favor. Don't act like this is some kind of party and you're happy to see me, okay?" Kate said.

"I'm trying to make the best of this, Kate. You could at least help a little."

Ugh, nothing ever changes, Kate thought. Jenny was still the priggish know-it-all of their youth; she was just more powerful and successful now, which made it worse. Jenny was the mayor of this one-horse town, with her finger in every plot. Jenny's husband's construction company had the winning bid on every Carlisle building project. How did that happen, you might ask? Kate could tell a few hair-raising secrets if she had a mind to, most of them involving her own father and his influence, and yet Jenny acted like Kate was the corrupt one. Jenny and Aubrey must know how Kate felt about them, about this place. Hadn't they noticed that she never visited? That the three of them saw each other only rarely, and only when Jenny or Aubrey came to New York and tracked her down? Kate hadn't even been in New York much over the last decade or so. Well, unfortunately the days when she went where she pleased were over, probably for good, and now here she was stuck with these two again, back in this shitty town.

Kate turned the engine off and collected her sandals from the back. Jenny pulled into the parking space in front of Kate. She had those annoying stickers on her rear windshield—the cartoon family complete with the mommy and daddy, the two boys with their sports equipment, and the dog for good measure. *Gag me*. As Kate watched Jenny get out and struggle with her packages, though, pulling boxes and bottles and finally a bouquet of Mylar balloons from the backseat in the middle of a downpour, she couldn't help but crack a smile. Jenny always had a plan, you had to give her that. She forced the world to conform to her expectations, where Kate wallowed in her disappointments, and Aubrey, let's face it, never dared to expect anything at all.

Kate got out and went to help with the packages. Together they ran up onto the covered porch. They were soaked by the time they got there, although Jenny looked none the worse for it. She had a sleek power haircut now that framed her face and made her look in control at all times. Which, of course, she was. The Great Manipulator, as Kate thought of her. On the days Kate didn't want to take responsibility for her own life—which was most days, lately—her favorite people to blame were Jenny and her father. Well, and her suffocating whiner of a husband; she couldn't stand him either. She was half tempted to do something crazy, just to *show* them, to get them off her back once and for all.

"Great location," Jenny said cheerily as Kate fumbled for her keys.

"What are you, a real estate agent? The only reason we're living here is, Keniston owns the place. He's my slumlord now. I'm warning you, it smells like cat piss in here."

She opened the door and they stepped into the front hall. It was dark inside, but Kate saw Jenny wrinkle her nose.

"And you thought I was exaggerating," Kate said.

She flipped a switch and the lights came on. Boxes clogged the front hall. Dark walls loomed over them. The house was a sad muddle of Victorian and Arts and Crafts styling, squat and dim and charmless.

"This way," Kate said.

In the kitchen, the table was piled high with more boxes. Kate started moving them to the floor, rummaging through them at random hunting for a corkscrew.

"You can put that stuff on the counter. I'll find us glasses for the wine," Kate said.

Aubrey called out from the front hall.

"Back here," Kate yelled.

Aubrey glided in, carrying a casserole dish, with multiple green bags from the food co-op looped over her wrists. Of the three of them, Aubrey had improved the most with age. (Of course, she had the farthest to come.) The lithe figure, the sharp cheekbones, the clear blue eyes with no makeup, belonged on the cover of a yoga magazine. Kate privately thought Aubrey's newfound serenity was just as likely to come from a prescription bottle as from chanting *ommm,* but hey, whatever worked.

"C'mere, you," Aubrey said, depositing her bounty on the counter and holding out her arms to Kate. "I'm so glad to see you. Welcome home."

Aubrey and Kate hugged. Tears stung Kate's eyes. As if Belle River could ever be home. As if her friends were true, and actually happy to see her. As if any of this was how it looked from the outside. She longed for those days when they were young, and loved each other like best friends should. Nothing had been right since they lost that. Correction, nothing had been right since the *night* they lost that—and lost so much else, too.

Kate extricated herself from Aubrey's grasp and set about opening the wine.

"Drinking in the afternoon," Aubrey said, shooting Jenny a glance. So Aubrey was judgmental now, too? Used to be, it was only Jenny who looked askance.

"It's five o'clock somewhere," Kate mumbled, coloring. Was she really letting these losers make her feel bad?

"Just a splash for me, I have to pick up the kids," Jenny said.

"Me, too," Aubrey said.

Kate poured an inch of wine for each of them and made a show of filling her own glass to the brim. If she needed the entire bottle to get through this conversation, she'd chug the damn thing, and they couldn't stop her.

"So," Jenny began. "We wanted to talk about how we can best help you settle in here."

"Thank you, but I don't want help."

"You need it, trust me," Jenny said. "This town has a long memory. People remember what happened, and they still care."

"I knew you'd throw that in my face. I didn't think you'd have the gall to do it the second I walked in the door."

"I'm trying to help. That's all," Jenny said.

"Did you not hear me the first time? I don't want your help."

Jenny sighed and looked at Aubrey. Of course the two of them were in cahoots on this. Kate was the one whose life had been ruined, and the two of them got to act like the victims.

"Kate," Aubrey said, "it may not make sense that people would still care, but Jenny's right. We want to help you—"

"You don't give a shit about me," Kate said. "You're covering your own asses, both of you. I get it. So let me set your mind at ease. Nobody's more upset than me that I'm back here. I hate this town. I hate this house. I hate the college. I hate my loser of a husband. And after everything that's happened, frankly, I hate the two of you. So no worries. I don't plan to stick around long."

8

Two Months Later

At 9 A.M. on Labor Day, Aubrey was doing yoga in the studio off her kitchen, desperately trying to quiet her mind. She had three hours till Jenny's big barbecue, and Ethan still hadn't come home from wherever he'd spent the night before. *Goddamn* him, he'd *promised*. Aubrey could hear the kids moving around upstairs. It was past time to get their breakfast, but she couldn't face them yet. Not again, not like this. Viv was still too young to understand, but Lilly was starting to see through the lies. And Logan had known for a while now. *Sorry pal, the story's not working,* she told Ethan in her mind. He could have the latest girlfriend buzz his pager and claim there was an emergency at the hospital, as had happened last night. But nobody believed him anymore, not even Aubrey, the stupidest fool in town.

Aubrey went into a deep backbend. Hot tears rolled down her temples and plopped softly on the mat. Why was she the one crying? She wanted to make Ethan cry, Ethan and whatever tramp he was with this time. She had this studio built ten years ago, after the first time she caught him. She'd done it to punish him, really. It replaced his home office, and cost a mint, with big windows and bamboo floors. He deserved to pay, after what he put her through. Ethan Saxman, MD, had seemed like the answer to Aubrey's prayers once, back when she was a starving grad student and he was resident at Carlisle General with a bright future ahead of him. She hadn't asked a lot of questions; she'd grabbed him and held on tight. The old adage was true in her case: Marry in haste, repent at leisure. In retrospect, it was clear that Ethan had always been a cheater, but Aubrey hadn't wanted to see it. She'd been happy at the beginning, for years really, when they were newlyweds, and after the kids were born. Aubrey stayed home and enjoyed her children, and didn't complain when Ethan was gone a lot. She closed her eyes. Well, she'd paid the price for that.

Aubrey had admitted to herself that Ethan was cheating only when she had caught him in the act. That was about ten years ago now. Ethan had claimed he was going to a conference in Philadelphia. The weather had turned hot, and she decided to take the kids to the lake, even though they hadn't officially opened the cabin yet. When Aubrey pulled into the driveway, Ethan's car was there—his, and another. She told Logan to stay put and watch his sisters, then walked up to the front door, breathing as hard as if she'd just run through the woods. She was terrified. She'd suspected for a long time, but to find out for sure would change things forever, and she knew it. Of what happened next, Aubrey recalled only fragments. A wineglass tipped over, clothing strewn across the floor in the harsh morning light. In the bedroom, Ethan with a shocked look on his face, and the redheaded nurse with her pale white breasts. Then the noise, the screaming—which turned out to be Aubrey herself, and then Logan, after he rushed in to help her. Poor, poor child, to bear witness to something like that. She tried to protect them. And that was the problem. Aubrey longed to walk away from her marriage, but she had her children to think of, and no way to support them. She knew how it felt to grow up with no father and no money. She refused to do that to them, so she stayed, and chose to believe Ethan's promises that he wouldn't betray her again.

But he did. The second time Ethan got caught (though she realized now that there must have been other times in between) was about five years later, and it wasn't by Aubrey. The young resident resigned when

Ethan dumped her and sued the hospital for sexual harassment. Ethan had to pay money to hush it up. He needed wifey by his side to ride out the scandal, so she had leverage this time. She also had the good sense to go to Jenny for advice. Mayor Jenny and her husband Tim were knee-deep in real estate deals in Riverside, the old industrial part of Belle River, which was gentrifying rapidly. Oh, there were whispers about the legality, but Aubrey didn't judge. With Jenny's help, she took their nest egg and bought a majority stake in a renovated loft building—in *her* name, not Ethan's. She'd been practicing yoga seriously for over twenty years at that point, and teaching it for almost as long. (She'd discovered yoga at Carlisle in her Eastern Religions class, and fallen in love with it because of its ancient roots. Besides, it was the one physical activity she was ever naturally good at.) She'd always taught part-time, just to get out of the house, and make a little money of her own. Now that she owned a building, Aubrey decided to open her own yoga studio. With the following she'd established over her years of teaching, Riverside Breathe was an instant success, and she had plenty of space left over to rent out to paying tenants. She was a businesswoman now, with a decent income. She had the means to walk away if she was willing to make some financial sacrifices, and here Ethan was, up to his old tricks. She'd promised herself she would leave him if she caught him a third time. But did she have the guts?

Aubrey did a round of sun salutations that failed to smooth her skittish heartbeat, then took child's pose, seeking peace and consolation. The cat walked in and started meowing at her, but she ignored him. That damn cat. He liked Ethan best, and always seemed to know when his master was coming home. At that moment, with her forehead pressed to the mat, Aubrey heard the garage door go up. Ethan was home, and she would have to deal with him now. Aubrey rolled her mat into a tight coil and shoved it in the cubby under the window seat. She'd go meet him in the garage, where the kids wouldn't hear them fight.

"Mom, Dad's home!" Viv shouted, bouncing into the studio in her pajamas and bare feet. "Can I have a Pop-Tart?"

"No."

Viv was seven, gap-toothed, adorable, and used to getting her own way. "I'll ask Dad. He'll say yes."

"Vivian, I said no."

Aubrey's voice came out so tentatively that Viv ignored her and skipped off toward the garage. Aubrey stood there wringing her hands. She couldn't confront Ethan with Viv watching. The reckoning would have to wait. She went downstairs and took up position at the kitchen island, facing the door that led to the garage, steeling herself. What would she say to him when he walked through that door? She wanted to scream, to throw something, wave the butcher knife. Every solution crossed her mind. To stay, to leave, to rush at him, screaming. But she wouldn't do any of those things right now. She would control herself in front of her daughter.

Ethan stumbled into the kitchen, laughing, with Viv clinging to his leg. His dark hair was mussed, his dress shirt rumpled, his finely modeled chin shadowed with stubble. He looked like a man who'd just rolled out of the sack after a wild night. How dare he touch her daughter in that state? Aubrey couldn't stand the sight of him. Her fingers twitched with the desire to slap him. She clenched her hands behind her back.

"Hey, babe. I got bagels," he said, tossing the paper bag onto the island. Just like nothing was wrong, like he wasn't the world's biggest asshole.

"Ooh, yummy," Viv said.

Ethan walked over to the desk by the window where they kept a basket for keys and such, and started emptying his pockets. She watched him throw his keys in there, then his sunglasses and wallet. He took out his phone, like he'd done a million times before. And she saw him hesitate. Normally, he would throw it in the basket, too, but he seemed not to want to, not today. He looked up and caught her watching. She smiled, but he must've seen something in her eyes, because she saw his Adam's apple bob. *Ha, ha,* he was scared. She knew exactly what he was thinking: Taking the phone with him would look suspicious, leaving it behind would risk Aubrey snooping.

He put it in the basket. Ethan hesitated by the desk for a minute, like he might say something. Then he glanced at Viv and seemed to think better of it. Aubrey's eyes were on him the whole time, the atmosphere between them thick with suspicion.

"I'm gonna take a shower," he said, "and maybe catch a nap before the barbecue."

Aubrey's smile didn't reach her eyes. "Of course, babe. You must be tired after your long night."

The uneasy look on his face as he exited the kitchen gave her a measure of satisfaction. As Viv bit into a cinnamon raisin bagel, Aubrey walked deliberately over to the basket and picked up Ethan's phone. Ethan had the latest iPhone, in space gray. Though the phone was only a few weeks old, she doubted he'd changed his passcode from the old model. He was sloppy that way. But she hesitated. Right now she had a strong suspicion that he was cheating again, but no solid proof. Once she knew for sure, she would have to take action, or hate herself.

Aubrey was still trying to decide whether to search the phone when it buzzed in her hand. Its blank face lit up with the first few words of an incoming text. "Hot damn, boy, you did a number" . . . The sender's name came up as "Kate." *What the—?* For an instant Aubrey thought of *her* Kate, but why would her Kate text Ethan? Why would her Kate's name be in Ethan's contacts, so it showed up simply as "Kate" when he got a text?

She typed in his passcode, and viewed the message in its entirety.

> Hot damn, boy, you did a number on me. I can still feel your hands on my body. I want more more more. Again, please. Just say when.

Rage blurred her vision. She wanted to smash this goddamn phone. But then an even more sickening feeling took over. Could the text actually *be* from Kate Eastman? Was that possible? No. No, it couldn't. Ethan's latest tramp had the same name, that's all. And yet . . . Aubrey had been fighting her suspicions for weeks now, blocking them out like she always did, looking the other way, except even more deliberately than usual because she didn't want to believe the worst of her friend. (Ethan, at this point, she could believe the worst of.) But now the doubts came rushing in. Glances exchanged between the two of them, stories that didn't add up, times they both went missing simultaneously. Things Aubrey had done her best to explain away. Even now, she was making excuses for them, telling herself this had to be a different Kate, hesitating to look at Ethan's contacts list when the truth was discoverable in an instant. She had to stop being such a freaking *baby*.

Aubrey stared at the phone in her hand, then looked over at Viv, who was absorbed in her bagel. She had to force herself to look at the truth—here, now, even with her daughter in the room. No more excuses.

Aubrey sank into the chair by the desk, and went to Ethan's contacts list. Kate's cell number (which Aubrey knew by heart) was right there, under "Kate." Couldn't he at least use a fake name, the piece of shit? Now Aubrey couldn't deny that the text was from her Kate, *the* Kate, Kate Eastman. Ever since freshman year at Carlisle, Aubrey had thought of Kate as her best friend. Even though Kate left school after freshman year. Even though Aubrey had done all the work of maintaining their friendship. When they visited or talked on the phone, when they messaged or texted or Skyped—which wasn't even that often—it was always Aubrey who initiated. Yet in her mind, Kate had always been a loyal friend who would never dream of hurting her. What did it say about Aubrey if not only her husband but her best friend would betray her like this? Was she not worthy of love? Did she have terrible judgment in friends? Or was she just a goddamn *idiot*, and people took advantage because that's how shitty people were?

It was like discovering Ethan's cheating for the first time, all over again. She felt so stupid. How long had she been denying the obvious? With shaking fingers, Aubrey went back through Ethan's texts. There were only three damning ones, part of an exchange with Kate from last night in which they set up their meeting at a local motel. (He'd obviously gotten smarter about hiding the evidence and deleted earlier texts; it was clear from their intimate tone that this wasn't the first time.) They agreed on the time and the place, and then Kate texted that she was at the motel waiting with nothing but her thigh-high boots on. Aubrey went cold and still. The evidence was undeniable. Ethan was cheating again. And he was cheating with Kate.

Aubrey carefully replaced Ethan's phone in the basket, wiped bagel crumbs from the island, and put the kettle on for tea. With each movement, visions floated before her eyes. Things she could do to *them*, to give them a taste of the pain they were causing her. She imagined Ethan coming home to find her in the bathroom with her wrists slit, or hanging from the wooden beam in the garage. Hah, he'd have to clean up the mess, explain to the kids. But that would leave Kate in the clear. Aubrey could go to Kate's house instead and shoot herself on the front porch, leaving a bloody mess spattered across the door sill. But why kill *herself*? Why should she be the one to suffer? She imagined Kate and Ethan in bed together, naked, in a passionate embrace. She would barge into the room, take the gun from her purse, pull the trigger—once, twice, a thousand times. She saw the scene in her mind's eye. Their corpses riddled with bullets, covered with blood, their blank eyes staring at the ceiling. They deserved it, oh, how they deserved it.

But Aubrey would never do it. There were the children to think of.

9

The wide green lawn of Jenny's house in Belle Hills teemed with the town's elite. Jenny made the rounds, greeting people by name, shaking hands, hugging and smiling till her cheeks hurt. The entire business community was here, a healthy number of local judges and politicians, and the upper tier of Carlisle's administration. Jenny was careful to give each VIP personal attention. She'd been lucky with the weather. Eighty degrees, bright sunshine, a light breeze. The band played oldies. Kids squealed as they jumped into the pool, and the good-looking young lifeguard she'd hired blew his whistle cheerfully. Lines of guests had formed at the open bar and at the grill, where the best caterer in town kept things humming along. Jenny had ordered up burgers (beef and veggie), hot dogs, potato salad, three-bean salad, watermelon, and ice cream. The beer was locally brewed. The party looked like a roaring success, and yet her palms were sweaty and she had a sick feeling in the pit of her stomach.

So many sharks swam beneath the pretty surface. Jenny hadn't seen Kate yet, but she'd RSVP'd yes. Their relationship had not been easy in the two months since Kate returned to town. Aubrey's husband and kids had shown up without her, saying Aubrey wasn't feeling a hundred per cent but might be along later. Aubrey was never sick, so what was up with that? Jenny had a bad feeling. And up on the deck, a reporter from the

Belle River Register had Jenny's husband Tim cornered—literally, had him backed up against the railing. The *Register* wanted dirt on Jenny and Tim and their real estate deals. Tim knew that, and she'd warned him a thousand times to keep his distance, yet he let himself get cornered anyway.

Jenny loved her husband. He was a local boy, handsome, with a good heart, but he had no game. He was a good father, a reliable builder, who did solid work at a fair price and didn't cut corners. Tim would've made a decent living without Jenny's help, and probably been happier without the high-profile success. But Jenny wasn't satisfied with that, so she took matters into her own hands. She called on her contacts, like any smart entrepreneur would, and pretty soon, Healy Construction started getting big contracts from the college. Maybe she did a few things Tim would not have been comfortable with if he knew the particulars, and so maybe she didn't fill him in on every detail. But she was only acting in Tim's best interests. He couldn't handle the truth.

Jenny made her way through the crowd and up onto the deck. Tim was laughing nervously at something the reporter said. He'd put back on his favorite ratty old Healy Construction hat, after she made him take it off before the guests arrived. Her fingers itched to swipe it off his head.

"Here she is now," Tim said.

The reporter whirled to face her. "Madam Mayor, nice to see you. I had a few questions—"

This reporter was an old-timer who came to all the town council meetings, and had interviewed Jenny several times. She gave him a warm smile.

"No interviews at the party, Bill. I'm off duty, and so is my husband," Jenny said.

"But if I could just ask about the new arts center project the college is bidding out in Riverside. Is Healy Construction planning to bid? You always seem to get these juicy contracts."

"Call my office if you'd like to schedule an interview, and in the meantime, have some food, have a beer. It's such a pretty day."

"I will take you up on that." He started to turn away. "Oh, but first, can you point someone out to me? I understand Kate *Eastman* is here today, and I'm interested in interviewing her."

Suddenly it felt very hot in the sun. Sweat prickled on the back of Jenny's neck. "Kate—?" she said.

"Kate Eastman, the trustee's daughter. I believe she was a friend of yours."

"Why do you want to talk to Kate?"

"Well, the Eastmans are important to the college. I thought her return might make a good story. That's all."

But as he spoke, the reporter shifted his gaze, not meeting Jenny's eyes, and her suspicions grew. Could this "local interest" story actually be about something else? Something in the past, that had happened their freshman year, that Jenny had worried would be stirred up by Kate's return? Or was she being paranoid?

"I don't think Kate made it to the party, unfortunately. Now if you'll excuse us, Tim and I have to mingle."

Jenny grabbed Tim's arm, pulling him toward the throng on the lawn. "Come on," she said, when he resisted.

Jenny hadn't seen Kate yet, but that didn't mean Kate wasn't here somewhere. She wanted to find her, and warn her to stay away from that damned reporter.

"No. Stop it," Tim said, and headed instead for the sliding glass door that led to the kitchen.

Jenny followed him. She knew Tim well enough to see that he was upset. Was it the reporter asking about the real estate deal that set him off, or the mention of Kate?

Inside, the kitchen was deserted and sparkling white, air-conditioned to an arctic chill.

"Don't let that reporter upset you," Jenny said. "I can handle the press. And didn't I tell you not to wear that hat? It looks shabby."

"Stop telling me what to do," he said.

Tim went over to the sink and ran the water, filling a glass and chugging it. She came to stand beside him, and glanced out the window to the deck. The reporter had disappeared. Presumably he was out in the crowd, searching for Kate. Jenny couldn't go after him, not until she calmed her husband down. Tim looked worn out. There were lines around his eyes that hadn't been there a few months ago. Her hours as mayor had taken a toll on Tim, and on their marriage. He had to pick up the slack with the kids, because Jenny was gone all the time. Meanwhile, bidding for the new Carlisle arts center project had reached the make-or-break stage. Tim wanted to take over the bidding, when in the past he'd been content to let her handle things. The timing could not be worse. Tim was too damn honest for the business he was in, and he would screw up everything. Into the middle of this tinderbox walks Kate Eastman, holding a lit match.

"Everything's under control, babe," she said soothingly. She reached out to touch him, but he backed away.

"I'm starting to think I can't trust you when you say things like that," he said.

"Come on. We're a team."

"Are we? Then why do you keep me in the dark, Jen?"

"We agreed that when it comes to the business, I handle bids and you handle operations."

"Not just about that. Tell me the truth. You know what that reporter was implying. We'll bid on the arts project, and we'll win, because we always win when the college is involved. Why is that, Jen?"

"Because you do good work at a reasonable price. You've built up a reputation. They trust you."

"You're telling me your pal Keniston Eastman has nothing to do with it?"

"What are you getting at?"

"I don't want to be in bed with him and his filthy daughter anymore."

"Kate has nothing to do with this."

"I don't believe you."

Tim's blue eyes were troubled. She felt bad for him, she really did, but he needed to suck it up and back off. Too much was at stake here. Next he'd be asking her about that incident again, from freshman year, when Kate got in trouble. When an innocent person died. They couldn't talk about it. It had to stay buried.

"Babe," she began, squeezing his arm.

Aubrey stepped through the sliding glass door. Thank God, just in time.

"Let's talk about this later, okay?" Jenny said.

"Yeah, whatever you say, Jen," Tim said bitterly. "You call the shots."

He brushed past Aubrey on his way out the door without so much as a hello.

"Sorry about that. We were in the middle of a spat, but I'm glad you're here. I need to talk to you about something," Jenny said, thinking of the reporter.

But her words barely seemed to register with Aubrey, who looked pale and ill.

"Are you okay?" Jenny said, looking at her friend with concern. "Ethan said you were sick."

"I've been better. He said I was *sick,* like physically? Hah," Aubrey said, with bitterness in her voice.

"Are you two having problems again? Ethan didn't—?"

"Oh, yes he did. And you'll never guess who the woman is this time," Aubrey said, sinking into a chair at the kitchen table.

Jenny filled a glass of water and brought it over to her.

"Who?" Jenny asked. Oh great, was this about to turn into some big drama? Aubrey's marital problems were nothing new, and Jenny had other things to worry about, like her guests, and the reporter who was looking to track down Kate Eastman and possibly start asking a lot of questions.

"It's Kate," Aubrey said simply. She looked through the glass of water like she didn't see it.

"Kate? You mean—?"

"Yes! Ethan is sleeping with Kate this time."

"*Oh,*" Jenny said. She did her best to appear shocked, but privately, she had suspected this for a while. Those two had a chemistry that, given their well-known proclivities, could only mean one thing.

"It's been going on for a while," Aubrey said, "but I just found out. I know Ethan is a—well, a sex addict I guess—and a liar. I've put up with that for the sake of the children. But to go after my best friend, it's too much."

Aubrey shook her head numbly. Her eyes were dry. Jenny might have been tempted to offer comfort anyway, to pull Aubrey into a hug, but instead she backed away, and leaned against the kitchen island. Aubrey's words stung. Kate barely gave Aubrey the time of day over the past twenty years, and now she was sleeping with Aubrey's husband. Jenny was there in every crisis. Yet Aubrey called Kate her best friend.

"What is wrong with me, Jenny? I've been playing the fool for years. I have to do something about this. I have to make them stop," Aubrey said.

"I don't mean to say I told you so," Jenny said, "but I've always said you should leave Ethan."

"Then he'd win. *They* would win. Ethan and Kate would get to be together, and I'd be alone. I'd probably have to sell the house. He'd get joint custody. It's so unfair."

"As far as Ethan and Kate running off together, I doubt they have any interest in that. They're so shallow. It's probably just a fling. And the rest—well, you need to talk to a lawyer. A good one. Take Ethan to the cleaners, and you'll feel better."

Aubrey shook her head. "After the way they betrayed me, that's not enough. I'm so angry at both of them. How could I have been so blind?"

"You like to see the best in people."

"You mean I'm a fool."

Jenny sighed. "Well, I'm glad you're finally seeing Kate for who she is. I'm not only talking about this affair, but—" Jenny glanced over her shoulder, then walked over and closed the sliding glass door. "You know what I'm talking about. There's a reporter from the *Register* out there looking for Kate right now. I'm worried about what he wants with her."

Aubrey focused on Jenny as if noticing her presence for the first time. Her eyes narrowed. "You mean, the reporter wants to ask Kate about—about freshman year?"

"I don't know for sure, but that's what I'm afraid of. We can't have that mess getting dredged up again, not now."

Aubrey picked up the glass of water and took a careful sip. Her eyes looked clearer suddenly. "Why not? Maybe that's exactly what Kate deserves."

"What? You can't be serious."

"Think about it for a minute. If we told people what really happened that night, Kate would be in big trouble. The police would get involved. She might even go to jail." A nasty smile appeared on Aubrey's face.

"That's crazy. You can't do that," Jenny said. She started to tremble.

"Why not?"

"We can't change our story now. You were her biggest defender, Aubrey. You always said it wasn't her fault. You've been saying that for twenty years."

"Just because I change my story doesn't mean I was lying before. Maybe I was wrong before. Maybe I remembered something new."

"No. If you tell anyone, or God forbid, go to the police, it will come back on us. We were both there that night. We both gave statements."

"Maybe I don't care about the consequences."

"*I* do. I'm the mayor of Belle River. I have a family, a business to run. I can't afford a scandal."

"I have things to protect, too."

"Okay, but—" Jenny paused, deciding how much to reveal. There was an angry, stubborn set to Aubrey's jaw. If Jenny didn't take a risk and tell her what was really at stake here, Aubrey might be crazy enough to go public. She couldn't allow that.

"Aubrey, listen. There's more to this than some old college scandal. I never told Tim the truth about what happened that night. If you change your story now, it could mess up my marriage in a big way."

"You never told Tim the truth?"

"No."

"How could you keep it from him? Wasn't Lucas his cousin?"

"Yes. That's exactly why I never told him."

Aubrey looked at Jenny with pain in her eyes.

"I'm sorry, Jenny. I really am. But I'm tired of being played for a fool. I simply can't do it anymore. I need to fight back."

"Fine, but pick some other way. Don't destroy my marriage to get your revenge."

"I don't mean to sound cold. But if you never told Tim the truth, that's your problem."

Jenny looked at Aubrey, dumbfounded. *The ingratitude*—after all she'd done for Aubrey.

"If Ethan's sleeping with Kate, isn't that *your* problem? He's been cheating on you for a decade, and she tumbles into bed with half the men she meets. You act like you're so shocked. It's been obvious to everybody for a long time that those two together were trouble."

A look of horror spread across Aubrey's face. "You *knew*?"

Jenny saw she'd made a misstep. "I'm sorry, I shouldn't have said that. I didn't know. Not exactly."

"Not *exactly*? My God, Jenny. You knew, and you didn't tell me."

"That's not what I said. I suspected, that's all. Can you honestly tell me you didn't suspect yourself?"

"Why didn't you warn me?"

"I didn't want to upset you for something that was just a hunch."

"Kate betrayed me, you knew about it, and you said nothing. The two of you were my best girlfriends. My *roommates*. I was supposed to be able to trust you."

"You can. Me, you can trust. Kate—well."

"No. You and Kate are alike. You think about number one, both of you. All you care about now is not shaking things up for yourself. Anybody else be damned. Stupid *Aubrey* be damned."

"I've always been a true friend to you, Aubrey. A lot better than Kate was, though you refused to see it."

"Better than Kate isn't saying much, is it? I get it now. Aubrey's a mess, that's what you always thought. Being friends with me made you feel better about yourself. Well, I'm not a doormat anymore, so look out."

Aubrey stalked out, leaving Jenny ashen. A few seconds passed in which she couldn't seem to catch her breath. She turned on the faucet, wet a paper towel with cold water, and pressed it carefully to her face until she calmed down. She had guests to attend to. She would pull herself together and do what was necessary to stop Kate and Aubrey from ruining her carefully laid plans. Just like in college. The two of them could cry and whine and self-destruct all they wanted. Jenny would keep her wits about her, and triumph in the end.

10

Freshman Winter

The winter of their freshman year was the coldest Carlisle had seen in ages. Snowdrifts reached to the windowsills, and giant icicles hung from the copper gutters of Whipple Hall. At night, drafts whistled through the creaky windows of the double, making Aubrey stir in her sleep. She'd turn over and burrow under the covers with a contented sigh. Like everything associated with Carlisle, the weather was magical to her. She had gotten a second job in addition to her work-study, and bought herself a down parka and snow boots with the money. She bundled happily into them each morning for the trek across the frozen Quad. The snow sparkled in the frosty sunlight as her feet crunched on the paths. Inside the overheated lecture halls, a wet-wool smell rose from her classmates' clothes as she strained to hear the professor over the clanging of the radiators. She wanted to remember this time and place forever, all the things she learned and felt, the people she knew, every sensation.

Aubrey had started spending her weeknights in the basement stacks at Ogden Library studying with Jenny. She adored it there. The sleet pelted against the glass of the high basement windows and reminded Aubrey of the scratching of mice. It was dim in the little corner they'd claimed as their own, and—against regulations—they plugged Jenny's space heater into an ancient outlet beneath a scarred wooden table. Aubrey warmed her feet and imagined herself sitting by a fire in the time of Dickens, with only a candle for her light. With the musty smell of old books filling her senses, she'd lose herself in their pages.

Aubrey was taking Novels of the Gilded Age, Eastern Religions, Intro to Astronomy, and Sanskrit (so she could read Hindu and Buddhist liturgy in the original). It was a heavy load, but she was eager to open her mind, to become worthy of Carlisle. She was writing a paper on the yoga-sutras of Pantanjali, ancient Hindu texts that promised the acquisition of supernatural mental powers through the regular practice of yoga. Was it true? She went to yoga class to investigate, so she could include her personal observations in the paper. That was the sort of amazing work you could do here. But when she tried to talk to her friends about what she was learning, most of them would say, "Cool," and change the subject to which parties were worth going to on Saturday night. It surprised her how few people at Carlisle cared about acquiring knowledge for its own sake. Her roomies didn't. Jenny studied to get As. Kate never studied. Kate skipped class when she felt like it and barely cracked a book. All term she would ignore her assignments, then spend Reading Week hopped up on stimulants—Dexedrine, the minuscule amount of coke she could afford since Keniston cut her allowance, and cup after cup of black coffee—so she could stay awake cramming for days. Then she'd regurgitate it for the exam and promptly forget it. Watching Kate pound uppers during fall term, Aubrey worried that her heart would stop, that she'd drop dead on College Street on her way to Hemingway's for an espresso to add to the toxic cocktail already flooding her bloodstream. But nothing bad happened. That's how it always went with Kate: no consequences. Her grades turned out decent, so she repeated the same scam for winter term—all play and no work, stockpiling a sizable stash of uppers for exam time.

One Wednesday night in early February, Aubrey was down in the stacks reading when she heard a knock on the window above her carrel. She'd been far away, lost in Edith Wharton's New York, which reminded her uncomfortably of Carlisle. The heartless rich kids, the genteel wraiths who'd fallen on hard times, the strivers looking for their next advantage—they were all here. It's not like there were no good people at Carlisle, but there were plenty of indifferent ones, as well as some who'd been corrupted at a young age through no fault of their own and couldn't help but misbehave. Aubrey put Kate in that latter category, if she was being honest. Lately, Kate had been thumbing her nose at her father and living off handouts from the fat trust fund that belonged to Griffin Rothenberg, her Odell swain. Griff was the son of a wealthy investment banker and a Swedish fashion model. With his striking blond head on his compact jock body, he bore enough of a resemblance to Kate that they were sometimes mistaken for brother and sister. As far as Aubrey could tell, Kate thought of Griff that way. Griff followed her around like a lovesick puppy while Kate treated him with a comfortable, dismissive indifference that Aubrey found hard to watch. Aubrey carried a torch for Griff herself, though she did her best to hide it. Griff was the male Kate, really. Not only did they look alike, but he had that same careless confidence, that ease in the world, that Aubrey both coveted and lacked utterly. Griff was the boy she'd most like to lose her virginity to, but she had no hope of achieving that. He was obsessed with Kate, and Aubrey was nothing but a third wheel to be patted on the head on those rare occasions when he noticed her at all.

At the sound of the knock, Aubrey looked up. Kate and Griff were down on their knees in the window well, making faces at her. Griff slammed a rectangular object up against the glass—a plastic tray from the dining hall.

Jenny leaned over from the adjacent carrel and gazed up at the tray pressed against the window.

"They're going traying *now*?" she asked. It was a rhetorical question.

The snow was deep enough that winter that the skiing at the local resorts was supposedly sublime. Aubrey had never been on skis and couldn't afford a lift ticket to save her life, but she'd gone mad for sledding. The speed, the abandon, the sharp taste of snow in her mouth when she crashed. Traying was the Carlisle version of sledding. You blasted a stick (smoked a joint), stole a tray from the dining hall, and walked a mile in the cold to Belle River Park to the crazy steep sledding hill, where you flew down the slope using the tray as your sled. The hill had been rigged up with all sorts of homemade jumps. The most popular jumps sent you rocketing high into the air, or directed you off into the woods to confront an obstacle course of trees. The broken limbs and the concussions were piling up, to the point that the college infirmary recently sent out a memorandum warning the students not to sled. But everybody ignored it. Traying was too fun.

"I'm going with them. Do you want to come?" Aubrey asked, shutting her book.

"No thanks, I have an essay due for Gov."

Aubrey gave a thumbs-up toward the window and grabbed her coat. "If I'm not back before the library closes, could you take my books home?" she asked.

"Sure," Jenny said grudgingly.

Aubrey skipped out of the bright library, down the marble steps into the crisp, cold air, pulling on her gloves as she went. She fell into step beside Kate and Griff, who were giggling uncontrollably. Obviously, they'd started the party without her.

"What are you guys smoking? Can I have some?" Aubrey said.

"On Briggs Street in broad daylight?" Griff said with a snort.

"Broad moonlight," Kate corrected.

The moon shone in the black sky and reflected off the snowbanks, strong enough to make Aubrey squint. Their breath came out in puffs of smoke as they walked.

"I have a fresh joint in my pocket," Kate said. "We'll smoke it when we get there."

"At least tell me what you're laughing at," Aubrey said.

"Griff claims there's a rumor we had a threesome in Dieckmann Hall."

"You and Griff did?" Aubrey asked, tingling with jealousy. She told herself Kate was above sleeping with Griff, and that as a consequence, he was celibate, and frustrated. But probably not.

"Not me and Griff. *Us,*" Kate said.

"Not a threesome, a foursome," Griff said. He was laughing so hard that it was difficult to understand him. "All three Whipple Trips with some fratbro from the ten-man, on more than one occasion."

"No, an orgy with the entire suite," Kate said, collapsing against Griff in giggles as she walked.

In Carlisle-speak, Aubrey, Kate, and Jenny were known as the Whipple Triplets, or the Whipple Trips for short. And the ten-man was a notorious ten-person suite in Dieckmann Hall that, year after year, remained occupied by the wealthiest, most dissolute prepster dudes on campus. Translating the slang, a rumor was circulating that Aubrey and her roommates had gone full slut with those notorious party boys. While on the one hand Aubrey was flattered to be gossiped about, on the other she was horrified.

They left the bustle of Briggs Street behind. Church Street was darker and quieter, lined on both sides with small apartment buildings that served as grad student housing, and two- and three-story multifamily houses, interspersed with convenience stores and gas stations. It was nearly eleven, and many windows were dark already. The occasional car passed, its wheels hissing on snow-slicked pavement. Jenny's parents lived nearby. Aubrey could only imagine how they'd feel if they heard this scandalous rumor about their daughter.

"Why would anyone say that about us?" she asked.

"Because you don't live in Dieckmann, but you're always there for brunch on Sunday. Ergo, you spend your Saturday nights bumping uglies in the ten-man," Griff said.

"We like the cinnamon rolls," Aubrey said.

"What is that, some kind of kinky sex position?" Griff asked, and cracked up again, laughing so hard that tears leaked from his eyes and snot from his nose.

"We go to Dieckmann for Sunday brunch because it's the only dorm that serves cinnamon rolls."

"Don't tell him that. You'll spoil the fun," Kate said.

"Baby likes her skanky reputation," Griff said, pulling Kate close.

"I don't," Aubrey said.

"Aubrey. People care enough to gossip about you. Appreciate the moment," Kate said, and jerked from Griff's grasp. "Let's *run*."

Kate took off racing toward Belle River Park, as Griff belted out the chorus to "Born to Run." Eventually Kate disappeared around a corner. Griff and Aubrey looked at each other, then took off after her. Griff shot Aubrey some side-eye and it became a race. They sprinted, neck and neck. Her legs were longer, but he was stronger and faster. Aubrey's lungs stung from the cold. She laughed and squealed, the rumor already forgotten.

A few minutes later the two of them passed through the gates into the hush of Belle River Park. The shadows of the trees on the snow were ghostly as Aubrey caught her breath. They wound their way to the sledding hill, where they found Kate standing in the shelter of a copse of evergreens, her face lighting up and going dark as she flicked her cigarette lighter. The park officially closed at sunset, but it was deserted and rarely patrolled, so they had no fear of detection.

Kate succeeded in getting the joint lit.

"Here," she said, and handed it to Aubrey, who drew the pungent smoke deep into her lungs.

Aubrey had never touched drugs or alcohol before freshman year, but under Kate's tutelage, she'd quickly become a connoisseur. Pot seemed like part of a Carlisle education, like studying Buddhism or going to art films dressed all in black. She'd smoked enough dope that she could now get a contact high just from breathing the air in the vicinity of someone else smoking, or putting her lips to the mouthpiece of a well-used bong. Or so she believed. A psychopharmacology major she knew from Sanskrit class swore there was no such thing as a contact high, that it was only a placebo effect. If that was true, why was Aubrey soaring off the first hit from Kate's joint? The joint came her way again, and Aubrey took another toke, then grabbed the dining hall tray from Griff's hand.

"Me first," she said, and ran for the sledding hill.

As she ascended the steep hill, Aubrey's feet sank into the snow, making each step an effort, and she slowed to a trudge. Man, she was high.

Every step sent strange vibrations up her legs and spine. The cold felt warm on her exposed skin, and the snow looked indigo in the moonlight. She lost track of time. The hike up the hill seemed to go on forever, but then suddenly she was at the top, looking down. Where were Kate and Griff? Her eyes were having trouble focusing. The spot where she thought they should be was swallowed in the darkness of the evergreens. What if they'd abandoned her, here in the freezing cold? Suddenly that seemed likely, and then virtually certain. Her heart seized up. She imagined the park police finding her tomorrow morning, frozen solid, in a fetal position, and alerting the RA in Whipple, that biology girl they barely knew, who'd have to inform Aubrey's roommates. Would Kate feel guilty at all? Would she cry? Probably not. Then something moved below. Aubrey stared right at them; she'd been staring at them the whole time. Wait, Kate was kneeling in front of Griff. Were they, could they be—?

Aubrey threw the tray onto the snow and plopped down on top of it. The impact against the hard ground made her teeth clatter. She tasted blood, and pushed off before she quite had her balance, immediately spinning around and barreling downhill backward.

"Aaagh!" she screamed.

As much as she kicked and flailed, she couldn't right herself, and in what seemed like a split second, she crashed into Kate and Griff at the bottom. They toppled over into the snowbank, limbs tangling, voices crying out, hoarse in the wind. Aubrey hit her head on someone's boot hard enough to see stars. Griff's pants were down around his ankles. Kate got to her feet, laughing.

"Gimme that, you spaz, I'll show you how it's done," she said in her luscious voice, made deeper by smoke and cold. Kate grabbed the tray from under Aubrey's thighs, and ran off toward the hill.

Griff picked himself up and turned away quickly. Aubrey saw a flash of smooth white butt as he yanked up his pants and rearranged himself. She stood up abruptly and staggered, reaching out for the nearest evergreen for support, rubbing her forehead.

"You okay?" Griff asked, turning back to her.

"I guess," Aubrey said. She was high enough that even though she knew intellectually that she'd really cracked her head, she couldn't feel it, and she wasn't alarmed. "What about you?"

"Fine."

"You didn't get frostbite in a sensitive place, did you?" she asked, and giggled.

Marijuana had amazing sedative properties. She was bitterly jealous of Kate, of the way Griff adored Kate, of how cavalierly Kate squandered his attentions. The resentment hibernated somewhere deep in Aubrey's chest, but at this moment, she couldn't access it, and it didn't matter. It just seemed funny, how their signals were so crossed. Kate would never love Griff, and Griff would never love Aubrey. Sad, sad, sad.

Griff laughed, but then stopped short. "She only has sex with me when she's high," he said, suddenly maudlin. "Do you think that's a bad sign? Sometimes I'm not sure if she really cares about me, or if she's using me for my money."

You're the only one who isn't sure about that, Aubrey thought to herself. Griff looked at her with such profound sadness that Aubrey worried she'd mistakenly spoken aloud.

"I'm sorry," she said.

"It's not *your* fault. I'm the idiot who lets her."

"Everyone thinks it's a privilege to get abused by Kate," Aubrey said. She thought she was trying to make him feel better. But as the words came out and hung in the icy air, Aubrey felt their truth in her own case.

The wind gusted, and Griff swayed on his feet, listing in Aubrey's direction. For one mesmerizing second, she thought he would kiss her. Then she realized: They were both totally baked, that was all. His balance was off. She was imagining things. Why would Griff kiss *her*? The guy was utterly crushed, he was so obsessed with Kate, who didn't give two shits about him. He wouldn't kiss Aubrey.

She could kiss him.

Aubrey was experiencing a strange disconnect between thoughts and actions, and didn't realize she'd acted on her desire until their lips met. His mouth was warm and firm. Her lips parted, and so did his. They were French kissing. He smelled of pot, but tasted like peppermints and snow.

Griff pulled away, rubbing his eyes. "Whoa. Did that just happen?" he asked.

"I'm not sure," Aubrey said. But she was sure. She had the memory now, and he couldn't take it away from her.

At the top of the hill, Kate turned around and settled onto the tray, calling out to them to watch.

"Please don't tell her we did that," Griff said.

Like she cares who you kiss, Aubrey almost said, but she wouldn't hurt Griff out of spite. He was like her, pining for a person he couldn't have. Maybe one day he would see how alike they were. In the meantime, Aubrey felt no guilt over that kiss. Normally, girl rules would apply here. Aubrey and Kate were best friends and suitemates. Until such time as Kate officially declared her lack of interest in Griff and designated him fair game, Aubrey should keep her hands off. But Kate had such bounty when it came to men, and didn't follow the rules herself. Kate was sleeping with more guys than poor Griff, and he had no clue. Or who knew, maybe he did and he let her walk on him anyway. One of Kate's hookups was that Lucas kid who Jenny was obviously still crazy for. Fair's fair. Why should Kate get everything, and the rest of the world go begging?

Kate skidded toward them on the tray, whooping, and came to a stop ten feet short of where they stood.

"Agh, that sucked. What a dud! I'm going again," Kate called. She stood up, stamping the cold from her feet, and looked past them down the path. "Jenny? You came!"

Aubrey and Griff turned in unison. Jenny hurried toward them, white clouds of breath streaming behind her. Aubrey instantly saw that something was off, something bad had happened, then told herself it was the weed talking. Pot made her paranoid. She ought to write that down on a piece of paper and carry it around so she could look at it when she was wasted, and remind herself not to fret.

But Kate looked worried, too. She strode over to meet Jenny.

"What is it?" Kate said. "Is everything okay?"

"Aubrey, your sister left a message on the room phone. Your mother's in the hospital. She says it's serious enough that you should go home."

Aubrey's brain was pleasantly foggy from the pot and the kiss. She had no sense of impending doom. How could anything bad happen on the same night that she kissed Griff?

"I talked to my mom a few weeks ago, and she sounded okay. Amanda's just being dramatic," Aubrey said.

But in the back of her mind, she knew that wasn't the case. Her mother had mentioned doctors' appointments a couple of times recently, and tests. Aubrey, with her college kid's blinders on, hadn't followed up. Besides, she knew her sister well enough to suspect that Amanda wouldn't bother to call without good reason.

"I hope you're right," Jenny said. "She didn't give any details. But she did say it was urgent and you should plan to go home right away. I think you should at least call her."

"I can't go home, not with finals coming up. Besides, I can't afford the plane ticket."

"Let's go back to the room, sweetie," Jenny said. "You can call Amanda and get the whole story. If it's really bad—I hate to say it, but if it is—the school has emergency funds for that sort of thing. We'll figure it out."

Aubrey looked from Jenny to Kate and back again, her face slowly crumpling as the news sank in. Leave it to her mother to go and get sick. Life had been too much for Brenda Miller to handle ever since Aubrey's dad walked out when Aubrey was three years old. Could you give yourself cancer? The yoga-sutras spoke of the connection between mind and body. Who knew, maybe you could. Maybe her mother had wished herself dead, because she was tired of the struggle, and managed to make it happen. *At least now I won't have to send her any more cash*, Aubrey thought. Then she started to cry, out of guilt more than grief. Like her father and sister before her, Aubrey had left her mother in the lurch. Brenda came to the airport to say good-bye when Aubrey went east. She pretended to be happy, but as Aubrey was about to disappear through security, Brenda hugged her tight as a vise and whispered over and over again, *Don't leave me, stay with me, please stay, I can't get by without you*. Aubrey gave her mother a quick peck on the cheek, then pried her arms away and ran. That was the last time they saw each other, and now her mother was going to die.

"She can't go alone. We can't let her. She's a mess," Jenny whispered.

Jenny and Kate sat together on Jenny's bed in the double. Aubrey had called her sister only to learn the worst. Her mother's cancer was advanced. The doctors gave her mere weeks to live, days maybe. Now Aubrey was huddled under the covers in her bed, her chest rising and falling rhythmically, her eyes shut tight. They assumed she was sleeping but in reality she was wasted out of her mind. Her head hurt from when she whacked it traying, or else from the drugs. They'd slipped her a couple of Valiums from Griff's stash to calm her down. On top of the pot she'd smoked, the Valium wrapped her in a fluffy cocoon where she could see the bad feelings, but not feel them. Her head pounded and vibrated, but it was happening to someone else. She listened to her friends discuss her welfare as if from miles away. The sounds reverberated strangely in her ears and dug into her brain. She would remember their words the next day, and for a long time after, but in the moment, nothing they said could cause her pain.

"She'll be fine tomorrow," Kate said.

"Her mother's dying. She won't be fine. She needs our help."

"Who's gonna pay for the tickets for one of us to go? She can't even afford *one* ticket."

"I told you, the college has an emergency fund. I'll do the paperwork in the morning."

"Maybe they'll pay for *her*. They're not gonna pay for two tickets. Sorry to inform you, but I'm flat-out broke. Besides, we have exams coming up, too."

"Like you give a rip about exams. What kind of friend are you, Kate?"

"How *dare* you, Jenny? I'm a good friend, thank you very much. Aubrey wouldn't have a social life if not for me."

"Congratulations, but I'm afraid another drunken frat party is not what Aubrey needs right now. We can come up with the money for an extra plane ticket if we put our minds to it. She has to deal with the doctors, and from the way it sounded—" Jenny paused and drew a breath. "—funeral arrangements, too. It's a lot for her."

"Why should that be our problem? She has an older sister, doesn't she?"

"The sister's useless, and a total bitch on top of it. I'm telling you, we can't let Aubrey go through this alone. One of us should go with her."

"Well, I *can't* go," Kate said petulantly.

"Why not?"

"I just can't."

Deep inside her drug-happy cocoon, Aubrey felt a jolt of worry. Jenny should back off before Kate agreed to come to Vegas. The last thing Aubrey wanted was for Kate to come home with her, and get a firsthand view of her pathetic trashy family. Kate would never look at her the same way again.

"You owe me an explanation, don't you think?" Jenny said.

"I don't owe shit to anybody, especially not to someone who just accused me of being a bad friend. After everything I've done for you, Jenny. I constantly invite you to stuff you could never get into on your own, and you never even say thank you."

Her mother was sick, and now her best friends were arguing because of her. She wanted to speak, to beg them to stop, to tell them how much it hurt to see them angry with each other. But the drugs were in the way, and she couldn't form words.

"Nobody ever helps *me*," Kate said.

"Helps you with what? I want to help Aubrey because her mother is dying. What's *your* problem?" Jenny said.

"My mother died, too, when I was only ten, and all I got was blame."

"From Keniston," Jenny said, skeptically.

"Exactly."

"Oh, come on, Kate. You always harp on that but we both know that's not true."

"How do *you* know? You weren't there. He blamed me because I wouldn't visit her. I *couldn't*. She'd been so beautiful, and then she was skin and bones. Tubes in her, and there was this bag attached to her, full of shit and God knows what. It *smelled*."

Aubrey heard sniffling. Kate was crying.

"I understand," Jenny said.

"No, you don't! Nobody does. Keniston forced me to visit her anyway. He never cared what it felt like to me. He just said I was a bad daughter. People always think the worst of me."

"This is not the time for self-pity."

"Oh, first I'm a bad friend, now I'm having a pity party. Admit it, you *hate* me."

"I don't hate you. This is about Aubrey. We should try to help Aubrey, that's all."

"I would be no help. I freak in hospitals. I said so. Shut up about it and stop forcing your goody-goody ideas on me."

"Can you please lower your voice?" Jenny whispered urgently.

"God, she can't hear us. She's wasted out of her mind. I'm tired of trying to measure up to your ridiculous standards."

"You're taking this way too personally."

"It *is* personal. Everything with us is personal. You do things to show me up, Jenny, to prove to everyone you're better than me. Well, two can play that game. I had sex with Lucas, you know."

Jenny made a strangled noise. "But . . . you said nothing happened. You said you had to pack."

"Not *then*. Not at Thanksgiving. Just the other day. And don't act like you don't care. I know he was the guy you talked about, the one you lost your virginity to. I knew and I did it anyway."

There was another long silence. Aubrey held her breath, listening hard, glad she had the drugs to make her feel nothing, or she would've hated Kate right then. She didn't ever want to hate Kate. Kate was her dearest friend.

"Why?" Jenny said finally, in a small voice.

"Because I felt like it. Because he wanted to. Because I am not constrained by your uptight, narrow-minded definition of friendship."

The silence stretched out.

"I was right," Jenny said, her voice harsh. "You are a bad friend. You're a bad *person*."

Jenny got up without another word and left the room. Aubrey peeked at Kate through her lowered eyelashes, which were wet with tears, and saw that Kate was smiling. A sick, ghoulish smile, like she'd been punched in the stomach, but a smile nonetheless.

11

Shecky's Burger Shack was the only place on College Street open twenty-four hours. Like generations of Carlisle students before her, when Kate got the midnight munchies, she went for a Sheckyburger. It was at Shecky's, at 2 A.M. on the Tuesday before her awful fight with Jenny, that Kate ran across Lucas Arsenault after not having seen him for a couple of months.

Kate was wasted at the time, although unlike her usual drug binges, this one had a purpose. She was working on a group project with Griff and the Three Rs (Rose Mackie, Rebecca Levine, and Renee Foster-Jones, who lived downstairs from the Whipple Triplets in mirror-image suite 302) for their Beat poets class. They planned to replicate known drug experiences of the Beats, document the spiritual and artistic insights they gleaned from the drug use by recording themselves saying profound things while stoned, and juxtapose their remarks to lines of Beat poetry in a slide show. Everybody agreed the idea was brilliant, but unfortunately the execution left something to be desired. It must've been the strain of weed. Every time one of them tried to say something profound, they said ridiculously pretentious stuff instead and gave each other the giggles something awful. When Kate's turn came, she intoned, "God created the earth. The earth created the Sheckyburger," and all hope of productivity was lost. They shut off the tape recorder, grabbed their coats en masse, and stampeded down the stairs for a Shecky's run.

The plate-glass window was steamed up when they arrived, and bright white light spilled through onto the icy pavement. Shecky's never slept—it was like a little slice of New York in Belle River. Kate walked in and smelled the charring meat and grilling onions and accumulated years of grease from the French fries and laughed out loud.

"Shecky's proves that God exists," she said to her companions as she got in line at the counter.

The scarred wooden booths, the cracked linoleum under the garish fluorescent lights—her home away from home. Her father's initials were carved on the table of the third booth from the door, the souvenir of a Shecky's run Keniston Eastman pulled thirty years before. When Kate did her admitted-student visit last spring, she'd carved hers right next to his (though she would never tell him this).

They placed their orders with the skinny kid behind the counter. Either all townies looked alike or the same exact kid also worked slinging crap from the steam tables in Eastman Commons. When Renee greeted the kid by name, Kate figured it was the latter.

"Look at you, Miss Socialist, making friends with the proles," Kate said.

She thought she'd said it in a nice way, but Renee gave her some righteous side-eye. "My brother works at McDonald's, and he's a human being. Timmy's a human being also."

"You'll have to excuse me. *I am profligate, because I'm a blonde.*"

"And I'm a socialist because I'm black, is that it?"

"Do your homework. That's Frank O'Hara, Beat poet."

"That's stupidity, is what it is," Renee said, and turned her back on Kate.

The townie kid must've overheard their exchange, because Kate's order was the only one that was delayed. By the time she got her bacon cheeseburger with fries, extra mayo, and double pickles, the others had finished eating and were nodding off at the table.

"Get it to go," Griff said, yawning. "I'm crashing."

"Me, too," Rebecca said.

"I'm outta here," said Rose.

Renee hadn't acknowledged Kate since she made that socialist remark, but she was leaning against Rebecca with her eyes closed and mouth open, quasi-passed-out.

"Go without me if you're so exhausted, but I'm eating my burger while it's hot," Kate said.

Griff sighed in annoyance. "If you get kidnapped walking home alone, I'll blame myself."

"I don't give a crap about your white liberal guilt."

"How can I be a liberal when my father has a hedge fund?"

Just then, the door opened, and Lucas walked in on a rush of cold air. He wore a lumberjack coat, and his ears were pink from the cold. Something in the fine tilt of his head, the athletic way he carried himself—bulky and graceful at once—caught her eye and reminded her why she'd taken him to her bed last fall. They'd never finished what they started, had they?

"Yo, what up, Timmy?" she heard him say to the kid behind the counter. The kid smiled so hard his whole face stretched, and Kate saw that Lucas must be some kind of hometown hero. Figures.

Kate turned to Griff. "You're off the hook, buddy. The guy who just walked in goes to Carlisle. I'll get him to walk me back to Whipple."

Griff looked pissed. If he didn't want Kate walking home alone, he certainly didn't want her going with that good-looking stranger. The Three Rs started pulling on their coats and hats and shuffling sideways to get out of the booth, taking a long time about it. Eventually, in his drug-addled state, Griff got carried along with the crowd. He waved to Kate wistfully as the door shut behind them.

Lucas sat down on a stool at the counter, waiting for his order. The townie kid had gone into the back to prepare it. Shecky's was empty now; the two of them were the only customers in the joint. Kate carried the red plastic basket with her burger and fries over to the counter and sat down on the stool next to Lucas. He was flipping through the leaves of a coin-operated jukebox.

"So," she said, barely glancing at him, as if they were continuing a conversation from a moment before. She picked up her Sheckyburger and took a bite. *Mmmm.* Maybe it was the weed, or the burger, or maybe it was the boy, because in that second, the planet turned on its axis and she felt like she was exactly where she was meant to be.

Lucas took a quarter from his pocket and put it down on the counter. "You like the Violent Femmes?"

She dabbed at her lips with a napkin and looked more closely at the writing inside the jukebox.

"I know that song. 'Why can't I get just one fuck,' right? Is that supposed to be like my theme song?"

He laughed. "No, I just feel like hearing it. It's an angry song. I'm an angry guy tonight."

"Yeah, I tend to bust an attitude when the going gets tough, too. Makes me feel better," she said.

"Exactly." He looked at her in surprise, nodding. His eyes were beautiful, a rich brown flecked with gold.

"Anyway, I suppose it's my own fault if you think I'm an easy lay," she said.

"I don't think that."

"No? I took you home like five minutes after we met."

He shrugged. "I went, didn't I?"

"What, no double standard? Most guys think it's okay for them to sleep around, but if girls do it, they're sluts."

His food still hadn't arrived, so he took a French fry from her platter and dipped it in ketchup. "Maybe some girls. Not you."

"Why not?"

He shrugged.

"I'll tell you why not," Kate said. "Because normal rules don't apply to me."

Lucas smiled. "You think highly of yourself."

"Don't you think highly of yourself?"

"Maybe."

They gazed at each other, a challenge hanging in the air between them.

The kid came out with Lucas's burger. He stood there, looking from Lucas to Kate and back again, like he wanted to say something.

"Thanks, Timmy," Lucas said, grabbing the platter from his hands. It was a dismissal. The kid shrugged and walked away.

"God, this music," Kate said, flipping through the jukebox leaves. "Country Western and oldies. Shoot me."

"I bet you listen to hip-hop, because you grew up on the streets," he said.

She couldn't decide if he was mocking her or flirting with her, or both, but she liked it.

"Hip-hop's great," she said. "You like Tupac? 'I'm the rebel, cold as the devil, straight from the underground.' The guy's a friggin' genius if you ask me."

"He's a criminal."

"So what, they're all criminals. Everyone's a criminal, really. My father's a criminal when you think about it."

"Your father the trustee's a criminal?"

"Oh, so you know who my father is?"

"Don't act all modest. Everybody knows."

"Well, he is. I mean, he breaks laws. I do, too."

Lucas laughed. "How could I forget, rules don't apply to you."

"Like you don't break laws? You never speed, or smoke a little weed on a Saturday night?" She picked up the quarter. "Pick a song, or I will."

"All right."

Lucas flipped a few more pages, then pressed the old-fashioned buttons, and Elvis Costello started singing "My Funny Valentine."

"Good choice. Just right for the dead hour in the middle of the night," she said.

"My favorite time of day," he said.

"Mine, too."

They finished their burgers in silence. By the time the song ended, their food was gone, and crumpled napkins filled the red baskets. The restaurant was quiet except for the buzzing of the fluorescent lights and the whirring of the pie refrigerator. The white noise cast a cloak of intimacy over them. They turned toward each other at the same moment on the rotating stools, and their knees touched. Neither one of them moved away. Kate tossed her head and played with her hair, catching sight of herself in the mirrored backsplash behind the counter. She was flirting shamelessly, and for the first time in a long time, her heart was in it. She had butterflies in her stomach; her armpits were moist.

"Tell me a thing," she said.

"What kind of thing?"

"Mmm, something I don't know about you."

She looked at him, waiting. He swirled the ice at the bottom of his glass and leaned back, pouring it into his mouth. He had one of those great jock necks, thick as a tree trunk. She watched his Adam's apple bob as he swallowed.

"I used to come here all the time in high school," he said, crunching the ice between his teeth. "After a game especially. Fuel up, you know. This place reminds me of that time. My team, my friends."

"You sound nostalgic."

"I am."

"Aren't you a little young for that?"

"Not really," Lucas said, shaking his head. "See, it turns out I can't play hockey anymore. I haven't told anybody yet. I just found out. So, kick me, I'm sad tonight."

"Why can't you play hockey?"

"I had a lot of concussions. Just got another, and the doc says it's my last. One more, and my brain might not recover."

"So no hockey. Don't you have other sports?"

"Yeah, football and lacrosse. I have to give those up, too. But hockey's the one I care about."

"Ah. The old Carlisle hockey obsession."

Hockey ruled at Carlisle, which had the strongest team in the Ivies but was outclassed in football and many other sports by bigger schools like Harvard and Princeton.

"It's not just Carlisle," Lucas said. "This is the north country up here. I learned to skate practically before I could walk. People think it's the violence I like, but it's the skill. The blade work, the stick work. And the ice. So pure and clean. It's a thing of beauty."

She leaned forward and raised her hand to his forehead, tracing a circle on the smooth skin with her fingertip.

"Your brain's beautiful, too. And you can live without hockey, but you can't live without your brain."

"That's the thing. I don't know if I *can* live without hockey," he said.

She was close enough to drink in the spicy smell of his shampoo, and beneath it, the warm scent of hair and skin. She remembered being in bed with him, feeling the bulk of him on top of her. She wanted to feel it again.

"You need to find some other source of excitement," she said, raising an eyebrow suggestively.

He gave her a slow, dreamy smile. "That could help."

It was a new experience for Kate, coming on strong to a guy rather than reacting to his advances, but she liked this one excessively. She'd let him get away the first time because of the complication with Jenny. She'd sensed by Jenny's reaction when she walked in on the two of them that there was a history. Her suspicion was confirmed not long after, when Kate and Aubrey ran into Lucas on the Quad on the way back from class. The three of them chatted for a few minutes, and the chemistry between Kate and Lucas was so palpable that Aubrey spilled the beans. Jenny had told Aubrey that Lucas was her high school boyfriend, but she'd been too proud to come to Kate and call dibs.

"Hey," Kate said. "Did you used to date my roommate? Jenny Vega?"

"You could call it that. We hung out. But it was a long time ago in a galaxy far, far away," Lucas said.

"Wasn't it just last year?"

"It was high school. Nobody should be held accountable for what they do in high school."

"Would she have a problem if *we* hung out?"

"We are hanging out."

"Are we? Okay."

"Look, Jenny broke up with me. As far as I'm concerned I don't owe her a thing. But if you're worried, ask her."

"What if she says to keep away from you?"

"I take it back. Don't ask her."

Kate laughed. Lucas was watching her intently.

"Forget about Jenny, okay? I promise you, she doesn't care," he said, and grabbed Kate's wrist, turning it over to examine the three small stars tattooed on its underside. "I like your tattoo. Does it mean something?" he asked, touching them.

"Funny, nobody's ever asked me that," she said, and paused, thinking about kissing his beautiful mouth. If Jenny wanted Kate to keep her hands off Lucas, she should've said something after she found them half naked together, right? But she didn't. Kate liked the feel of Lucas's fingers digging into her wrist enough that she lowered her head until her cheek rested on the back of his hand, rubbing her face against his skin like a cat. She expected that being close to him would make her heart beat faster. Instead her pulse slowed down, and she felt like she breathed easier. He caressed her hair, and she sat up, pointing to the star farthest to the left.

"This one is for my mom, who died. This one on the left is for my best friend Maggie, who ate a bottle of pills and OD'd when we were in tenth grade. I think of her every single day. And the last one is me."

"Why are you there with them? You're still alive."

"For the moment. No promises," she said, and looked up into his eyes so he felt the full weight of her remark.

"What, like you'd kill yourself?"

"Sometimes I get really sad. If I want to, nobody can tell me not to, because I'm the boss of me."

He smiled. "Great, just what I need in my darkest hour. A batshit-crazy girl, with a ruby in her belly button and a death wish."

Kate laughed. "Don't knock crazy till you try it, my friend."

After that, the conversation got deep fast. As different as they were, they had everything in common. They were born two days apart. Lucas lost his dad at the same age as Kate lost her mom. He hated his stepfather even more than Kate hated Victoria, and had a passel of bratty stepsibs who sucked up attention and food and took all his stuff. They both thought Carlisle was full of shit, and that Carlislers who "bled orange" were losers and fools. Neither one of them could imagine caring about a subject enough to declare a major. And they both cherished a fantasy that they'd never breathed a word of before to anyone: of hitting the road, no money, no destination, no phone. Vagabonding around with nothing but a couple of changes of clothes in a backpack until they got bored of it, which might be never. Maybe they would go away, together, far away, and chop wood and live off the land. They might never come back.

"Hey, you know what's on here? You'll love this," Lucas said, pulling another quarter from his pocket. He pushed the jukebox buttons from memory, and Roger Miller drifted out, with that sublime finger-snapping.

"Trailers for sale or rent, rooms to let, fifty cents."

"I do love this!" Kate squealed. "I know all the words."

"Me, too," he said, and laughed.

They started singing along. " 'Third boxcar, midnight train. Destination, Bangor, Maine.' "

"Ever been to Bangor?" Lucas asked.

"I've been a lot of places, but Bangor, Maine, is not one of them."

"It's like a five-hour drive. I know a great doughnut shop, opens at six. We could get 'em fresh from the deep fry."

At that moment, Kate would have gone anywhere with him. She stood up and grabbed her coat. "I'm in."

Lucas's car was a faded old ragtop with bench seats that looked like it was held together with chewing gum and wire. He drove with one hand on the wheel and kept the other arm tight around her. She leaned into him, shivering, as the heater coughed and snorted. Once they hit the interstate, Lucas put his knee to the steering wheel and took Kate's head in his hands, kissing her deeply, stopping only for occasional peeks at the road. They made out at seventy miles an hour, their tongues intertwined, their hands stealing underneath one another's clothes, until the median came rushing at them and Lucas had to fight to keep control of the car. He righted it at the last second, and they looked at each other, hearts racing with panic, and burst into hysterical laughter.

"Let's go park somewhere before we wipe out for real," he said. "I know a place."

He took the next exit, and got on the main road that ran along the river, heading back toward campus. A few minutes later, they pulled off onto a narrow dirt road that led to a gravel parking lot facing out over the water. A full yellow moon hung low in the sky, throwing off an eerie glow. The river was clogged with giant blocks of ice, bobbing and glinting, silvery in the moonlight.

"The cops won't bother us here, not at this hour," he said, smoothing her hair back from her face.

"Where are we?"

"Not too far from school, actually."

"You've been here before."

"A million times. This is the deepest part of the river. We swim here in the summertime. You can't see it through the trees, but a little ways upriver's the old railroad bridge. We jump off it and race to the float. It's like a dare, every year after ice out. First man to the float gets a beer."

"Sounds dangerous."

"Yeah, people drown sometimes. But kids around here still do it. It's like a rite of passage."

"Cool, I want to try. Not now, obviously. Once it warms up."

"Yeah, I don't think so."

"I'm an ace swimmer. Lifeguard certified, five summers of sailing camp."

"It's not that. A winter like this, ice out isn't till May. Swim before June, the water'll paralyze you in minutes, and you'll sink like a rock. By the time the river's swimmable, I'm gonna bet you'll be off on Martha's Vineyard sipping cocktails."

"I don't have any plans for the summer that I can't change. Who knows, maybe I'll stay in Belle River."

He laughed. "Right, and hang out with me and my townie friends down by the Dairy Bar."

"Why not?"

"That'd be a sight. I'd like to see it, actually."

Their eyes caught and held, and they melted together, kissing until they were both breathless. She started to take off her clothes, but he stopped her.

"We'll be more comfortable in the back."

He opened his door, smiling, and beckoned her out. The frigid air came as a shock, a faint aroma of skunk adding to its sharpness. They stood together for a moment looking toward the opposite shore, his arms wrapped tightly around her as they listened to the ice grind and crack on the river.

"That sound," she said. "It's like it's alive."

"Oh, the river's alive. Never doubt it. C'mon," he said, and opened the back door.

It turned out Jenny *did* care. Kate had no intention of giving up Lucas at this point. She couldn't if she wanted to. But she felt bad that she'd thrown her hookup with him in Jenny's face. And at such a time. With Jenny and Aubrey gone, Kate was lonely and anxious. She wanted to drown her sorrows in sex with Lucas, but since their night by the river (no surprise, they never made it to Bangor), he seemed to be avoiding her. Between Lucas's disappearing act and her roommates' absence, Kate didn't know what to do with herself. She liked an audience; solitude freaked her out. Griff was available to sit with her nonstop, holding her hand and staring into her eyes if she let him, but that got cloying after about five minutes. He took hanging out way too seriously. Grabbing a milkshake together meant they were getting engaged, as far as Griff was concerned. So two days after her awful fight with Jenny, at her wit's end, Kate called Aubrey's mother's apartment and left a message on the answering machine begging Jenny to call so she could apologize. Later that day the phone rang in suite 402, and it was Jenny calling from Nevada.

"I'm so sorry, can you forgive me?" Kate cried.

She paused for breath and then, hearing only the buzz of silence on the line, plowed ahead.

"After you said I was a bad friend for not helping Aubrey, I felt really small. That's why I brought up Lucas, to get back at you. That was a shitty thing to do, and I apologize."

"Ugh, let's just forget it, all right?" Jenny said.

"Yes. Yes, thank you. So you forgive me."

"About Lucas? Fine. It's harder to forgive the timing. Aubrey was suffering, I was trying to help, and you were just so—nasty."

"I tried to explain. I'm terrified of hospitals."

"We never even went to the hospital. She died before we got there," Jenny said.

"She *died*? Oh, no, I can't believe it. So fast?"

"Yes. We ended up going straight from the airport to the funeral home."

"Well, I couldn't have known that, could I? I'm sorry if you think I was heartless. I just got really defensive and lashed out. I care so much about our friendship, Jenny."

"Yeah, sure, me, too. Listen, if this is all you're calling about, I should go. We need to pick out an urn, and order food for the memorial service."

Kate felt like she'd been slapped. She didn't like to grovel. If she made the effort to apologize, she expected a grateful response from Jenny, not a bitchy tone and getting off the phone.

"I'm very sorry to hear about Aubrey's mom," Kate said stiffly. "When is the funeral?"

"Tomorrow morning."

"Should I send flowers?"

Jenny sighed audibly. "Honestly, Kate, do what you want."

"Tell Aubrey I'm sorry about her mother," Kate said, and slammed the receiver down.

Her roommates were a conundrum. As much as she loved them, she also hated them, especially that impossible Jenny.

12

Finals had already started back at Carlisle. Jenny was desperate to study on the flight from Las Vegas to Boston, but she couldn't set her mind to it, so troubled was she by what she'd witnessed of Aubrey's home life. Or lack of one. Brenda Miller had been living in an SRO motel, in a single room with a hot plate and the bathroom down the hall. Aubrey said she hadn't known how bad things had gotten, or she would've found a way to send her mother more money. (How? Aubrey had nothing.) Brenda Miller's bank account had been overdrawn, and any valuables sold or pawned already, which, looking on the bright side, meant there wasn't much work to be done to sort out her things. Aubrey took a couple of old photographs and an ugly, crocheted afghan that she said had sentimental value, to remember her mother by. Her pretty sister Amanda, hostile and hard-eyed and impatient, took nothing, though Jenny privately suspected Amanda had pocketed anything valuable before they arrived.

There was no money for a funeral. Aubrey had none, obviously. Amanda, who drove a Mustang and had awfully nice clothes for a cocktail waitress, claimed to be flat broke. As far as Jenny could tell, Amanda would've been happy to leave her mother's ashes in the trash can outside the funeral home. But Aubrey insisted on having some sort of ceremony. So at ten o' clock that morning, with the mercury already at eighty-five and the desert sky a harsh blue, Jenny and the two sisters rented a rickety motorboat at a lake about an hour from the city, a place Aubrey said her mother had loved. Aubrey and Amanda didn't know any prayers, so Jenny recited the Twenty-third Psalm while Aubrey and Amanda took turns reaching into the plastic bag and tossing handfuls of gritty, gray ash into the water. Aubrey sobbed all through their makeshift memorial and all the way to the airport, where Amanda waved a curt good-bye, obviously relieved to see the back of them. Jenny got the feeling Aubrey and her sister wouldn't speak again for a very long time, if ever.

Now, at thirty thousand feet, Aubrey was passed out, eyes shut, mouth open, in an exhausted sleep. She had thanked Jenny constantly, proclaiming her tearful gratitude, saying Jenny and Kate were her only family now. The responsibility of that weighed on Jenny's mind, simply because she knew it was true, and Kate wasn't bloody likely to shoulder her half of that burden.

But maybe Jenny was wrong about that. Their flight had been delayed, first by air-traffic congestion in Las Vegas, and later by a blizzard at Logan Airport that kept them circling for an hour until the runway could be plowed and de-iced. By the time they landed, the last bus back to Belle River had left without them. Jenny looked at her watch when they got to baggage claim and started to panic. Her econ exam was the day after tomorrow. She needed to get back to school fast, but there were no good options. She could call an expensive car service. She could roust her parents from their warm bed and ask them to drive for hours in the middle of a snowstorm to rescue her. Or, she could sleep in the terminal tonight, in which case she wouldn't make it back to campus till tomorrow afternoon and be too wrecked to study. That was her reward for being a good friend to Aubrey.

"Look, there's Kate!" Aubrey said, taking off toward the automatic doors.

"Where?"

Kate's bright hair stood out like a beacon in the gray-faced crowd waiting on the other side of the glass doors. By the time Jenny caught up, Aubrey was sobbing in Kate's arms.

Jenny met Kate's eyes over Aubrey's heaving shoulders. "I didn't know you'd be here," she said. The words came out sounding accusatory.

"I thought you could use a lift," Kate replied. "I borrowed Griff's Jeep. It's four-wheel-drive."

Kate looked tired and pale. Outside the plate-glass windows, the snow fell steadily, and Jenny felt a tentacle of forgiveness creep into her heart. It was no small undertaking, driving from Belle River to Boston, and back, in weather like this. A ride home in time for a decent night's sleep beat the hell out of camping on the floor of the terminal, using her suitcase for a pillow, and being too exhausted to study the next day. It was hard to stay mad at a person who'd drive four hours in a snowstorm to rescue you from a fate like that.

"Thanks, that's really nice of you," Jenny said, somewhat grudgingly, since Kate was still that same arrogant bitch who'd knowingly slept with her ex. She half expected a nasty retort. Kate was doing this for Aubrey, not for Jenny, et cetera and so forth. But Kate smiled in delight.

"What are roomies for? C'mon, I'm parked in the short-term lot."

On the ride home, Jenny sat in the backseat with her head lolling and her eyes closed, drifting in and out of sleep. In her lucid moments, she eavesdropped on Aubrey and Kate's conversation. They say eavesdroppers never hear good of themselves. That was a myth. Aubrey told Kate in detail about all the ways Jenny had helped out in her moment of need, and to Jenny's surprise, Kate joined in the praise. Jenny was smart and together and a loyal friend, Kate gushed. Nothing fazed her. They were lucky to have her in their lives. Hey, maybe Kate suspected Jenny was awake, and was saying sweet things in order to get back in her good graces. But still. Jenny dozed off, feeling generous toward Kate. When she awoke, they had just crossed the New Hampshire border. The world outside the windows was white and desolate, and Kate was steady at the wheel.

"I'm sad for my mom," Aubrey was saying. "She had such a hard life, and now it won't get better. I always thought someday, things would finally be right between us, but now it's too late."

"I think a lot about my mom, too," Kate said. "What would she be like now? What would *I* be like, if she'd lived? It's not just that she died too young, but she left me too young. I needed my mother."

Jenny wondered whether, if Kate hadn't lost her mom at a young age, she would be a better person now. Maybe she wouldn't take other people's things, or lord it over them, or ruin their self-confidence. Kate's relationship with her father and stepmother was dismal and wrenching. Jenny liked to think Kate had things easy, but maybe that wasn't entirely true.

"We're *orphans*," Aubrey said.

"I'm not. There's still Keniston."

"Technically, my father is still alive, too. But I have no idea where, so he doesn't count. And your dad disowned you, so he doesn't count, either."

"He didn't exactly disown me," Kate said defensively. "He held back my trust payments. I mean, yeah, that's outrageous, but it's Victoria's doing. He's under her thumb. I feel sorry for him, the old fool." Kate's condescending tone couldn't hide the hurt she obviously felt at her father's disloyalty.

The windshield wipers swished against the melting snow as they drove on. It got quiet inside the Jeep, and Jenny melted a little, too. She liked to think of herself as a fair person, and it seemed only fair to forgive Kate. As jealous as she might be over Lucas, the fact was, Jenny broke up with him before Lucas and Kate even met. Maybe Kate had lorded her conquest of Lucas over Jenny, but she did that in retaliation for Jenny saying mean things to her first. Ultimately, Kate wasn't so bad. Her life was harder than it looked from the outside. Jenny decided to cut Kate some slack, at least for now.

The three of them made it through exams, and the new term began. The weather was icy and bleak. Jenny trudged on, fighting a cold and the winter doldrums, while Kate and Aubrey gave in to the gloom. Jenny watched with dismay as they partied every night and slept through classes, ate mounds of junk food for days on end, then ate nothing at all. Their hair looked greasy and their sheets smelled of sweat, and it seemed to Jenny that they would fail out of school if somebody didn't intervene. So she took to scolding them, which accomplished nothing except to make them close the door to Kate's room and ram a towel in the crack when they smoked weed. At least it was an improvement over smoking in the living room. Jenny tried not to care about their decline. If they couldn't be bothered to help themselves, why should she knock herself out trying to help them, when she was so crazy busy?

In addition to five classes and four extracurriculars, Jenny worked fifteen hours a week in the provost's office. It wasn't one of those mindless work-study jobs, like checking IDs at the gym or signing out books in Ogden Library, where you sat on your butt in your sweatpants, schmoozing cute guys. It was clerical work, and demanding. The bosses noticed every typo. You had to wear office attire. You couldn't be late or trade hours with other students even if you had a big paper due. But the job gave her access to inside information and face time with important people in the administration. It would be killer on her résumé and hopefully earn her a letter of recommendation. So she stuck with it. No question, though, it added pressure, and contributed to how fed-up she felt with her roommates lately.

On a dark afternoon at the beginning of March, Jenny was called in to the provost's office unexpectedly because both secretaries were out with the flu and the trustees were in town. The gray sky spit snow as Jenny hurried over the icy paths toward Founders' Hall, her legs freezing in thin nylons. She rode up in the creaky elevator to the dark-paneled provost's office, where she found Gloria Meyers—the provost herself—waiting for her with her fingers tapping impatiently. The provost was a sturdy woman with steel-gray hair, whose wardrobe tended toward jewel tones and bold earrings. She looked as if she should be nice, like somebody's artsy grandma, but in actuality she was brusque and intimidating. Before Jenny even had her parka off, the provost was rattling off a complicated series of instructions for assembling the meeting binders. The board of trustees' meeting began in fifteen minutes. Assembling the binders in time was not humanly possible, but Jenny was afraid to open her mouth and say so, so she simply nodded and walked over to the Xerox machine. The next forty minutes of her life was spent furiously copying documents and inserting them into three-ring binders.

Jenny loaded the binders onto a cart and headed down the hall to the large conference room feeling like she was going to the firing squad.

Byron Ogletree, the president of Carlisle, was standing at a lectern at the head of a long table when Jenny struggled through the heavy wooden door, pushing the binders on the cart. Ogletree was a famous economist, and looked every bit the academic with his mane of white hair, goatee, and bow tie. He paused in midsentence and looked at Jenny, which made her freeze like a deer caught in headlights. Gloria Meyers came to her rescue.

"You hand them out to this side of the table and I'll do the other," Gloria whispered, grabbing an armful of binders. "Then take a seat in the back in case I need you."

Inside the cavernous room, weak light filtered through ancient leaded windows. Gray-haired, gray-suited men sat around the long mahogany conference table. Jenny was frazzled, and too timid to make eye contact. She didn't realize she was handing a binder to Keniston Eastman until he thanked her by name.

At the break, she was put in charge of overseeing the coffee station. The trustees milled about, chatting and laughing. Some left the room to make phone calls or use the bathroom. She was mopping up a spill with paper towels when Mr. Eastman came over to her. He glanced over his shoulder before speaking.

"Jenny, I need to talk to you, privately," he said in a low tone, with an urgent air.

She was too surprised to reply, so she nodded, and kept cleaning.

"I'm staying at the College Inn. When the meeting ends, I'll wait for you in the bar there. Come as soon as you can, all right?"

She said nothing, but he seemed to take that as a yes. The meeting resumed. Jenny spent the second half of it staring at her hands, too self-conscious to look in Eastman's direction, not hearing a word that was uttered. What did Keniston Eastman want with her? What could he possibly mean by asking her to meet him in a *bar*? He must know she was underage; she was the same age as his daughter. If an older man invites a girl who's not of drinking age to a bar, does that signal an improper advance? If Keniston was making an improper advance, what should she do about it? He seemed to her too old and intimidating to be physically attractive, but maybe physical attractiveness wasn't relevant here. What would be the benefits to her if she said yes to a proposition from Keniston Eastman, or the repercussions if she said no? It wasn't like Jenny never thought about him. She fantasized about him regularly, but these fantasies were not the same kind she had about Lucas. In her daydreams, Keniston was her mentor. He offered her a job, made introductions, took an interest in her career. She wanted that from him, badly. What if he offered her such things in exchange for an occasional assignation? Would she really turn him down? Or would she say yes? That was a horrifying thought and an exhilarating one at the same time.

It was four thirty and getting dark by the time Jenny walked through Briggs Gate. Trading the quiet of the Quad for the bustle of College Street, she felt on the verge of something big. The wheels of passing cars had melted the day's snow into a gray slush that soaked through the soles of her shoes, but she ignored the chill on her toes. The College Inn had pride of place at the corner of College and Main, its elegant brick and limestone façade designed to mimic the look of the dormitories lining the world-famous Quad. In her years growing up in Belle River, Jenny had never set foot in the Inn. It was the hotel of choice for the Carlisle power crowd—parents with fat wallets, Carlisle class of this-or-that returning for reunions or tailgates, visiting scholars on expense accounts. The lobby was old-school. Persian rugs and a brass chandelier, deep leather armchairs. The man behind the reception desk wore an orange-and-white striped tie—Carlisle's colors—and looked at Jenny expectantly. She felt conspicuous in the down parka she wore over her office clothes, but she squared her shoulders and tried to look confident. After all, she belonged here as much as anybody. Keniston Eastman had invited her.

Before the desk clerk could speak, Jenny saw the entrance to the restaurant on her right, and ducked inside. The room was dimly lit and mostly deserted, with rich wood paneling, and a faint tang of cigar smoke in the air. Keniston waved at her from a booth near the back. She took a deep breath and went to join him.

"Jenny, hello," he said, with forced heartiness, and shook her hand. She saw again how much he looked like the portrait of his ancestor that hung over the grand staircase in Founders'—the same forbidding profile and heavy eyebrows.

"Hello, Kenist—I mean, Mr. Eastman," she said, sliding in across from him and shrugging out of her coat. She felt hot and breathless and slightly ill. If this was really a proposition, she didn't think she could go through with it.

"I was surprised to see you this afternoon, but then I recalled you mentioned that you work for the provost's office," he said.

"Yes, sir. How nice that you get to visit for your trustees' meeting. Kate must be thrilled that you're in town," she said, awkwardly.

This wasn't feeling like the beginning of an illicit relationship, but even so, she was thrown off balance, being alone with him like this.

Keniston grimaced. "Kate doesn't know I'm here. That's why I asked to speak with you. I'm a bit out of touch with her, and so I wanted to ask you something."

Of course—this was about Kate! What an idiot Jenny was, and how full of herself. Her cheeks burned. She was grateful for the dim lighting, so Keniston wouldn't see her blush, or read in her eyes the ludicrous assumption she'd made. The idea that Keniston Eastman, with his millions and his expensive suits and his pretty young wife, might try to seduce *her*—little old Jenny Vega from the wrong side of the tracks in Belle River. Who did she think she was? Completely ridiculous. Not in a million years. And thank God for that! Right? She was profoundly relieved—although a tiny bit disappointed to lose her shot at Eastman's patronage.

Caught up in her own embarrassment, Jenny missed what he'd just said.

"—since Thanksgiving, so—"

"I'm sorry," she said, faltering. "Can you repeat that? It's been a long day."

"Of course. Forgive my rudeness, just plunging into things. Can I get you a drink?"

A glass of amber liquid sat before him. Scotch, probably. She could smell its sharp, smoky scent from across the table.

"I'm not of legal age," she said.

"I wasn't suggesting you order alcohol." He signaled to a waiter, who came over instantly. "The young lady will have a—?"

"Diet Coke, please. With lemon," she said, blushing anew. What a ditz she was.

Within minutes, her drink appeared, and Jenny sipped the ice-cold soda gratefully as Keniston launched into his tale of woe. She was too distracted at first to realize that he was confiding in her, telling her the private details of his troubled relationship with his daughter. Some stuff Jenny already knew or could have guessed. Kate and Keniston had quarreled bitterly over Thanksgiving and weren't on speaking terms. Kate had a difficult relationship with Victoria that led her to view Keniston's efforts at guidance as vindictive attacks. Keniston was terribly worried about her drinking and drugging and spending and cutting class. He wasn't a monster. He remembered what it was like to be in college, and a certain amount of misbehavior was expected in a normal child. But Kate wasn't a normal child. Kate was different. She was troubled.

"I asked you here because I have to tell you something, and ask a favor of you, but this is highly confidential. You have to promise me it will stay between us," he said.

"Of course," she whispered, leaning forward. "You can count on me. I won't breathe a word."

His face was grim. Jenny wasn't thinking about what he would say, or how he felt. She was too caught up in the drama of being taken into his confidence. Keniston took a swig of his drink, girding himself for the revelation.

"Did Kate ever tell you about what happened to Maggie Price, her best friend at Odell?" he began.

"Not that I recall."

"Oh, you'd remember if she had. Maggie committed suicide her sophomore year. A beautiful girl, very smart, everything ahead of her. From a prominent family. Her parents were friends of mine. It's beyond comprehension what they went through. She did it with pills, an intentional overdose. And she left a note. The note mentioned Kate by name."

Jenny looked at him in surprise. "What did it say?"

"It said, 'See, I showed you, it doesn't hurt. I'll be waiting.' "

Jenny stared at Keniston, too shocked to reply. So Kate had been part of a suicide pact? That seemed impossible. The Kate Eastman Jenny knew was so alive. And so full of herself. She would never choose to die.

"Was the note for real?" Jenny asked. "Maybe Maggie was making it up."

"Oh, no. I confronted Kate. She admitted they were planning to do it together, but Kate got cold feet and backed out at the last minute. It's the only time I was happy she didn't keep her word. I sent her to a psychiatrist after that, naturally, but my suspicion is, she's no longer following the prescribed treatment." He paused and looked Jenny in the eye. "Is she?"

"I wouldn't know. I mean, we're close, or I thought we were. She's never mentioned any of this to me. I'm pretty shocked to hear it, actually."

"I see."

"What treatment is she supposed to follow?"

"Medication, talk therapy. A structured schedule including regular sleep and exercise. And refraining from the consumption of drugs or alcohol. That's very important, because Kate is prone to addictive behavior and binge drinking. When she relapses, she gets depressed, and she's extremely susceptible to . . . all right, I'll say it, self-harm."

"For what it's worth, Mr. Eastman, Kate doesn't seem suicidal to me. Not at all."

"I'm glad to hear it, but you're not a professional."

"No, I'm not," Jenny admitted.

"I know she's back to her old habits. Victoria told me Kate came home drunk from the nightclub when you were in New York over Thanksgiving."

"Yes. I'm sorry."

He waved dismissively. "Don't apologize. I know my daughter. I'm sure she was the ringleader. The point is, we argued about it. I was trying to help her, but I'm afraid I merely succeeded in driving her away."

"She made it sound like you argued over money."

"Any time I intervene, Kate pretends I'm motivated by something venal, something other than concern for her welfare. That makes it easier to ignore me. You know, she once told Victoria that I've hated her ever since my first wife died because I hold Kate responsible for Kitty's cancer. I can't figure out if she actually believes these wild accusations or if she's just trying to manipulate me."

Jenny didn't think it was her place to tell him how sincerely Kate believed that.

"It sounds like you really need to talk to her," Jenny said. "Have a heart-to-heart and clear the air."

"I wish that were possible, but she won't speak to me. That's why I need you."

"No problem, Mr. Eastman. I'm happy to help. I can go back to Whipple right now and ask her to come over here and talk to you."

"No, no, not that," he exclaimed. "If she knew I was here in town, if she knew I was meeting with you—don't you see? She'd never speak to either of us again. She can't know we talked, ever."

"Oh. Then—? I'm confused."

"What I need is for you to keep me posted on her situation," he said.

"What do you mean, keep you posted? Are you asking me to spy on her?"

"That's an unfortunate choice of words. As her father, I need to know, is she doing a lot of drugs, drinking a lot? Is she sleeping around, with a lot of boys? The doctor says that's bad for her self-esteem."

Sleeping around with a lot of boys seemed to be quite good for Kate's self-esteem, but that wasn't the point.

"Mr. Eastman, you're asking me to inform on your daughter."

"I'm asking you to help me help her. Think of it as an act of friendship."

"I don't think she'd see it that way," she said.

"Kate doesn't always know what's best for her."

"I'm sorry, I wish I could do what you're asking, but I don't feel right spying on Kate. That's not what friends do."

He sighed, and signaled the waiter for another round of drinks. Only once they'd come, and he'd taken a long pull on his second scotch, did he speak.

"I admire your integrity, Jenny, really I do," Keniston said.

He was probably buttering her up. But she liked the feeling of having this important man admire her, so it was difficult not to fall for it.

"I would never ask you to go against your principles," he said. "The problem is, if you don't help me, Jenny, I'm afraid Kate might do something very foolish. I'm afraid she might harm herself. If you could just see your way clear to helping me out on this one thing, if you could find it in your heart to keep me in the loop, I would be very grateful. I don't mean money. I would never try to bribe you. I know you're an honorable person. I recognize that what I ask is a bit of an uncomfortable undertaking. You would be putting yourself out. I would consider it my duty and my privilege to repay you someday, in whatever form is of most use to you. Advice. Introductions. A first job out of college, if that would be of interest."

"Of course. I would love to work for you after college."

"Very good then. Shall we shake on it?"

He held out his hand. Jenny hadn't intended to agree to inform on Kate, but Keniston Eastman's hand—and his job offer—exerted a magnetic pull.

"I can't. I shouldn't," she said, with some difficulty.

"I promise she'll never find out."

"Sir, if there was anything truly wrong, I'd tell you. But I'm not comfortable calling you up and saying, oh, there was just a guy in Kate's room, or she smoked pot, or—you know, stuff like that."

"What if we were to touch base by telephone once a week, and you give me a general picture of how she's doing?"

"You mean, give a thumbs-up or thumbs-down? I could do that."

"If I have follow-up questions, I'll ask, but you can decline to answer if the subject is too sensitive. If we do that, I'll feel reassured, and you don't need to feel that you're betraying Kate's confidence. All right?"

Keniston's hand hung there, waiting to be shaken. What he proposed was so much less drastic than reporting on Kate's every move that Jenny felt obligated to agree. It would seem churlish not to, after his hospitality in New York, and his taking an interest in her career. She wanted to work for him after college, so much. This would put them in regular contact. She could always say no to ratting Kate out over boys or drugs or that sort of thing. He'd just said so, hadn't he?

Jenny reached out and shook Keniston Eastman's hand. The look of relief in his eyes gave her a moment of queasiness. She was working for him now. They had an arrangement. He would have his expectations. Jenny liked to do a good job, to please the people in authority. When Keniston started asking sensitive questions, as he surely would, was she really going to refuse to answer?

13

The Eastmans had a house in Jamaica, an old plantation owner's spread, perched in the lush green hills to the east of Montego Bay with breathtaking views of the sea. Kate thought of it as *her* house, since the stepmonsters never visited and didn't give a crap about it. For Kate, it was the place where she'd frolicked with her mother as a child, but Victoria would sell the house in a heartbeat if she could find a buyer. Luckily, she couldn't, since the snowbirds had long since departed Jamaica in favor of more fashionable isles like Anguilla and St. Bart's. The house had been in the Eastman family since early in the previous century, ever since Kate's great-grandfather took an interest in a cane plantation and rum factory at the tail end of Prohibition. Later generations of Eastmans decided the alcohol business was too low-class, and sold the family interest and rolled the money into a beach resort that had been quite chic for a time, back in the heyday of James Bond and martinis and such. Then the socialists came to power in Jamaica and threatened to nationalize everything, and Kate's grandfather let the resort go for a song. Somehow through thick and thin they'd held on to the house, and Kate had taken to saying that Keniston should give it to her as a twenty-first-birthday present, that she would go live there and care for the place and start a bed-and-breakfast or something. She would never actually do that—Kate, changing the bedsheets of strangers?—but she hated the thought of losing a house that held precious childhood memories.

Spring break was coming up and nobody had plans yet. Kate was sick of the wretched, endless winter, and tired of the fishbowl life of Carlisle, where she felt constantly watched and spied on. Keniston always seemed to know what she was doing—how? Getting on a plane to anywhere sounded good right now, but getting on a plane to Jamaica would be paradise. One night, as she sat with her roommates and Griff Rothenberg over the unappetizing remains of tacos in the Commons, she idly mentioned her desire to visit her house. She wasn't serious, but Griff glommed on to the idea instantly.

"I'm game. Let's go," Griff said.

"I was just daydreaming," Kate said. "The house is closed now. The caretakers would have to open it."

"So, that's nothing, right? Taking off the dust covers and turning on the air-conditioning? Why does your dad pay them if not to be able to do that on a whim?"

"I don't even know if the pool is filled."

"Call and ask."

"All right."

Kate had her qualms. Griff was getting so possessive lately. She had no interest in a vacation where the two of them played house for a week and he became even more convinced that Kate was his girlfriend. She was obsessed with that gorgeous, moody townie boy Lucas, whom she'd barely seen since that night they had sex in his car near the icy river.

"No need to worry about a plane ticket," Griff said. "My dad's flying to the Caymans next week. We can hitch a ride on his plane."

"The house is in *Jamaica*," Kate said.

"Jamaica and the Caymans are right next door to each other, babe. I can ask him to add a stop for us," Griff said, with a puppy-dog eagerness on his handsome face that Kate found cloying.

"Free vacation?" Aubrey said. "Can I come?"

"Why not, we can all go," Kate said sourly, never imagining it would come to pass. She had no intention of following through.

A few days later, when Griff told her the private jet was a go, Kate reconsidered. She'd had a particularly gruesome couple of days—oversleeping after a night of partying and missing a midterm, realizing she'd used up her March allowance by the twelfth of the month—and the urge for escape was more powerful than ever. She imagined lounging by the pool with views of the ocean, rubbing lotion on Lucas's back. Lucas's perfect body in a bathing suit, with a tan, would cure her winter doldrums. She would lie out on the lounger with him at night, talking under the stars, or swim with him in the salty ocean, clinging together as the waves battered them. There was only one problem: Lucas seemed determined to avoid her. Since that time they ran into each other at Shecky's, Kate had succeeded in spending only the occasional night with her townie, and always in her room. He never invited her to his. The next morning without fail he would slip from her grasp and disappear back into his own life so completely it was like an air lock sealed behind him. His detachment took Kate by surprise. After their first night together, she expected the sort of adulation other guys gave her, but Lucas was elusive. Nobody had ever been so indifferent to her before, and she was caught by it. She loved the head games, loved the chase, loved how he ignored her in the Commons and sat with his boys instead. She developed a sixth sense for his presence. She could recognize him from the corner of her eye from the far side of the Quad based on the color of his jacket or the tilt of his head. The thought of spending time with Lucas in Jamaica was intoxicating. *Lucas,* not Griff.

"I don't think it'll work," she said. "I'm not on speaking terms with my father. He'd never approve."

"From what you've told me, you're the one who's refusing to speak to him," Griff said. "I bet if you asked, he'd say yes, as a gesture of reconciliation. What have you got to lose?"

"I'll give it a shot," Kate said, thinking that if Keniston did say yes, she would figure out some way to get Lucas to come along. But getting

Griff not to? That part seemed like a long shot. He was like gum on her shoe.

Kate e-mailed Keniston, and as Griff had predicted, he wrote back right away. He would allow her to stay at the house in Jamaica provided that responsible people would accompany her. For example, her roommate, Jenny Vega, had impressed him at Thanksgiving as a girl with a good head on her shoulders. If Jenny accompanied Kate, he would approve the trip.

Keniston had solved Kate's problem. She had an excuse to turn this into a group trip, with free airfare and a free place to stay. Who would say no to that? Not even Lucas, not once she told him that a lot of people were going. Enough people to make it nonthreatening to Lucas. Enough people so she could create a buffer between her and Griff, and have time to indulge her Lucas fixation.

She showed Griff the e-mail.

"I have to bring Jenny," Kate said, laying the groundwork. "I can't invite Jenny without inviting Aubrey, too. I'm sorry, but this means it won't be just you and me."

"No problem. The plane seats ten," Griff said.

"I wouldn't want my girls to feel like third wheels, so we'll need to invite guys for them."

"I can ask around at the frat to see who's available."

"Let me take care of the invitations," Kate said.

A week later, six of them stepped from the air-conditioned sterility of the terminal in Montego Bay to the hot, humid chaos of the pavement—Kate, Aubrey, and Jenny; and Griff, Lucas, and some dweeb named Drew that Jenny picked up somewhere, whose chief assets were being male (ostensibly; Kate had her doubts) and being available to go on vacation with no notice. Vans and taxis and minibuses jockeyed for position at the curb. People accosted them, holding signs for hotels and cruise lines. Kate led the way to a taxi stand, where she asked around for a van big enough to carry them out to the countryside. Nobody wanted to take them to the Eastmans' house, which was up in the middle of nowhere in the hills. Taxi drivers preferred going to the big hotels or the port where the cruise ships docked, so they could count on a fare back. Finally Kate agreed to a rip-off price for a ride in a dilapidated old station wagon with the word "taxi" hand-lettered on the side, driven by a guy with no front teeth.

"C'mon, we'll sit in the way-back," she said, taking Lucas's hand. She wanted him badly enough to be brazen about singling him out. She would throw Griff together with Aubrey, who'd been crushing on him noticeably for months—so much so that Kate might have minded if she'd given a rip about Griff.

The way-back of the station wagon smelled like a dead animal.

"Hey, roll the windows down, it stinks back here," Kate yelled, as the others piled into the car.

Soon they were speeding along a potholed highway heading east. The azure ocean sparkled beside them, breaking in delicate lacy waves on the white-sand beach. Wind roared through the car, drowning out any attempts at conversation. The first few bumps tossed Kate and Lucas around the rear compartment, rattling their bones and making them grunt at every impact. They hunched down together, using each other's bodies to brace themselves against the floor. Kate turned toward Lucas with her lips parted, hungry for his kiss, and found his hand against her chest, holding her off.

"What?" she whisper-shouted into his ear.

"I need to ask you something."

"Okay."

"Are you with me or with him, the frat guy?"

"You mean Griff?"

"Yeah, what gives?"

"Are you asking whose bed I'm sleeping in on this trip?"

"Uh, well . . ."

"Yours," she said, her heart thrilling as she looked into his golden-brown eyes. She couldn't remember being this excited about a guy—well, ever.

"Does *he* know that?" Lucas asked.

"He'll figure it out."

"No. I don't put moves on another dude's girl."

"Look, Griff's a big boy. And this isn't high school. I don't belong to anybody. I just do what feels right."

He looked at her disapprovingly. "I think you mean, do what feels *good.*"

"Huh?"

He shook his head and sat upright, disengaging his limbs from hers. The sense of desolation she felt as he removed himself was so intense, and such a new sensation for her, that she almost enjoyed it.

They turned off the highway onto a smaller road. Goats foraged by the roadside. The hills in the distance were impossibly green. Coconut palms swayed in the front yards of half-finished concrete bungalows. The villages were collections of a few buildings at a crossroads. They drove through one, then another and another. Groups of men stood or sat in knots in front of tin-roofed shacks with wares displayed inside, the signs advertising fresh fish and bananas. The trees were heavy with strange fruit, and the air smelled like burning. Kate looked at Lucas, who gazed out the window with wide eyes. She wondered how often he'd been outside the state of New Hampshire, or even out of Belle River. Surely he would fall into her arms tonight. How could he not, in a place as lush as this? She would show him how sweet life could be.

Finally, they turned onto a steep gravel road and headed uphill. At the top of the rise, wrought-iron gates stood ajar. They drove through them into the cobbled courtyard of a large, graceful white house. A covered veranda faced a wide lawn that sloped down to the palm-fringed swimming pool, and beyond it, the sparkling sea. Hearing the sound of the vehicle, a middle-aged Jamaican couple came down off the veranda and waved. As her friends spilled stiffly out of the taxi after their uncomfortable ride, Kate introduced them to Ethelene and Samuel, the caretakers who ran the place. Samuel wanted to know where to put the luggage—which bags in which rooms? Kate told him not to worry about it for now—pile everything in the living room and they'd work it out later—because the first order of business was jumping in the pool.

"My only request is, keep the rum punches coming," she said.

"Rum punches coming right up," Samuel said.

Ethelene and Samuel had a son named Marlon, the same age as Kate, whom she'd known forever. He was tall and skinny, with a wide smile and connections that could get Kate whatever she wanted. Ethelene said her son was going into town and could stop by the grocery store, so they should place their orders. Kate wrote up a grocery list and whispered in Marlon's ear about the special-delivery items she was looking for. He wanted her to front the cash. Groceries and alcohol could be charged to Keniston's monthly bill at the store in town, but not the drugs. So Kate took up a discreet collection, and everybody contributed greenbacks except Jenny, who claimed she'd never once tried any illegal substance and wouldn't break her perfect streak, not even for the extra-powerful Jamaican weed. Especially not for that: God knew what it would do to her virgin head.

"Kate, you shouldn't be doing this. It's a bad idea," Jenny said.

"We're not in Turkey," Kate replied. "Weed is like a sacrament here, you don't get arrested for it. And if we do a little X, maybe, or the local equivalent, nobody will be the wiser."

"I'm not only talking about getting arrested—although yeah. But how do you know what this stuff will do to your head?"

"Relax, babe, when it comes to pill-popping and A-bombing, I'm an old pro," Kate said, and gave Jenny a big wet kiss on the cheek. "Loosen up. Drink something with an umbrella in it, go to bed with your makeup on. Live dangerously. At the very least, don't queer my vibe."

If Kate was to have any chance of claiming Lucas, everybody had to throw the rules by the wayside—*everybody*, including Jenny. Jenny brought along a boy of her own, and yet Kate caught her eyeing Lucas with that hungry look, the same one that shone out of Kate's own eyes when she gazed at him. God, how could they still be caught up in a stupid conflict over a *boy*? They were above that. Kate thought that but she also thought *Hands off my man, bitch*.

There was talk of going down to the beach. By walking to the edge of the lawn, taking the dirt path out onto the cliffs, and leaning over, you could see it: a perfect crescent of white sand, despoiled by legions of tourists from the nearby cottage colony who pitched their umbrellas and left their garbage. To access the beach, Samuel would drive them back down the steep road they'd just come up, but nobody had the stomach for that after their spine-jolting journey. Instead, they spent the waning afternoon getting blind drunk on rum punches by the swimming pool. Kate cuddled with Griff on his lounge chair, but it was a ruse, a distraction. She planned to get him comfortable, then fob him off on Aubrey. The sun began descending on the horizon, and she decided to make her move, rising idly and diving into the kidney-shaped pool. She swam over to where Aubrey stood looking out at the view in a borrowed teensy bikini that belonged to Kate. The swimsuit revealed Aubrey's figure in its glorious gauntness, each rib countable, hip bones protruding, long, spidery limbs—like a swinging London model from the sixties, or a concentration-camp survivor.

"Having fun?" Kate asked softly.

"Sure." Aubrey's voice rang hollow.

"*Are* you?"

"It's paradise here."

"You're not answering my question," Kate said, glancing over her shoulder, then leaning closer. "I know you're still grieving your mom, hon. I brought you here to make you feel better. This trip is all about you. I have a special present for you."

"Oh? What's that?"

"*Griff*. I know you like him, don't deny it."

"C'mon, Kate. Don't tease me. Griff's with you."

"Not really. We've always been more friends than boyfriend and girlfriend. I care about him, and I want to see him with somebody who makes him happy. I think that person might be you."

"Yeah, how does *he* feel about that?" Aubrey asked skeptically.

"Well, I know he likes you. He has his eye on you."

"He doesn't act like it."

"He's shy."

"Really?" Aubrey asked, with the tilt of an eyebrow.

"Really. Go talk to him. He wants to get to know you better."

"I don't know, Kate."

"Why not?"

"I'm a wimp, I guess. Afraid of rejection. I don't have a clear shot with you in the picture."

"But I'm giving him to you."

"That takes care of the girl rules. I won't feel bad on your account. But you can't give a person like a present. He's into you, still."

"I promise you, he's done with me. He wants someone steadier. He needs that. Seriously, I *said*, go."

"You're sure?"

"Yes, I am sure. Come on, now. No time like the present," Kate said.

Aubrey hesitated.

"Go already," Kate said, rolling her eyes, and poked Aubrey hard in the side.

Slowly, tentatively, Aubrey made her way over to the steps and emerged from the pool, water dripping from her long hair. It almost hurt to watch as Aubrey wrapped herself in a towel and walked bravely over to Griff's lounge chair, sitting down gingerly on the edge. If only Kate could ease Griff out of her own life and into Aubrey's, she'd be doing everybody a favor. Griff looked past Aubrey's shoulder and tried to catch Kate's eye. She dove under and swam a few laps, but when she came up for air, he was still watching her, barely paying attention to what Aubrey said. Meanwhile, Lucas lay in the last bit of sun with a towel over his eyes, indifferent to everything around him. He hadn't spoken a word since they arrived at the house. Jenny and her friend Drew were wandering around taking photographs of the view.

After a while, Kate got out of the pool and went to lie on the lounge chair closest to Lucas. Samuel came out and lit the tiki torches. Their acrid, lighter-fluid smell reminded Kate of summers of her childhood. Ethelene called them to the veranda, where a feast of jerk chicken with rice and beans had been laid out on the long mahogany table. Citronella candles flickered up and down its length, giving off their sweet scent. They ate in their wet bathing suits and bare feet, drinking chilled sauvignon blanc and talking about how crazy school was. They all loved and loathed Carlisle. At some point during dinner, Marlon came by and put a brown paper bag in Kate's hand conspiratorially.

"Pipe's in there," he whispered. "Papers, too, take your choice. And those special extra treats you asked for. Be careful with those, they mess with your head."

"I can handle it."

"All right, all right. Just wait till the old folks gone inside so we don't have no fuss."

"Will do. Thanks, my friend," Kate said, and kissed his cheek.

After laying waste to the food, they were ready to go back to the pool. A glorious sunset spread out to the west, the sky glowing in brilliant hues of orange, red, and violet. The mosquitoes were coming out, even though they were way up in the hills. They wrapped fluffy, striped towels close around them and huddled together on the chairs in the cooling air.

"Beautiful night, but I can think of a way to make it better," Kate said, and pulled out the paper bag Marlon had given her.

"It's getting chilly," Jenny said, standing up. "I think I'll go inside. Anybody want to come?"

Kate gave her a withering look but didn't try to stop her. Then Lucas stood up.

"I'm beat," he said.

"No," Kate said. "Sit down."

"But—"

"Jenny can leave. Not you."

Everybody stared at Kate, and she stared right back. Her blue eyes, rimmed with purple liner smudged from the water, were defiant and wild.

Jenny shrugged. "Be careful," she said, to no one in particular, and walked off toward the house.

Lucas remained standing. He glowered at Kate, saying nothing. His whole moody routine was getting less cute by the minute. Kate filled the bowl of the pipe, lit it, and took a deep drag. As the THC hit her bloodstream, she could tell that this was some powerful shit, different from anything she'd smoked before. It would loose chaos upon their group, but she was ready for that.

"Here," she said, and held out the pipe to Lucas.

14

On the second day of the trip, Aubrey woke up alone in a lounge chair by the pool, in terrible pain from a sunburn. She had no sense of what time it was but the sun hung low enough in the sky that she suspected late afternoon. She sat up stiffly, every move agony. How had she let that happen, when she knew her pale skin blistered in the sun? She couldn't remember a thing. The drugs and drinking last night had left her mind a blank.

Desperate for some aloe vera gel and needing to pee, she stood up on shaky legs and forced herself to go into the house. Her eyes burned and her stomach felt funky. Aubrey found a bathroom, then wandered the empty rooms of the first floor for what seemed like a long time, looking for her friends, who'd vanished into thin air. At least it was cool in here. The floors of the large rooms were made of white tile, and the heavy shutters were drawn against the sun. But the silence unnerved her. She felt like she'd stumbled into some vast, ghostly mansion, like she might walk here forever without encountering another soul.

When finally she heard a murmur of voices, she followed the sound to the kitchen. The housekeeper, Ethelene, was gabbing away in incomprehensible patois with the young girl who had cleaned up dinner last night. They looked up suspiciously as Aubrey poked her head in.

"Look at you now," Ethelene said, clucking her tongue as she took in Aubrey's lobster-red skin.

"You wouldn't happen to have any aloe vera gel by any chance?" Aubrey asked timidly.

"We don't got no drugstore fancies. I can give you a banana peel."

"A—what?"

"Banana peel. Rub it on your skin, it take the pain away."

The young maid giggled, which made Aubrey think Ethelene was making fun of her. Still, a banana peel was better than nothing.

"Okay, sure. Thank you. And I'd like a banana to eat, too, if that's okay."

"That's just fine."

Aubrey took what Ethelene handed her, and backed out of the kitchen.

On the second floor, endless bedrooms opened off a wide hallway. Kate had told them yesterday to take their pick, and Aubrey chose the poky one at the end of the hall. Servants' quarters, Kate called it. But the others were much too grand, if a bit musty and neglected. She'd worry she might break something and have to pay for it if she slept in one of those. Kate had taken the same room she'd used when she was a girl. It was large and airy, with a four-poster bed and tall windows that looked to the sea. Plus it had an air conditioner, which, Aubrey discovered too late, hers didn't. Who cared anyway? She hadn't slept in her room last night, and if her plans worked out, she wouldn't sleep there tonight either. But where was everyone?

Aubrey went to the closed door of Kate's bedroom, raised her knuckles to knock, and stopped short. Wild cries filtered out into the quiet of the afternoon, startling her. Who was in bed with Kate? Her eyes welled up at the thought that it might be Griff. Last night, something had happened between Aubrey and Griff, who'd long been the object of Aubrey's all-consuming crush. Admittedly, they'd both been high out of their minds, but still, Aubrey hoped with all her heart that it meant something. That it at least meant he liked her, a little. But was Griff in bed with Kate now? Kate and Griff were so alike. The sun-streaked hair, the fine profile, the glossy skin. They'd traveled the whole wide world, and knew the same people and places. With Kate in her way, Aubrey had no shot with a guy like Griff, and having a shot with him mattered very much to her. Kate already had everything a person could want, where Aubrey had nothing. If there was a chance with Griff, she would throw herself at his head with no regrets. But if there was no chance, she really shouldn't humiliate herself. She should try not to, anyway.

Aubrey reached for the doorknob. She had to know who was in bed with Kate. She opened the door slowly, taking care not to let it creak, and breathed out in silent relief. It was Lucas on top of Kate, thrusting, gleaming with sweat, his naked butt white against his tan. (Why did everybody tan except her?) Neither of them noticed her, and she shut the door softly and retreated to her room, mollified.

Last night, after Jenny and her date went off to an early bed in separate rooms, Aubrey and Griff and Kate and Lucas had stayed by the pool and smoked the most powerful weed Aubrey had ever encountered in her life. After that, when they were already floating, Kate convinced them all to drop half a tab each of—what was it? Ecstasy? Something else? Aubrey liked drugs. She liked how they made her forget the difficult things—her dead mother, her dim prospects, the deficits in her personal appearance. And she loved how they brought her closer to Kate. But she needed to learn her limits. Last night got out of hand. They were straight-up tripping. Aubrey lay paralyzed on the lounger and watched constellations expand and contract, unable to speak or even move her arms, for a very long time. After that she remembered standing on the cliff's edge, watching the waves crash below in the moonlight, holding hands with Griff and talking about whether if they jumped from there they would land in the water. In the light of day she knew how crazy that was, how close they'd come. The beach was a hundred feet below; they would have died. But they didn't. Later, when the sky was pink with cool dawn, she and Griff were alone by the pool. He sat on a lounger. She knelt on the hard concrete deck, doing what she'd seen Kate do to him in the snowy park, the night she found out her mother was sick. She could still feel his hands, stroking her hair. She looked up at him and saw the tears on his face, and thought, *He's so sad.* Aubrey couldn't stand it if that was their only encounter and he cried during it. She reached for her backpack and took out a hairbrush and a tube of lip gloss. She would go find Griff, and make him feel better.

15

On the morning of the third day of their trip to Jamaica, Aubrey opened the blinds in the bedroom where Jenny was sleeping and shook her by the shoulder.

"Jenny, wake up. Wake up. Griff left," Aubrey said urgently.

Jenny mumbled to leave her alone and turned over, throwing her arm over her eyes to blot out the light. Samuel the caretaker kept the rum punches flowing all night. She was hungover for the third morning in a row, and the sunlight hurt her eyes.

"Griff left without us," Aubrey said.

"Huh?"

"Griff went to the airport without us. He's gone!"

"Shit," Jenny said, sitting up so fast that her head spun and her stomach lurched. "He's our ride. How will we get home now?"

"That's all you're worried about?" Aubrey said, a note of hysteria in her voice.

"What else?"

Jenny looked more closely at Aubrey and saw what a wreck she was—sickly pale under a nasty sunburn, with purple circles under her eyes and fingernails bitten to bloody stumps.

"Did you sleep with Griff?" she asked.

Aubrey nodded and started to cry.

"How did that happen? Was it last night?" Jenny asked.

"No, it was actually yesterday afternoon. You remember, when you went to the beach?"

"Yes?"

"I'd been asleep by the pool. Kate, I guess, went off with Lucas."

Jenny looked away, upset. "Yeah. I know."

"I woke up, and went looking for—well, anyone. I found Griff—packing. I tried to talk him out of leaving. I succeeded, at least temporarily. One thing led to another, and we . . . did it. But I'm afraid it was just, like, consolation for him, you know?"

Or revenge, Jenny thought. "Oh, Aubrey. And it was your first time."

"Please, don't tell anyone that. My God, whatever you do, don't tell Griff I was a virgin. I'd be mortified."

Jenny shook her head in bewilderment. "It's not a crime."

"You know what I mean. People already think I'm weird. Promise me."

"Of course I won't tell Griff. What did he say to you exactly?"

"That he couldn't take Kate's attitude anymore. That she was crazy, and he had to get out of here."

"So he left us in the lurch?"

"He wasn't thinking about us. You know how Kate messes with his head. He wasn't himself."

"Stop making excuses for him. You should worry about yourself."

Jenny's well of sympathy for her roommate was running dry. Normally she would reach out and hug Aubrey at a moment like this, but a new feeling of distaste at Aubrey's hopelessness overtook her. She had enough stress, keeping an eye on Kate's drug use and erratic behavior, brooding over whether it was time to tattle to Keniston, without worrying about Aubrey, too. On top of that, she had a raging headache, and the bedroom had no air-conditioning. It was ninety degrees and close despite the open window, and she could smell Aubrey's stale sweat.

"Look, I need a shower, and strong coffee. We'll talk later."

Jenny dragged herself from the bed and walked away from her own room, leaving Aubrey to gaze after her with tears in her eyes.

Half an hour later, after a lukewarm shower that made her feel somewhat better, Jenny headed down to breakfast. The veranda was thankfully deserted, the others hiding from the day in their darkened rooms. Looking toward the sea, Jenny took a deep breath of jasmine-scented air and told herself to at least try to enjoy her few precious remaining hours in this tropical paradise. Every morning, Ethelene put out rolls, coffee, and fruit, and the kids helped themselves—assuming they bothered to wake up. Jenny went to the sideboard and picked up a plate, thinking she might eat something after all. The vacation had been a sickening kaleidoscope of drunken nights and bleary days, yet its luxuries would be permanently etched in her mind, and make her want things. The palm trees and the aqua water, the gracious home with the sweeping vista of the ocean, the staff to feed her and clean up afterward. She wanted to be rich like Kate, but without the drama and the heartache. Was such a thing possible? Kate was the iconic poor little rich girl, living so far out on the edge that her feet were starting to skid off the cliff. She'd take them down with her if they let her. Since arriving, every one of them had been drunk or high every night, sleeping in the wrong beds, saying things they didn't mean and couldn't take back. Jenny wound up in bed with Drew two nights ago despite the fact that—she was pretty sure—he was gay. Nothing much happened, and they laughed about it in the morning, but still, she'd risked an important friendship. (Drew and Jenny saw eye-to-eye, and if she was honest with herself, she was more likely to keep in touch with him after Carlisle than with her wild and crazy roommates.) She didn't blame herself. They acted out at Kate's instigation. A dark magic emanated from the girl, from her Pre-Raphaelite hair and golden skin, from her marijuana pipe, that dazed them, and made them obey her whims no matter how self-destructive.

By the time Kate and Lucas staggered downstairs, it was late afternoon. They were red-eyed and catatonic, with matted hair, smelling of sex. When Jenny told them about Griff leaving, they merely nodded. There had been an ugly scene the night before, in the small hours while everyone else slept. Jenny heard the yelling, rolled over, and went back to sleep, but she hadn't been surprised when Aubrey broke the news of

Griff's departure. Whatever happened was bad enough that Kate and Lucas had obviously been expecting him to take off, too.

"We have to get back home on our own now," Jenny said, looking at Kate accusingly.

Kate shrugged and stared into her coffee. "People come and go as they please. What do you want me to do about it?" she mumbled.

"Griff left because of the way you treated him. You could at least take some responsibility for the fact that we're stranded."

Kate put her fingers to her temples and grimaced. "Lower your voice."

"Meanwhile I've spent the day on the phone trying to clean up your mess, as usual. I reserved tickets for everybody on a United flight tomorrow morning," Jenny said. She'd also placed a call to Keniston in New York, though she didn't mention that.

Kate's pretty mouth settled into a sullen line. "I'm not leaving till Sunday," she said.

"They were the only seats I could find. Seven A.M. departure. It's spring break. Everything else is booked. Drew and I want to get back to Carlisle on time, so we'll be on it. If you want to stay, that's your choice, but you won't find an open seat until next Tuesday at the earliest."

"Who paid for the tickets?" Lucas asked.

"Nobody. You can pay for yours at the airport," Jenny said.

Jenny watched the alarm spread across Lucas's face. It gave her a sick pleasure to think the expense would cause trouble for him. She wanted Lucas to suffer, she realized. They were all going crazy cooped up here on this hilltop, broiling in the sun and frying their brains with drugs and booze. How long until they were at each other's throats? She had to get away; tomorrow wasn't soon enough.

"I'm going to the beach," she announced, and stood up.

She didn't think they'd follow her. They were so lethargic they could barely hold their heads up. But as she collected her towel and sunscreen in the living room, Lucas skulked up to her.

"Hey, Jen," he said under his breath, "I'm kinda short on money for the flight. I was wondering if you could maybe spot me something. I'll pay you back, I swear."

"You should ask Kate. She's your girlfriend, isn't she?"

"She says she's broke."

"This isn't my problem, Lucas."

"Kate told me the trip was free, or I would never have come."

"And you believed her? You should've known better. Everything costs something," Jenny said, and turned her back.

Jenny recruited Drew to come with her to the beach. The two of them had been going every afternoon—the only ones of the crew who'd bothered leaving the hilltop. Samuel was on his way to town and gave them a lift in his old Plymouth sedan, dropping them at the entrance to the cottage colony that they could see from the cliff's edge. Small, brightly colored bungalows spread up the hillside. Jenny and Drew walked down a steep dirt path to the white sand beach, which was crowded with Americans and Brits of all shapes and sizes, some bright red, some pasty white, some a rich, deep tan. They wound their way through beach chairs and umbrellas down toward the waves, where they found an unoccupied spot to spread their towels.

"What a relief to be out of the lion's den," Drew said.

"Is it that bad?" she asked, pulling sunscreen from her beach bag and offering it to him. He squirted some into his palm and looked at her quizzically.

"I know they're your friends. But honestly? Yes, it's bad."

Jenny rubbed sunscreen on her arms and legs, then lay down and closed her eyes, letting the sun bake the alcohol out of her. Drew's comment hung in the air.

"Can you be more specific?" she said after a few minutes. "What's bad about them, exactly?"

"Promise you won't get mad."

"Okay," Jenny said with alarm, her stomach sinking.

"You're one of the smartest, most ambitious girls I've ever met, and yet you're known around campus as one of the Whipple Triplets. Is that what you want—to be mentioned in the same breath as a spoiled, druggie rich girl and a basket case?"

Drew's words exploded in her head like little truth bombs. And yet, she couldn't stand to hear her most ungenerous private thoughts spoken aloud. No matter what their flaws, Kate and Aubrey belonged to her, and she to them.

"That's unfair," she said.

"You said you wouldn't get mad," Drew said.

"I know, but they're my roommates! I love them. I want to protect them."

"Yes, exactly. You're the responsible one, always saving their butts, while they behave however they want and break every rule. Don't you worry something bad will happen?"

"Bad how?"

"I don't know, but they're reckless people. They do a ton of drugs, sleep with each other's boyfriends, leech off people, piss people off. It's off the rails. Bound to explode eventually. Just saying, be careful. Honestly, if I were you, I would think long and hard about rooming with them next year. But now I've had my say and I'll shut up. Those waves are calling to me. Want to go in?"

Drew hauled himself to his feet and held out a hand to her. They ran together down to the edge of the water and waded into the crashing waves. The water was surprisingly cool and refreshing against Jenny's skin. They swam out to where it was calmer, treading water, as a school of tiny silver fish swam by, tickling them. The water was so clear that she could see straight down to the pink polish on her toes. She looked back toward the crowded beach, and followed the line of the road up the mountainside. Far above, the mirage of Kate's house glittered white against the green hills. The sight of it gave her a fierce twinge of foreboding.

When Samuel came to pick them up at sundown, Kate, Aubrey, and Lucas were in the car with him.

Kate leaned out the open back window. "We're going to a pig roast, get in," she said, smiling exuberantly. A strand of her long blond hair caught the wind.

"We're in wet swimsuits," Jenny said.

"It's fine, you'll need a bathing suit anyway. The restaurant's next to this magical bay that glows in the dark. It's bioluminescent, from these microorganisms that live in the water. You *have* to see it before you leave."

Kate's excitement was contagious. She pushed open the door and scooted over, and against her better judgment, Jenny climbed in.

"C'mon, Drew, you too," Kate said. "I'll sit in Aubrey's lap." She climbed on top of Aubrey, who put her arms around Kate's waist and rested her chin on her shoulder. Everybody had magically made up. Well, maybe not everybody. Lucas sat in the front seat next to Samuel. He turned around and gave Kate a disgusted glance. Jenny tried to catch his eye, but he wouldn't return her gaze.

Samuel dropped them in a crowded parking lot and they walked down the steps to an open-air restaurant by the water. The place had a concrete floor, a thatched roof, and a steel-drum band playing Caribbean music. They snagged a picnic table with a view of the bay and ordered a round of rum punches. Needless to say, nobody asked for ID.

The water of the bay was calm and muddy, and quite unbeautiful compared to the crystalline waves at the beach.

"Where's the glow?" Jenny asked.

"When it gets dark, we go out on a boat," Kate said. "You'll see."

A guy with dreadlocks and gold teeth turned a pig on a spit over a grill made from a giant oil drum. His long goatee was adorned with beads and a ribbon in the colors of the Jamaican flag. Every once in a while he would get up and croon a ballad, accompanied by the steel-drum band. Now he sang "I Bid You Good Night," the plaintive lyrics set off perfectly by his high, sweet voice. "*Lay down, dear brother, lay down and take your rest . . .* "

"I love this song," Kate said.

"It's a funeral song, you know," Jenny said.

Jenny had vowed not to drink so she would be able to manage the 5 A.M. wake-up call and long flight home the next day. But time dragged as they waited for the sun to go down and the pork to be ready, and her resolution fell by the wayside. Lucas had taken the seat beside her, and when he ordered another, so did she. It had been many months since they last talked. With two rum punches easing the way, they found themselves in deep conversation, reminiscing about high school, their Belle River friends. The conversation turned eventually to what they were doing now, and how each of them found Carlisle. Lucas was anxious and depressed. He told her about his hockey injury and how it had effectively ended his athletic career, something she hadn't known. He seemed lost without hockey in his life.

"I'm so sorry," she said, leaning toward him, squeezing his hand. "Kate never mentioned it."

By the time the waitress brought them heaping plates of roast pork, rice, and beans, Jenny's head was spinning from all that rum on an empty stomach. She'd eaten nothing all day but an ice cream at the beach and a couple of slices of mango for breakfast. Lucas's face, his rich brown eyes, anchored her to the surface of the planet and prevented her from flying off into space. They talked and talked as if no time had passed, and her chest ached with how much she missed him. She looked out at the water, and the sky was dark. She'd been so wrapped up in Lucas that she forgot to watch the sunset.

"The boat's leaving. Let's go," Kate said.

Jenny stood up reluctantly. They were the last five people to board, and had to take separate seats, wherever they could find empty ones, on the ledge that ran around the perimeter of the boat. Jenny ended up sitting beside the crooner from the restaurant, who also served as the captain of the tour boat. His name was Chesley, and he kept up a running patter of jokes and information as he steered the creaky old ferry out into the bay. Once they were under way, he turned off the lights on the ferry and told them to look back at their wake, which glowed yellowy green in the black water.

"Now lean down and drag your hands in it," Chesley instructed. They all did that, and oohed and aahed at the sparkling trails they left. Jenny pulled her hand in from the warm water and stared at it, awestruck. It sparkled momentarily, bright as a disco ball, then faded and died.

The lights of the restaurant receded into the distance. A few minutes later, they came alongside a sandbar, and Chesley dropped anchor.

"Now we swim," he said. "You got fifteen minutes, then I blow the horn. Get back to the boat within five minutes or I drive away and leave you to the sharks." He laughed uproariously at his own joke. "Just kidding, they take my license for sure if the sharks get you."

People stood up and began diving one by one into the water. They would hit with a splash, sending rings of glowing color radiating outward. Jenny peeled off her cover-up and swung her legs over the side of the boat, dropping down easily into the water. It was warmer than the ocean, and shallow enough to stand comfortably, the bottom made of fine silt that squished between her toes. There was no moon tonight. The sky and the water merged together into blackness. But wherever people moved, a luminous brilliance flared and then disappeared, like a candle being snuffed out. The invisible creatures clung to Jenny's skin, outlining her limbs in electric radiance. She turned and Lucas was beside her, recognizable from his glowing outline in the blackness. They were alone behind the boat, the splashes and giggles of the others audible from around the corner.

"We're in fairyland," she whispered, running her hands through the water and setting off sparkling waves. His hair and eyelashes glittered as he came closer. "You're made of magic dust," she said.

He took her in his arms and held her close, and the world stopped spinning as they stood there. But when she raised her lips, looking for his, he pulled away.

"I miss you," she whispered.

"Jenny, I need help."

"Why?"

"It's Kate. It's like we're in this sick game that I don't know how to get out of."

A powerful wave of bitterness swept over her as she heard the truth in his voice. The stupid fool was in love with Kate.

"If you think she's bad for you, break up with her, or stop whining about it already."

"You don't understand. She's inside my brain, under my skin. Even if I wanted to, I couldn't escape."

"What is wrong with you? You have no backbone? Leave me out of it, Lucas."

Just then, the horn sounded, three long blasts, loud enough to make them jump.

"I'm going back to the boat," Jenny said, and took off swimming toward the ladder.

16

In high school, Aubrey imagined that once she got to Carlisle, life would be perfect. She would finally fit somewhere. She would find her true friends, and they would love her for herself. But Carlisle proved to be a new treadmill, faster and more slippery than any she'd encountered before, with no way to get off. She had no recourse, no other vision for her future. Either succeed here or give up forever. So naturally, she tried to prove herself in Jamaica by matching Kate shot for shot, toke for toke. She ingested any pill or powder or smoked any bong that they put into her hands to show them she was one of them. She gave up her virginity to Griff because he was of that place and she craved his stamp of approval. (Sometimes she thought she maybe even loved him.) Now, back at school, Griff walked the other way every time he saw her coming, and she'd accomplished nothing, except to pick up an expensive Ivy League drug habit. Not that she was alone in this. Drugs were an everyday vice at Carlisle. Nobody thought twice about it, everybody did it, but Aubrey seemed to have more trouble managing it than other kids did. Her hands shook all the time. She felt headachey, feverish, unable to eat or sleep, and the only thing that made her feel better was getting high again. So she started going to parties where she knew there would be drugs. Not just on weekends. She went on weeknights, too, even when she had a paper due or a midterm the next day.

Aubrey never intended to stop going to class. She loved her classes. At first she had a rule that no matter how late she partied, she'd force herself to get up for class the next morning. Trouble was, she kept sleeping through her alarm. She'd wake up when it was dark outside and find that she slept the clock around. The dorm was quiet not because it was early morning (how could it be—it had been early morning already when she collapsed on her bed fully clothed and lay there watching the ceiling spin), but because everybody was at dinner without her. The first time this happened, she was terribly upset. But the second time, she didn't think as much of it. She missed one day of classes, and then another, and before she knew it, the thought of going to class provoked greater anxiety than the thought of not going. Without the touchstone of the lectures to keep her grounded, she fell behind on her reading. And once she missed reading for a few days in a row, the syllabus became like a tall mountain to climb. She couldn't catch up; she wouldn't know where to begin.

Aubrey imagined that something very bad would come of all this. She wanted to escape the consequences, but there was nowhere to go. She couldn't go home. Her mother was dead. *Dead dead dead dead.* Her only home now was her rumpled bed in the double with its stale-smelling sheets, or the bathtub she sat in until the water went cold, looking at the veins on her wrists and wondering how much it would hurt to slash them. For the first time Aubrey realized how much her occasional telephone calls with her mother had grounded her. Quick and contentless, just—*Hi, how you doing, what's up, babe?* A few brief facts about how much and where her mother was working, which courses Aubrey was taking, how she'd done on a test. They never talked about anything deep. But if her mother was alive still, and asked her what was going on, this time, Aubrey would confess. She would spill her troubles, get help. She faulted her mother for not doing more for her when she was alive. But her mother had loved her, and the mere fact of that love would have been enough, she was sure, to arrest her tailspin. Without it, there was only open air to grab as she fell.

During the long afternoons when she should have been in class, Aubrey took the ugly, crocheted throw that was her only legacy from her mother, pulled it over her head, and lay in the hot, scratchy darkness, pretending she was dead. She was sort of hoping to commune with her mother that way. But it was never dark enough under the throw to imitate the grave. The loose rows of stitches let in too much light. And besides, her mother was in a cold, clear lake, with watery light shining down. Aubrey was wasting her time, trying to reach her this way. But she kept doing it anyway, because imagining that she was dead comforted her somehow.

One afternoon toward the end of April, Aubrey was lying on the couch in the living room with the throw over her head when the doorbell of suite 402 rang. It was late in the day, and she was alone in the suite.

"Abby Miller?" asked Chen Mei, the Whipple RA, when Aubrey opened the door.

"Aubrey."

"Huh?"

"I'm *Aubrey* Miller."

"Here," Chen Mei said, thrusting a clipboard at her. "Sign the paper, on the line. Then I can give you the letter."

"What letter?" Aubrey said.

"Just sign."

Aubrey took the clipboard and read the paper attached to it. It was an acknowledgment that she'd received a Notice of Hearing Regarding Academic Probation from the Committee on Academic Standards. Her heart stopped.

"What does this mean?" she asked Chen Mei.

"You got ac pro. Either shape up, or they'll kick you out."

"But—"

"Don't tell me. I don't have any say. Sign it and take the letter," Chen Mei said, holding out an envelope.

Aubrey scribbled her name, and ripped open the envelope with shaking hands. The letter advised her that she had been placed on academic probation because her GPA after midterm examinations stood at 1.95. *What midterm examinations?* Time had gotten away from her. She'd missed *tests*. Aubrey felt nauseous. A hearing date was scheduled for the week after finals. If at the time of the hearing, her GPA was 2.50 or higher, she would be removed from academic probation. If it was between 2.00 and 2.50, she would be required to withdraw for a semester and complete a prescribed course of remedial instruction before reenrolling. If it was below 2.00, she would be expelled.

Expelled. The word echoed in her mind. Aubrey staggered and grabbed the doorframe.

"Oh my God, what do I do?"

Chen Mei shrugged. "Study and see what happens. Maybe you make it, maybe not. Not everybody belongs here," she said, and walked away.

Aubrey slid down to a sitting position on the floor, too shocked to cry, and stared blankly into the dimly lit hallway with her hand over her mouth. *Not everybody belongs here.* Aubrey didn't belong. She'd always known it. There it was in black and white on the paper she held in her hand, so everybody else could know it, too. She felt like she might throw up, and ran to the bathroom, but when she got there, she caught sight of herself in the mirror and stopped dead. Who was that girl, with the lank, dirty hair and paste-white skin? She moved closer, staring into her own eyes, looking for signs of life, but they were flat and colorless. Was she already dead? Had the moments under the blanket been more than pretend? She touched herself, and her skin was cold and clammy. Her face felt rigid, her skin stretched tight over her bones like a drum. She flicked her cheek with her finger and saw her whole face jump. When the pain felt good, she flicked harder. Suddenly she was slapping herself across the face with both hands, hard enough to leave angry red marks. She sank down against the bathtub, wailing. Whipple was an old building with thick walls, and nobody heard her cry. She could put the chain on the door, get in a warm bath, sharpen her penknife, draw it across her wrist, and . . .

Of all the dangerous things Kate had turned Aubrey on to, suicide was the most intoxicating. You'd think a high-strung, sensitive girl like Aubrey would have read *The Bell Jar* in high school, and had time to inoculate herself against its siren song before coming to a soul-sucking place like Carlisle. But no, her first encounter was with Kate's dog-eared copy, two weeks earlier, and the damage was done in two hours flat. She couldn't manage to do any reading for class, but she'd read *The Bell Jar* five times since then, and listened over and over again to this one Tom Waits song, where he said the world wasn't his home, he was just passing through. Words about death got stuck in her brain while everything else poured out. She was obsessed with the inscription on the inside cover of Kate's copy of *The Bell Jar*. "M to K with ♥♥♥—*We desire the things that will destroy us in the end.*" Aubrey liked to sit and run her fingertip over the girlish handwriting, imagining Kate in her room at Odell, lying across her narrow bed, whispering to Maggie in her breathy voice. Kate gave the book to Aubrey the same night she told her Maggie's story. In Kate's telling, it was a romantic tale. Two young girls, closer than sisters, half crazy, at odds with the world, make a pact. They'd show everybody, make them sorry, and in death, they'd be together forever, young and beautiful. One kept her word. The other didn't, and was left alone, mourning her friend and regretting her cowardice. But it wasn't too late. Aubrey could step into Maggie's place. They could still fulfill the promise. Aubrey wanted that—surely Kate wanted it, too. Aubrey was jealous of Maggie, a girl whom she'd never met, dead for years, who held this special place in Kate's heart. She wanted that place for herself.

Aubrey reached up, grabbed the hard, porcelain edge of the sink, and hauled herself to her feet. She saw the path now. A way to belong at Carlisle once and forever, to lock her fate to Kate's. She would become a story they would tell for years to come.

Once she saw the answer, there wasn't a moment to waste. Kate had gone to Shecky's to meet Lucas. Aubrey would find her and convince her. She had to: her plan made no sense without Kate. It shouldn't be impossible. Kate was in a bad way herself these days. Her affair with Lucas was spiraling out of control. Griff had finally gotten fed up with her and kicked her off the trust-fund gravy train. Kate's father seemed to know things about her behavior that he shouldn't know. Kate believed her profs were spying on her for Keniston, and it made her paranoid and jumpy. She was depressed and sick of the world. All Aubrey needed to do was remind her there was a way out.

Aubrey left a note on Jenny's bed, right where it couldn't be missed, along with the letter from the Committee on Academic Standards underneath. Let them know what they'd done to her. Let them see that she and Kate had won in the end, by taking matters into their own hands and settling their fate on their own terms. They might not print her picture in the brochure, but damn it, they wouldn't forget her.

17

This place is driving me crazy," Lucas said, as they sat at the counter at Shecky's Burger Shack, waiting for the food he'd ordered. It was a warm late-spring evening, perfect for dining al fresco on the lush lawns of Carlisle, and the burger joint buzzed with students ordering takeout. The festive atmosphere was at odds with the dejected look on Lucas's face.

"Shecky's?" Kate asked, between sips of a vanilla milkshake.

"No, not Shecky's. Carlisle."

"What are you talking about?"

"It's like this sick social experiment. All these different types of kids. Rich, poor, black, white, smart, jocks, idiots, whack jobs. They throw us in the deep end and expect us to swim. If we drown, that's actually a good thing as far as Carlisle is concerned. They winnow out the weak links."

"You can't blame Carlisle for everybody's problems. Look at me. I was fucked up before I ever walked through Briggs Gate."

Even a week or two ago, Lucas would have laughed at that comment, and leaned in for a vanilla-flavored kiss. They would have sat at the counter making out until the manager told them to knock it off or get a room. Now Lucas just stared at her sullenly. He had asked her to meet him here tonight because he had something to tell her. Another girl would worry that he planned to break up. But no guy had ever broken up with Kate Eastman before.

"What was it you wanted to tell me?" she asked.

He wouldn't meet her eyes. "Look, this term has been hard on me, what with my injury, facing up to the end of my athletic career."

"At least they're not taking your money away."

"No, I mean, it's an Ivy. The financial aid is mine to keep. But I told you before, hockey's who I am. Without it, I don't know what to do with myself."

"Babe, you need to relax, take your mind off it. I scored an eight-ball last night. We could go somewhere and snort it and fool around."

"I don't want to get high, Kate. It just messes me up worse."

The skinny kid handed Lucas the bag with his food, giving them both a searching look. The kid bugged her. He was always watching.

"Whatever, if that's how you want to play it," she said, trying not to sound too annoyed. But she *was* annoyed. From the start, Kate had been attracted to Lucas's moodiness—the clouds in his eyes, the disappearing act he pulled when she wanted him most. Add the jocky looks and townie pedigree, and Lucas was her dreamboat small-town hunk. Most guys bored her fast, but Lucas stayed interesting. She hoped he wasn't about to turn needy and draining. She had enough of that from crazy Aubrey, who was a basket case these days.

"Look, it's not just Carlisle getting me down," Lucas said. "Ever since I've been with you, I'm doing too many drugs. I'm losing my grip."

Kate sighed irritably. "So don't get high. It's your choice. Don't put it on me."

"I need a break, Kate."

"A *break*? Wait a minute, are you breaking up with me?" she asked in astonishment. The skinny kid, who'd been mopping the counter next to them with a limp rag, turned and stared.

"Mind your business," she hissed at him. "Why are you so obsessed with me? You're like a goddamn Peeping Tom."

"Leave Timmy out of this. Let's go somewhere we can talk," Lucas said.

"Fine! I hate this fucking place."

"Give me a minute."

The skinny kid had gone back to the cash register to take an order from some Omega Chi girls Kate knew. They were dressed to the nines, on the way to some party, stinking up the place with their clouds of perfume. They waved at Kate and she waved back, flashing a smile so fake it was like a death grimace. Kate reached into her pocket and pulled out the baggie she'd scored the night before from Rudy down the hall, who was from Corona and had mad connections. Lucas was acting weird and stressing her out. A little bump would smooth things over. She snorted it off her pinkie fingernail, sniffed hard, and relished the rush.

Lucas walked over and had a brief conversation with the skinny kid, who reached into his pocket and handed Lucas his car keys.

The Omega Chi girls made whooping noises as Kate walked out with Lucas.

"Who's the hottie, Eastman?" one of them yelled.

"I recognize him. He's a hockey player," another one said.

Kate let the door slam behind her. She saw the disgusted look on Lucas's face. "Oh, please, I'm not like them," she said.

An old rusted-out Subaru was parked in the alley behind the restaurant. Lucas unlocked the passenger door and opened it for Kate. Wadded-up Sheckyburger wrappers littered the floor. The backseat was piled high with schoolbooks and sports equipment. The engine started with a whine that didn't sound good, and Lucas pulled out of the alley onto Palliser Street, which ran parallel to College. He took a back route Kate was not familiar with. She didn't know where they were going, and she didn't care. She was *pissed*. Who the hell did this townie fucking nobody think he was, breaking up with Kate Eastman? She'd blown off Griff Rothenberg for this guy—Griff, with his house in St. Bart's and his private jet, easy on the eyes to boot—and now Lucas had the audacity to dump her? No way. No fucking way. The coke made her feel like she could arrange the world how she wanted, and she wanted Lucas. She wasn't done with him yet. Nope, not done with his mouth, his eyes, his body. She was hung up on the boy, and she was keeping him till she got tired of him. End of story.

"Lucas, listen," she said, soothingly. "You're freaked out about not playing hockey. I get it. But this has nothing to do with me or what drugs I do. There's no need to break up over this."

"I need to get my head straight, okay? I'm taking next year off. I'm gonna live at home and work for my uncle's construction business. He needs somebody to help out with landscaping, and I need time away from this place, before it kills me."

"Wait, you're taking a year off from Carlisle?"

"Yes."

"To *mow lawns*?"

"Yes, okay? So I'm beneath you, we can agree on that. I knew you wouldn't understand."

"Stop with the victim routine. If I don't understand, then explain it to me."

"You either get it or you don't."

"Would you just try, for Chrissakes. This isn't fair."

"I need time, okay? I'm in a bad place mentally, and I need to figure out why. Am I just messed up because of losing hockey? Is it this place? I mean, we can agree—we have agreed—that Carlisle sucks shit."

"Yes and no," Kate allowed.

"Okay, but then there's this other possibility. Maybe—just maybe—you're too much for me to handle. When I'm around you, I lose myself. I do things I wouldn't normally do."

He glanced at her. She saw need and fear in his eyes, and she liked it. She put her hand on his thigh—it was hard and solid and alive—and felt him shiver.

"Come on, babe, admit it," she said, her voice full of come-hither promise. "You love what we do. You love every second. It's not my fault that you're obsessed with me."

She inched her hand further up his leg, and he leaned back, opening himself to her touch. When she got where she was going, he nearly ran off the road.

"Stop it, I'll crash," he said, shaking her hand off as he righted the car.

"Serve you right."

They retreated to their corners and took deep breaths.

"Hey," she said, "can we just forget all this angsty bullshit and go somewhere and screw? You don't have to get high if you don't want to. I won't, even."

She didn't need to, because she already was. The coke made her see things very clearly. Lucas could be managed, with words and with sex, like any man. They were speeding down the river road, fat bugs splatting on the windshield. The road looked familiar. She realized they'd been here before, in a different season.

"Huh," Kate said, grinning. "What do you know? This is the place we went to that night, right? When we listened to the ice on the river."

"Yeah."

"Well, all right."

Their crazy fling had started here. They would return to that deserted parking lot, and she would do things to him that would change his mind. Simple.

But when they pulled into the gravel parking lot by the river, it was crowded. Kate shouldn't have been surprised. Back then it had been pitch dark and below zero; now it was a sultry late-spring evening. Still, she was pissed off that strangers had invaded their special place. Kids ran around the parking lot screaming with excitement. A couple of teenagers pulled a canoe from the bed of a pickup truck. One of them waved to Lucas.

"Who's that?" she asked.

"A bud from high school," Lucas said.

"So much for private. It's a goddamn zoo."

"I know where we can go to be alone, but it's kind of a walk," Lucas said.

"Fine. I have feet."

He leaned across her and rummaged in the glove compartment for a flashlight, which he stuck in the back pocket of his jeans. "Come on."

They exited the car, and Kate breathed in the scent of evergreens and mud. Everything felt so intense. The air rang with the sounds of frogs and crickets. The sun was a gassy yellow ball hanging low over the river.

The day had been humid and lush, a first taste of summer, but here by the water, the air had an edge of chill. The temperature would plummet when the sun went down. At moments like this, Lucas seemed exotic to her. The boulevards of Paris were old hat to Kate, but a parking lot in the north woods was new, full of possibility. She would not let him go. Not when he filled her senses like this. Whatever it took to change his mind, she would do it—anything.

Instead of following the signs to the sandy beach and boat launch, Lucas led her to a dirt path that hugged the riverbank. A notice at the trailhead warned, *Trail not maintained. Proceed at your own risk*, which delighted her. Kate wore flip-flops with her cutoffs and tank top, and ignored the brambles and pebbles that assaulted her feet as she clambered quickly up and over the trunk of a fallen tree at the path's mouth. Lucas slipped ahead of her, holding back branches as they progressed so they wouldn't spring back and hit her in the face. The path was narrow, crossed every few feet by the gnarled roots of giant evergreens. To their left, the forest was a dense wall. To their right, the ground dropped off steeply to the river. Kate looked down and the vertigo thrilled her. One wrong step and you'd tumble, rolling head over heels through sharp granite outcroppings and the broken-off spikes of tree stumps till you hit the steel-colored water forty feet below. Nothing like the threat of death to make you feel alive.

After a few minutes, the path began to climb upward. Sweat trickled down Kate's back, and Lucas's T-shirt clung to his body. Kate's eyes lingered on him as he walked ahead of her, to the point that she lost her footing and stumbled, catching herself before she tumbled down the cliff.

Five minutes in, she asked how much longer.

"Just a little ways."

"We're all alone. Why not stop here?" she said. Beside the path, a fallen tree beckoned, perfectly horizontal and covered with cushiony moss. They could lay their clothes down and have the perfect bed. The sight of him was too much. She wanted him now, wanted to feel his smooth skin against hers as the humid afternoon cooled to dusk.

"The old railroad bridge is just ahead."

"Oh. That place the kids jump off of? You told me about that."

"We can talk better there. It's overgrown, and it makes a sort of shelter. Like a tree house. Come on."

They walked faster. The thought of that epic jump urged Kate on. That's how she would win him back. They'd hold hands and step into the abyss together. Feel the rush of air as they fell through space, and the shock of the icy water when they hit. She wanted to come to the surface beside him, swim to the riverbank and peel his clothes off.

Within a few minutes, the path curved sharply and opened onto a wide vista of the river. Kate's breath caught at the sight of the ruined bridge. Two stone supports rose from murky water, holding up two wooden spans that had once joined in the middle, each surmounted by the spectral remains of an arch. The entire central portion of the bridge had collapsed away to nothing. Just empty air. A train trying to cross would cascade down into the water, car by car, and get swept away by the current. She could hear the powerful rush of water from way up here.

They stepped off the path and onto the bridge, walking carefully between the rusty tracks and rotted boards. Trees had taken root at the foot of the bridge and grown up all around it. Vines and weeds rose from the bank out onto the wooden trestle and climbed the metal posts, where they spread out, lush as a Cambodian jungle, and formed a green bower. As Kate moved forward toward the garden alcove, Lucas's arm shot out and stopped her. She looked down at the chasm yawning at her feet and gasped. They had come farther than she realized, near to the point where the bridge fell away, leaving nothing but air between her and the water.

"Careful," he said, and their eyes met. Her heart pounded, with adrenaline and with lust.

"I love it here," she whispered.

Her fingers closed on the smooth skin of his arm. She pulled him closer, and their lips met. Her mouth moved down his neck to the hollow of his collarbone where a pulse beat. His skin tasted of salt and smelled warm, like the sun baking on a beach blanket.

He pulled her away. "This isn't why I brought you here. We need to talk."

Lucas pulled her into an area where the leafy curtain was the thickest. The spot was well used, and they stepped over the detritus of other people's hookups—condom wrappers, beer bottles, cigarette butts. Lucas cleared a space for them, kicking the trash over to the knife's edge where the bridge ended, and launching it down into the water. When the garbage was gone, he stripped off his T-shirt and swiped at the floor, whisking away any last specks. She watched his back as he moved, the smooth expanse, the power of it. When he was satisfied that the floor was clean, he shook out the T-shirt, then laid it down like a blanket.

"Sit down, let's talk."

"Oh, with your shirt off. I know what you want. The same thing as every other boy."

"Fine, I'll put it back on and you can sit on the tracks. I was trying to be a gentleman about it."

"About breaking up with me?"

"Like I said, I need some head space."

"It's not me, it's you?"

"Exactly."

"Do you know what a fucking cliché that is?"

"Yeah, I get it, I'm a cliché."

She felt short of breath and shaky. Desperate, on the verge of tears. Was it the coke, or was it Lucas? Kate cried rarely. It was an unusual sensation for her, and she didn't like it.

"There are things I could do for you," she began.

She knelt on the T-shirt beside him, took his face in her hands, and lifted her mouth to his.

"This won't change anything," he said, but his body relaxed under her touch, and his mouth opened.

He couldn't mean it. He gave in to the kiss too enthusiastically. She ran her hands down his broad back and settled them on the backside of his jeans, pulling him tight against her and shifting to straddle him. His body couldn't lie: he was hard already. His mouth was hot on her skin, and his hands were urgent as he tore at her clothes. He pushed her backward, and she cried out as he yanked off her panties and plunged into her. With the leaves rustling in the hot breeze, Kate felt like she was living some other girl's life. This is what it would be like if she'd been born in Belle River, with a normal family, and Lucas was her sweetheart. She would feel joy, she would be able to love someone, tears would wet her cheeks as they made love. But this was a dream, an interlude. She wasn't from here, she wasn't like that, and this thing with Lucas was over already.

When they had finished, he rolled off her, and they lay apart, the cooling air taking the heat from their skin. Kate turned her head and gazed at the open sky, where the gap between the broken trestles yawned, mere feet away. The sun had set, but the moon hadn't risen yet, and stars were just appearing in the heavens. High up in her bower, she could hear the rush of the river and the noise from the highway that ran along the opposite bank. All those people going about their business, unaware that she was lying here with Lucas, both of them spent and panting. This couldn't be the last time. She wouldn't allow it.

Kate sat up and crossed her arms, hugging herself against the chill. She reached for her cutoffs, pulled out the baggie, and did another bump for courage. She had to change his mind somehow.

"I thought you said no drugs," Lucas said.

"That was before."

"Before what?"

She didn't reply, but stopped to listen to the water rushing below. As the coke hit her bloodstream, she felt it in her toes, her eyeballs, the ends of her hair. She was at one with this place, with its power and its beauty. She was strong. And she had an idea.

"I want to do the jump," she said.

Lucas cocked his head like she was crazy. "Are you nuts? It's wicked cold."

"It was almost eighty degrees today."

"I'm talking about water temperature. Ice-out came late this year. The water's still below freezing. I mean, take a look, there's still ice along the edges."

"Don't be a wuss. Jump with me. We'll hold hands."

He sat up and watched as she dressed. She moved more languorously with his eyes on her, certain that she could bend him to her will by showing him something he liked. Men were so visual, after all.

"Where's the primo spot to jump from—just right here, where the bridge ends?" she asked.

"I'm telling you, you can't swim in the Belle at this time of year for more than a few minutes without cramping up. Trying to jump now would be epically stupid."

"Stupidity never stopped me before, and I'm quite sure it never stopped you."

He made an exasperated noise, then stood up and started pulling his clothes on. Darkness was falling hard. Lucas flicked on the flashlight and finished dressing in its glow.

"Where are you going?" she asked, a quiver of alarm in her voice.

"Home. You want a ride back to the Quad, fine, but then we're done."

"But—we just had sex. And you liked it, I know you did."

"I always like it with you. That doesn't make us right. Go back to your rich boyfriend. He's the one for you. You can abuse him and he won't complain, he'll pay for your coke. It's perfect. I don't know why you can't see that."

"Lucas, I didn't mean to say you were stupid. I'm sorry if it came out wrong. Lucas, *please*!"

He tried to move past her but she grabbed at his arm. The flashlight flew from his hands, bouncing once and flying off the edge of the bridge. The water was so far below that they heard no splash. Lucas exclaimed in alarm. Kate peeked over the edge and got a sick, excited fluttering in her stomach. In the fading light, the water below looked black instead of silver. She could hear the roar, and see the sparkle of light on water. She saw the force of the current.

"Jesus. Be careful," he said.

"What if I want to jump?" Kate said, her voice full of sick excitement.

The world felt off kilter, and her instincts said to lean into that feeling, to welcome it. If she couldn't have Lucas, they could both jump, and let the chips fall where they may. Maybe they'd live, maybe they'd die, but they'd be together.

"You're crazier than I thought," he said.

"*Kate!*"

The shout rang out from the path behind them, startling them both. For a terrible instant, Kate lost her balance and tottered, arms helicoptering, much too close to the edge, until Lucas grabbed her. She felt the electricity in his arms as they stepped back from the brink. The two of them were connected, in fear, in excitement, and she loved the sensation. Kate turned toward the voice. Aubrey stood at the foot of the bridge, her tall, pale form lit up against the backdrop of dark trees. Just what Kate needed. Her loser roommate showing up at the critical moment when she and Lucas were about to get somewhere ultimate. Aubrey would ruin it.

"What the hell is she doing here?" Lucas said.

"I'll get rid of her," Kate said under her breath.

"He's breaking up with you, isn't he?" Aubrey said, coming toward them.

"No, he is not. You don't have the first fucking clue about it. How did you find us?" Kate demanded.

"Timmy told me." When Kate looked blank, Aubrey said, "The kid from Shecky's. I rode my bike all the way from town. I knew you would need me, Kate."

"I don't need you. Lucas and I want to be alone, so go away."

"Your roommate's right, Kate," Lucas said. "I said what I came to say. Enough already, I'm out of here."

"No!" Kate cried. She turned on Aubrey. "Get out of here, you psycho bitch! You're ruining everything."

"Kate, he's just some townie asshole. He doesn't matter. Don't you see?"

"He's the only thing that matters. Get lost. Get out of here!"

"Face it," Aubrey said cruelly, "he doesn't want you. But it's okay.

This place is perfect. We can jump, we can stick it to them all. We can end it, just like you and Maggie planned," Aubrey said.

"Leave Maggie out of this," Kate said.

"Who's Maggie?" Lucas said.

Kate motioned to the tattoo on her wrist. "My best friend from high school who died. Remember? I told you about her."

"The one who OD'd?" Lucas said. "Wait a minute, did she kill herself? Is that why you're so keen to jump? You want to off yourself, and take me with you? God, I'm sick of all you Carlisle freaks. You're all crazy."

"Don't talk to me like that," Kate said, turning on Lucas, hysteria building in her voice.

Aubrey's mention of Maggie had knocked something loose inside her, something terrible and dark, that had been building all night. The people Kate loved always left her. Her mother, Maggie. Lucas was trying to walk out on her, too. She couldn't let that happen. She would be so alone. She would have nothing. She refused.

Lucas shook his head disgustedly and tried again to walk past Kate. She grabbed his arm with both hands, and held tight.

Her eyes were wild. "Lucas, you're not leaving. We're not done. I have more to show you," she cried.

"You don't own me, rich girl. Let go."

Lucas tried to shake her off, but Kate's grip was superhuman.

"*Let go,* I said, you crazy bitch."

He pried her hands loose forcibly, but instead of retreating, she advanced, striking and clawing at him wildly. Lucas shrank back and raised his fists to his face, like a boxer on the ropes.

"Stop it! Stop, you're out of control."

"Don't . . . you . . . leave . . . me!" Kate screamed, scratching at him with her long nails.

She couldn't stop hitting him. He'd hurt her, she'd hurt him back. Lucas hunched over and stepped back to escape the onslaught of Kate's fists. Her field of vision filled with rage, and she forgot everything. She forgot that Aubrey was standing there watching. She forgot that there was a giant abyss where the bridge had once been right behind Lucas's feet. She was not aware that two more people had arrived at the bridge; she didn't hear them shout at her to stop, to watch out, to be careful. Kate saw and heard nothing except for Lucas and the rush of blood in her ears. Focused on him as she was, she did see the moment when his foot found only open air and he began to slip backward. Oh, she remembered the gap then. Hidden in her panic was a rush of satisfaction. A wild fear spread across Lucas's face as he began to fall, and Kate thought—in the split second before she started to scream—*you'll be sorry now.*

18

Jenny turned the key and stepped into the living room of suite 402. Somebody had shut the windows she'd purposely left open when she left for class this morning, and now it was hot in here, and smelled funky. Aubrey and Kate had gotten lax about laundry, and started leaving food lying around. Jenny wasn't a maid. If they couldn't observe basic standards of cleanliness, maybe she'd take the plunge and sign up to room with Rebecca Levine next year. But in her heart, she doubted she could do it. That night in Jamaica, when Lucas confessed that Kate had gotten under his skin, Jenny knew exactly what he meant. Her roommates weren't good for her, but she was hung up on them, like on a bad boyfriend.

Jenny threw open the windows, and turned on the fan, then did the same in the double. There was a piece of paper lying on her bedspread that hadn't been there this morning. She picked it up. It was a note, in Aubrey's handwriting, with a second piece of paper folded up and tucked beneath it.

"*Jenny,*" she read, "*they're trying to kick me out of school. I can't can't can't handle that. I can't take it anymore. Kate knows what to do. We are ready to die. Life is too hard. I'm not brave like you. Kate will help me end my troubles. I love you, and thank you for always being there for me. Aubrey.*"

Her first reaction was not to believe it. Aubrey was a drama queen who'd cried for help many times before, and Jenny was tired of the theatrics. Then she unfolded the second piece of paper, which had been furled into a tiny rectangle like a piece of origami. It was a letter from the Committee on Academic Standards informing Aubrey that she faced expulsion from Carlisle if she didn't post a miraculous turnaround in her grades. That part was true, then—Aubrey was on the verge of getting kicked out. Jenny thought about the terrible things that had happened to Aubrey in the past few months. Her mother's death. That humiliating mess in Jamaica with Griff Rothenberg. Now, the prospect of getting expelled from Carlisle, when Carlisle was the only thing Aubrey had left. That would be enough to break a strong person, and Aubrey wasn't strong. This suicide threat could be real. What's more, Kate was supposedly in on the suicide pact, and helping Aubrey. And Keniston Eastman had specifically warned Jenny that Kate had a history of self-destructive behavior.

Shit. Jenny was supposed to be watching for signs of exactly this sort of thing, but if there had been any, she'd missed them. She'd screwed up.

Jenny ran to the phone in the living room and dialed Keniston's private number. No answer. She left an urgent message on the answering machine, laying out the facts, and prayed he'd call back quickly. When the phone didn't ring immediately, Jenny started to feel sick to her stomach. What if Aubrey was already dead? Or Kate was? Should she call the police? As she picked up the phone to dial, there was a knock on the door. Jenny felt a surge of relief and ran to open it, thinking it would be Aubrey coming back. But it was Rebecca Levine.

"What's the matter?" Rebecca asked, her smile fading as she saw Jenny's expression.

"Oh, my God, Rebecca. Aubrey left me a suicide note. Here, read it."

Jenny thrust the note at her. As Rebecca read, a look of horror spread across her face.

"This sounds like it's for real."

"That's what I'm afraid of," Jenny said.

"I saw Aubrey on the Quad a little while ago. She was going to Shecky's to look for Kate. You should go after them, Jen. See if you can talk them out of it. If they're really suicidal, they should go to the Health Center."

"You're right."

"I'll stay here in case they come back."

"I think we should call the police," Jenny said.

"Good idea. I'll call. You hurry! Try to catch them before anything bad happens."

Jenny ran down the stairs, across the Quad and out Briggs Gate, her hair flying. Her heart pounded as she dodged traffic on College Street. At Shecky's she threw herself, panting, against the glass door, making the bell jangle as it flew inward. Tim Healy looked up from the cash register. Tim was Lucas's cousin, a sweet kid who was a few years behind them in school. She ran over to him, struggling to catch her breath so she could get words out.

"What's wrong, Jenny?" Tim said, looking concerned.

"I'm looking for Kate Eastman and Aubrey Miller. You know them, right?"

"Sure, why?"

"Were they here?" she said.

"Yeah, a little while ago. Kate came in with Lucas. He broke up with her right in front of me. She was flipping out. He borrowed my car so they could go to the old railroad bridge for some privacy."

"The railroad bridge. When?"

"Maybe like"—he glanced over his shoulder at the clock on the wall—"an hour ago, more or less. Aubrey came by after they left. She wanted to know where Kate was. I told her, and she took off on her bike."

"I have to get to the bridge right away. Can you give me a ride?"

"Lucas took my car, and my shift's not over till eight. Is something wrong?"

Jenny smashed her hand on the counter, on the verge of tears.

"Tell me what the problem is," Tim said.

"Aubrey's gone off the deep end because she's in trouble at school. Now you're telling me Lucas broke up with Kate. I'm worried about them,

Tim, really worried, like they might be a danger to themselves. Please help me."

"Wait here. I'll figure something out," Tim said.

He disappeared into the kitchen, returning with a set of keys, shucking his apron and tossing it so it caught on a hook behind the counter.

"Let's go," he said.

They raced toward the river in somebody's ancient pickup truck. Jenny's once-crisp white blouse showed through in places with sweat, and her knees bobbed up and down frantically.

"Can't you go faster?" she said.

"Not unless I want to get stopped," Tim said. "Hey, are you telling me the whole story?"

"I told you, they're in trouble. Aubrey left a suicide note. My other friend called the police to look for them."

They were on the river road now, and Tim stepped hard on the gas. Jenny's hair whipped into her eyes in the rush of air from the window. Darkness was falling. The moths looked like snowflakes rushing into the glare of the headlights.

"She's bad news," Tim said, over the roar of the wind.

"Who?"

"Kate, who do you think? If Lucas wasn't messed up in this, I wouldn't even try to help her. But he's my cousin."

"Lucas can take care of himself," Jenny said, still angry at him from Jamaica.

They parked near the boat launch and ran toward the hiking trail. Sprinting down the narrow path, Jenny was soon out of breath and sweating. Branches caught in her hair and scratched at her legs. More than once, she stumbled on the uneven surface, and had to call to Tim to slow down so he didn't leave her behind in the gathering dark. Finally, the path curved as she remembered, opening to the right to reveal the ruined bridge, backlit against an indigo sky. Just enough light remained to make out the forms of Aubrey, Kate, and Lucas halfway across its span, standing at the point where the railbed fell away to nothing. She made it to the foot of the bridge in time to see Kate advancing on Lucas, raining blows on him as he backed toward the edge of the bridge.

"Holy shit, stop it, stop!" Tim yelled.

Lucas took a step backward to get away from Kate's punishing blows, and began to flail and slip backward. Tim screamed Lucas's name. Lucas let out a terrible shriek as he disappeared off the edge of the bridge, a shriek that hung in the air for an endless, sickening moment, stopping abruptly when he hit the icy black water below.

Tim reached the spot where his cousin had stood a split second before. Jenny caught up with him, skidding to a top, unable to believe her eyes. Did that really happen? Did Lucas really fall into the river? Did he come back up? Kate stared down into the abyss with her hands pressed to her mouth. Beside her, Aubrey screamed hysterically. Jenny looked down and saw only black water.

"You pushed him! You pushed him, you crazy bitch!" Tim shouted, grabbing Kate's hands away from her face and shaking her.

Kate's eyes were unfocused. Her mouth hung open but no words came out.

Tim let go of Kate and whirled toward Jenny. "We have to do something. He's a great swimmer, but not in water this cold. I'm going after him. You go to the parking lot. Try to get help. There's a pay phone. Call 911."

Tim sprinted back to the foot of the bridge before Jenny could get a word out. A tumbledown metal fence cordoned off the steep hillside. He clambered over it and ducked under the bridge trestle, disappearing from view.

Kate sank to the ground, shaking visibly. Aubrey knelt beside her and took her in her arms. Jenny had come here to stop Kate and Aubrey from harming themselves, but now Kate had gone and hurt someone else. Screw her roommates, and the damage they caused. Jenny had dragged Tim Healy into this mess, and now he'd gone after Lucas and might be in danger, too. She wanted to help Tim look for Lucas, but she was afraid to leave her roommates here, in this condition. Of the two of them, Aubrey seemed in better shape, though that wasn't saying much. Jenny shook Aubrey by the shoulder and looked her in the eye.

"Aubrey, listen, we have to help Lucas. If he's hurt, or God forbid, if he dies, Kate could go to jail. Do you understand?"

"She didn't mean to push him."

"It sure looked like she did," Jenny said. "But there's no time to argue. He could die if we don't do something. I know you don't want that. I'm going with Tim, to try to help. You go to the parking lot and call the police. Can you do that?"

Aubrey nodded, but she looked so shaken that Jenny doubted it. This was a girl who had just left a suicide note, and here she was sitting on a broken bridge, at the edge of an abyss.

"I read your note," Jenny said. "I can't leave you here."

Aubrey glanced toward the spot where Lucas had fallen. "The note was a mistake. I know that now."

"I'm glad. But you and Kate need to get away from here, okay? I won't leave you in a place where you could jump."

"We won't jump! Not after what just happened."

"I believe you, but please, stand up, get moving. Both of you."

Jenny held out her hands and helped Aubrey to her feet. Aubrey's eyes looked a little clearer, giving Jenny a measure of reassurance.

"I'll take care of Kate," Aubrey said. "We'll leave here as soon as she calms down. Go look for Lucas."

Time was running out. A person could die in minutes in water that cold. Jenny had no choice but to take Aubrey at her word. She nodded and walked to the end of the bridge, to the place where she'd seen Tim go over the fence.

The fence was damaged here, fallen low to the ground so that Jenny was able to walk right over it. She stopped short on the other side and looked down. The hill fell away at a treacherous angle. Far below, Tim stood at the bottom of the embankment. Jenny ventured forward a few steps, her heart in her throat. It looked too steep to attempt. But she couldn't bear the thought of plucky Tim Healy going to Lucas's rescue with no help, and maybe getting hurt himself. She'd known Tim since he was a kid. He was three grades behind her, funny, decent, and from a nice family. She had to help him if she could.

Jenny stayed low and cut back and forth across the face of the slope. Halfway down, she hit a slippery patch. Her feet flew out from under her and she slid the rest of the way on her butt.

At the river's edge, she stood up, brushed off, and looked for Tim. But he was gone.

"Tim! Tim!" Jenny called, but the only reply was the rush of water.

The river ran so high that it had swallowed the bank. Jenny clutched a tree branch and leaned out as far as she could to get a view. A foot below, vicious cold emanated from the water. The moon had risen, and it played tricks on her eyes. She thought she saw something bobbing in the water, and her heart leapt, but when she looked again, nothing was there. The water had closed over Tim and Lucas as if they'd never existed.

Not far downriver, close in to the bank, a metal swim float bobbed in the water, catching rays of moonlight. If Jenny could make it to that float, she could stand on it and get a long view downstream, and see enough to know better how to help. Jenny was a competent swimmer, but the Belle at high water scared her to death. Before she could change her mind, Jenny took a deep breath and jumped. The bite of the water as she plunged into the blackness knocked the wind out of her. She came up gasping for air, her fingers and toes tingling. She tried to stroke, but the suck of the current pulled at her arms, and she had to fight to keep her head up. Pointing her body in the direction of the metal float, Jenny let the current take her. The float came rushing at her, the force of the water slamming her into it headfirst. Jenny saw stars. The river was in her eyes, in her mouth, choking her, as the current did its best to suck her under the raft.

Jenny jackknifed sideways and cleared the float, fighting for air. She felt a sharp pain as something caught her across the midriff. The force of the water had thrown her against the steel cable that anchored the float to the riverbed. She folded her body over it to avoid getting swept away. Holding on to the steel cord with stiff fingers, she pulled hand-over-hand, dragging her body closer to the raft. Jenny swung her legs up and braced them against the side of the float, then with all her strength, grasped the cable and hauled herself upward. She cleared the side and collapsed onto the hard metal surface, gasping and sobbing in between breaths. Her teeth chattered violently, and water streamed from her hair into her eyes. She dragged herself to a sitting position, then staggered to her feet on the swaying raft. The river raced by on both sides. Fifty yards downstream, around where the gravel parking lot should be, lights flashed red and blue against the black of the trees. The police were here. Jenny jumped up and down, screaming and waving her arms to attract their attention. After a few minutes, she saw a rubber rescue raft put in at the boat launch and head in her direction.

As the rescue boat approached, something caught Jenny's eye, and she looked down into the water. Right below the surface, on his back, looking up at her with his eyes wide open and his hair streaming around his beautiful head, was Lucas. Jenny started screaming and didn't stop until the fireman pulled her into the boat.

She woke up in a hospital bed under layers of cotton blankets. Her mind was foggy from sedatives, and she felt more tired than she had in her life. She turned her head to see her mother sitting beside her, tears standing out in her dark eyes.

"I'm gonna be okay, Ma," Jenny croaked, and her tongue felt large and cottony in her mouth.

"Shh, quiet, *m'ija,* you got a concussion and bruised ribs. *Ay,*" her mother said.

"What about Tim?"

Jenny needed to focus on Tim, to drive the image of Lucas's face—of his staring eyes—from her mind.

"Don't think about him now," her mother said, and from that, Jenny concluded that the news about Tim was bad.

She must have slept, because when she opened her eyes again, her mother was gone, and Gloria Meyers, the Carlisle provost, sat by her bedside.

"You're awake," Gloria Meyers said, and put aside the file she'd been reading.

"Provost Meyers? Where's my mother?"

"She looked tired. I told her to get some dinner and a change of clothes, and come back in an hour."

"But why are *you* here?"

"I was concerned about you."

"That's very nice of you," Jenny said.

But something about the situation felt wrong. Gloria Meyers—with her iron-gray hair and brusque manner—didn't come across as *nice*. She was Jenny's boss, and a distant one at that, not her friend. In fact, they'd rarely spoken. So why was she here, really? Jenny thought about what happened at the bridge. It wasn't just that Lucas had drowned, but that *Kate* had pushed him to his death. Gloria Meyers was good friends with the Eastmans. Gloria Meyers showed up at Jenny's bedside. Could those two events be related?

"Are you here because of Kate?" Jenny asked.

"I'm here because a boy jumped off the old railroad bridge and died. A Carlisle student. I understand you and a local boy tried to save him, and you were injured in the process. I came to check on you."

"Thank you, but—"

Jenny tried to sit up, but a searing pain behind her eyes drove her head back to the pillow.

"Don't get up," the provost said, leaning over Jenny like she might push her down if she tried again.

"But I need to tell you, you're wrong about what happened at the bridge," Jenny said weakly.

"Well, that's what the police told me. The boy jumped. They said it might be a suicide, or a dare. That bridge is a hazard. It ought to be torn down."

"He didn't jump," Jenny insisted.

Gloria Meyers held up her hands as if to ward off Jenny's words. "Don't say anything right now. You suffered a head injury. You're confused, and tired. I should be going. You rest. I'll tell the nurse that you shouldn't be disturbed."

The provost stood to leave. Jenny shut her eyes again, and felt them fill with tears. Someone had told the police that Lucas jumped, but that was a lie. Jenny ought to set the record straight, tell Gloria Meyers what had really happened, and what's more, tell the police. But she didn't have the strength right now. Her head hurt too much. She couldn't think straight. She let the provost leave without saying any more.

The next morning, Jenny's headache was still there, but it was bearable, and she was released from the hospital. Her parents wanted her to come right home, but Jenny insisted on going to Tim Healy's room, where his family kept vigil by his bedside. Tim had struck his head on a rock and been knocked out in the river. He would've drowned if the police hadn't been on the scene already. Tim hadn't regained consciousness, and they were doing everything possible to relieve the swelling on his brain. They hoped he would come out of it, and not suffer any brain damage, but it was impossible to predict.

Jenny couldn't stand the thought that a second person might die because of Kate. It was on the tip of her tongue to tell Tim's parents what really happened at the bridge. But standing by his bedside, seeing how distraught his parents were, she couldn't bring herself to tell them that their nephew had been—what? Murdered? That was such an ugly word, but wasn't it the truth? She wouldn't burden them with this now, but she would go to the police.

In the car, Jenny asked her parents to take her directly to the police station, but they insisted she come home and rest. If Jenny had something to report about what happened last night, her father said, she could call, and an officer would come interview her.

They arrived at the house to find a long, shiny black Mercedes parked in front of it. As Jenny's dad pulled into the driveway, a uniformed chauffeur got out and came around to open the door for Keniston Eastman, who was followed out of the backseat by a distinguished-looking man whom Jenny didn't recognize.

"That's my roommate's father," Jenny said in surprise.

"We know," her mother said. "He came last night, and paid for your hospital room. Such a nice man."

Keniston waved at them, and her mother waved back.

"Why did he pay for my room?" Jenny said, with a sinking feeling.

"Because you helped his daughter. You know we can't afford a private room. The insurance doesn't cover it."

"Who's that with him?"

"His lawyer. He wants to thank you. Let's go inside, I'll make coffee."

His lawyer? This was not a get-well call.

"Mom, I'm tired. Can you talk to them for me, so I can go up to bed?"

"Just spend five minutes. Be polite, say thank you, then you rest."

Inside, Jenny sat down at the kitchen table with Keniston and his lawyer, whose name was Warren Adams, as her mother bustled around making the coffee. Keniston looked her mother's way, then exchanged fraught glances with Adams.

"Jenny," Keniston said, "I wanted to express my gratitude. You've been a good friend to Kate. I know the police are going to want to speak to you about Mr. Arsenault's suicide, and as a token of my gratitude, I wanted to offer Warren's help as you go through that process."

"Mr. Eastman, thank you, but I don't need a lawyer."

"It's a stressful situation, speaking to the police about a suicide," Keniston said.

"Yes, well, before we go any further, you should know, it wasn't a suicide. What I saw—"

Keniston stood up suddenly. "It's best if you speak to Warren about this. He's the legal expert, and I have to make an important phone call. Mrs. Vega, could I trouble you to show me to a telephone?"

"There's one right here," Jenny's mother said, pointing to the phone on the wall.

"A private one, if you please."

Jenny watched as Keniston shepherded her mother from the room. He carried a cell phone, so why did he need to use their telephone? It occurred to Jenny that this was a ruse to leave her alone with the lawyer.

"Miss Vega," Adams said, "I know you've just gone through a difficult experience. If you like, I can take a signed statement from you right now and relay it to the Belle River Police so you don't have to go down to the station. Our understanding, based on eyewitness accounts from Kate Eastman and Aubrey Miller, is that the young man threw himself off the bridge. He was apparently distraught over a recent injury that ended his hockey career."

Jenny cleared her throat nervously. "I'm sorry. That's not what I saw."

"Well. You were standing farther away, so perhaps you didn't have a clear view."

"Was it Kate who said Lucas jumped? He wasn't pushed?"

Adams fixed her with cold, blue eyes. A nerve pulsed in his cheek. "Pushed? Absolutely not. Nobody said anything of the kind. Both Miss Eastman and your other roommate, Miss Miller, are very clear that he jumped, and that, frankly, he wanted to die."

Jenny wasn't surprised that Kate would lie to save her own skin. As for Aubrey, she worshipped the ground Kate walked on, and wouldn't say a word against her. Besides, Aubrey was in trouble at Carlisle. Big trouble. Trouble that Keniston Eastman could make go away with one phone call. It would be Jenny's word against theirs.

"Just so you know," Adams continued, "the conclusion that Mr. Arsenault's death was a suicide is backed up by other sources. We have doctors' reports concerning his head injury. The hockey coach confirmed that he was forced to leave the team. Provost Meyers says that Mr. Arsenault filed an application for permission to withdraw from school, which is a very serious step to take. The facts, in our view, show a young man who was going through a very difficult time, difficult enough that he chose to take his own life."

"People in Belle River don't kill themselves. We suck up the hard times and go on."

"Miss Vega, I'm sure his death comes as a shock. But your roommates' statements have been vetted and verified, and as far as we know, nobody contradicts them. Unless *you* know someone who does."

Jenny understood that he was asking what her own account to the police would be, but she wasn't ready to answer that yet.

"What about Tim Healy?" she asked. "He saw everything. You might be surprised at what he has to say when he wakes up."

"I'm sorry to say, he may *not* wake up. We're very concerned for Tim, and his family. We've offered to fly in specialists. But given the severity of his head injury, I've been told that should he recover—which we sincerely hope he does—it's unlikely he'll have any memory of what happened."

"Tim's doctor actually told you that?"

Adams's eloquent shrug reminded Jenny that Tim was in *Carlisle* General Hospital, in the *Eastman* Wing. Patient confidentiality would count for squat there if the hospital's great benefactor started asking questions. The Eastmans had many allies; Jenny had none. If she wanted to go to the police and turn Kate in, if she wanted to make enemies of the Eastmans, she would take the consequences on her own.

"Miss Vega, I have to ask," Adams said, "what are you planning to say to the police?"

The question hung in the air. If only she could reverse time—make Kate not push Lucas, make him not fall, not die. But she couldn't. It was time to decide: Tell the truth and pay the price, or fall in line.

"What if—" she began, and hesitated.

"What if what?"

"What if I said I had seen Kate . . . I won't say *push* Lucas, that's too strong. What if I saw her hitting Lucas, and he was backing up, and then he fell off the bridge? What about that?"

"Well, I would say you were wrong, that your version of the facts is untrue. Beyond that, I might think you bore some grudge against Miss Eastman for alienating Mr. Arsenault's affections, and that you were lying out of spite. Other people might think that, too. Maybe they'd even think you were so twisted from romantic disappointment that you needed psychiatric help. Or that you had a substance abuse problem."

"Substance abuse? Me?" Jenny exclaimed.

"Several witnesses say they regularly detect the smell of marijuana coming from your room."

"From my suite. *Kate's* suite."

"Miss Vega, let me be frank. I haven't had time yet to go through a full process of collecting material on you. Maybe you think your reputation is beyond reproach. But any witness can be discredited. Making accusations against my client will draw a very robust response. A response that could damage your reputation at the least, and at the worst, could lead to your expulsion from Carlisle if we find evidence of drug use, say, or giving a false statement. If you were to be expelled, you'd find it difficult to gain admission to another college, and quite impossible to get a job in finance in the future, which I've been told is something that you want."

Jenny's nerve deserted her, and her throat went dry. She couldn't believe this was happening, yet on the other hand, she wasn't surprised at all. This was how Keniston Eastman rolled. Bring in a lawyer to make the threats. Leave the room. Keep his hands clean. She wouldn't even be able to pin this shakedown on him.

"And if I tell the police the same thing Kate did?" she asked.

"If you tell the *truth*, you will remain a great friend of the Eastmans, with all the benefits that entails for you and your family."

Adams looked meaningfully around the kitchen, his glance taking in the twenty-year-old appliances, the pictures of Jesus and John F. Kennedy hanging on the wall, the much-laundered checkered curtains. He was letting her know that the huge disparity in wealth and power between Jenny and the Eastmans had double consequences. Not only would he be happy to destroy little Jenny Vega if she dared to stand against his clients, but if she chose to do the opposite, things could be very sweet for her. Having Keniston Eastman owe you a whopping favor was kind of like winning the lottery.

Keniston walked into the kitchen. "Sorry for the delay. Have you two had a nice chat?" he asked, coming over to the table.

The condescension in his manner made her furious. He was so certain she would roll over that she wanted to throw his daughter's sick, twisted actions in his face.

"Did Kate really look you in the eye and tell you Lucas Arsenault jumped?" Jenny asked.

"Wait a minute, didn't you hear what I said?" Adams said, looking alarmed, as if he might get in trouble for not having everything wrapped up by now.

But Keniston met Jenny's eyes, unperturbed. "Kate and I didn't get a chance to speak before she left, Jenny. She's gone to stay with her stepmother."

"With Victoria?"

"No, her former stepmother. My ex-wife Simone lives in Geneva with my younger daughter. Kate was distraught, and we thought it would do her good to get away from this environment for a bit, and be with family. She may even enroll in school over there."

"In *Geneva*?" Jenny asked.

"Yes," he said.

"Switzerland?"

"Indeed."

There was a glint of victory in his eye. Jenny had taken a course in European history and politics. Switzerland was a neutral country, she recalled, with bank secrecy, and a reluctance to extradite those accused of crimes. So Jenny could throw away her entire future in an attempt to make Kate pay for her sins, and it would come to naught in the end. This was what true wealth bought you. Kate Eastman was beyond the reach of the law. She could kill someone and get away with it. Let that be a warning to the likes of Jenny Vega.

"All right," Jenny said. "Write the statement. I'll sign it."

part two

19

Present Day

The dog ran off the side of the jogging trail, heading straight for the riverbank.

"Baxter! Get back here now!" the jogger yelled, as his dog disappeared into the fog. Baxter was a rescue mutt, part hound, and the scent of animals in the woods could prove irresistible to him. But he knew better than to leave the trail during a training run.

"Baxter!" the dog's owner called again through rapid breaths, as he slowed his pace. He scanned the woods for any sign of his pet, and found none. "Damn dog."

From somewhere to the left, Baxter started barking like mad. The jogger heard the note of alarm in the sound, and the hair on the back of his neck stood up. *Bears?* he thought, and picked up a stick. He'd never once seen a bear in ten years of running the river trail, but it wasn't impossible.

"Baxter?" he said, his own voice shaky now, as he followed the sound of barking through the fog, making his way down the steep side of the bank.

Closer to the water's edge, the mist lifted, and he saw his dog standing guard over the thing that had caught his attention. The body of a woman had washed up on the bank. Her skin was blue-tinged and her eyes were wide open. Her golden hair spread out around her like a mermaid's. He took a step closer and saw the mess that had been the top of her head.

"Jesus," the jogger whispered, as the dog looked up and began to whimper.

20

Owen Rizzo took a last, lingering look at the blond woman on the coroner's slab before replacing the sheet tenderly over her. He'd met her once before. Six months before, to be exact, when he came up to Belle River from New York to interview for the chief of police job. He remembered that evening vividly. He remembered *her.* After he took the job and moved to town, he'd tried to find her. But it turned out the name she gave him was a fake, and once he figured that out, he stopped looking. Now, finally, here she was. It made him so sad that he needed a minute to compose himself before he could face talking to the ME.

At the moment they met, Owen remembered, he'd just come off that entire day of interviews. He'd passed with flying colors, and he knew it. Owen interviewed well, and he had a résumé that blew away anything they'd seen before in this Podunk town. The mayor hinted that she expected to be calling with an offer soon. He walked into Henry's Bistro feeling wired and excited, despite the oppressively hot and sticky weather. He was scheduled to have dinner with the current police chief, a guy named Peter Dudley, Jr., who was retiring. Dudley, who'd shepherded him to his interviews all day, had a country-cop shtick that wore on Owen's nerves, so he wasn't disappointed to get a text saying Dudley had to cancel. A tornado warning had gone into effect, and Dudley needed to oversee the town response. Owen was happy to be left alone. He'd order a steak and a bottle of red wine on the town's tab, and think over whether he could tolerate a job that seemed more geared toward handling weather emergencies than fighting crime.

He sat down at a booth in the bar area. The restaurant was completely deserted, which probably had something to do with the black, threatening sky outside the big plate-glass window. From where Owen sat, he would have a primo view of the town's main street as the storm rolled in. He placed a drink order with the waitress. Pretty soon the thunder started, and within minutes, flashes of lightning lit the dark sky. A few fat drops spattered against the window, and then came the deluge. Water fell in sheets. Traffic lights swayed in the wind. Drivers pulled to the side of the street as tree branches and other debris blew past. Pedestrians ran for cover, and Owen felt guilty being warm and dry inside instead of out there battling the storm. But this wasn't his town to police, not yet anyway.

He was still waiting for his wine to arrive when she ran up under the awning. With the rain blowing sideways, the awning couldn't keep her dry, and a few seconds later she walked in the front door, shaking water from an inside-out umbrella. Her silk blouse had soaked through to show the outline of a black brassiere underneath. He'd been alone for two years now, since his wife died, and he couldn't help but notice. It wasn't just the glimpse of the bra. She was a beautiful woman.

"You need a paper towel?" he said, getting to his feet.

The waitress had not returned, and there was nobody behind the bar, so Owen walked over and grabbed the roll of paper towels that sat beside the beer tap.

"Thank you," she said breathlessly, ripping off a long piece and patting her face and arms dry. "Do you work here?"

"No, just a customer."

He went back to his booth. She sat down on a barstool near the door and tied her wet hair into a messy knot at the nape of her neck. Something in her hands, in the graceful way she moved, reminded him of Nicolette, though they looked nothing alike. He was just about to ask her name when a flash of gold on her ring finger caught his eye. So she was married. Even though he'd only known her for a moment, he was disappointed.

"Is anybody working here?" she asked. "I'd love a drink. Can you believe this weather?" Her voice was smoky and seductive.

"The waitress disappeared a while ago. They're probably battening down the hatches in the kitchen," he said.

Outside, a bolt of lightning lit the sky, followed by a deafening crack. The woman jumped. "That was close," she said.

"There's a tornado warning in effect. You should move away from the window," he said.

"Oh, so you're a weatherman?" she said, smiling, a challenge in her eyes.

"Nope. A cop."

"Well, I'd better do what you say, then."

He liked the sound of that. She got up and moved to another barstool right across from him. As rain lashed the street, a strange green light filtered in through the big window, and lightning flashed blue in the sky. The waitress came back with his wine. He'd ordered a bottle of malbec that she'd recommended, and she opened it and poured a splash for Owen to taste. He swirled the glass and sniffed it like he'd seen people do, conscious of the blond woman watching him from her barstool. She looked like the type who went to wine tastings. He didn't want her to think he was a rube.

"Very nice," he said.

The waitress filled his glass. Just then, the overhead lights began to flicker, and they all looked up at the ceiling. Thunder crashed outside and the lights in the bar went dark.

"Whoa," the waitress said. "We don't lose power too often around here. I'd better go see what's going on in the kitchen." She walked away hurriedly toward the back of the restaurant.

"So much for my drink," the blond woman said.

In the half-light, he picked up his bottle of wine and gestured at the empty second glass on his table. "You can have some of mine if you like."

"You don't mind sharing?"

"Not at all. My associate stood me up because of the weather, and I can't finish a whole bottle by myself. Well, I *can,* but I shouldn't."

"All right," she said, and came over to the booth, sliding in across from him. "Thank you. I hate being alone in the dark anyway."

It wasn't really dark at that hour, even with the black clouds and the heavy rain, and she hadn't exactly been alone. But whatever got her to sit with him was fine by Owen. He poured wine into her glass, and watched the strange light from the window cast a moody shadow across her face.

"Let me see if I can find a candle," he said, and went behind the bar again. He fished around and found one, and a book of matches. He brought the candle over to the booth and lit it.

"There you go. Let there be light," he said.

"You sure you don't work here?" she asked.

"No, in fact, I don't live in this town. I'm here interviewing for a job," he said.

"Working for the college?" she asked. "Cheers, by the way." They clinked glasses.

"No, it would be working for the town. Police chief, actually."

"Very impressive. It fits. You look like a G-man."

"A *G-man*?" He laughed.

"Isn't that what they're called? Like Dick Tracy or something, from the comic books? With the dark hair and the strong jaw."

"That's a little before my time."

"Mine, too, but everybody knows Dick Tracy. Nobody ever said you look like him before?"

He chuckled. "Maybe once or twice."

"Mmm-hmm, thought so, you were being modest. So, Chief, tell me. From what I recall, back in the day, there wasn't much in the way of crime in good old Belle River, unless you count underage drinking, or toilet-papering houses on Halloween."

"Less crime is what cops like."

"Won't you be bored?" she said. "You look like a man who goes where the action is."

"What, because of my strong jaw?"

She laughed. "Exactly."

She ran a fingertip around the rim of her wineglass and smiled up at him. They were flirting, he realized. He hadn't flirted since Nicolette died. Not seriously, anyway, not like he meant it.

"It sounds like you haven't spent much time in Belle River recently. What're you, a Carlisle grad, back for a visit?" he asked.

"Yes and no. I started here my freshman year but never graduated, to my father's everlasting shame and disappointment. I ended up bumming around Europe for a while, getting my degree over there."

"That sounds like more fun. Carlisle's stuck-up anyway, right? Who needs it."

"I'm with you on that one. You're *not* an alum, I take it?" she asked.

"St. John's. You probably never heard of it."

"In Queens? Sure I did. I'm a New Yorker, born and raised. You are, too. I can hear it in your voice."

The comment about the New York in his voice touched Owen. He was a New Yorker in his bones, and he had his doubts about leaving his home and moving to this remote college town. If it was just him, he'd stay put. Stay in his job, move up the career ladder in the big-city police department, keep the house in Long Island he'd bought with Nicolette when they got married. But he wanted his kids to grow up somewhere peaceful and pretty, where he didn't have to worry about them walking home from school on their own. This town fit the bill. He didn't love it for himself, but it would be good for them. And if there were women like her here, maybe he could get used to it.

"Owen Rizzo, by the way," he said, extending his hand.

She hesitated for a second. "Maggie Price," she said, and shook it.

Her hand was warm and alive. He held it a second too long, and glanced down and saw little blue-green stars tattooed on the underside of her wrist. Man, she was sexy. He wanted to know her better. Yes, she was married, but they were stuck here together in a storm, far from home. He could enjoy her company without crossing any lines, couldn't he?

Their eyes met.

"You live in New York, then, like me?" he asked, already imagining asking her to dinner in the city. *She's married.*

"Not anymore. I moved back to Belle River about a week ago after more than twenty years away. Unfortunately."

"Unfortunately? This seems like a nice enough town. Quaint, peaceful, decent restaurants if you don't mind eating in the dark."

"Peace and quiet never did much for me," she said. "And things didn't go so well when I was in school here. Belle River is—well, it's bad luck for me, I'm afraid."

"Why come back, then?" he asked, studying her eyes. They were cool and blue, shadowed by long lashes in the half-light.

"Reversal of fortune, you could say." She looked around restlessly.

From her expression, he saw that she didn't want to tell that particular story, so he didn't press. Outside, the rain came down in torrents, and lightning flashed. Maggie set her wineglass on the table. It was nearly empty. He refilled it, and poured himself another while he was at it.

"What happened to the waitress?" she said, and as if on the cue, the waitress reappeared.

"Sorry, folks. Power line went down. It may be a while before the lights come back on, and the kitchen is closed for now."

"That's a drag," Maggie said. "If I don't eat something soon, I'll have to stop drinking this very nice wine, or I'll end up plastered."

"We could order a pizza," Owen said.

"There's an idea. Go for it, Chief," Maggie said.

Owen pulled out his phone and looked at it. "Sorry. No signal."

Maggie took hers from her bag. "Look at that. Mine's out, too."

"It's probably from the storm," the waitress said. "College Pizza's not gonna be delivering in this mess anyway."

Maggie looked out at the downpour. "It's getting worse, isn't it? Miss, do you think you could dig up some peanuts or something?"

"I can do a bread basket. Hold on, I'll be right back with that."

"And another bottle of this, please," Maggie said, holding up the malbec, which was already nearly empty.

A couple of minutes later, they had their bread and wine, and settled in to drink and watch the storm rage. A pretty flush suffused Maggie's cheeks as she asked Owen why he would ever leave New York to come to a place like this, so small and dull. Her interest in him was like a warm light; he opened under its influence. He told her about Nicolette dying. About how hard the cancer had been, and what it was like now, trying to raise his son and daughter by himself. Ty had been eight and Annie six when Nicolette passed, and there was no family to help. His parents had both died not long before his kids were born; Nicolette's lived in a retirement community in Florida and weren't interested in more than the occasional visit.

"Sounds lonely," she said.

"Yeah, now that you mention it, I have been lonely," Owen said, and realized that right this minute, here with Maggie, he wasn't lonely at all.

They got to talking about his work. Owen loved his job. He was the senior detective on a joint state-federal narcotics task force, and the work was thrilling—half high-level investigation, half cops and robbers on the street. He'd just taken down a Salvadoran gang that had cornered the meth trade in Brooklyn and Long Island and had thirty murders to their credit. But as much as he loved it, the work was dangerous, the hours he kept on the task force were brutal, and his kids were suffering. He tried to get time off, but his boss was old-school, an ex-marine now with DEA, who thought your wife dying didn't make your kids his problem. Nothing could fix that except a new job, preferably one where Owen didn't answer to anybody, which was why he applied here. Chief's jobs in wealthy college towns with a salary like this one didn't come along too often, and even if it wasn't a perfect fit, he should probably jump on it.

Owen looked up at the clock and saw that nearly two hours had passed since they started talking. The second bottle of wine was down to the dregs. He'd been running on and on about himself—though, hell, that felt great—but he hadn't learned a thing about her.

"Long story short, I'm here because I'm looking for a fresh start. But I'll stop talking about myself now. Tell me about you."

"Me? Well, I could use a fresh start, a second chance. Or a third or fourth. I'm not sure *what* chance I'm on, come to think of it. Nothing ever quite works out for me."

"Looking at you, I find that hard to believe. You must have the world at your feet."

"Thanks for the vote of confidence, but no. My mother died of cancer when I wasn't much older than your kids are now. I never had the guidance I needed after that, and I guess you could say I went astray. I screwed my up life pretty badly. Maybe I would have done better if I had a father like you. Caring and strong. Your kids are lucky."

"I try. But it's hard. It must've been hard for your dad, too, raising you alone."

"Oh, he wasn't alone, and he didn't really raise me either. I had a succession of wicked stepmothers. Well, two of them anyway. They hated my guts. The first one divorced my father after less than a year and took a boatload of his money. The second one, Victoria, she was my stepmother when I was a teenager. We butted heads constantly, you can't imagine."

"I think I can," he said, envisioning Maggie as a teenager. She must've been a magnet for the boys, with that face, that body, that voice. You'd have to lock a girl like that in a tower to keep her out of trouble.

"It was partly my fault that Victoria and I didn't get along," Maggie said. "I realized that eventually, and I owned up to it. Victoria died of cancer about a year ago. I was really sad when it happened, which surprised me. I guess I'd finally grown up enough to understand how hard *I* was on *her*."

"Did you tell her that?"

"Yes, I went to see her. We had a talk, and made up—well, sort of. I blame my father for playing us off against each other, so I apologized, but I wanted her to acknowledge the role he played. She wouldn't go there. She was his loyal retainer to the end."

"So he's the bad guy, your father?"

"Oh, yeah. Classic bad guy. Cold, harsh, distant. Always gets his way. He was never available when I was growing up. He messed me up big-time."

"And let me guess," he said, leaning toward her. "You married a man just like him."

She looked down at her left hand. "Married? Oops, did I forget to take that damn ring off?"

"You're not married?" Owen asked, his heart leaping.

She laughed. "Just kidding. Usually when a married woman cozies up to a man in a bar, she takes off her ring. If she's smart, that is."

"Is that what you're doing, cozying up to me in this bar?"

"What do you think?" she asked.

Under the table, her feet snuck in between his.

"I hope so," Owen said, looking into her eyes, his pulse racing.

"We get a pass, don't we, because of the storm? If two people were marooned on a desert island together, they'd be allowed to console each other until the rescue helicopter came."

"I agree completely."

Normally Owen was circumspect in these situations. But here in this place, so deserted and intimate, with the rain lashing against the window, and the light outside fading, he felt so close to her. In the candlelight, he took her hand, and turned it over to look at the stars.

"I used to have a big diamond, but we had to sell it," she said, taking her hand away. "Times change, and all good things must come to an end. Though, when it comes to my marriage—" She sighed, and threw her head back against the banquette. "It's not so easy to end that, I'm afraid. I've been trying to get away from him for years, but it never happens."

"Why not? You have kids?" he asked.

"No."

"You own property together?"

"No. Not anymore."

He shrugged. "So leave him, then. Sounds like you could if you wanted to."

She leaned forward and looked at him from under her lashes. "Listen to you, Chief, encouraging me to leave my husband. And we've only just met."

She leaned closer, and their fingers intertwined again.

"I'm just saying. Life is short. If you're unhappy, you should make a change," he said.

"Oh, but you don't know me. I've always been unhappy." Her voice was breathy and low, and he seemed to hear it deep inside his head.

"Always?" he asked.

"Not now, not right this minute, but that's because I'm distracted. You're a pretty good distraction, you know?"

Her lips were parted. He was desperate to kiss her, and there was nobody here to see. He pulled on her hand, and as if by magic, she came around to his side of the booth and slipped in beside him. He took her face in his hands, and they had a kiss straight out of his teenaged wet dreams. Mouths open and hungry, tasting of red wine, their hands exploring each other. It wasn't until he started to unbutton her blouse that he remembered where they were, and pulled back. Her eyes and her mouth were blurry with lust, and he had a raging hard-on. He'd never cheated on his wife (though this wouldn't exactly be cheating), and he'd never slept with a married woman. But even if what they were doing was wrong, he didn't want to stop.

"I'm staying at the inn, right down the street. Come back to my room with me," he said, and his voice sounded strange and thick to his own ears.

But before she could answer, in one of the worst instances of timing in Owen's life, the lights came back on. They sat back, blinking in the sudden brightness, their hands falling to their sides. Maggie rearranged her clothes, and moved back to the other side of the booth. He felt abandoned.

"I don't know, Chief. Maybe we shouldn't," she said, smoothing her hair.

The waitress walked into the room, exuding cheerful efficiency, and broke the mood for good.

"There you go, folks. Power's back on. Not too bad an outage, huh? Give me a minute and I'll be right back for your food order."

Somebody pounded on the plate-glass window. Owen looked up and saw a man standing there—a good-looking man of about his own age, slightly disheveled, with blond hair wet from the rain. He was staring at Maggie, and he looked angry.

"Oh, that's my husband. I'd better go," Maggie said breathlessly, and grabbed her bag.

She started to slide out of the booth, but Owen stopped her with his foot. He saw something in the man's eyes that troubled him, a glint of rage, of hysteria almost.

"Hey, will you be okay? Is he—does he get *violent*?"

"No. That's not his style, and he's caught me in bars with strange men before. He's more the sulk and guilt-trip type." She looked at Owen wistfully. "Hey, sorry I have to run. But you should take the job, move to town. Belle River could use a man like you."

The man banged on the window again. Maggie slipped out of the booth. And then she was gone.

Owen did move to Belle River. He gave up his high-powered career, sold his house, packed up his kids, and took the helm of this small-town police department. And the whole time in the back of his mind, he imagined that he'd get a blazing-hot affair with Maggie Price out of the deal. He knew that if he found her again, he wouldn't care about his position, or the risks. He'd want to be with her, to kiss her again, to distract her from her unhappiness.

When she didn't materialize, when fate didn't throw them together walking down College Street at high noon, he went looking. He searched for her in every registry and every database at his disposal. When there was no Maggie *Price,* he thought maybe she'd given him her maiden name, and he started looking for Maggie Anything, or Margaret. Turned out there were quite a few Margarets in Belle River. For every one, he took the time to pull a driver's license photo if there was one, or to scour the Internet for a picture that would rule the woman out. (He could've gotten fired for some of the things he did, if anybody had known.) Owen was a busy man. A single father, in a new job, with the eyes of the town upon him. But he worked his way through every Margaret in Belle River between the ages of twenty-five and fifty (he put her age at mid-to-late thirties, but he was casting a wide net) before he threw in the towel. At some point it dawned on him that she'd given him a fake name on purpose—he remembered that moment of hesitation when they shook hands—because she didn't want to be found. Still, he didn't quit until he was forced to, by virtue of running out of Margarets.

And now, after all that fruitless searching, she'd turned up on his watch. Some jogger had found her washed up on the riverbank a few hours back, at a location that fell within Owen's jurisdiction to investigate. Owen regretted not asking for her number, not taking her back to his room, not becoming her lover, her friend. He remembered her wistfulness that night, and her glamour and her breathy charm. He remembered their kiss, and the feeling of her breasts under his hands. And he remembered her husband, standing outside the bar, staring at her through the plate glass with rage in his eyes. Owen could have saved her, he was certain, but it was too late now. Now all he could do was figure out what happened, who did this to her—the husband, presumably—and bring that piece of shit to justice.

21

Griff woke to the sound of pounding on the front door. He groaned and rolled over onto his back, struggling to open his eyes through the crud that crusted them shut. He'd spent the last two days and three nights on the white sectional in the living room, in his boxers, surrounded by crushed beer cans and an increasingly empty bottle of Absolut. He was in no condition to receive visitors, so he pulled a sofa cushion over his head and waited for whoever the hell was at the door to give up and go away.

More pounding followed, compounded by the incessant ringing of the doorbell. He felt like his head was about to explode.

"What the fuck . . . get lost!" he shouted, clapping his hands over his ears.

"Mr. Eastman!" a deep voice yelled through the door. "Open up, police. We need to speak with you."

Police? *Shit.* As if they hadn't done enough damage to Griff's life already.

He sat up and peeked through the living room blinds. It was afternoon already, what time he couldn't say. Dead leaves blew down the street in a stiff breeze. The sun sat low and weak in the sky, but the light of it on his burning eyes was still enough to make him wince. Two people stood on the front steps. A tall guy with dark hair who looked vaguely familiar, and a young black woman in a trench coat. They were both in plain clothes but they looked like cops right enough. He thought about whether to get off the couch and find out what they wanted with him. Once upon a time, Griff's father had a clever lawyer named Burt Lippmann, and Lippmann had offered Griff this piece of advice: You were not required to let a cop in without a warrant, but you should probably do so—unless of course you were sitting on piles of evidence that needed destroying. Otherwise, it was smarter to play nice, or the cop would get the warrant anyway, and come back looking to screw you over for the inconvenience.

Griff knocked on the window, and the cops turned to look at him in unison.

"Just a minute," Griff mouthed, holding up a finger.

He cast around the living room for clothing, and found none. It was damn cold in here. He'd forgotten how much he disliked this godforsaken climate. There was a bathrobe, he remembered, hanging on the hook on the back of the door in the moldy downstairs bathroom. He went to get it, stopping to splash some water on his face. Griff combed his hair with his fingers, and it felt stiff and dirty to the touch. He was forty years old, life as he'd known it was over, and it was feeling increasingly like a hassle to carry on with things. He looked green and ill in the harsh light. His eyes were bloodshot and yellow. Drinking your dinner for three nights running was not the best thing for the liver. He needed a shave. There was a bruise on his left cheek, and his lip was puffy. He probed it gingerly with his finger, and winced. Using his tongue, he poked around his mouth and found that the entire left side of his jaw was tender.

At the front door, he hesitated. Did he really need to let these bloodsuckers in? He decided to compromise, opening the door but leaving the chain on.

"Can I help you, Officers?" he said, through the chain. A bitter wind swept through the gap, and Griff's eyes began to water.

The man stared at Griff intently, which naturally made him uncomfortable, given that the guy was a cop and Griff was in a bathrobe and bare feet in the middle of the day.

"Do you know it's after two o'clock?" the cop asked.

"Right, Officer. Is there something I can do for you?" Griff said.

The man pulled a leather wallet from his jacket pocket and flashed a badge.

"Chief Owen Rizzo of the Belle River Police Department. This is my colleague, Detective Keisha Charles. Are you Keniston Eastman?"

"No," Griff said.

"Is Mr. Eastman available?"

"No."

"When is he expected to return?"

"Mr. Eastman doesn't live here. He owns this house. I'm the tenant," Griff said.

"Oh. Mr.—?"

"Rothenberg."

"Mr. Rothenberg, do you mind if we come in?" the officer asked, glancing at the chain lock suspiciously. Nobody in this one-horse town so much as locked their doors. Griff must look paranoid, but he had his reasons for hating cops.

"What is this about, Officer?"

"This is in reference to a Katherine Eastman," the police chief said, and Griff's stomach dropped to his feet.

"What about her?"

"You know her?"

"Yes." Griff was using the Burt Lippmann approach to talking to cops. *Say nothing, or say as little as possible.*

"How about if you invite us in, and then I'll explain. It's damn cold out here."

Griff was leery of letting cops into his house, but the mention of Kate's name had an effect on him, as it always did. Maybe it would be a foolish move to let them in, but he needed to know what they had to say.

"All right. Come in."

Griff stepped back and removed the chain. A wintry draft blew into the hallway along with the cops, making him pull the bathrobe closer.

He watched with mingled amusement and embarrassment as they took in the surroundings.

"Cleaning lady's day off," Griff said.

That was an understatement. The place looked like the health department should pay a visit. Griff and Kate had done nothing to fix it up in the months they'd lived here, other than moving in their sleek New York furniture, which looked ridiculous in the dilapidated rooms. Neither of them could bear to think that this Belle River misadventure was anything but temporary. And of course, Kate was above doing housework. They'd never had to get along without help until recently, but at least Griff tried—for a while anyway. Lately, not so much.

"Is there somewhere we can sit down?" the police chief asked, with a dubious look at the living room. It was like a frat basement in there, the floor studded with beer cans and pizza boxes.

"The kitchen. I can make some coffee if you like. I could use a cup myself. This way," Griff said, trying to sound accommodating.

In the kitchen, the cops took seats at the table while Griff puttered around gathering the coffee things. He needed a minute to clear his head before he talked to them. He caught the girl cop glancing at his laptop, which sat out on the kitchen counter. She could search it all she wanted and she wouldn't find anything interesting. Just some porn and a few pathetic relics of his useless job search. Griff had given up on finding work months ago. Big surprise—nobody wanted to hire a financial consultant whose father was locked up for a notorious financial crime.

Griff started the coffeemaker and took a seat across from the two cops. Their names had gone in one ear and out the other. All he remembered was that the man was chief of police, which worried him. If the chief of police was paying a house call, that must mean something big. Plus, it was bothering him—where had he seen the guy before?

"You asked about Kate. Did she do something I should be aware of?" Griff asked.

The cops looked at each other.

"So she went by Kate?" the chief asked, looking pained as he made a note in a spiral notebook.

"Yes."

"Kate Eastman?"

"Yes."

"And what was your relationship to her?"

"She was my wife."

"*Was?*"

"Is my wife. Kate Eastman *is* my wife."

"Eastman. Not Kate Rothenberg?"

"No. She never took my name."

"Ah." The chief was silent for a moment, taking Griff's measure. He made a motion toward his own face. "What happened to your face, if you don't mind my asking? You look like you took a punch."

Griff touched his jaw again. "Oh, I uh, must've walked into something. I should probably cut back on the beer. Old college habit."

"Uh-huh," the chief said.

Griff's hands were shaking. That could be chalked up to excessive alcohol consumption or might be the first sign of an impending anxiety attack. The attacks were a recent thing with him. They started when his father and the money went away simultaneously, and picked up steam once he realized that Kate was likely to leave, too. Griff had been steady all his life, but of course, he'd had an easy life until recently. Maybe if he'd had things rougher, he would've been a bag of nerves all along. He'd tried Prozac for a bit, but quit when it interfered with his drinking, alcohol being his preferred refuge in a crisis.

The shaking attracted the chief's attention to Griff's hands. There were noticeable scratches on the backs of his hands and on his forearms. The chief saw the scratches, and exchanged a meaningful look with the female detective, who pulled a notebook from her purse and wrote something down. Griff got up to check on the coffeemaker, wishing he had never let them in.

"So what is Ms. Eastman's relationship to the Keniston Eastman who owns this house?" the chief asked.

"Keniston is Kate's father," Griff said. "You said if I let you in, that you would explain what this is about."

"We're getting to that," the chief said, staring at Griff with dislike, or maybe it was suspicion.

"Mr. Rothenberg," the female detective said, looking at her notebook, "a couple of nights ago, one of our officers found a vehicle abandoned in a parking lot off River Road, near the town boat launch, just downriver from the old railroad bridge. A 2014 red BMW three-series convertible with New Hampshire plates, registered in the name Katherine Elizabeth Eastman. Are you familiar with that vehicle?"

"Yes, that's Kate's car. What was it doing there?"

"We're hoping you can help us figure that out," she replied.

"I'm sorry, but I don't know."

"When did you last see your wife?" the chief asked.

"Uh, hmm. How do you take your coffee, by the way?" Griff asked, to buy time.

"Any way is fine," the chief said, watching him closely.

Their questions were beginning to alarm him. He needed time to organize his thoughts. He needed moral support, or better yet, legal advice. Too bad Burt Lippmann was serving five-to-forty in Allenwood for conspiring with his father.

Griff filled three cups and carried them to the table. He was shaking so hard that coffee sloshed onto the tablecloth.

"I asked when you last—"

"Yes, I heard you," Griff said, taking a seat and a big gulp of coffee. It burned his mouth, and he winced. "Uh, let's see. I last saw Kate . . . maybe a day or two ago. Maybe three."

"You're not sure?" the chief asked.

"Let me think," Griff said. "Thursday. I'm pretty sure I last saw her on Thursday. What day is today?"

"Today is Sunday."

"Really?"

"Yes. Do you still think you last saw her Thursday?"

"Yes, it was the day before her birthday, and her birthday was on Friday."

"So you didn't see your wife on her birthday?" the chief asked.

"No."

"That's pretty unusual, for a man not to see his wife on her birthday. Were you having marital problems?"

"What business is that of yours?"

"Based on what you just said, you haven't seen your wife in three days, but you didn't report her missing. Why not?"

Griff's heart started to pound, and he felt like he couldn't breathe. "Did something happen to Kate? Just tell me."

Griff glared at the cop, and he glared right back. The female detective cleared her throat.

"Mr. Rothenberg, I'm afraid we have some bad news," she said.

Griff went cold, and then hot. He'd been avoiding acknowledging to himself the likely reason behind their visit, but the moment had come when denial was no longer an option. He looked into the female detective's eyes, which were kind, and tried to speak, but found he couldn't. *Kate, Kate, Kate, I love you so.*

"Yesterday, a jogger on the river trail found a body washed up on the bank of the Belle River," she said. "The 911 call initially went to fire and rescue, who responded and took custody of the body of a female subject, approximately five-four, a hundred ten to a hundred twenty pounds, blond hair, thirty to forty years old, deceased. Does that match the description of your wife?"

"Yes," Griff said softly, looking down at the tablecloth. "I mean, it generally does, but that doesn't mean it's her. Right?"

The detective flipped through her notebook again. "The medical examiner took fingerprints from the body, which is standard procedure. The fingerprints were matched to one Katherine Elizabeth Eastman, previously arrested in New York five years ago on suspicion of DUI. We were able to trace her to this address, which is how we found you. The conclusion is that the deceased is most likely Ms.—"

"*Yes,*" he said, and the syllable came out like a plea for her to stop.

"We were hoping you might be able to come down to the station," she said gently. "You won't be viewing the actual body. The ME photographs the victim prior to autopsy, and we have the official pictures at our office. We need you to make a formal identification for the record."

Griff put his head down on the table and cried like a baby.

22

Aubrey was touched when Griff called her from the police station. Touched, but not surprised that she was the one he'd turn to in his moment of need. He didn't call Jenny, even though Jenny was the mayor and tight with the chief of police and could pull strings. He called Aubrey, because Aubrey had always been on his side. Aubrey had the integrity not to blame Griff for his father's mistakes. She never thought less of him because he'd lost his vast fortune. She never stopped thinking he was gorgeous, and interesting. She never wavered in her support and friendship even when his family name became synonymous with "crook" in certain circles. When Jenny and Tim lost the money they'd invested with Marty Rothenberg's firm, Jenny turned her back on Griff. She was afraid of associating with the likes of him, as if the stigma would rub off. Griff moved up to Belle River and couldn't find a job to save his life, but did Jenny offer to help? Nope. Everybody in town owed her a favor and she couldn't be bothered to make a single call. What kind of way was that to treat an old friend?

Jenny wasn't the worst offender, though, not by a long shot. Kate had vowed to take Griff for better or worse, richer or poorer. On their wedding day, as Aubrey recalled, Griff was richer and Kate was poorer. She'd run through her trust fund, and her father wouldn't pony up any more beyond the cost of the fancy wedding, but Griff went ahead and married her anyway, without so much as a pre-nup. Was Kate grateful to him for coming to her rescue? Hell, no. The second the feds raided Rothenberg Capital and slapped the cuffs on Griff's dad, Kate turned around and started treating her husband like dirt. He could no longer support her in the fashion to which she was accustomed. Coming down in the world is a bitch, and Kate took her frustration out on her husband. Forget the vows. Marriage vows meant nothing to Kate. That part about forsaking all others? Optional, as far as Kate was concerned, as Aubrey had learned to her own pain and disappointment. Aubrey spent her entire adult life thinking the sun rose and set on Kate Eastman, but she'd learned the hard way that Kate was not worthy of her admiration.

Griff apparently didn't know that yet, since he was crying on the phone. She wondered if she should enlighten him about Kate and Ethan. But it didn't seem like the right moment.

"*What* happened to Kate?" Aubrey said. "I can't understand you, Griff. Calm down, speak slowly."

Ethan was sitting at the kitchen island, working on a jigsaw puzzle with Viv. He'd been out all night Thursday and didn't come home till the wee hours on Friday. He probably still thought she was in the dark, but she'd been keeping tabs on Kate and Ethan for months now. Watching, thinking, dreaming of turning the tables. Ethan had a slight greenish bruise that looked suspiciously like a black eye. What was that all about? Aubrey had pretended not to notice—why give him the satisfaction?—and they'd barely spoken all weekend. He crept around like this wasn't his house, spending most of his time watching football in the basement, emerging only ten minutes ago when Viv begged him for attention. The second Kate's name was mentioned, however, Ethan came to life.

"What's that?" he asked, looking over at her.

"Oh, my God. Oh, my God. No!" Aubrey said.

Ethan's face went white. "What is it? What happened?"

She waved at him to shut up.

"How did it happen?" she asked Griff.

"How did *what* happen?" Ethan cried, and she made him wait while she listened to Griff's tale in gruesome detail.

"You shouldn't go through this alone," Aubrey said into the phone. "No. No, really. I'm coming down there right away. I'll be there in fifteen minutes. Okay? You just sit tight, honey." Aubrey hung up and turned to Ethan. "I have to go to the police station," she said.

"Jesus, Aubrey. Didn't you hear me asking what happened?"

"Griff needs moral support."

"Aubrey, *what happened to Kate*?" Ethan demanded.

Aubrey glanced meaningfully at Viv. "Little pitchers have big ears. I'll call you from the road," she said, though she had no intention of doing that. Let him stew. Like all those nights she sat up wondering when and if he was coming home, and the whole time he was out screwing her best friend. Aubrey had always prided herself on being so smart, and yet she'd let them play her for a fool. Not anymore.

Viv had been following the adults' conversation closely. "What happened to Aunt Kate, Mommy?" Viv asked.

"She was in an accident, baby. I have to go help Uncle Griff. Hopefully I won't be late, but if I am, Dad will give you dinner." Aubrey turned to Ethan. "There's a pizza in the freezer, and veggies in the crisper to make a salad."

Ethan stood up. "I'm coming with you."

"No," she said firmly. "Somebody needs to stay with the kids. Lilly has an algebra test tomorrow. You need to make sure she studies."

"I'm a doctor. If there was an accident, I can help."

"It's too late for that."

He went white. "What do you mean, too late?"

"Are you really gonna make me say it in front of her?" Aubrey said, and grabbed her car keys from the basket. She slammed the garage door extra hard as she went out to the car.

Aubrey was sick and tired of making nice with that scumbag cheater piece of shit. All the love she'd ever felt for Ethan was gone. And that was tragic, because she'd loved him a lot once. When they met, she was a grad student in comparative religion, and he was an orthopedics resident at the hospital. He came to a yoga class she taught at the student center, because he was interested in yoga as therapy for joint injury. He ended up asking her to dinner, where Aubrey wowed him with her knowledge of the Vedic spiritual roots of various poses. At the time, Ethan seemed like the answer to her prayers. He was handsome and successful, and she was lonely and broke. Her college friends had moved away, and there was nobody to warn her to put the brakes on with Dr. Heartthrob. She fell for Ethan hard, and the more invested she got, the more he backed off. He probably wouldn't have married her if she hadn't gotten pregnant with Logan. But once Logan was born, Ethan seemed really happy—so long as family life didn't interfere with his work. She quit her PhD program to stay home with their growing family, because Ethan was so busy with his career. Aubrey went from being a Carlisle brainiac to being a doctor's wife, ignored and taken for granted, and she was still in the process of digging herself out from that.

Aubrey slid behind the wheel of the Volvo and looked up to find Ethan right beside her, holding the driver's-side door open so she couldn't leave.

"Please, Aubrey. Tell me what Griff said."

He looked like somebody had punched him in the stomach. Over Kate! Aubrey had had three difficult childbirths. Lilly almost died of croup when she was eighteen months old. Logan broke half the bones in his body playing sports, and Viv had been hit in the face with a softball and nearly lost the vision in her left eye. Yet Ethan never had this look on his face till tonight. *Your girlfriend's dead, asshole, happy now?* People got what they deserved. Aubrey had the money to kick him out months ago, and instead she'd let him live here while she ironed his shirts and cooked his meals. He'd taken advantage of her generosity, but the party was over.

"Griff said he hadn't heard from Kate since Thursday night. Where was she? Do *you* know?" Aubrey said.

"Me? Of course not. Why would I?" Ethan said, but she saw a shadow pass across his eyes.

"You seem awfully broken up given that Kate was *my* friend."

"What's that supposed to mean?"

"I don't know! I'm upset, Ethan, okay? Let go of the door. I'll call you when I can."

Aubrey hit the garage-door opener and pressed the ignition. When Ethan didn't let go, she put the car in reverse and stepped on the gas, forcing him to jump aside.

The Belle River police station was housed in a historic brick building in the heart of town, but inside it was bare-bones, government-issue ugly, with linoleum floors and harsh fluorescent lighting. Griff sat in the waiting area, bent over with his head in his hands. Aubrey took the seat next to him and put her hand on his shoulder, but still he didn't look up.

"Hey," she said softly. "I'm here, Griff. Are you ready to go?"

He raised his head. His eyes were flat and dead-looking, and he smelled like the bottom of a bottle, but Aubrey didn't care about any of that. She saw him as he'd been two decades earlier, on the dance floor at Spring Fling, their freshman year. It wasn't long after that trouble at the old railroad bridge, because Kate was recently departed, and Griff was hurting. He'd just heard from a friend in Paris who'd run into Kate in Saint-Germain-des-Prés at two o'clock in the morning, riding on the back of some guy's motorcycle. Kate had said to tell Griff hi, and he couldn't stop talking about what that meant. Was Kate thinking about him? Was she sad to be so far away from school? *Doesn't sound like it,* Aubrey thought to herself, and, *Honey, she dumped you already, you just don't know it yet.* But in Griff's eyes, he and Kate were on separate continents against their will, torn apart by the vagaries of fate. Aubrey let him talk for as long as he needed to. Griff looked amazing that night, in a cream-colored jacket that set off his tan and his sun-kissed hair. They slow-danced, and he buried his face against Aubrey's neck. Later, they went back to his room. Yes, comforting Griff had always been sweet. And now she'd have a chance to do some more of it.

"They found Kate's body down by the river," he said.

"The river? My God."

"I didn't see her in person. They took her to some facility to do an autopsy. They had me look at pictures for the identification."

"That's awful. I am so sorry, sweetheart."

"Aubrey, it didn't even look like her. Her face was this strange color, like—"

He put his head down and started to cry. Aubrey rubbed his back for a few minutes, then, getting impatient with the hard plastic chair, took his hands in hers. Griff's hands were freezing cold, so she rubbed them.

"Hey," she said. "I can't imagine what you're going through. I want to help. Let me take you home, all right? I'm gonna get you a hot shower, a cup of herbal tea, and put you to bed. My car is outside."

Griff wiped his eyes with his coat sleeve. "There's no way I could sleep tonight."

"I understand. But let's get you out of here anyway. Unless—I'm assuming you're free to leave?"

"Why wouldn't I be?"

"I didn't mean anything by that. Just wondering if there are any more formalities."

"No. They wanted to interview me. But I refused to talk to them. After what happened to my dad, I thought I should consult someone first. Do you think that was a mistake?"

"Oh, gosh. I'm not the one to ask about legal stuff."

A woman with bright-red hair sitting behind the courtesy desk was watching them with a little too much interest.

"Let's talk about this in the car, Griff," Aubrey said firmly. "Come on."

Darkness had fallen early, and with a northern ferocity. The sky was black and full of stars, and the temperature hovered around freezing. Aubrey breathed deep and felt clean, cold air rush into her lungs. Griff, wearing only a T-shirt and jeans, hugged himself and shivered.

"You didn't bring a coat?" Aubrey said.

"The cops came to the house to tell me that they found her. They said to come downtown so I just walked out. I wasn't thinking."

"The heat takes a second to come on," Aubrey said, once they were in the car.

Griff huddled against the passenger door. Aubrey wanted to be a supportive friend, but now that they were away from prying eyes, she couldn't hold her tongue.

"What did the police say, Griff? What do they think? Do they think she killed herself?"

"Please." He raised his hands to his face as if to protect himself from her words.

"No, but really. They must have some explanation. Some theory. They don't think someone *killed* her?"

"Aubrey."

"We were supposed to have dinner Friday night. I think you knew that. Just us girls, for her birthday. But she never showed up. Did you see her that night? Did she say anything that made you think something was wrong?"

"Would you *shut up*?" he cried, making her flinch.

She would hate for this intimate feeling between them to be spoiled over something stupid like when Griff saw Kate last, or what he knew about her death. After a moment, Aubrey recovered, and patted his knee reassuringly.

"You're right. I'm sorry. This isn't the time. It's just—I'm in shock. I know you are, too."

They fell silent. Aubrey pulled out of the parking spot. As usual, there was no traffic downtown—there never was, after six thirty or so. The stoplight at the corner of Briggs Street had been turned to blinking yellow, so Aubrey didn't even have to stop. The right turn onto Faculty Row came up so fast that she nearly missed it.

"I forgot how close to town you live," she said.

Griff nodded miserably. Aubrey pulled up in front of his house.

"We're here," she said.

The lights were off inside the ugly brown house, and it loomed over the street, hulking in the darkness. When Aubrey opened her door, cold air rushed in, pushing out the warm air from the heater. Griff shrank back into his seat.

"Aren't you coming?" she said.

"That fucking house," Griff said. "I hate it. I can't stand the thought of going back in there."

Aubrey closed her door again and looked at him. "You know, it's probably not a bad idea for you to stay somewhere else tonight. Not be alone. I can go upstairs and pack a bag for you if you like," she said.

"The problem is, I have nowhere to go. Can you believe that? I can't even afford a hotel room. Griffin Rothenberg, golden boy, homeless. That's a shocker, huh?" he said, with a bitter laugh.

It hurt her heart to see him like this. "You can come home with me, honey," she said.

"To your house?"

"Yes."

He looked up, and their eyes met. Griff's were bloodshot, but blue as ever in the glow of the street light.

"Aubrey, I appreciate the offer. But I couldn't stand to see your husband."

The hatred in his voice felt familiar to Aubrey. It took her a second to realize that Griff felt the same way about Ethan as she did herself, and another to understand that must mean Griff *knew*. *Griff* knew about Kate and Ethan's affair. Jenny had admitted she knew, and now Griff. How many others? Was Aubrey the only fool who hadn't seen what was right before her eyes? She'd hate herself, except she hated Kate and Ethan more.

"You knew," she said aloud.

He nodded. "You did, too?"

"I figured it out just recently, but I never said anything to anyone. Ethan doesn't know I know. Did Kate—"

"Please. I can't talk about her," he said.

"Of course. I understand, it's too upsetting, and you need your strength. We'll save it until after you've had a decent night's sleep. I thought of someplace I can take you that's quiet and peaceful. My cabin at the lake. The heat's off but there's plenty of dry firewood, and a woodstove."

"Thank you, that sounds good," he said.

Griff reached out and squeezed her hand, and Aubrey felt a rush of love. You couldn't really think of this as a bad night, despite Kate dying and all. In the long run, people who did evil got what they deserved, and everything worked out for the best.

23

When Aubrey called to give Jenny the news about Kate late Sunday night, Jenny grilled her for information. Who found the body? What did the police think? When was the funeral? But all Aubrey could talk about was Griff, Griff, Griff, how worried she was about Griff. Who gave a shit about Griff? What about Kate, their friend, who was dead? Jenny hung up and started to cry. She'd loved Kate once. The wild child with the golden hair, full of chaos and laughter. Kate made life exciting, she made things sparkle. It shouldn't have come to this.

It was late and the boys were in bed. Jenny went looking for Tim, because she needed someone to comfort her. She knew better, but she did it anyway, hoping. He was sitting in the den, half watching the ball game, a surveyor's report from a jobsite on his knee. She told him Kate's body had been pulled from the river.

"The river, huh? Poetic justice," he said, stony-faced. Then he got up and walked away. She heard him in the kitchen, opening the fridge, and popping a beer, and she felt alone with her sorrow.

Jenny went to her room and slammed the door. She got in bed, pulled the blankets up, and started sobbing. After a while, Tim came in. Jenny rolled over and looked at him with wet eyes, but he turned his back and went into the bathroom to get undressed, something he never did. He was making a point: She would suffer this loss by herself. Tim had never liked

Kate. No—that wasn't strong enough. Tim *hated* Kate. He'd never forgiven her for whatever role he imagined she'd played in Lucas's death. He was glad Kate was dead, and he wouldn't pretend otherwise, not even for Jenny's sake. Which was crazy when you thought about it, because he had no facts to back him up. Tim didn't remember a single thing that happened that night at the bridge twenty-two years ago. The doctors had been right. His head injury had wiped his memory of that event, and to this day, it hadn't returned.

Tim came back into the bedroom, and got into bed with his phone, scrolling through e-mails, ignoring her. The bulk of his body beside her felt as unyielding as a brick wall. Jenny sat up, reached for the box of Kleenex on her bedside table, and blew her nose. She longed to yell at him, to accuse him of heartlessness, of insensitivity, of being a bad husband. But she couldn't, because she was the one in the wrong. There was a lie at the center of their marriage, a worm in the apple. And it was her fault. Years ago, when she lied to cover up Kate's crime, Jenny took sides against Tim and his family. She was only eighteen at the time, and the pressure had been intense. To this day, it gave her the shakes to think about that meeting in her mother's kitchen with Keniston Eastman and his lawyer. A young girl, naïve, up against the sharks of Wall Street—what was she *supposed* to do? She might have forgiven herself by now, except it wasn't just the police she lied to. She lied to her own husband. She was still lying to this day.

But if Jenny was truly honest with herself, she would admit that she hadn't been naïve, not back then, not ever. She got rewarded for her lie year after year. It's not like Keniston gave her money—nothing so crass as that. He gave her a job out of college. He gave her sterling references and important contacts. And years later, when she was looking to expand Tim's small family construction company into something bigger and more lucrative, Keniston gave her access to the people at Carlisle who had the power to award contracts. Jenny handled those bids; Tim didn't know the details, he didn't even know the basics. Carlisle's business took Healy Construction from a mom-and-pop concern into a successful company with nearly a hundred employees. Tim never knew that Keniston Eastman played a key role in that. Tim hated the Eastmans, period. If he'd known of Keniston's role in the contracts, he would never have accepted the work. So Jenny kept Tim in the dark. But she did it for a good reason. She was trying to build the business—for both of them, for their family, for the boys' futures.

Jenny was just plain better than Tim at planning ahead, at making things happen. Their relationship had started years earlier when Jenny befriended Tim as he struggled to recover from his head injury, and it still retained a bit of that big sister–little brother flavor. Once Tim got better, and went back to school, Jenny would stop in to Shecky's a couple of times a week to say hi and check up on him. When Tim turned eighteen, she brought him a pint of Jack Daniel's with a bow on it (she was twenty-one by then, and legal), and they drove out to Dunbar Meadows on a muggy night to celebrate. They got trashed on a blanket under a big yellow moon to the sound of crickets chirping, and made out like crazy. The next day, they pretended it never happened. He came to her graduation and sat with her family, but after Carlisle, Jenny moved to New York. Tim went off to UNH, and they kept in touch only sporadically.

When her father died unexpectedly, about five years after her college graduation, Jenny came home to help her mother sell the hardware store. It was supposed to be temporary. But one night, bored and casting around for something to do, Jenny dialed Tim's number for the first time in a long time. Tim was not long out of college then, working for his dad's construction company as a job foreman, learning the ropes. When Jenny saw him that first night, outside the movie theater on College Street, she actually said "wow" out loud. Maybe it was all that physical labor. He was taller and bigger and tan from the sun. He was *handsome*. They went to Shecky's for a burger for old times' sake, and, sitting opposite Tim in the booth, Jenny realized that she'd never felt as comfortable with any other guy. In that moment, she knew what she wanted, and she wanted Tim Healy. She never stopped to think that there was a lie between them that could never be made right.

Tim switched off his bedside lamp without saying a word. Usually they kissed good night, but not this time.

"Good night," she said tentatively. But he didn't reply.

Jenny's stomach hurt, and she tossed and turned. For a long time, Tim had been able to put Lucas's death out of his mind, but with Kate back in Belle River, he couldn't do it anymore. It ate away at him. That's why Jenny cared so much about keeping the secret buried. Not because the scandal would rock her political career, or imperil their business, although those things mattered to her a great deal. Her biggest worry was for her marriage. Jenny would love nothing better than to come clean and fix things. But how could she, when she'd been lying to Tim for so many years?

With Kate dead now, the problem should go away. That would be a relief.

24

Owen Rizzo had handled plenty of murder cases, but never one where he knew the victim personally. He hadn't known Maggie Price long or known her well—known *Kate Eastman*, that is. But the intense evening they spent together had stayed with him to the point where he wasn't entirely objective when it came to working her case. It didn't matter, though. He could recognize and make allowances for his own bias. Owen was a better investigator blindfolded and with his hands tied behind his back than any of the men who worked for him. But they might not see it that way, and he didn't need them questioning his judgment, so he was careful not to let slip that he had a personal interest in the case. Especially given *how* personal his interest was. In the few short hours they spent together, Kate had gotten under his skin.

His task this Monday morning was to rally his troops, such as they were, and they weren't much. These guys were better at finding lost dogs than solving crimes. But you went to war with the troops you had, and if the troops were weak, then the commander better be strong. For starters, Owen needed to make them understand that this was indeed a murder case. The forensic evidence left room for doubt—though not really, not if you knew what you were looking for. A woman might fall into a river by accident, or she might decide to end her life and jump of her own accord. Then again, somebody might bludgeon her with a rock and throw her lifeless body into the water. Those three scenarios might produce similar-looking head injuries, so that the local coroner (who, Owen learned to his shock, hadn't autopsied a single murder victim in his entire career) couldn't tell the difference. Owen had appropriated money from an overtime fund to pay an independent expert to review Kate's autopsy report. (That was his prerogative as chief, and he saw no need to run that decision by anyone.) He was expecting a fax any minute that would back up his strong feeling that Kate didn't kill herself, or carelessly fall into the Belle, but rather that somebody violently ended her life. Like maybe that lying drunkard of a husband of hers, whom Owen had the pleasure of meeting yesterday in the flesh. The guy clearly hadn't remembered him from that night at the bar, but Owen remembered him all right.

Owen walked into the conference room at nine on the dot on Monday to find his three male officers lounging around shooting the breeze and eating doughnuts from a box that he'd paid for out of his own pocket. (He wasn't above using food to get their attention.) His lone female detective, Keisha Charles, was out working leads already, as she should be. She was the only one he trusted. But then, he'd hired her himself, so he'd have at least one officer familiar with modern investigative techniques. Keisha was supremely qualified—graduated from Carlisle in criminal justice, aced the state police training, got picked to go to Quantico for extra training with the FBI. She also happened to be the daughter of a fine narcotics detective from the Bronx who, yes, all right, happened to be a good friend of Owen's. The hire hadn't sat well with the rest of the department, since it used money that had previously been allocated for a secretarial position. As far as he was concerned, they could type their own damn reports. And if Pam What's-her-name lost her job—well, no harm, no foul. Rob Womack had gone behind Owen's back and spoken to the mayor about that decision. When Owen made clear he wouldn't brook any interference or second-guessing, the mayor wisely solved the problem by hooking Pam up with another position, which actually paid her more. So there was really nothing to complain about, and they should let it go already.

As Owen took the seat at the head of the table, Gene Stevens shoved the Dunkin' Donuts box across to him.

"Saved you the last cruller at grave risk to my own safety, Chief. You don't ever want to come between this guy and a doughnut," Gene said, pointing at Marv Pelletier, who laughed so hard his beer belly jiggled. They were Mutt and Jeff, those two, Marv short and round and Gene tall and spare, and they gloried in the foolish chitchat.

"Look who's talking. You wouldn't know it by looking at him, but he ate half the box," Marv said.

"What's this about, Chief?" Rob Womack asked. "We heard you caught a floater last night. Is that true?"

"Can we please not refer to her in a disrespectful manner?" Owen said.

"Sorry," Womack said, his jaw setting. "A *her,* you say? So it's a girl, then?"

"A woman. Yes."

"We don't get too many females jumping," Gene said.

"Who says she jumped?" Owen said.

All three of them looked at him with surprised expressions.

"Come on, get real, Chief," Womack said.

There they went, leaping to conclusions already. When Owen originally pondered this move, he'd worried that he or the kids wouldn't like the town, or that he'd find the job boring. None of that turned out to be true. Instead the problem was the friction between him and the men—only the *men;* Keisha was great—under his command. He simply couldn't get them to conform to his standards for what good police work looked like. Of his four full-time, non-traffic-patrol officers, Marv Pelletier and Gene Stevens were the biggest pains in his butt. They spent their time carping about how the former chief ran things better and how the town and the department were going to hell. Worst of all, they were competent with paperwork but lax with actually getting their butts on the streets, which meant they were either lazy, or cowards. Fortunately they were both near retirement age. This guy Rob presented the opposite problem. Rob was young and ambitious, a musclehead type with a starched uniform and a spic-and-span cruiser who'd been passed over for the chief's job when they hired Owen. He was borderline insubordinate, and regularly told Owen how they did things around here rather than doing what he was told. None of this was a great setup for working an important case, a case Owen cared about more perhaps than any other in his career.

"She jumped, Chief, I guarantee it," Rob said. "The kids love to jump off the old railroad bridge. They do it on a dare, and they don't always come back up."

"Not too many girls do it, though," Gene said. "Girls are too smart for that shit."

"Local girl, or Carlisle?" Marv asked.

"She wasn't a *girl.*" Owen flipped open the case file. "Victim is Katherine Elizabeth Eastman, aged forty, Nineteen Dunsmore Street—"

"Faculty Row," Marv and Gene said simultaneously.

"What?" Owen asked.

"Nobody calls it Dunsmore Street, it's Faculty Row," Marv said. "Used to be, the college actually owned the houses and they'd give 'em to the profs as part of their compensation package. Now they're all private, but they're still orange on the inside. Orange being the Carlisle color, see?"

"Yes, I know that, Marv," Owen said.

"So what's her Carlisle connection?" Rob asked.

"I don't know that she has one," Owen said.

Owen hadn't forgotten Kate telling him in the bar on that rainy night how she'd disappointed her father by not graduating from Carlisle. But if he repeated that, his officers would know he'd met her.

"No Carlisle connection?" Marv said.

"Who knows?" Owen replied. "That's not the question that should leap to mind when you respond to the scene of a death."

"Around here, it should be," Marv said. "Nineteen Dunsmore. Keniston Eastman owns that place, if I'm not mistaken. The Eastmans are a big Carlisle family, Chief, one of the biggest. You got your Eastman Commons. Your Eastman Field House. The Eastman Wing at the hospital. You don't want to mess with that family without talking to the general counsel's office first."

"General counsel of what?"

Marv and Gene looked at each other like, *Who the hell is this guy?*

"Of the *college*," Marv said. "You know if we ever arrest a Carlisle kid, we give the GC a heads-up as a courtesy, right?"

"Chief Dudley mentioned that. I couldn't believe it was true."

"Oh, it's true. I know you got your pride, Chief, but trust me. It's not worth pissing off the college just to mark your territory. If you're telling me you pulled a *Carlisle* kid from the river, that's huge. You'd better call the mayor, too. She doesn't like to get blindsided."

Owen made a dismissive gesture. He would call the mayor in his own good time.

"Wait a minute, *Kate Eastman*," Rob Womack said, and slapped the table.

Owen turned to Rob. "You know her?"

"Kate Eastman was the girl who was with Lucas Arsenault the night he died, am I right?" Rob said.

"With who?" Owen said.

"Local kid," Marv said. "Jumped off the bridge in the off season, as I recall, just like this female jumper you got here. It was a big to-do when he died. Nobody wanted to believe a local boy would be that stupid."

"Yeah, because he wouldn't," Rob said. "I knew Lucas. He didn't jump."

"When was this?" Owen asked.

"Maybe twenty years ago," Rob said.

"Twenty *years*?" Owen exclaimed. "Jesus, will you people lay off the ancient-history bullshit? We have a real case here. Now. Today. Do you have any interest in working it?"

"Yeah, of course we do," Rob said, bristling.

"Then stop bringing up irrelevant nonsense and focus."

"Sorry, Chief. You're right," Marv said.

Rob looked pissed and Gene grumbled something, but Owen had a case to solve. He couldn't worry about hurting grown men's feelings.

"You don't think she jumped?" Rob said. "Why not? What does the ME say?"

"What the ME says might not be correct," Owen began.

Seeing the skeptical looks around the table, Owen realized he needed definitive proof to back him up. He pressed the intercom and asked his secretary if a fax had come in for him from a Dr. Michael Chan in Boston. Within minutes, his secretary (and yes, Owen still had a secretary, but that's because he was the chief) came in and put the report in his hands. Owen leafed through it quickly and immediately found the answer he'd been looking for.

"Gentlemen, this is a report from a highly respected forensic scientist who's testified in some of the biggest murder cases in the country. I had him take a second look at the autopsy results, because our county medical examiner, believe it or not, has never handled a homicide case in his entire career."

"We don't get too many murders around here, Chief," Marv said.

"You paid for an outside expert?" Rob said. Owen decided to ignore him.

"The county ME," Owen continued, "noted that no water was found in victim's lungs, signifying that she was dead before she hit the river. But he drew no conclusion from that fact about the manner of her death, other than to say it was caused by blunt-force trauma to the head. Fine, but then what? We need to know, does that mean someone hit her with a baseball bat and threw her in, or does it mean she jumped and hit a rock on the way down? The county ME didn't have the guts to make a decision on that. Like a lot of mediocre bureaucrats, he pulled his punches. So I brought in Dr. Chan. Dr. Chan's report, which I just received, concludes that Kate Eastman was killed by a blow to the head. The conclusion is based on the position of the injury to her cranium. That injury could only have been inflicted by an assailant who was standing behind her and striking downward. The bottom line is, we have a murder case to work."

"What about crime scene evidence?" Rob asked. "Shouldn't we be out searching around the old railroad bridge?"

"Why? I've now proved to you she didn't jump. She was murdered. Her vehicle was found abandoned at the boat-launch parking lot off River Road, which is almost a mile away from that bridge you keep talking about, and over difficult terrain. She went missing on Friday night, when it was raining pretty hard. That makes it even less likely that she hiked to the bridge. I believe she was killed elsewhere, moved to the boat-launch parking lot in her own vehicle, then dumped into the river."

"Where did the killer go after he dumped the body?" Womack asked. "If he moved her in her own vehicle and then abandoned it, he didn't have a ride." The asshole was obviously looking to shred Owen's theory instead of fall in line. Owen knew he had to keep his cool.

"Don't know," Owen replied. "Maybe there was an accomplice. Maybe he took a cab for all we know. Feel free to look into that, Rob. I had Kate's vehicle transported to the state police crime lab for a thorough search and analysis, so if the killer left a trace in there, we'll find it."

"If you're so convinced nothing went down at the bridge, and that she was murdered, then where did it happen?" Rob asked.

"That's the million-dollar question. One possibility is, she was killed in her own residence. Yesterday, Detective Charles and I responded there to notify the next of kin and request an official identification. We met her husband, a Mr. Griffin Rothenberg. He was passed out drunk at two o'clock in the afternoon, and had an ugly bruise on his face that he couldn't explain, and scratches on the backs of both hands. Scrapings were removed from under the victim's fingernails, so hopefully we'll get a match. The state police forensics lab is working with the ME to analyze evidence from the body. Since she was in the water for a while, hair and fiber evidence may be degraded, but we hope not. Oh, and the husband refused to cooperate beyond ID'ing the body."

"He lawyered up?" Marv said.

"Not even. It's not like he said he wanted a lawyer present but then he'd talk. He walked out on us. Wouldn't consent to a search of premises so we could look for evidence that might explain what happened to her. To me, that's a red flag. What kind of grieving husband doesn't want to get to the bottom of his wife's death?"

"It sounds like you already decided the husband did it," Womack said. "So I guess you don't have much use for us."

Owen wanted to punch the guy, but he forced himself to take a deep breath instead. "Not at all. In fact, I have assignments for every one of you. Gene, you're good with paperwork. I'd like to start working on a warrant application for Nineteen Dunsmore Street. I recognize that we don't have probable cause yet. But we can lay out what we know so far and make contact with the county attorney to start the process. As additional facts come in, we add them to the warrant application so we can be ready to go as soon as possible. Every minute we delay is another minute Rothenberg could destroy evidence."

"Yes, sir," Gene said.

"Rob, you canvass the neighbors on Dunsmore Street and find out if anybody heard anything unusual on Friday night, which is when we believe Ms. Eastman went missing. Screaming, yelling, throwing things, bumps in the night. Anything indicating domestic violence could give us probable cause to search the house, as well as for an arrest warrant. But be discreet. We don't need to spook Rothenberg and have him skip to Mexico."

"All right," Womack said, nodding.

"What about me, Chief?" Marv asked.

Marv was the one in whom Owen had the least confidence, but he had to assign him something or the guy would get miffed.

"Tell you what, Marv. You investigate any prior domestic violence complaints against Griffin Rothenberg. They moved to town recently. Before that, they were in New York. So check both places."

"What about Keisha?" Marv said. "Can she check New York? Just because she doesn't bother showing up for the meeting doesn't mean she oughta get off without an assignment."

Lazy POS, Owen thought.

"Keisha has plenty to do, all right? She's out working a lead for me, something I asked her to look into. In fact, here she comes now."

Through the glass partition, they watched as Keisha Charles yanked off her coat and scarf and dug through her briefcase. She strode into the conference room, bringing with her the bright, cold morning.

"Sorry I'm late, Chief, but when you hear what I found, I guarantee you'll forgive me," she said.

"Have a seat," he said. "Fill us in."

Keisha took an open chair and rummaged through her folders, picking out one and laying it open on the table.

"Last night you gave me two assignments. First, find out everything there is to know about Kate Eastman's husband Griffin Rothenberg. So let's start there. Griffin Rothenberg, Carlisle graduate in economics, is the only child of one Martin Allen Rothenberg, whose name you're probably familiar with—"

A string of whistles rang out around the table, accompanied by a "Holy shit," from Rob Womack.

"—because he was prosecuted for a major insider-trading scheme and financial fraud. Rothenberg Capital Partners. Not quite Bernie Madoff scale, but close. His entire company went under, and ten of his closest associates went to jail with him."

"You know, that doesn't surprise me one bit," Owen said. "That guy had an attitude, didn't he?"

"He sure did, Chief," Keisha said.

"Like father, like son," Owen asked. "Do you think there could be a connection between Kate's death and that fraud case?"

"You mean, was the son involved in his father's crimes? Did the wife know something she shouldn't? That sort of thing."

"You never know."

"I'll look into it. It could provide a motive."

"Even if there's no direct connection, we know Griffin Rothenberg was once a rich sonofabitch, and now he's down on his luck, living in a dump and drinking all day. That could be a motive, too. Who knows, maybe his wife had money. Maybe he took out an insurance policy. We need to look into all these angles," Owen said.

"Speaking of angles," Keisha said, "Maureen, the night dispatcher, told me an attractive blond woman came to pick Rothenberg up last night. She only caught the first name. Aubrey. I think that might be this woman who teaches at the yoga studio in Riverside I go to sometimes. I'm gonna check into it."

"Good," Owen said.

"Next, you asked me to find out what I could about the marriage. Smart, Chief. I hit pay dirt."

She pulled a sheaf of papers from a folder and handed it to Owen. "Kate Eastman filed for divorce from Griffin Rothenberg at the Belle County Courthouse. *She* filed, not him. That's a copy of the divorce complaint. Take a look at the date stamped on the top."

"That's—it can't be. Is that this past Friday?" Owen said.

"Yes!" Keisha said triumphantly. "The victim filed for divorce on Friday morning, and the papers were served on the husband at his home address a few hours later. The same day she disappeared. Is that motive, or what?"

"Not only is it motive, that's probable cause right there," Owen said. "A woman goes missing the same day she serves her husband with divorce papers, then she turns up with a fractured skull, dumped in the river. The husband has a big bruise on his face and scratches on his hands. That settles it. We're going to the judge right away to get a warrant on that house," Owen said, and stood up.

Owen wasn't about to drag his feet and risk letting that creep Rothenberg get away with killing the lovely Kate. He knew something the others didn't, something sensational that had been in the ME's report. He'd kept it on the down low so it didn't get splashed across the front page of every newspaper in the state. Kate Eastman was murdered on her fortieth birthday, the same day she filed for divorce. And on that day, Kate Eastman was ten weeks pregnant. That bastard had murdered his pregnant wife. Owen planned to lock him up for that crime if it was the last thing he did.

25

The day after he identified Kate's body from photos at the Belle River police station, Griff woke up on the sofa in Aubrey's cabin, feeling like he was coming down with the flu. He had a sore throat and burning eyes, his entire body ached, and the left side of his face was puffed up and tender, like he'd cracked a tooth. Griff got up and searched through the medicine chests in the bathrooms and the cabinets in the kitchen and came up empty. How was it possible that in this entire house there was not one godforsaken item that could help him? No furry old Advil at the bottom of a drawer. No vodka stashed in the back of a cupboard. Not even an expired box of mac and cheese that he could mix with water and eat from the pot to try to dispel the chill. Instead he found dried-up toothpaste, old bottles of ketchup and Sriracha, and a half-eaten jar of blueberry preserves in the fridge. He stood at the sink and ate the preserves with a spoon. After that, he still had a growling stomach, and endless time on his hands to mourn what was lost.

That list was long. Griff had no wife, no money, and no friends except Aubrey (who was really more hanger-on than true friend). His phone was out of battery and he didn't have a charger. He was stranded without a car—didn't even own a car, since Kate had taken the BMW and now the cops had impounded it. He had no idea when Aubrey was coming back and no way to reach her, since there was no landline that he could see. He had no advisers and no lawyers at a moment when he surely needed them. He didn't even have religion to comfort him, because he lost his faith years ago when his mother left them out of the blue to go back to Sweden.

This dark moment was always coming for him. Maybe it was where he was fated to spend the rest of his life, or maybe it was a test, the first step on a perilous journey to some other, happier existence.

Griff built a nest of cushions on the floor as close to the woodstove as he could get without singeing his clothes, and lay down on top of it, wrapping himself in an ugly afghan from the sofa. He stared up at the cathedral ceiling and tried to think straight, but drew a blank. The ceiling was made of a raw, silvery wood that Aubrey told him had been salvaged from a historic local barn. That's how the people were around here—they wanted to tell you about the provenance of the wood in their houses. They would explain how they'd grown the tomatoes you were eating using only organic methods, and that their children went to schools that had no walls, where they made musical instruments from found objects. In a moment of delusion when they first moved up here, Griff thought it might be worthwhile to be a part of that. He'd investigated buying a small organic farm, and when that proved too expensive, getting some chickens for the backyard, though it turned out raising chickens in downtown Belle River was against the law. He'd even talked to Kate about having a child.

Hah.

When Griff's father's empire collapsed, the only part he truly minded was seeing his suddenly old and frail-looking father go to jail. That was partly for his father's sake and partly for his own, because Marty Rothenberg was a surprisingly loving dad, and Griff missed him very much. (His mother was a different story.) The money, on the other hand, he was glad to see the back of. Nobody believed that, but it was true. All the money had ever done was separate him from people, make it hard to tell who actually cared about him and who just wanted something.

Take Kate, for example. He always thought they were exactly alike. They'd grown up together, in the same rarefied air. The doorman buildings on park blocks. The gated communities filled with lavish second homes standing empty till their owners cared to visit. The islands whose runways accommodated only private jets. Naturally they kept bumping up against each other over the years. There were some differences. Her family was merely wealthy, where his had the riches of sultans. But the class difference between them made up for that. Her people came over on the *Mayflower.* His father was born in Brooklyn, had stubby fingers, and always wore cheap suits to prove he wasn't ashamed of where he came from. Griff's fashion-model mother had bequeathed him her blond hair and bone structure, but he had his father's heart (and short stature). His father was a mensch, a man of the people, and his crimes had been driven mainly by the desire to make other people happy. Nobody else saw that, but Griff did. He saw the good in everyone. For instance, he'd always seen the good in Kate Eastman.

The first time he laid eyes on her was at a middle school dance. People thought they'd met at Odell, but no, it was earlier, just a few months after his mother left. He was in seventh grade at St. Alfred's and she went to Miss Kent's, and the two schools held mixers sometimes to justify the expensive dance lessons a lot of the kids still took. He'd been smoking cigarettes in the bathroom with a couple of buddies to avoid talking to the girls, and they got chased out by one of the chaperones. As he stepped back into the dimly lit gym, he had a vision that changed the course of his life. People moved aside like the Red Sea parting, and there was this girl standing alone, bathed in a white light. She was dazzlingly beautiful, and she looked bored. Of course, he later realized that Kate was by herself that night because she thought the other girls in her grade were beneath her. But at the time, Griff was enough of a romantic to believe she was waiting for him. He was a loner in a crowd even then, and desperate for a soulmate. But he didn't tell her that. Instead he told her that he had a car and driver waiting downstairs if she was up for going to Brooklyn to get a slice of decent pizza.

"Do you have any rum?" she asked. "I'd love a rum and Coke."

"The car has a mini-fridge. We can probably dig up something."

They made out in the backseat all the way down the FDR and over the Brooklyn Bridge. The Manhattan skyline viewed out the back window of the car looked so beautiful that it made him want to cry. After that, they were never really apart. Except for weeks and months and years here and there, and all the time she spent with other men. But he didn't count that.

The years Kate was in Europe were the hardest. He felt robbed of his Carlisle experience because he couldn't spend that time with her. She never wrote to him and never called, so he stopped trying to contact her directly. Always he was missing her, longing for her, maneuvering to get information about her. When he did hear about her, it was worse, because of course Kate was fine without him. She'd been at some party, or gallery opening, with some handsome Frenchman (and they were always *men*, much older, sometimes married), and she'd—what?—said something impossibly witty, or looked incredibly chic, dyed her hair pink, or dropped a wad of cash on a crazy bet. She was always doing breathless and exciting things, it seemed, in Paris, without him.

For Griff, there was never anybody else. He'd been imprinted at too early an age. Oh, gaggles of girls chased him, of course; he was extremely rich and not bad-looking, and wherever he went, a party followed, because he paid for it. He never enjoyed it, though. He let other girls blow him to ease the frustration, a few he even fucked, but none of them did he really notice. He resented the loneliness, mainly because Kate's absence seemed unnecessary. Something unfortunate had gone down at the bridge that night, but couldn't they have paid the other family off? That's what his father would have done. Really, was it worth giving up a Carlisle degree and ending up with some useless piece of paper from that place in Switzerland where the louche aristocrats of Europe sent their least promising children? Kate was never able to get a proper job after that, just PR things and fashion stuff through friends of friends, where her looks and pedigree were sufficient credentials. Forget the financial sacrifice; it was a waste of a fine mind. He thought she was one of the smartest people he'd ever met.

Griff graduated and went to work in New York. He had just about resigned himself to his hollow life when he literally ran into Keniston

Eastman on the street. It happened downtown, during a hot June lunchtime, in the dark shadows of the skyscraper that they both worked in, about a year after his Carlisle graduation. They worked twenty-six floors apart, it turned out, for different firms. Griff was a junior analyst at a firm headed by a friend of his father's, learning the ropes. (Griff's dad had instituted an antinepotism policy the year Griff graduated from Carlisle, and refused to let Griff come work for him. It was only later that Griff realized this was done to protect him.) Griff exchanged pleasantries with Mr. Eastman. He asked about Kate, but then, he always asked everyone about Kate. Maybe something in his eyes as he said her name gave him away. They parted ways, and he thought nothing more of it. Then, a couple of days later, he got a call from Keniston's secretary asking him to lunch. He thought at first that it was a recruiting call. Everyone was constantly trying to recruit Griff, since Marty Rothenberg was one of the most sought-after finance connections in all the world. He declined politely, saying he was happy where he was, and five minutes later, the secretary called back to say that actually, Mr. Eastman had something of a personal nature to discuss, and would he reconsider.

The executive dining room of Keniston's firm was on the forty-seventh floor of the building, with harbor views. You could see all the bridges, and Lady Liberty holding her torch. It was a fine, clear day, but Griff couldn't enjoy it, nor could he appreciate the trout meunière or the excellent white Burgundy, because he was waiting for Keniston Eastman to come to the point. This had to be about Kate, right? Finally, over coffee, once the room had cleared out, Keniston brought up his daughter's name. And Griff got the opening he'd been waiting for for years.

According to her father, Kate was in a bad way. He'd done his level best for her, supporting her in a fine style in Europe ever since she left Carlisle. He'd sent her to the right school, let her spend time in Paris and the Côte d'Azur and places where she would be noticed, paid for her clothes and travel. Keniston had done all this, it became apparent, in the hope that Kate would make an advantageous marriage with some wealthy European. Now, Griff could have told him that idea was at least a century out of date. If that happened at all anymore, the Europeans were the ones preying on the rich Americans, not the other way around. But mostly people just fucked and nobody ever got married, which was why the birthrate in Western Europe was in the tank. But there was no need for Griff to tell Keniston this, since he'd already learned it for himself, the hard way. Kate had picked up a parasite. A Dutch musician named Markus Rijnders, who had a minor recording contract and a major heroin habit, which it was Keniston's greatest fear that Kate might come to share.

"I don't know why I don't just give up on her," Keniston said, and there was a haunted look in his eyes that Griff recognized.

"I do, sir. I understand why."

"Yes," Keniston said. "I thought you would."

Keniston couldn't go to Europe himself to reclaim Kate, for a host of complicated reasons. Kate would never listen to him. His wife had lost patience with Kate's antics. Business obligations, social engagements, and so forth. But Griff was a young man of means, still carefree, whose employer surely valued his contributions enough to be willing to grant him a leave of reasonable if uncertain duration. And if not, Keniston would be happy to put in a word. His extensive business dealings with Griff's boss made him think he had some influence there.

In other words, Keniston hoped that Griff was enough of a stooge, and sufficiently hung up on Keniston's crazy daughter, to fall into an obvious trap. Which he proceeded to do with alacrity.

Next thing Griff knew, he was on an airplane, watching dawn break over the Atlantic, too excited to sleep. Memories of Kate washed over him like a delirium. It had been nearly four years since he'd been in her presence, but her face was etched in his mind. He couldn't believe he would get to look at that face again, so soon. It was almost too much to contemplate. That whole first day, he wandered around Paris in a daze, letting the reflected light from the limestone buildings dazzle his eyes, stopping here and there for a coffee or a pastry to restore his flagging energy. He had her address in his pocket but he couldn't bring himself to call on her yet. The anticipation of seeing Kate was so sweet that he didn't want it to end. Plus, naturally, given the things Keniston had told him, Griff was afraid of what he might find.

The next day, Griff timed his visit for late afternoon, when he'd been told Kate would be alone in the apartment. She was living in Montmartre in a dump of a fifth-floor walk-up with that musician guy. Keniston must have had the detectives on them, because he knew all the details of their comings and goings. She answered the door herself, in jeans and a dirty T-shirt, looking like she'd just woken up.

"Griff? I can't believe it. What are you doing here?" she said, but she looked happy to see him.

"Passing through on business," he said, and mentioned the name of a mutual friend he'd been told she was in touch with by way of explaining how he'd gotten her address.

He was shocked at her appearance but careful to hide his reaction. She looked much worse than he'd imagined—emaciated frame, lank hair, shadows under her eyes. He glanced at her arms and thankfully didn't see needle marks. That would've been too awful. Cocaine, yes, but heroin was a trailer-park drug, wrong for her. She wasn't the Kate he remembered, but she was still recognizably herself. He almost loved her more like this. Maybe, finally, she needed him.

"Aren't you going to invite me in?" he asked, when they were still making small talk at the door after a couple of minutes.

"The place is a wretched dump. I won't inflict it on you."

"Come out with me then. I saw a tabac on the corner. Let me buy you a coffee and we can gossip for a bit. I have an hour to kill before my next meeting."

She hesitated.

"Come on, Kate. It's not often I get to Paris."

Griff had thought through his approach very carefully. He knew better than to tell her that her father was concerned and had asked him to come over, or that Griff had missed her terribly, or anything that placed her under any obligation. He smiled nonchalantly, and finally, she nodded.

"All right. Hold on a second," she said.

She marched off to the next room, and came back a moment later covered up in dark sunglasses and a baggy jacket.

The tabac was dim inside, with a greasy tile floor and a couple of small tables crammed in a corner. They sat down at one, and his heart rolled over in his chest at the touch of her knees under the table. The place reeked of cigarette smoke. Kate smoked one cigarette after another, Marlboro reds. Griff cast his memory back but couldn't recall a time when she'd had a tobacco habit like that. Another bad sign. He bought her a coffee laced with brandy. As she sipped it, spots of color returned to her cheeks and the tremor disappeared from her voice. He talked of trivial things that he knew would entertain her. The apartment he was having decorated, which friends would be in the Hamptons this summer, a boat show he'd been to with a cousin of a friend of Kate's from Odell. He kept up the patter, which felt a bit like trying to lure a timid bird out of a tree.

"New York seems so far away," she said wistfully. "I miss it."

"Why not come back for a visit?"

"I can't. I've been staying away."

"Yes, I noticed. Why is that?" he asked.

"That trouble at the bridge freshman year. Don't you remember?"

"That's what's keeping you in Europe? Not because you prefer it here?"

She nodded. "I'm afraid to go back."

"Seriously? Why?"

She wouldn't answer.

"Kate, I don't know what happened that night, and I'm not asking you to tell me. But I'm certain that if you were in trouble over anything, they would have come after you by now."

"Do you really think so?"

He watched the pulse beat in the hollow of her throat. He'd forgotten that pulse. He used to kiss it sometimes.

"I do," he said.

"I don't know," she said, and shook her head miserably. "I can't believe it would just go away."

"Do you want to tell me what happened?" he asked, his voice gentle. "Maybe I could advise you better if I knew."

She brought the coffee cup to her lips, then put it down again and stared into it. "Lucas died," she said finally, in a tiny voice.

"I knew that. But it was a suicide. Right?"

She raised her eyes to meet his. He'd never seen her look so desperate before. Her hand on the table moved toward the pack of cigarettes, but before she reached it, he stopped it with his own.

"You can tell me anything. I would never think less of you," Griff said.

"You should."

"I won't. What happened that night, Kate?"

She looked past his shoulder, to the bright outline of the door. He turned to follow her gaze, surprised to see daylight outside. In here, it felt like the depths of night.

"I don't know what happened," she said, in a dead tone. "I was out of my mind, I guess, from a lot of stuff. He broke up with me. I did too many lines, and my breathing got funny. Carlisle got to me. The fishbowl."

"I know, I know." He squeezed her hand tighter.

"Anyway," she said, and fell silent, pressing her lips together.

Griff saw that was as much as he would ever get out of her about what happened at the bridge. It was enough to give him the picture. She'd killed the guy, basically, pushed him off the bridge. He'd suspected; now he knew. It bothered him somewhat. Not enough to change his feelings about her.

"What does your father say?" Griff asked.

"We don't talk much. But one time recently, he said I should come home. That everything was quiet, was how he put it."

"You should listen to him, Kate. I think you feel guilty, and that's why you're hesitating."

"Shouldn't I feel guilty?" she asked, meeting his eyes tentatively.

"Maybe you should. But not so much that you ruin your life. Everybody else has graduated and moved on."

"Not Lucas."

He shrugged. What could he say to that?

"I never paid for what I did," Kate said.

"It seems to me that you're paying very much. Look at you, look how thin you are." He pulled her hand toward him, and circled her wrist with his fingers. "So thin. You're killing yourself over this, slowly but surely. That won't do anybody any good."

Two crystal tears rolled slowly down her cheeks, illuminated by the light from the door. He wanted to catch them with his tongue, to press his lips to her pale forehead. But he knew better, and sat back in his chair.

"You want to make amends," Griff said. "That's good. You *should* want to. But don't waste your life over it. Come home to New York, and do something positive with your time. I have a friend who runs a nonprofit that works with girls in the projects. I'll introduce you to her."

Kate gave a sad laugh, but it was still magic to his ears. "What, so I can, like, organize charity balls?" she said.

"*No.* Mentor kids. Give back."

She smiled, but then her face clouded over. "I'm living with my boyfriend. He wouldn't want me to."

"Oh, come on."

"Really. He doesn't like me to go places without him."

"That's a hassle. Well, come for a week then. Just for a visit. He can't object to that."

"For a week?"

"Sure, why not? I've got a million frequent-flier miles. I'll spot you the ticket. First class, as much champagne as you want. How's that sound?"

She shook her head. "He'd throw a fit."

"He sounds like a pain in the ass. Don't tell him, then."

"What?"

"Is he home now? It didn't seem like anybody was at home."

"No. His band plays at this lounge on Wednesday nights. He won't be home till the morning."

"Since when does Kate Eastman answer to anyone? Pack a bag and we'll grab a taxi to the airport. By the time he gets home in the morning, you'll be halfway to JFK. Leave him a note, if you must."

"I thought you had a meeting."

"Nothing I can't cancel. What do you say?"

Griff made it sound like a grand adventure, a great escape, but he was still surprised when she agreed to come along. They were back in New York the next day. He would have to pretend not to be in touch with her father, so she wouldn't realize that the whole plan had been orchestrated by the two of them. But that wouldn't be difficult.

As they taxied, and the skyline came into view, Kate smiled, and tears stood out in her eyes.

"I'm glad I came. Thank you," she said, and kissed his cheek spontaneously. He thought his heart would explode, that's how joyous it was to be with her again after so long.

Kate stayed in an apartment Griff had in the financial district, one of several he'd bought in a brand-new condo building, thinking he'd flip them for a nice profit in a year or two. The building was sleek, all stainless steel and smoky blue glass, with million-dollar views. He left her alone there to sleep and to think and to look out at the city. She begged him for some drugs to tide her over, so he got her things that wouldn't make her worse—some Ambien, a few Xanax, a pint of vodka. He had food sent in, things she liked from when they were in school together at Odell and would come back for holidays. She seemed nostalgic for that time in her life. Griff would visit frequently. Riding the elevator up to the thirty-second floor, he'd get butterflies at the thought of seeing her. They'd stay up late, sprawled across the white suede sofa with wineglasses in their hands, talking. She seemed so sad, but he'd never been happier. Eventually he convinced her to call Keniston and let him know she was back (of course, Keniston had known that from the moment their flight landed), and then to check into rehab. Keniston paid for a place in Connecticut that had an excellent reputation, well-appointed rooms, and wide lawns. It was more a spa than a hospital. Kate stayed there for two months, and Griff visited constantly. By the end, they were together for real, lovers again, and Kate never went back to Paris.

Griff and Kate got married a year later, on the beach in Anguilla in a small ceremony limited to close friends and family. His father's lawyers had a conniption when he refused to ask her for a pre-nup, but he wasn't giving Kate any excuses to call off the engagement. Their wedding made the magazines. Kate looked so beautiful, in a simple, elegant white dress, barefoot in the sand with flowers in her hair. For a long time, they were happy. At least, *he* was happy. It was terrible the way things ended.

The sound of a car in the driveway punctured Griff's reverie, dragging him unwillingly back to the present. He wasn't on the beach in Anguilla with his bride. He was in Aubrey's drafty cabin. Outside the picture window, the lake looked evil and black. He sat up and watched Aubrey come up the back steps, a bag of groceries in her arms. She looked troubled as she fumbled for the key. Griff felt feverish, but his manners kicked in. He staggered to his feet to help her with the bag.

"Thanks," she said, opening the door as he reached for the bag. "Are you okay, Griff? You don't look so good."

"I had a rough night."

"I can imagine. I got this," she said, holding the bag against her chest, shutting the door. "I brought you some food, but I couldn't get those clothes from your house that you asked for."

Their eyes met. He saw the unease in hers. "Why not?" he asked.

"The police were there, searching the place. They had it blocked off with tape, so I couldn't've gone in if I tried. I decided not to stop. I just drove by. I didn't want them following me and finding you out here."

"Good," he said, leaning against the wall, feeling faint. He slid down to sitting and put his head on his knees.

"Honey, do you need a doctor?" Aubrey asked, alarmed.

He looked up and saw the adoration in her eyes. It had been quite some time since anybody looked at Griff Rothenberg that way, and it made him feel relieved. Not because he reciprocated her feelings, but because he knew he could count on her. He had nobody else in his corner, so that was a good thing.

"No, Aubrey, sweetheart, thank you. But I probably need a lawyer, so if you know a cheap one, I could use a name."

26

Monday morning, Jenny and Tim barely spoke as they went through the motions of getting ready for work. At breakfast, everybody was out of sorts. T.J. was coming down with something, Reed was nervous about a test. They ran late. The boys missed the bus. Tim left to drive them to school before Jenny could try to make up.

On the drive to town, the horror of Kate's death settled over Jenny like a cloud. She had to find out what the police knew. The obvious move would be to stop at the police station and get a briefing. But she didn't have the kind of relationship with the new chief that made that possible. Chief Dudley, the old chief, would have been on the phone to brief her within minutes of pulling a body from the river. But Chief Rizzo hadn't called, and worse, he hadn't returned the three separate messages she left for him last night requesting information. Who the hell did this guy think he was?

Jenny had supported Rizzo for chief. Yeah, all right, the town council vote was unanimous, and maybe he could have won without her support. But maybe not, because the town council followed Jenny's lead. She could've chosen to back the very deserving internal candidate, Robbie Womack, instead. Robbie happened to be a friend of hers and Tim's. That might very well have turned the tide against the newcomer, but instead she overlooked her personal preference and supported Owen Rizzo because she felt he had a superior résumé. He ought to be grateful to her for that.

And Jenny had done more for Rizzo than just vote for him. She hooked him up with an apartment, so he could move to town without the stress of buying a house on short notice. Not just any apartment, either. This apartment was on the ground floor of Jenny's mother's house. Below-market rent, perfect location, and Jenny's mom was the type who'd bring by a casserole, or babysit in a pinch, free of charge. Rizzo didn't seem to appreciate any of that. But that was nothing compared to the solid Jenny did for Rizzo when he caused an uproar by firing Pam Grimaldi with no warning. Pam had been the department secretary for twenty years, and people loved her. Rizzo let her go so he could afford to hire some new detective to work on his pet projects. Did he consult Jenny about this first? No, he didn't consult anybody. And if he was so hell-bent on having an extra detective, did he promote one of the very deserving traffic cops who'd been waiting in the wings for years? No, he hired a young girl straight out of Carlisle who was the daughter of a friend of his. Jenny should've made a move against Rizzo then, but instead, God knows why, she saved his butt. She found Pam Grimaldi another job, and smoothed things over with the rank-and-file officers. Then she tried to talk some sense into Rizzo about how to get along with folks in Belle River, and suggested that he would be well advised to run major decisions by her. She was right about that; he *would* be well advised, and he was lucky she still cared enough to try to set him straight. But instead of taking her words to heart, he lost his temper and told her to mind her own business. Well, maybe Rizzo didn't realize it, but this town, and everything that happened in it, *was* Jenny's business.

Their tense relationship left Jenny in a difficult position when it came to getting inside information about Kate's death. If Jenny went in now with guns blazing and demanded a detailed briefing, Rizzo might overreact. He might start to think things that were unwarranted, or start looking into old rumors when he shouldn't. So she decided against paying Chief Rizzo a call. As soon as she pulled into her parking space at work, she texted Robbie Womack instead.

At her desk, Jenny spent a couple of hours pretending to work. Soon it would be time to run for reelection, and her campaign manager, Drew Novak (her old buddy from Carlisle student council days), had given her a list of potential campaign events to plan. But she didn't have the emotional fortitude today, and anyway it was illegal to do any electioneering from her office in Town Hall. Jenny ordered in a salad and ate it at her desk. After she finished, she stopped fighting her feelings, and picked up an old photo album from freshman year that she'd found in the back of a closet last night. Then she sat behind her big desk facing onto Briggs Street and paged through the photos with tears leaking from her eyes.

A picture of the young Kate stretched out in her bikini on a lounge chair by the pool in Jamaica made Jenny smile. There was Griff, right beside her. They were so innocent then, all of them, and Kate and Griff were gorgeous. Kate was still beautiful when Jenny saw her three days ago, on the morning of her fortieth birthday, walking into the Belle County Courthouse. Jenny had a full-on view of the courthouse from her office window, and on that particular Friday morning, Kate had turned up unexpectedly. Jenny watched her go into the courthouse, then watched her come out afterward. People visited the courthouse for lots of reasons. You filed lawsuits there, probated wills, paid traffic tickets. Also, the county attorney's office was located on the first floor, should you happen to be accused of a crime—or want to confess to one.

What the hell was Kate up to? She spent almost thirty minutes inside the courthouse Friday morning, and for that thirty minutes, Jenny was beside herself with nerves. Had Kate somehow decided after all these years that she wanted to come clean about Lucas's death? That would send Jenny's entire life down the toilet. Aubrey was the one whom Jenny had been worrying about on that account, ever since she'd threatened to expose Kate after finding out that Kate was sleeping with her husband. As far as Jenny knew, Aubrey had not acted on her threats, but here was Kate, visiting the courthouse. The rest of that Friday had passed in a blur for Jenny, as she contemplated the destruction of her career and her marriage, and wondered what she could do to prevent it from happening.

And now Kate was dead.

Her secretary buzzed. Jenny wiped her eyes and sniffed hard. "Yes?"

"Officer Womack is here to see you. I told him you're not taking meetings today, but he says it's urgent police business."

"Send him in," Jenny said, stashing the photo album in a desk drawer.

Jenny stood up as Robbie Womack entered. She leaned across her desk, and they clasped hands for a long moment. She and Robbie went back years, though he was always more Tim's friend than hers. Robbie and Tim were the same year from high school and did a regular guys' poker night with some of their old crew. Jenny served on the PTA with Robbie's wife, Val. She was always careful to include the Womacks in her big events—they'd come to her Labor Day party with their four kids and Val's parents—even though they didn't move in the upper echelons of the town like Jenny and Tim did. When she decided to support Rizzo for chief, Jenny sat Robbie down and explained her decision to him. She made it sound like she had no choice, because the entire town council was so dazzled by the city boy and his fancy credentials. But she promised Robbie that she'd have his back if Rizzo gave him a hard time, and she tried to live up to that.

"Thanks for coming by," she said.

"Of course," Robbie said, as they sat down. "I forgot until I got your text that Kate Eastman was a friend of yours. I'm sorry for your loss."

"Thank you. We were close at Carlisle, so it comes as a shock. The reason I called, Robbie, is that I need to get the facts straight about her death before the shit hits the fan."

"You mean the press?"

"Exactly. Kate was young and attractive, she was from a prominent family. There's bound to be serious press interest, and I haven't heard a peep out of the chief of police."

"Rizzo isn't keeping you in the loop? We told him specifically to give you a heads-up."

"Well, he didn't, and I don't get it. Chief Dudley would have called me first thing. Is there some reason Rizzo is keeping me in the dark?" Jenny asked.

"Other than being a dick?" Robbie said, with a grin. But he immediately turned serious. "That's not a joke, I'm afraid. The only opinion Owen Rizzo cares about is his own. He doesn't listen, and he doesn't consult."

"It's not anything other than that?"

Robbie looked at her closely. "Like what?"

"I don't know. That I was close to Kate and might not be objective."

"I doubt he knows you were friends with the victim. He's not big on learning about the town he's policing." Robbie paused. "I'm getting the sense you want to tell me something about the case. Is there anything I should know?"

Jenny made an effort to keep her expression blank and her voice steady. Robbie might look like a dumb jock, but he was actually a very shrewd cop, and he surely remembered the rumors that had swirled around Lucas Arsenault's death. She didn't need to arouse his suspicions.

"I'm trying to understand what happened to my friend, that's all. I assume it was a suicide?"

"I'll tell you what I know, Jenny, but it has to stay between us. Rizzo's the type who'd come after me for leaking information."

"It's not a leak if you're talking to the mayor."

"He wouldn't see it that way."

She made an irritated noise. "That's ridiculous. But you have my word, I won't tell a soul."

"Okay, then. To me, I agree, this death is most likely a suicide. I think we ought to wrap it up nice and quick, and spare the family the embarrassment."

"You think that. But Rizzo doesn't?"

"No. As a matter of fact, he's convinced Kate Eastman was murdered."

Jenny drew a sharp breath. "Why the hell would he think that?"

"Apparently—forgive me, Jen, this may be hard to hear."

"Go on."

"Apparently the autopsy says skull fracture, no water in the lungs, so she died from blunt-force trauma before she hit the water. I'm thinking, so what, right? She jumped, and hit her head on the way down. But Rizzo went and hired some fancy outside expert, who claims this particular fracture came from somebody bludgeoning her from behind. I think Rizzo likes the idea of having a murder case in town, you know. Makes him feel like a big man."

Jenny's hands clenched in her lap. She forced herself to unclench them, and cleared her throat, which was thick with anxiety.

"Outside expert?"

"Yeah, some famous forensics guy."

"How did he manage that? I never saw any request for an appropriation."

"To be honest, I don't know where he got the money. That's a good question."

"Does he have a suspect?" Jenny asked, holding her breath.

"He does. The husband."

"*Griff?*"

"I'm sorry, is he a friend of yours?"

"We're not close. I'm just surprised. He was crazy about his wife," Jenny said.

"Those are the ones who turn violent when things head south. You knew they were getting a divorce?"

"No! That can't be true."

"It is true," Robbie said. "I saw the complaint. The wife's the one who filed, so presumably she's the one who wanted out. Some guys flip out when they get hit with divorce papers. Rizzo might have a point there."

A divorce action against Griff? Could that explain Kate's courthouse visit last Friday? If so, Jenny had been freaking out for nothing.

"What do the papers say? Is there anything specific about why Kate wanted the divorce?" Jenny asked.

"No, just basic irreconcilable differences. It's the timing that has Rizzo bent out of shape. She filed this past Friday, the same day she went missing."

"Oh," Jenny said, and her eyes widened.

So that was definitely why Kate visited the courthouse. Jenny never considered the possibility that Kate and Griff might split, but it seemed obvious in retrospect. Aubrey made that scene at the Labor Day party about Kate and Ethan's affair. But then the controversy seemed to melt away. Jenny figured Aubrey had decided to look the other way. She'd done that enough times before. And Griff didn't seem to know anything about the affair. On the surface, everything was placid. They had even planned for the three couples to have dinner together in the back room at Henry's Bistro on Friday night, to celebrate Kate's birthday, though then they'd changed it to girls' night out, no guys. And when Aubrey called with word that Kate was sick, they ended up calling the whole thing off.

"Rizzo thinks the husband might've been having an affair," Robbie Womack said.

"That *Griff* was having an affair?"

"Yeah, apparently Aubrey the yoga teacher came to collect him from the station yesterday, and somebody spotted them looking pretty cozy. She's a friend of yours, too, right?"

"No. I mean, yes, she is a friend, but Aubrey and Griff? That's not possible."

"Maybe it's just Rizzo talking out of his hat."

"That's insane. He has it completely backwards."

"I believe you, Jen. Rizzo's running off half-cocked, and good people are gonna get hurt. He's out there right now, executing a warrant on the husband's house."

"The house on Faculty Row? Keniston *Eastman's* house?"

"Yes, that's what I'm telling you."

"Oh, this is out of hand," Jenny said. "I can't believe he would do that without consulting me."

"We told him not to. He doesn't listen."

Keniston had an old WASP's horror of public embarrassment. He would be furious that Jenny had allowed things to escalate to the point that his daughter's death would be fodder for the tabloids, that his house would be invaded and his furniture and personal effects pawed over by the police. Jenny had spent years carefully cultivating her relationship with Keniston. He was her most important patron. She couldn't afford to jeopardize his goodwill by having the town mishandle the investigation into his daughter's death. Rizzo was out of control, and she had to do something to rein him in.

"Where's Chief Rizzo now?" Jenny asked.

"Still searching the house. He's not even using Belle River officers. Doesn't trust us, I guess. He brought the state police forensics unit to serve the warrant."

"That's crazy. That place leaks like a sieve. Every detail will be in the press tomorrow morning."

"I know, it's a problem," Robbie said, nodding. "If I was you, I'd be very worried. I might even drive over to the search location and call a halt."

Jenny considered whether there was any way she could stop the search of Keniston's house before it hit the news. On the town's organizational chart, the mayor sat above the chief of police. Unfortunately, that was in name only. Jenny had no day-to-day authority over the police department. She could vote to fund them or defund them, and she could vote to hire or fire. That was about it.

"I'd need a vote of the town council to get Rizzo to stop. I'd basically have to remove him from office," she said.

"Well," Robbie said, sitting back in his chair deliberately. "Maybe you should."

And there was the rub. Robbie wanted Rizzo's job; he'd always wanted it. Jenny was beginning to see that she'd made a big mistake when she elevated a newcomer whom she couldn't control to a position as important as chief of police. She needed a reliable source of information inside the department. She needed someone who would follow her lead when it came to big cases. It was becoming apparent that Owen Rizzo would never do that. But Robbie Womack might.

"Chief Rizzo has caused some trouble, lately, Robbie. I agree. But removing him from office is a big step. Even if I decided I wanted to, it wouldn't be easy."

"I understand. Things take time."

"We'd need to build a real case before going to the council. We'd have to show misconduct," she said.

"He fired Pam Grimaldi for no good reason," Robbie said.

"True, but it's not like that was discriminatory or anything. We need something that looks really bad. Misappropriation of funds. Sexual harassment. Something of that nature."

"I get the picture."

"Anything you find that might help, I want to hear about it," Jenny said. "The more I know, the more ammunition I'll have against Chief Rizzo."

"Consider it done," Robbie said.

They made plans to talk on the phone once each night so Robbie could report on the case, then said their good-byes.

As the door closed behind him, Jenny took the scrapbook from her desk and opened it to the photo of Griff and Kate in Jamaica. So Owen Rizzo was focusing on Griff as a suspect in his wife's murder. To anyone who knew the two of them, that seemed laughable. No man had ever loved a woman so devotedly. But if Rizzo wanted to call Kate's death a murder and try to hang it on someone, better he look to Griff than start digging into what happened at the bridge twenty years ago.

27

Searching Kate's house was strangely moving for Owen. He marched around in a paper suit and shoe covers, barking directions at a bunch of guys from the state police. But in the midst of the bustle, he felt a strange communion with Kate. He enjoyed looking at photos of her from when she was a kid, and searching through the clothes in her closet, which smelled of her perfume. (He left no trace on the things he touched, since he wore latex gloves.) It was intimate, a way to get to know her better, since he'd been cheated of the chance to do that while she was alive. She'd been dazzlingly beautiful as a girl, but in the pictures she never looked happy to him. She'd always been unhappy. She'd told him that. There was one picture in particular he loved. In it, Kate was maybe seventeen or eighteen. She was sitting on a stone wall with a big white mansion behind her, wearing riding clothes. It was a bright, sunny day, but the tree beside her cast a shadow across her perfect face, making her seem doomed, like a princess in a story.

What a body, though.

Ah, he was getting sentimental. He needed to get his shit together and focus on making the case against the man who killed her. Owen had been slightly perturbed when they rolled up to serve the warrant, and Griffin Rothenberg was nowhere to be found. Had he cut and run already? That was what the prosecutors called consciousness of guilt, but it was also frigging inconvenient. Owen had Gene and Marv out cruising around looking for Rothenberg now, although if they found him, they were instructed to back off and surveil from a distance because Owen didn't have enough evidence to make an arrest. Yet.

Owen studied their wedding picture, taken on a beach somewhere. Kate's smile for the camera seemed fake. Was she ever in love with the guy? Rothenberg's father had been filthy rich. Maybe she married him for the money. She wouldn't be the first girl to do that. Owen wasn't about to judge her for it; she'd paid a big enough price already. He dropped the wedding picture into an evidence bag, sealed it up with tape, and put it on the cart for transfer to the state police lab. Prosecutors loved stuff like that to show to the jury, set the stage, create a little atmosphere. The couple in their happier days, before it all went wrong. The one of Kate in riding clothes he tucked inside his shirt.

The forensics guys were here to handle the technical stuff. They had gone up to the second floor and were working their way down, looking for anything that smacked of crime scene. A murder weapon, obviously, but also—blood spatters, suspicious stains, mud on shoes, cleaning supplies, places that looked staged or like they'd been mopped up or swabbed with bleach. They sprayed their luminol and collected their samples for the lab. Hair strands from Rothenberg's comb, water glasses that could be dusted to lift his prints. That asshole wasn't likely to come in and give a DNA sample voluntarily. But there was more than one way to skin a cat.

With the state police handling the technical side, Owen was free to focus on documents. He liked documents. There weren't enough of them in narcotics cases. Maybe you'd get a slip of paper that said "Chino, 20 kilos," with a cell number on it, but nothing that required a man to solve a puzzle, to use his brain. He was looking for anything that gave Rothenberg a motive, or put him near the River Road boat launch on Friday night, when they believed she disappeared. Phone records, a bus ticket in a coat pocket, a receipt from a gas station. Anything. Or an insurance policy on Kate's life with Rothenberg named as the beneficiary. Wouldn't that be nice? Owen walked the first floor, looking for a desk or filing cabinet or anything, even a junk drawer where they stashed their paperwork. The house was a jumble of rooms, poorly organized, musty and dark, not at all the sort of place he imagined Kate living. She belonged in that mansion in the picture, not in a dump like this. Rothenberg must've really hit the skids if this was the best he could do. Hell, Owen could've done better for Kate himself, and he'd never come within a hundred miles of the kind of money that guy had.

In the kitchen, where he and Keisha had interviewed Rothenberg just the afternoon before, Owen went through the drawers and came up empty. Then he opened the pantry door and stopped and stared. Owen's pantry had about ten boxes of cereal, a few cans of beans, maybe some spaghetti. This one was full to the brim with the most amazing stash of booze he'd ever seen outside a bar. Owen rummaged through it, the bottles clinking as he read the labels. There were many types of artisanal gin and some very expensive vermouth. Bourbon, both Kentucky and local, as well as five kinds of scotch, including a famous single malt that cost a pretty penny. Dark rum, white rum, and cachaça. Liqueurs and cordials in every flavor, brandy and cognac, margarita mix and Bloody Mary mix and simple syrup and bitters. You could throw a party for a hundred people and not make a dent in this haul. Owen wondered what the total price tag was. If Rothenberg could afford a liquor cabinet this extravagant, maybe he wasn't hurting so bad after all. Maybe he had money stashed. *Lightbulb*—maybe he had money stashed, and he used it to pay for a habit that was maybe booze, but maybe something more. Could there be drugs in the house? The answer to that, in his experience, was there always could. Owen didn't have enough to lock Rothenberg up for murder. But if he found drugs, he could sure as hell lock him up for that, and he'd get the breathing room he needed to make the murder case at his leisure.

Owen dialed the state police for what felt like the tenth time that day, and requested dispatch of a canine team. He hated going to them with hat in hand, but this town had no goddamn resources, and if he borrowed from the overtime fund again, someone was bound to find out. He swallowed his pride and asked the state police for another favor. Owen was not about to let a possible drug arrest of Rothenberg fall by the wayside just to save face.

When they told him it would take an hour to get the canine there, Owen photographed the booze (you never knew what might come in handy at trial) and went back to searching for documents. Eventually he located a screen porch off the kitchen that he'd missed on his first walk-through. The storm windows were up, but as Owen stepped down to the porch, the temperature dropped a good twenty-five degrees. If Kate was his, he would've spent a Saturday insulating the porch so she didn't have to sit in the cold. Presumably a guy like Rothenberg had never heard of Home Depot and couldn't swing a hammer to save his life.

The desk in the corner was covered with papers. Owen switched on the desk lamp and started wading through them. It was a freaking bonanza. Phone records, credit card bills, bank records, correspondence. Rothenberg hadn't gone digital yet, apparently. Owen sorted them into piles. The bank records and credit cards were key, because Owen needed to be able to prove that Rothenberg profited from his wife's death. He found the October statement for a joint checking account, which showed a dangerously low balance, less than was needed to pay off the credit card debt he found in their bills. Now that he had the account numbers, he would subpoena every record he could get his hands on, and if there was a financial motive, he would find it.

Owen moved a sheaf of papers and under it discovered a shiny silver laptop. He knew better than to lay a finger on it himself. An expert needed to retrieve the data under controlled conditions. (Another expense he'd have to find the money for somehow.) His hands twitched with excitement as he sealed the laptop into an evidence bag for chain of custody. There was bound to be something on there to sink the husband. Sexts with a girlfriend. Google searches for how to dump a body. Directions to the River Road boat launch, or something else Rizzo hadn't thought of yet. Computers solved cases, because people were stupid. Owen couldn't count the number of times he'd searched a guy's phone and found it loaded with pictures of drugs and guns and cash. Which, okay, maybe meant drug dealers were *especially* stupid. But no—it was the rich, stuck-up assholes like Rothenberg who felt so far above the law that they'd never bother to destroy evidence of their crimes.

Next came the desk drawers. He yanked open the top right-hand one and stopped, breathless. This was Kate's drawer. A small tray held pink paper clips, hair elastics, a lip gloss, matches from a bar in New York City, a pack of Marlboro reds. (Did she smoke? He didn't remember that from the bar.) It was just the sort of stuff a woman would keep in her handbag. He'd thought about the handbag before, of course. It was missing. They were hoping to find it in this search, but so far they hadn't. Something was wedged under the tray. Owen moved it aside and pulled out a small red-leather date book. It was a dainty thing, with gold edging on the pages and a red silk ribbon marking Friday's date. Friday, her fortieth birthday, the last day she walked this earth. He had to sit down in the desk chair. She'd written "40" in black ink at the top of the page, surrounded by little lines that looked like fireworks exploding. And below that, in a bold, slanted hand, in the space for seven o'clock: "Bday dinner at Henry's w/ J&A." Henry's? Was that the name of a person, or did it refer to Henry's Bistro? He'd send Keisha down there with a subpoena for their reservation book to find out.

His walkie-talkie squawked.

"Yo, Chief. We got something here."

"Where are you?"

"Master bedroom."

"On my way."

He'd looked through the bedroom before the forensics team showed up, but it had been a cursory search, to get a feel for things. He thought he would've spotted something major, but that's why you brought in the crime scene team. They were the experts.

In the bedroom, Owen found the team leader and another guy hunched over the laundry hamper, clothing scattered on the floor at their feet. They turned when he walked in.

"Get a load of this, Chief," the team leader said. "Matthews found it wadded up in the bottom of the basket."

The team leader stepped aside. Laid out on the top of the hamper,

Owen saw a men's shirt, purple-check, with a Brooks Brothers label. The left-hand side was marred by a large spatter of dried blood.

Owen grinned and clapped the team leader on the back. "Thanks, bro. I think you just solved my case."

28

Griff woke from a troubled sleep. Thoughts of Kate rushed in, and it took a couple of minutes before he could breathe again. The last thing he remembered was Aubrey feeding him soup and promising to find him a lawyer. She'd neglected to bring any booze, however. He hadn't had a drink since Sunday and it was—what, Tuesday? Wednesday? He wasn't feverish any longer. His mind was clearer than it had been in a while. That was not necessarily a good thing.

In the quiet of the cabin, he heard the soft lapping of the lake against the dock. A ray of light from the picture window pierced his eyes, irritating them. The sunlight forced him to sit up; otherwise he might not have found the will. He felt Kate in it, calling him outdoors. Pulling the afghan tight around his shoulders, Griff stepped out onto the back deck, and the cold enveloped him. It was a damp, blustery day, with a taste of snow in the air. Was Kate out here? He saw no hope in this dead landscape. The sky was silver, the lake was black, and the bare trees made ugly slashes against the sky. All around, piles of wet leaves gave off the sickly-sweet smell of death. Maybe that was her message to him.

He was staring at the lake, thinking about Kate's body in the freezing river, when the phone in his back pocket rang, making him start. Aubrey brought him a charger, he remembered. He pulled the phone out and saw that it was Jenny calling.

"Hello?" he said.

"Griff. I can't believe I reached you. I tried so many times."

"My phone was dead," he said, and his voice was dead, too.

"Are you all right?" Jenny asked.

The question was so surreal that he couldn't answer.

"Griff?" she said.

"No, Jenny. I'm not all right."

"Everybody's been looking for you. A lot is going on. I can't get into it over the phone. When the medical examiner's office couldn't get in touch with you, they had to call Kate's brother to make arrangements for her body."

"Her brother? Why?"

"Because they couldn't find you, and Keniston was in the hospital."

"Oh. Kate said he was going in for tests."

"Well, he has cancer, so they talked to Benji Eastman instead, and Benji called me, trying to find you. I arranged for Kate to be moved to the funeral home in town, but now the funeral director wants to meet with you."

"That's terrible about Keniston."

"Yes it is. But Griff, where the hell have you been?"

"At Aubrey's cabin, at the lake."

Jenny made an annoyed noise. "I can't believe she didn't tell me that."

"I haven't been feeling well. She was letting me rest," Griff said.

"There's no time for that now. I hate to be blunt, Griff, but if you don't show your face, it looks bad. You need to make your wife's funeral arrangements, or else people might draw the wrong conclusions."

He paused. She was implying that people thought he killed Kate. If that's what they thought of him, why was Jenny even bothering to help him? He wished she would leave him to his fate.

"Are the police—?" he began.

"Are they what?" she asked. But he let the question lie there.

"Let's talk in person, all right?" she said. "Stay where you are. I'm coming to get you. We'll go to the funeral home together."

She hung up before he could say no. It would take her half an hour to drive to the cabin from Belle River. Griff had no car to make his getaway.

But he found that he no longer wanted to run. He didn't want to die either. It hadn't occurred to him before Jenny's call, but Kate was still here, not just in his mind, but in body. He could see her, touch her, talk to her, say the things he'd been longing to say but thought he'd never get the chance to. Maybe if he said them, he would be able to go on. There was a small part of him that still imagined a future.

Suddenly Griff couldn't wait. He went back inside and tried to take a shower, but the water that came out of the shower head was ice-cold and rusty, so he settled for washing his face. That bruise was fading, and the swelling on the left side of his jaw had gone down. He was ravenously hungry. He made scrambled eggs and wolfed them straight from the pan. By the time he was done, Jenny's minivan was in the driveway. She honked. He threw the pan in the sink and ran out.

The road down from the lake was narrow and winding, and for the first bit Jenny concentrated on her driving. Once they hit the highway, she stepped on the gas, and glanced over at Griff with concern.

"Nobody told me you two were splitting up," she began.

"It came as a surprise to me, too."

"You asked me on the phone about the police," she said. "They think it's suspicious that Kate went missing immediately after filing for divorce."

Griff shrugged. "I don't know why they think that. She served me with papers and then she took off. She wasn't about to come back home like nothing happened. I assumed she left town."

"Well, you were wrong. She didn't go off on some Caribbean cruise. She turned up dead. Aren't you worried they'll come after you? Because you should be."

"I have no control over what the cops do. Aubrey told me they already searched my house."

"Anything I say about that, I'd be disclosing confidential information."

"Don't tell me then. I don't want to put you in a bad position," Griff said.

"I'll do it, Griff. I just want you to understand, you can never say I told you."

"Honestly, Jenny, it doesn't matter to me. I don't care what happens next. I just want to see Kate."

"I have a contact inside the police department. He called me a little while ago with the results of the search. You should know, the police found a shirt of yours, with bloodstains on it."

He leaned back in the passenger seat and closed his eyes. "It's not Kate's blood. It's mine. I didn't kill her, Jenny. I loved her."

"I know that."

He opened his eyes. "But *somebody* killed her?"

"The chief of police thinks so. He's a royal terror. I wish I could control him, but I can't. Honestly, he's focused on you, Griff."

"Figures." Griff shook his head in disgust. *Fucking cops.* "What about you? What do you think?"

Jenny sighed. "Personally, I hope it gets ruled a suicide. That would be best for everybody. Let her rest in peace."

He didn't contradict her. By the time they reached the funeral home, it had started to snow, in sharp, icy crystals that struck the back of Griff's neck and chilled him to the bone. The funeral home was new construction, meant to look quaint and New Englandy with white-clapboard siding and green shutters, but inside, smelling of cheap carpeting and air freshener.

"Who picked this place?" Griff asked.

"It's the only funeral home in town. Once the medical examiner released her body, she had to go somewhere."

"It's so bleak," he said, and his voice caught.

"You don't have to do the service here. We can do it at a church and go straight to the cemetery, then do a reception at my house, if you like."

"Mem Church?" Griff asked.

Memorial Church, in the center of the Quad, with its soaring transept and stained-glass windows, was where Carlisle held its sacred events. Graduations, swearings-in, weddings. Griff had wanted to get married there, but Kate wouldn't hear of it.

"If you think that's what she'd want," Jenny said, reading his mind.

Of course Kate wouldn't want that, but Griff wanted it on her behalf.

She should've graduated. It was a travesty that she didn't. Let her at least have a Carlisle funeral.

"She wasn't an alum," Jenny said, "but Keniston could probably arrange it. He's getting released tonight, and Benji's driving him up here in the morning. It's only—"

"What?"

"The press has their teeth in the story, Griff. If you hold the funeral in the middle of campus, it could turn into a circus. I'm even worried they'll show up here."

"I've been through worse," he said with a shrug, thinking of his father. "You just ignore it."

"Kate's in there," Jenny said, nodding toward a side room. "I'll wait in the lobby. I'm sure you want some time alone with her."

It was the only thing he wanted.

As Griff stepped into the room and caught sight of Kate lying on the bier, his breath left him. They'd dimmed the lights, so the space seemed candlelit, almost romantic, and she looked so beautiful. He approached her reverently. The undertaker had done a remarkable job. She was herself, except with a heavy sheen of pale foundation makeup, which Kate never wore, and carefully brushed hair, where Kate's hair was free and wild. Otherwise, it was just Kate, looking fast asleep. Jenny must have selected the outfit. She wore her favorite dress, a chic black sheath by a famous designer that hugged her figure, from the days when they could afford to spend thousands on a single item of clothing. Griff gazed down at her, ignoring the faint chemical smell that pervaded the air. He'd expected to want to throw himself on her body, to rant and rave, but instead he felt calm and light. He felt peace and joy. Until he touched her.

He drew his hand back as if he'd had an electric shock, but it was just the opposite. The life force had left her. Her flesh felt cold, plastic, inert. Like a refrigerated doll. Like she was dead. Only in that moment did it become real, and he sank to his knees beside her and sobbed.

"*Why?*" he shouted, through his tears, then remembered where he was. This place could be bugged. The cops might be listening.

"Who did this to you?" he said aloud. "Was it *him*? Or did you do it to yourself?"

He went to sit in a nearby folding chair, staring at her in the oppressive silence as an Eagles song played in his head. *And the storybook comes to a close, gone are the ribbons and bows.* Their love affair had been a storybook, to Griff at least. But if he was honest, they'd only had four or five good years before things went downhill, followed by nearly a decade of a slow, agonizing unraveling. But Kate was Kate. What could you do? He never stopped loving her.

Their best times were in New York, those first few years. There was a moment, after rehab, after they got married, when he truly believed she'd changed. Her guilt over Lucas was the cause, but if it helped manage her demons, he'd take it and be grateful. At some point in Paris, Kate had added a fourth star to that tattoo inside her wrist. Griff would come upon her sometimes, sitting quietly with a faraway look in her eyes, tracing that fourth star with her finger. He never asked her if it represented Lucas; he never let on he noticed it at all. But he knew. The guilt seemed to do her good. Kate took Griff up on his offer of an introduction to his friend who ran the charity, and for a while she volunteered in a shelter for homeless kids. She went so far as to write away for brochures on master's programs in social work.

But then . . . what? It was hard to say what went wrong. The corrosive effect of his money surely played a role. It took willpower to instruct your driver to bring you to the homeless shelter in the Bronx when you could be sitting in the front row of the couture shows instead, and willpower was never Kate's forte. Griff felt partly responsible, for setting a bad example. His job on Wall Street was a charade, his duties limited to playing matchmaker between his own firm and various powerful clients who were associates of his father's. It was an endless round of lunches, drinks, and dinners—contentless, well suited to a charming schmoozer who wasn't smart with numbers, which was how he thought of himself. He should've resisted the path laid out for him and done something else, something he liked, though he'd never liked anything much. He'd been a devotee of the gentleman's C at Carlisle; call it the gentleman's B-minus with grade inflation. The only classes he ever aced were Intro to Marine Bio and Literature of the Sea, because he loved boats and the ocean, and he loved to sail. Maybe he should have made a meaningful career out of that somehow, instead of being content to cruise the BVI in his yacht, watching the sun set with a mojito in his hand. Although boats turned out to be part of the problem: he took Kate away from New York when she didn't want to go, so they could spend time on the water.

Around the time of her thirtieth birthday, Kate had begun to slip away from him. It started with a trip they made to Belle River, after Griff was asked to serve as financial chair of his tenth-reunion committee. They were only in town for a few days. She was excited about it at first, planning girl time with her old roommates, but at some point, something went awry. He never found out exactly what, or even if there was a particular triggering incident, though he imagined it had to do with Lucas Arsenault. In any event, depression overwhelmed her, and Kate fell into a deep, dark hole. He got her doctor to prescribe antidepressants, but Kate claimed they made her bloated and stupid. She stopped taking them, and turned instead to her old friends drugs and booze. He hated to see her to get wasted alone, so he joined her, as if that made it better. Pretty soon, they were both partying too much.

There were no natural brakes for their bad behavior. No children who needed care, no fixed hours at work, no financial constraints. Whatever substance they felt like indulging in, they could afford the purest, and in unlimited quantities. They'd go out to clubs or to friends' estates in the Hamptons, start doing lines, and before Griff knew it, Kate had left with some other guy. He was usually trashed out of his mind by then, and numb to the pain of it. If she left with someone, he'd leave with someone, too. Pretty soon they'd both slept with pretty much everyone they knew, Kate was on the verge of blowing out her septum, Griff's liver was in trouble, and the whole scene had gotten toxic. They could either get out of town, go to rehab, or get divorced. Kate said rehab was a drag. Griff couldn't stand to lose Kate. So the solution was obvious—leave New York.

For her thirtieth birthday, he bought her a house in Anguilla, not far from the beach where they'd married. The house was set high in the hills, with views for miles to the aqua bay where the yachts were anchored like so many toys. He whisked her down there on his father's jet and had her wear a blindfold in the car. They walked in the front door, and she could see straight through the double-height living room to a twenty-foot-high wall of glass, where he'd set up a telescope trained on the bay. He guided her over to it, and directed her gaze at a particular boat sitting proudly in the water, a sleek seventy-foot Hinckley, exquisitely crafted of mahogany, with a navy-blue hull and a white bridge. It was a classic—drop-dead gorgeous under full sail, not too big for Griff to skipper himself (with the aid of a small crew).

He said, "Take a look at the name on the side. I named her the *Kate,* she's your boat, baby."

They spent their days sailing her around to wherever the weather was fairest and the beaches the most secluded. They'd cruise the Caribbean all winter, then have the crew take the boat across and fly to catch it again in the Med, where they'd spend the long summers flitting among whitewashed islands. In between, they'd catch up with friends here and there at posh resorts, over gin and tonics, or land for a while in the best hotels in Palm Beach, Capri, or Gstaad—avoiding New York like that made their problems go away, as if New York was the only place you could be unhappy. Griff was having too good a time to realize they were living his dream, not Kate's. Yet she didn't complain. She didn't seem unhappy with their life, until his father fell from grace, and the money spigot got shut off. Until that moment, Griff never understood that Kate was really only with him for his money. He believed it of everybody else, yes. But never her. He was wrong about that, as it turned out.

There was a knock at the door, and Jenny stuck her head in.

"Griff, I'm really sorry, but there are TV trucks out front. Three of them."

"How do they know we're here?"

"I'm not sure they do know, but they know *Kate* is here. I talked to the funeral director. He's got private security people coming over right now to lock the place down and make sure she's not disturbed."

"*Disturbed*?" Griff said, going pale.

"I just mean, that nobody sneaks in to take pictures or anything."

He leapt to his feet. "Where are they? Scumbags. I'll give them something to photograph."

Jenny came forward and put her hands on his shoulders soothingly. "Honey, trust me, that'll just make things worse. We're going to sneak you out the back, through the garage, and you can discuss the arrangements with the funeral director over the phone. Just give me a minute to set it up. Say your good-byes, I'll be back in a few minutes," she said, and closed the door.

Say his good-byes? He walked over to the bier where she lay, and looked down at her knowing that good-bye was impossible. He was going to come out of this situation intact, except for his heart and soul and anything else about him that mattered. Oh, he'd go on—there was money for that. At noon on Friday, Kate's fortieth birthday, at a moment when they were still legally married, she'd come into the balance of her trust. Griff suspected that that fact explained the timing of her divorce filing. After all those years when he supported her in style, Kate was planning to take her trust money and split. That money was Griff's now, as her legal heir. It wasn't much, two hundred and fifty K. Enough to buy a small boat that he could live on in a marina somewhere, to sail again on blue waters, have a drink at sunset and toast to her. Maybe eventually he'd get lonely enough to find some intrepid woman to keep him company. A Mexican girl who took things in stride and knew how to cook, or a South African or Australian who could go for months without seeing port and not mind. But he'd never love her. He'd never love anyone again. If only there was some way around it. If only he could bring Kate back to life.

Jenny was at the door. "Let's go," she said.

Griff leaned over and kissed Kate's cold, pale lips. But unlike Sleeping Beauty in the fairy tale, she did not wake.

29

Sleet pelted the plate-glass windows of the yoga studio as Aubrey rose from her mat at the front of the class. Outside, the river ran gray and cold. She dimmed the lights and flicked on the music. The sound of wind chimes and birdsong filled the airy room, which smelled of exotic woods and incense and was heated to a tropical intensity. Aubrey passed among the closely spaced mats passing out cool towels to be used as eyeshades, gliding with such grace that she appeared to float. Women gazed at her adoringly and accepted her offering, then closed their eyes, and let out a luxuriant breath.

"As we relax into our *savasana,*" Aubrey said in her most soothing tone, "allow the warmth of the room to penetrate into your breath and through your breath. Cherish the warmth of your body. Relax your fingers and your toes. Open yourself to gratitude. Gratitude for your body. Gratitude for your decision to practice today despite inclement weather, despite other calls on your time and attention. Honor yourself. Honor the winter, that cleanses and redeems. Honor this moment of peace, that restores and fortifies you for the day ahead. And rest."

Aubrey flowed toward the front of the room, stopping here and there to make gentle adjustments to a student's posture. A moment later, she was back on her mat, seated in a perfect lotus, her serene expression belying her anxious heartbeat. The police were in the office across the hall, talking to her assistant. She could see them through the glass door.

A powerful gust of wind drove sleet against the window as Aubrey looked at the clock. It was five minutes too early, but she decided to dismiss the class. She couldn't stand the suspense a moment longer.

"Allow your eyes to come back to focus beneath your eyelids," she said, her voice less soothing, more rushed, than usual. "Allow energy to flow back into your limbs. Stretch your arms, wiggle your fingers and your toes. When you're ready, open your eyes, and come to a seated position."

When the majority of the class was upright, Aubrey struck the small gong that she used to end each class, and listened as the note flowed out, rich and sonorous. She drew her hands together at her heart and bowed her head.

"*Namaste.*"

A chorus of *namaste*s echoed back from the smiling students. Usually she lingered after class to answer questions and accept personal expressions of gratitude from her students. Not today, not with the police waiting. Aubrey expertly rolled her mat, rose to her feet in a graceful motion, and walked from the room, leaving a few of the regulars gazing after her in puzzlement.

As she entered the glass-walled office, her assistant Mikayla, round and freckle-faced and normally cheerful, turned to her with alarm. A man and a woman stood in front of Aubrey's desk. Aubrey recognized the man from the TV news. He was the chief of police.

"These officers are here to ask some questions about your friend who died. I explained I don't know anything," Mikayla said.

"Thank you, Mikayla. I'll take care of this."

Aubrey shut the door firmly behind Mikayla. "What can I do for you, Officers," she said.

"You're Mrs. Saxman?" the man asked.

"Aubrey Saxman, yes. And you are—?"

"Chief Owen Rizzo, Belle River PD, and my colleague, Detective

Keisha Charles. We're investigating the death of Kate Eastman, and we'd like to ask you a few questions."

Was she required to speak with them? Aubrey wondered. Should she refuse, or call a lawyer? Or would that look bad? If only she'd thought about this before the police showed up. She'd expected them to question her at some point, but she never thought it would be so soon. And she'd been too caught up in taking care of Griff to look out for herself.

Aubrey decided the best course of action was to appear cooperative.

"Certainly, have a seat. Can I offer you some tea? Such unpleasant weather," Aubrey said, taking a seat behind her desk.

"No, thank you, that's not necessary. We were told you knew Ms. Eastman, is that correct?" Chief Rizzo asked.

"Oh, yes. We were close friends, for twenty years, give or take. I'm *devastated* at her death," Aubrey said, looking away, her face puckering.

Rizzo nodded at the female detective, and Aubrey noticed that she started taking notes. That was unnerving. Why would they think anything Aubrey had to say was worth writing down?

"I'm very sorry for your loss," Rizzo said. "When exactly did you last see Ms. Eastman?"

"I—well, I'm not sure," she said.

"Any guess?"

Aubrey's stomach fluttered with nerves. She wondered if this was one of those situations like on TV cop shows where they already knew the answer and were trying to catch her in a lie.

"I wouldn't want to say the wrong thing," she said, her eyes trailing the detective's pen as it moved across the page.

"An approximate date would be fine," he said.

"Let me see. I remember we had lunch a few weeks ago."

"Just the two of you?"

"No. Jenny was with us. Jenny Healy."

"The mayor?"

"Yes."

"Why was *she* there?" the chief asked.

"Because we're good friends."

"You and the mayor?"

"All three of us. We roomed together freshman year at Carlisle. You didn't know that?" Aubrey said, trying to gauge whether they'd done their homework.

He ignored her question. "So the three of you had lunch several weeks back, and you haven't seen Ms. Eastman since then?"

"That's right."

"What about this past Friday?" Rizzo asked, and Aubrey's heart stopped.

"Uhh, you mean—?" she asked, stupefied, and shook her head.

"Weren't you planning to see Ms. Eastman this past Friday? It was her fortieth birthday, and I understood you had a dinner scheduled."

"Oh! Right, yes. *Yes.* We did have a plan to take Kate out for her birthday. Jenny and I. It was originally supposed to be the six of us, the three roommates and our husbands, at Henry's Bistro, but we changed it to a girls' night."

"What time were you supposed to meet?"

"Seven o'clock."

"But it never happened?"

"No."

"Why not?" the chief asked.

"It got called off."

"When did that happen?"

"I'm not sure. Maybe that same day."

"This was only a few days ago. You don't remember?"

"No, sorry, I'm not good with dates and such," Aubrey said, with an innocent flutter of her eyelashes. If she played up the airhead-yoga-instructor stereotype, maybe they would go away and leave her alone.

"Why was it canceled?"

"I think Kate was sick."

"Did you hear that from Kate herself?"

"I'm not sure. Maybe you should ask Jenny. Details aren't my strong suit. I might be remembering wrong."

"No worries," the chief said. "We're talking to a lot of people. We're simply trying to develop a timeline of Ms. Eastman's actions on the day she disappeared, so we can answer questions like who saw her last, and so forth," the chief said.

"But why does that matter? Wasn't Kate's death an accident?" Aubrey asked.

"Maybe, but maybe not. That's what we're trying to figure out," the chief replied.

Aubrey folded her hands, trying to appear calm. There was nothing to worry about here. It was always likely that the police would investigate, and that they might question her. The chief just said, they were talking to a lot of people. It was always a possibility that they might decide Kate's death was suspicious. None of that should concern Aubrey unduly, since nothing they would find could implicate her.

"If you don't think it was an accident, then it must have been a suicide, right?" Aubrey said.

"Not necessarily," Chief Rizzo said. "She didn't leave a note. So there's nothing definitive that suggests this was suicide, unless you know something about her state of mind, in which case, please, tell us."

Aubrey hesitated. If they didn't think Kate's death was an accident, and they weren't considering the possibility of suicide, then that meant they were considering murder, for sure. Could they be thinking that, already? Did they already have a suspect?

"Mrs. Saxman?" the chief prompted.

"Oh, yes, sorry," Aubrey said. "I'm just a bit hesitant to discuss Kate's private . . . troubles." She had almost said *affairs*.

"I understand. But this is very important. We'll keep what you tell us confidential if at all possible," he said.

"All right, then. If you must know, Kate did have what you could call suicidal tendencies. She made a pretty serious attempt in high school, and talked about killing herself a lot in college. She seemed serious about it. I wouldn't be surprised, if she got upset, that she might contemplate something like that to this day. It's something you should be looking into."

"I see. Do you have reason to believe she was particularly upset recently?"

"I'm not sure. I've been so busy with my kids, and the yoga studio lately. Of course, I regret it now, not making more time for her," Aubrey said.

"We have reason to believe Ms. Eastman's marriage was troubled," Rizzo said. "Can you tell us anything about that?"

Did he know something specific, or was he fishing? If the police hadn't already found out about Kate and Ethan's affair, Aubrey wasn't about to enlighten them. It would only turn the spotlight on her own life.

"I had no idea," Aubrey said.

"You weren't aware that she recently filed for divorce?"

Aubrey looked at him in surprise. Was that possible? Was it even true? Surely somebody would've told her something as important as that.

"No," she said. "I didn't know. I find it hard to believe I wouldn't have heard."

"Well, you said you hadn't talked to Ms. Eastman much lately. Mr. Rothenberg didn't tell you?" Chief Rizzo asked, watching Aubrey closely.

"Mr. Rothenberg? No, why would *he* tell me? Kate would've been the one to tell me, and she didn't mention it," Aubrey said.

"Did you know Kate—*Ms. Eastman*—had just come into a substantial sum of money? Two hundred and fifty thousand dollars, according to bank records that we've subpoenaed."

"I'm not sure Kate would consider that a substantial sum of money. But no, I didn't know that."

"It seems like a relevant fact, don't you think? That leads me to another question. You came to the station Sunday night to pick up Mr. Rothenberg."

"Yes."

"So you know Mr. Rothenberg?"

"Sure. I've known him since college. Kate was my roommate. Since they were married, I ended up keeping in touch with Griff as well."

"Do you know, was Mr. Rothenberg . . . seeing anyone?"

"You mean, was Griff involved with another woman?"

"Yes."

Aubrey laughed in shock. Griff, the devoted husband? "No, absolutely not," she said.

"You sound very certain of that. How can you be so sure?"

Aubrey had no idea where the police chief was going with these questions. Was Griff having an affair, and Aubrey didn't know? Impossible, she didn't believe it for a second. She spent way too much time watching Griff, thinking about him, to miss something that major.

"I'm sure because I know how much Griff loved his wife," she said. "Chief Rizzo, I have to say, I feel like you're fishing for gossip. Is this really how the police investigate a case?"

"Look, I'll be honest. Our dispatch secretary mentioned you and Mr. Rothenberg seemed unusually cozy when you came to pick him up from the station the other night. Please understand, I have no desire to offend you, but I'm obligated to ask. Mrs. Saxman, are you romantically involved with Mr. Rothenberg?"

In the mirror over the sofa, Aubrey saw her reflection, all bright eyes and sharp spots of color in pale cheeks, looking as rattled as she felt. The idea that the police might zero in on Aubrey, or on *Griff*, not because of Ethan and Kate's affair, but because of some imagined entanglement between the two of them? That had never occurred to her in a million years. Yet, if they did, it would have the same result as if they knew the truth about Kate and Ethan. They'd still be messing around in Aubrey's private business, with all the risks that presented. At this point, she realized she'd said enough, and anything more would be counterproductive. She wasn't in control of this interview, and she ought to shut it down.

"You think Griff and I were having an affair, simply because I picked him up from the police station after the man found out his wife died?" Aubrey asked, allowing a note of anger to creep into her voice.

"I'm not saying I think that. I'm just asking," Rizzo said.

"Well, the answer is no. I was trying to be a good friend, that's all."

"All right," Rizzo said.

"I have to say, I'm finding your questions somewhat offensive, Chief Rizzo. I feel like you're looking for a scandal where there's only a tragedy. Kate was simply a woman with a history of depression who in all likelihood took her own life. She is—*was*—a dear friend of mine, and I have to ask you not to disrespect her memory with your wild allegations."

Rizzo flushed, looking stung. "That's not my intention at all. I'm trying to find out the truth about how she died," he said.

"You won't get the truth by asking such absurd questions."

"They're not absurd," he said, in an angry tone, then took a deep breath. "Mrs. Saxman, look, we're on the same side. I'll explain my thinking, if you give me your word you'll keep it in confidence."

"All right. Fine, go ahead," Aubrey said.

"First of all, the forensic evidence in this case is consistent with homicide. Not with an accident. Not with the victim taking her own life. I know you say Kate had a history of suicidal behavior, but it sounds like that was many years ago. And there's something else, a very important reason that she wouldn't kill herself. You might not have known this, but Kate was pregnant at the time of her death," Rizzo said.

As the sick expression spread across Aubrey's face, Rizzo nodded.

"So now you understand," he said. "I wouldn't normally disclose such sensitive information, but given that you were close to both parties, I feel that you could shed some light and be a very useful witness, if only you'd help. I need you to see that your friend was probably murdered, possibly by her own husband. Things were very wrong between the two of them. We know that, because she filed for divorce. So I have to ask you to think hard about their relationship. Was there anything you saw or heard, in the weeks leading up to her death, that I should be aware of, that might shed light on the situation? If so, I urge you to tell me. Don't protect him."

Aubrey stared at her hands, folded in her lap, unable to give Rizzo any answer. *Kate pregnant with Ethan's baby.* She couldn't believe it. Something else she hadn't known, something huge they'd kept from her.

"You look upset," Rizzo said. "I understand, you're in mourning for your friend, and this news may have added to the shock. I just felt it was important for you to have the complete picture. We'll get out of your way now, so you can have time to think things over. Here's my card," Rizzo said, standing up, and nodding to his partner, who rose also. "You think about it, and if you remember anything, you give me a call. All right?"

Aubrey nodded helplessly, and Rizzo left the card on her desk. When they'd gone, Aubrey locked herself in the bathroom and threw up.

The baby had to be Ethan's; Kate and Griff weren't sleeping together as far as Aubrey knew. Aubrey had figured out, from her clandestine monitoring of Ethan's texts, that Kate was begging him to run off with her. This must be why—because Kate was *pregnant*. This made everything so much worse. The betrayal was greater, and yet so was the tragedy of Kate's death. Aubrey had *tried* to live with their affair, she really had. But the humiliation had been too great, the betrayal beyond what she could tolerate. She had to take a stand. Yet—an innocent child had died. Aubrey felt feverish, light-headed, sick at the thought of the baby.

When Aubrey emerged from the bathroom, Mikayla took one look at her and decided that she was coming down with something and needed to be driven home immediately. Aubrey went to her room, got in bed, and pulled the covers over her head. The kids fended for themselves for supper—there were enough organic veggie pizzas in the freezer to keep them for a week if need be. Lilly came by with a mug of tea but Aubrey sent her away, saying she was contagious. When Ethan came home, Aubrey first pretended to be asleep, then instructed him to sleep on the couch in his study so he wouldn't catch what she had. Instead of asking after her symptoms, he jumped at the chance to be away from her and alone with his grief for his mistress. He thought she was too stupid to understand. He *still* thought that. But that was fine now, it was all right. Aubrey had a plan. Ethan would get what he deserved.

The next day, Aubrey went through the motions of her day as her mind raced. She went to work, came home, fed the kids, helped with homework, washed the dishes. She told everyone that she'd had a bout of food poisoning, but it was over now. She told Ethan he could come back to their bedroom. When he resisted, she bullied him into it, and forced herself to lie beside him no matter how much she despised him, so she could know for sure when he fell asleep.

Ethan wasn't sleeping well; imagine that. Poor thing tossed and turned and got up more than once to go to the bathroom. Around one thirty, when his breathing finally quieted, Aubrey swung her legs over the side of the bed and got to her feet gingerly. She tiptoed to the door, closing it softly behind her, and made her way down the stairs in the dark. By the glow of the appliances, she hurried through the kitchen to the laundry room. The laundry room was Aubrey's turf, even more so than the yoga studio. Nobody came in here but her, and if she wanted to hide something, this was the place. There was a tall cabinet with louvered doors to the right of the washer-dryer. It normally squeaked to high heaven when you opened it, but she'd gotten out the oil can today, and now the hinges flowed like silk. Wrapping her hand in a dish towel to avoid leaving fingerprints, Aubrey reached into the cabinet with her long arm, all the way to the back, behind the Tide and the dryer sheets, and pulled out a small purse. It was a pretty thing, a little black shoulder bag with a long gold chain. Kate didn't stint: it looked expensive. Her things were still inside—wallet, keys, lipstick, hairbrush, compact, a miniature atomizer of perfume. Aubrey raised the bag to within an inch of her nose and breathed in. It smelled like Kate, which made her feel a rush of love. And of hatred, and grief, and victory. Every emotion at once.

From the laundry room, Aubrey had to pass through the kitchen to get to the garage. On the way, she stopped at the basket to retrieve Ethan's car keys. A noise made her jump, but it was just the cat. He meowed. She ignored him. Aubrey stepped into the garage, where the comforting smells of rubber and gasoline soothed her fraying nerves. Aubrey opened the passenger door of Ethan's Audi and shoved the handbag as far under the seat as it would go, then stepped back to check. *Good.* The handbag was invisible, but not if you knew where to look for it. She'd kept the police chief's card. She would make the call anonymously, and Ethan would finally learn that actions had consequences.

30

Jenny woke up a minute before the alarm was set to go off, her chest tight with anxiety. She was scheduled to deliver Kate's eulogy from the well of Mem Church in a matter of hours. Lines from her speech rattled around her brain all night and kept her awake, but delivering the eulogy was not her biggest worry this morning. Just as Jenny had feared, somebody leaked the search warrant to the press, and she was expecting an onslaught of cameras and TV trucks at the funeral. The warrant named Griff as the prime suspect in Kate's murder and gave salacious details about the crime. The beautiful blond wife goes missing on the day she files for divorce, the same day her trust fund vests, leaving her with two hundred and fifty thousand that would now go to the husband. The wife is found washed up by the side of the river with a fractured skull. The husband—whose father is a notorious fraudster once worth hundreds of millions—hides a bloodstained Brooks Brothers shirt at the bottom of the laundry hamper. It was catnip, and Jenny had no hope of containing the story now.

Keniston Eastman's voicemail from last night still rang in her ears. He wasn't just irate over the leak; he was distraught over his daughter's death, and beside himself at the implication that his son-in-law was involved. Jenny would have to face Keniston this morning, and she dreaded it.

Then there were the problems closer to home. Tim slept beside her, his face in repose exhausted and troubled. He'd been out of sorts for days now. They hadn't made up. Jenny kept her distance, walked on eggshells. She had enough trouble, between the funeral and trying to keep a lid on the publicity surrounding the murder case, to face another argument.

She got out of bed with a sigh and went downstairs to start the coffee. The boys would be up in half an hour, but before that she had time to check the news and review her speech. She threw a coat over her nightgown, stuck her feet into her UGGs, and went out to collect the *Belle River Register* from the curb. Overnight, snow had fallen, and the driveway was slick. White clouds of breath trailed behind her. She shook the snow from the paper in its plastic wrapper. The sky was pink and brightening rapidly, and the air was sharp as crystal. Kate would have a pretty day for her funeral, at least. But of course, Kate hated the cold.

Back in the kitchen, she unfurled the newspaper. "Brooks Brothers Killer," the headline shrieked, over a giant, four-color photograph of Kate and Griff on their wedding day. Poor Griff. Jenny felt awful for him, but it was the box story to the right of the main article that made her gasp. "Murder Victim Previously Present at Local Man's Death," it read. There was a tiny, blurry BRHS yearbook photo of Lucas under the headline.

Someone had put two and two together, and connected Kate to Lucas's death. The byline said the author was Bill Buckwald, the same reporter who'd been interested in interviewing Kate at Jenny's Labor Day party months ago. Buckwald reported that, twenty-two years before, the coroner ruled Lucas's drowning a "death by misadventure," and the Arsenault family fought unsuccessfully to overturn that verdict and open a homicide investigation. Jenny read the rest of the article with her heart in her throat, relaxing only when she got to the end and hadn't found her own name. The article merely said that Kate had been present at the bridge the night Lucas died, and that the circumstances of Lucas's death were the subject of dispute. The *Register* didn't seem to be arguing—heaven forbid—that there was any connection between Lucas's death and Kate's. So why even publish such a story? Was this just for local color, or was Buckwald fishing for dirt on the Arsenault case? She'd have to keep her eye on that.

Jenny went into the den and clicked on the television, flipping back and forth between the local stations and the national morning shows to see what they were saying. Kate's murder was everywhere. The local stations talked of nothing else, but even the national networks were covering it. Most of them seemed to be calling it the "Carlisle murder," though a few had picked up "Brooks Brothers killer," and one even had it as the "country club murder," though neither Kate nor Griff belonged to a country club. One of the national networks flashed a picture of Kate taken when she was a teenager, in riding clothes in front of a mansion, looking gorgeous, rich, and extremely blond. Jenny knew that picture. It had been in the house on Faculty Row, the house Rizzo had just searched—Keniston's house. Ditto the next picture, of Griff on the deck of a yacht looking like Thurston Howell the Fourth. How had the press gotten hold of those photos? Had Chief Rizzo taken them from the house and leaked them? He still hadn't returned her phone calls, and she was increasingly uneasy with how he was handling the case. As she watched, the television news anchor started talking about yet another piece of evidence that should have remained confidential. A DNA test had apparently proved that scrapings of human skin taken from under Kate's fingernails belonged to Griff. Evidence straight from the state crime lab, fed to the press. Now, maybe that was some rogue lab technician, but maybe it was Rizzo, trying to gin up public sentiment for a murder investigation so nobody would be able to slow him down. Jenny recalled her conversation with Robbie Womack about trying to build evidence to argue for Chief Rizzo's removal. She'd been having her doubts about opposing the chief, but the press reports made her very nervous.

Jenny turned on her phone. Her voicemail box was full, and she had sixty-seven e-mails, mostly from reporters—some from as far away as Italy and Japan. There was also an urgent e-mail from the head of Carlisle Safety and Security saying that the town green and the Quad were overrun with TV trucks, that Belle River PD was completely AWOL and he couldn't get through to the chief of police. Now *that* was something she could use. In a town like Belle River, the one thing people expected from the police was decent traffic control. Jenny forwarded that e-mail to every member of the town council, with the subject line "Carlisle concerns about Chief Rizzo's performance." Then she woke the kids and told them to grab a granola bar for breakfast.

An hour later, clad in a new black suit, her hair and makeup perfect and her speech memorized, Jenny headed down the hill into town. Traffic snarled the streets of Belle River beyond anything she'd seen in all her years here. Jenny had a meeting soon with Griff and the Eastman family to review funeral arrangements, and what normally was a ten-minute drive was already taking twenty. She decided to park at the office and walk to Mem Church so she wouldn't have to fight the gridlock for that extra few blocks. After waiting nearly five minutes to make a left across traffic into the town garage, Jenny found an unknown car with out-of-town plates parked in her space, right under the big sign that said *Reserved for Mayor Healy*. That was the last straw. She whipped out her phone and dialed Owen Rizzo, who hadn't answered her calls for the past two days. She planned to leave an angry voicemail, but to her surprise, he picked up.

"Chief Rizzo. *Finally*," Jenny said.

"I see you forwarded an e-mail about parking problems to the entire town council," Rizzo said, indignation in his voice.

"Yes, I did. I just drove through the downtown, which is overrun, and there was not one single patrol car in sight. I need to know what you're doing about this situation."

"So talk to me about it. Don't go behind my back," Rizzo said.

"How can I talk to you when you won't return my phone calls?" Jenny said.

"I've been a little busy, as you may have noticed."

"Unfortunately, I *have* noticed. We need to talk about how you're handling Kate Eastman's death. I thought we had a good relationship, Chief. But you don't even call me when she's found. You unilaterally decide that this is a murder instead of a suicide, and you go to the press without consulting me. I'm beginning to have some serious doubts about your judgment," Jenny said, trying to keep her voice calm.

"Police matters are my department, Madam Mayor," Rizzo said.

"You may be chief, but I'm the mayor of this town, and you need to work with me, simple as that."

"Look, we had this discussion before when we had that ruckus over a simple staffing change. Ma'am, with all due respect, I need my independence, or I can't do my job. I run the department my way. Now, if you don't mind, I would like to ask you a few questions about Kate Eastman, given that you were a friend of hers."

"You have questions? Well, I have an answer. This was a suicide. Everybody who knows Kate thinks that. It was not a murder. Her husband didn't kill her. You're off on a frolic and detour, with no proof."

"I have proof. I have an expert report—"

"Right, I heard. How exactly did you pay for that, by the way?" Jenny demanded.

"Excuse me?"

"I'm asking, where did you get the money to pay for an outside expert?"

"I really can't brook this kind of interference," Rizzo said.

"From what I see, you're failing to look out for the well-being of this community, and that's my business. This case could've been handled privately to spare the family the pain. Instead you're off on some crusade, investigating some nonexistent crime, while the entire town is overrun by TV crews."

"Madam Mayor, I'll say it again. Managing the department is my job."

"Then manage it. Or we'll end up with some poor old lady getting run over, and you'll be out of a job. Now I have to go. I'm delivering Kate's eulogy."

Jenny hung up resolutely. Maybe she hadn't come right out and said it, but she'd hinted sufficiently to give Rizzo fair warning: If he didn't change his tune and start working with her instead of against her, she'd have him removed from office. As mayor, Jenny wasn't a dictator, but she wasn't a pushover either. She took care of business when the situation called for it. Speaking of—she got on the phone to the town's tow-truck concession and told them to boot that damn car and get it out of her parking space, ASAP.

Walking down Briggs Street, taking care not to slip on the ice in her high-heeled pumps, Jenny marveled at the size of the crowds. Cars were parked haphazardly on sidewalks, TV trucks blocked driveways, and reporters with recognizable faces did sound checks on the town green. Briggs Gate had been closed off by two Carlisle Safety and Security vans parked lengthwise across its expanse. One of the officers recognized Jenny and waved her through. The massive Gothic bulk of Mem Church sat just inside the gate, anchoring the west end of the Quad. Its grayish limestone façade was a drab contrast to the mellow brick buildings around it, and looked sober and gloomy against the fresh white snow. But you couldn't deny its majesty. From the tall stained-glass windows to the soaring steeple to the sweeping stone steps that fronted it, the church impressed. This was the place Carlisle reserved for its greatest dignitaries—Nobel laureates, presidents, literary lions, *Eastmans*. Jenny had to wonder if Keniston regretted the decision to hold Kate's funeral here. It was looking more like an ambush than an honor. Keniston must be wishing he'd chosen some obscure country graveyard for his daughter's funeral so he could mourn her in peace.

The massive wooden front doors were locked, so she went around to the side entrance, where another Carlisle safety officer stood guard. From there she took the elevator down to the basement, and walked down a long, echoing stone hallway to the suite of offices at the back, which smelled of burnt coffee and heating oil. When she walked into the conference room and caught sight of Keniston, Jenny struggled to keep the dismay from showing in her face. He sat hunched in a wheelchair, frail and shrunken, a yellow cast to his skin, his son Benji on one side of him, and Griff on the other. Keniston had aged almost beyond recognition in the year and a half since she'd seen him at Victoria's funeral. Griff looked awful, too—pale as death, with a day's growth of beard and dark circles under his eyes. Jenny knew Griff intended to be at the funeral, but with the press accusing him of murdering his wife, she'd wondered if he would change his mind. It took guts to show his face under the circumstances—and show it not only to the public, but to his wife's family. Keniston seemed to be treating Griff with grave civility. Maybe he'd decided that the best way to handle the negative press attention was to present a united front?

Jenny went to Keniston and leaned down for an awkward half hug. "I'm so sorry for your loss," she whispered.

Then she made her way around the table, hugging Griff and Benji, and shaking hands with the Right Reverend Maurice Jeffries, Carlisle's chaplain, who would be conducting the service. They spent a somber fifteen minutes reviewing the order of the proceedings. When that business was concluded, Keniston asked for a moment alone with Jenny. The others left the room, though Jenny wished she could beg them to stay. She'd been dreading this conversation for days.

"I know what you're going to say," Jenny said, before Keniston could speak. "Let me say it for you. I'm beside myself at the press coverage, Keniston. I've tried to control it, but the chief of police is new and he's an outsider. He doesn't understand the town, or the college. I believe he's responsible for the leaks to the media, and I swear to you, I'm trying to rein him in."

"You think I'm upset about the *press coverage*?" Keniston said, his craggy eyebrows drawing together. His voice might be weak with age and illness, but to Jenny, he was as intimidating as ever.

"I thought so. *I* am," she said.

"At my age, you stop worrying about how things look," Keniston said, "and focus on what really matters. I'm upset that my daughter is dead, and my son-in-law is accused of *murdering* her. That's what I care about."

"Of course," Jenny said. "I never meant to suggest otherwise. I just thought, since you wanted to speak to me alone—"

"That I planned to scold you."

"Yes."

"And I do. But not about the press coverage. What kind of police department are you running here, that they go after an innocent man who's grieving the loss of his wife?"

"I'm not running it. I told you, it's this police chief." She paused, letting his words sink in. "Are you saying you don't believe Griff killed Kate?"

"Never. Griffin Rothenberg would not harm a hair on Kate's head. That boy saved her life a million times over. He's a saint. I was angry with Griff's father, and I let that come between us for a while, but no longer. I have complete faith in him, and I plan to stand by him through this mess."

"Oh, I agree with you," Jenny said. "And yet—" Jenny paused, not sure she liked the repercussions for her if Griff was innocent—if the focus of the press, and the police, shifted away from him.

"Speak up," Keniston said.

"I'm not saying Griff is guilty. But there is evidence. Kate filed for divorce and disappeared. There's blood all over Griff's shirt, and Griff's skin is under Kate's fingernails. She just came into some money—well, you know about that."

"Griff has perfectly good explanations for all of these things. I'm hiring a private detective to work on backing up Griff's side of the story. What I care about is having my son-in-law left alone and my daughter buried in peace. That's where you could do a better job, Jenny. Control the press. Call off the police. Put this nightmare to bed."

"I'll try my best, I promise," she said, nodding.

Keniston looked at his watch. It was nearly time for the funeral to begin.

"Let's get on with it, shall we," he said, as if he was gaveling a business meeting to order rather than going to his daughter's funeral.

By the time they were seated on the dais, the church was full, and a frenzied buzz of conversation echoed back from the vaulted ceiling. There must be over a thousand people here. Who *were* they? Strangers and pretenders, mostly, along with Eastman friends and relatives, rubberneckers from the town who'd never met Kate, and a load of Carlisle faculty. The press was cordoned off in the north transept, away from the main action, but constantly threatening to swamp the velvet ropes. As the organist began to play the Chopin funeral march and the sonorous notes rose high into the air, the congregation turned as one toward the door. Kate's coffin was rich mahogany with polished brass fittings, piled high with white lilies, and borne by eight somber, dark-suited pallbearers. The three

Eastman boys, four men whom Jenny didn't recognize, and at the front right, Griff, with tears shining in his eyes. The flashbulbs sputtered like mad as the photographers went wild trying to get his picture. She could imagine the headlines: "Killer Husband Fakes Tears!"

Once the coffin had been placed before the dais, Griff took his seat beside Keniston as the chief mourner, and the chaplain rose to begin the service. The service lasted a very long time, and when finally it was Jenny's turn, she walked to the podium feeling drained and emotionally depleted. She clutched her notes, but she couldn't remember a word of her prepared speech, and the print on the page swam before her eyes. After a long, terrible pause, Jenny cast the notes aside and spoke from her heart. Her love for her friend came pouring out of her. Open on Kate, holding her father's hand at her dying mother's bedside. Then Kate with her bright hair on the wide green lawn of the Quad on their first day at Carlisle. Kate, always the belle, whether in jeans and sneakers, or a miniskirt and stilettos. Kate studying but not studying, goofing off, partying yet still getting As because she was so damn smart. (She'd wasted her talents, but Jenny never said that.) Kate holding court at a long table in the Commons, eating that nasty pink yogurt she loved that wasn't even a real flavor, and talking about Freud so that even the dullest among them finally got it. Kate on her wedding day to Griff, full of hope. Kate, leading a life of glamour and luxury. Kate this past summer, returning to Belle River to start over after misfortune struck, in the bosom of old friends, holding her head up. Kate, taken from her loved ones much too soon. But take comfort, for she was at peace now, resting in the arms of God.

Tears rolled down Jenny's cheeks, and there wasn't a dry eye in the house. Jenny believed every word as she said it, even though she was simultaneously conscious of the flip side—the negative, the tragic, the ugly. But you didn't speak ill of the dead, and after years in politics, Jenny believed in giving the audience what they wanted. A funeral was no place for the bitter truth. They would say a proper good-bye and pray for Kate at the hour of her death. Scandal would have to wait.

But it didn't wait long. Griff and the other pallbearers got up to carry Kate's coffin to the hearse outside, leaving Jenny to wheel Keniston down the handicapped-accessible ramp. They were only a minute behind the others. But by the time they got outside, the coffin was in the hearse, and Griff was spread-eagled against a police cruiser while Owen Rizzo slapped the cuffs on in full view of the national press.

31

The cell was cold and grimy. It reminded Griff of that godawful house on Faculty Row. That place was a pigsty and depressing as hell, with old steam radiators that rattled and spit, and drafty windows that leaked frigid air on cold nights. For a while Griff had tried to maintain the place, but it was a losing battle. Every time he did something, Kate undid it. She didn't understand the basics of taking care of a house, or taking care of herself for that matter. He couldn't blame her. She'd had help all her life. First in New York with her family, and then with him. Kate's favorite thing of all was living in hotels, which they did for months on end. She liked her sheets ironed, and changed every day, her crumpled towels whisked away, fresh flowers, a chocolate on the pillow. In the best places, the staff tiptoed in when you were down at the pool, and you never saw them. She didn't want to have to tell someone what to do; she just wanted it done. Room service at odd hours, breakfast on the terrace in her bathrobe with dark glasses on to block the tropical sun, aspirin from the gift shop for her hangover—that's the life Kate was used to. Griff could hardly blame her if, when all that disappeared, Kate had difficulty learning to cook or clean or do laundry. Kate was a New Yorker. She didn't like to drive, so if there was no deli on the corner, if nobody delivered, how could she be expected to buy groceries?

Griff did all the shopping, and when he did, he noticed things. He knew Kate was pregnant, because he knew when she got her period. He knew whether there were tampons in the drawer, because he made the drugstore runs. He noticed the puffiness in her face, and her breasts, and the flush that came to her cheeks. He knew she wanted this baby, because she changed what she ate, and cut back how much she drank. He knew what those special vitamins were for. She didn't have to say. He also knew that the child wasn't his, because she'd never agreed to get pregnant even though he'd begged her, and because they hadn't had sex in a year. He knew that Kate didn't want his baby, but that she wanted this one. And Griff knew whose it was, because he'd been watching that little romance from the beginning.

Ethan Saxman was Aubrey's husband, so Griff and Kate had met him on several occasions before moving back to town. But mostly, they'd kept their distance from the Belle River crowd. Kate hated the place. It reminded her too much of that unfortunate business at the bridge, and as much as Belle River itself reminded her, her freshman-year roommates reminded her even more. Kate had only seen her ex-roommates for the occasional weekend or birthday or holiday here and there over the years, and even that was at their instigation. If Aubrey and Jenny hadn't pursued Kate, the connection would have been lost. Griff himself was in close communication with old chums from his frat, as well as a number of other Carlisle men from his graduating class. He liked having a history with people. Kate didn't. It made her feel too exposed. He understood that. He accepted her idiosyncrasies.

When they moved back to Belle River—under a cloud of suspicion, in dire straits financially, in need of friends—Ethan Saxman was the shiny new toy that distracted Kate from her troubles. They saw him again for the first time in several years in some mediocre restaurant when the three couples met for dinner early in the summer. The tables were too close together; it was hot and noisy and unpleasant. Ethan stood up and moved his chair to make room for Kate at the table. Griff watched the whole thing happen. She looked at him, he smiled at her—done. The look in Kate's eyes, the timbre of her voice as they talked to each other. Ethan was tall and dark, with those thick, girlish lips, like Lucas Arsenault had. Kate went for that sort of thing—tall, dark, and obvious, with an ostentatious sex appeal. Griff was not as tall, he was blond, his looks were more refined. Women still followed him with their eyes when he walked into a room. *Women* did; not Kate. You'd think physical appearance wouldn't matter after a lifetime of devotion, but people were shallow. Kate was the shallowest of all.

Griff followed the details of the affair like he was hate-watching some awful, addictive TV show. Kate refused to learn about technology or be bothered paying bills, so their various accounts were set up and handled by Griff. They shared an Apple account, which meant that he could set her texts to show up on his iPhone and she didn't even realize it. They shared an Uber account, so he could see where the cars took her. And they shared their one remaining credit card, so he saw every charge she made. No need to pay for a private detective when he could follow her with the swipe of a fingertip. He knew which hotel Kate frequented with her lover. A *motel* really, a seedy place called the Pinetree Inn, out on Route 17 in Mill Junction where they hoped to escape prying eyes from Belle River. Kate was kind enough to leave Griff the car on these occasions. This was because the first time she stayed out all night with her new beau, Griff had been hesitant to confront her directly, so he threw a fit about being stranded with no ride. Kate took that to heart, and never made that mistake again, which meant Griff had the BMW to drive out to Mill Junction and spy on them. Half the time they didn't bother closing the blinds. Griff saw them together. He saw what they did.

Griff recently realized, from reading Kate's texts, that she was pressuring Ethan to leave his wife. He couldn't tell if she'd told Ethan yet that she was pregnant. (Indeed, Griff had no official confirmation that Kate actually was pregnant, beyond his own observations. She certainly hadn't talked to him about it.) The fact that Ethan had three children with another woman meant nothing to Kate, for whom other people's needs didn't register. The interesting thing was that Ethan was not on board with Kate's plan. In his texts, Ethan seemed to be hesitating, backing off, even hinting at ending things. And it might have gone that way, had Griff not intervened and snatched defeat from the jaws of victory.

Sitting in the cold jail cell, Griff had plenty of time to relive the confrontation in all its awfulness. It was last Thursday night around nine o'clock, cold and windy with a chance of rain. Griff sat drinking in the gloomy kitchen, wondering if Kate was coming home. The clock on the wall ticked loudly, and the bottle of vodka was almost empty. Griff was just about to get up and raid the pantry for another bottle when his phone buzzed with the duplicate of Kate's text to Ethan Saxman.

"I decided to file," Kate wrote. "I know you said not to but I have to. I want to explain so meet me at Pinetree ASAP."

Then nothing.

Five minutes later, Kate texted her lover again. "Babe r u coming? Please answer. So important."

Poor Kate was feeling insecure. Had Saxman ditched her already? Aww, how sad. Griff took a swig straight from the bottle and waited, but his stomach felt funny. One word in her text had leaped out, and it troubled him. *File*. What did she mean, *file*?

"Can't get away tonight. Don't do anything until we talk," Ethan replied, several minutes later.

"No, too important," Kate texted back almost instantly. "Have to tell you something big. You'll understand once you know."

"I can meet tomorrow but don't do anything yet," Saxman texted back.

Don't do *what*? What the hell were they talking about?

"Lawyer says I need to file in the morning bc $. At Pinetree now pls come!!" Kate wrote.

Understanding broke over Griff like a tidal wave. "File" meant file for divorce. Kate was about to reveal to her lover that she was pregnant with his child, and planned to file for divorce from Griff the next morning. Kate wasn't simply having another in a long string of affairs. She was leaving Griff—correction, *divorcing* him, on a timeline designed to deprive him of his fair share of her trust fund money. Griff and Kate had been talking for months about what to do with that money when it came in, which would be on the day of her fortieth birthday. He had a plan for a fresh start for them, both of them, together, far away from the pernicious influence of Ethan Saxman. In the Keys, or maybe the Virgin Islands, captaining a little boat, booking fishing charters. He could earn their keep, he was confident of that. Griff was excited about the plan but Kate refused to commit to it. Maybe, let's wait and see, she'd say. That had obviously been a lie, a stall, a scam. She never had any intention of going away with him. She was stringing him along while she made other plans. Griff lavished years of his life and millions of his father's fortune on Kate, and this was how she repaid him.

Griff hoisted the vodka bottle and discovered that it was empty. The car keys sat in the middle of the table where Kate had left them. His next step unfolded with perfect logic. There was no thought process involved. He simply picked up the keys and walked out the front door. He didn't even stop to get his wallet.

He didn't remember driving to the motel, but sometime later, Griff was there, parked in his usual spot. He liked to hide at the far side of the lot, next to the Dumpster, beyond where the streetlights reached, and watch without being seen. The Pinetree Inn was the sort of single-story, low-rise dump where the rooms opened directly onto the parking lot. Each room had a different-colored door. About half of the spaces were taken tonight, but nobody had gone in or out recently. Saxman's car was parked in front of the cheerful yellow door to room 21. The blinds were closed, so Griff used his imagination to visualize what they were doing in there.

Time moved very slowly, as drunk as he was. Half an hour passed as Griff pondered whether to get out of the car. Why was he here, if not to barge in and win his wife back? He ought to stop stalling. But if Griff went over there, would Kate agree to come home with him, or would she hold to Saxman tighter, out of some rebellious sense of pride? He might be sending her further into Saxman's arms.

Eventually nature called. The cold air woke Griff up as soon as he opened the car door. He stepped behind the Dumpster to take a piss, and while he was back there, he made a decision. He zipped up and hurried back around the Dumpster, then marched across the blacktop, heading for room 21, to take his wife back from that asshole Saxman.

At the yellow door, Griff paused. Ethan was speaking—rapidly, urgently, roughly. Griff couldn't make out the words, but the tone alone was enough to piss him off. How dare that creep Saxman speak to Kate that way? Griff raised his fist and pounded on the door.

"Who is it?" Ethan said, in an annoyed tone.

"Manager," Griff said, putting on some vague foreign accent. "We had noise complaint. Open door, or I call the police."

Saxman opened the door. As he caught sight of Griff, his expression morphed from irritation to shock. He moved to slam the door a second too late. Griff threw his weight against it, and they went tumbling into the room in a tangle of limbs. Kate screamed. Griff leapt to his feet, kicking away Saxman's grasping hands, and started toward her.

"Did he hurt you?" Griff cried.

"Did you follow me, Griff?" Kate demanded. She sat on the bed fully clothed, her face red from crying, which only incensed Griff further.

"Did *I* hurt her? You're the lunatic causing a scene," Ethan said, as he got to his feet, his face flushed with anger.

"Stay out of this! Kate is my wife, and she's coming home with me right now," Griff said.

"No, I'm not," Kate said.

"Yes, you are."

Griff grabbed Kate's arms and yanked her to her feet, dragging her toward the door. She dug her heels into the ugly carpet.

"Let . . . go . . . you crazy stalker!" she cried, twisting from his grasp, flailing at him.

Griff felt the sting as Kate's fingernails gouged his arms and his hands. Saxman grabbed Griff by the back of his shirt, and pulled him off Kate, shoving him across the room. Griff's head cracked against the wall. He fell sideways and crashed into a lamp, which toppled over beside him, its lightbulb exploding in a blue flash. Griff staggered to his feet, breathing heavily, just in time to see Saxman rushing him. They grappled, in a clinch, neither of them able to land a punch. Saxman was taller and had a longer reach, but Griff was heavier and stronger. Griff mustered the strength to push the guy off him. Ethan staggered backward, recovered instantly, and came back at Griff. Griff threw a poorly aimed punch that glanced off the side of Saxman's face. Saxman swung at Griff hard and connected with his jaw. Momentarily stunned, Griff took a step back and put a hand to his lip. It came away bright red.

"*Get out now*," Kate said, her voice thick with rage. "If you don't leave right this minute, I swear to God, I'll get a restraining order."

She looked at him with such disgust that it took his breath away. The manager stood in the open doorway. He was a Sikh man in a turban, tall and dignified, and informed them gravely that the police were on the way.

Griff stared at the blood on his fingers. He knew he was blind drunk and reeked of alcohol. He was the one who forced his way into the room. With Griff's luck, when the cops showed up, he'd probably be the one they arrested, no matter how unfair that was.

"You'll regret this," he said bitterly, though he didn't know if he was speaking to Kate or her lover. All he knew was, he'd made it more likely Kate would leave him for Saxman, not less.

Griff forgot that he had the car. Next thing he remembered, he was running down the road, blind with rage and pain. He wound up in a bar, where they refused to serve him, and called a taxi for him instead. He went home and stripped, stuffing his shirt into the laundry hamper. He noticed the blood on it, but he didn't think twice about it. Ethan was the one who slugged him, so why would he worry? Griff fell into bed and passed out. He never imagined that shirt would be seized by the police and become the centerpiece of a murder case against him. But then, he never thought any of this would come to pass—Kate dead, him sitting in a jail cell charged with her murder.

Griff heard the clanging of metal doors.

"Rothenberg," the guard said, unlocking Griff's cell. "Lawyer here to see you. Let's go."

Griff was escorted to a small, windowless interview room. He recognized the man who waited for him, because he was famous. Leonard Walters, an aggressive New York criminal lawyer with a national profile, a shock of white hair that set off his perpetual tan, and a fondness for trying cases in the press.

"Mr. Rothenberg, good to meet you," Walters said. "I'm here to represent you at your father-in-law's behest. No need to go through the formalities about retainer and such. He took care of all that."

"I'm very grateful," Griff said. "Keniston knows I would never hurt his daughter. I loved Kate—"

Walters held up a hand. "Let's skip that and cut to the chase. It doesn't matter how you felt or even what you did. What matters is what the police can prove, and how effectively we can undermine their case against you."

"I want you to know, I'm innocent."

"Glad to hear it. If you're guilty that's fine, too. Everybody deserves a defense. Only I'd advise you not to confess to me, because that makes my job harder, avoiding perjury and so forth." Walters glanced at the gold Rolex on his wrist. "No time to waste. Here's my plan."

As Walters explained it, he intended to demolish the case against Griff by painting Chief Rizzo in the media as a trigger-happy rube who'd missed important pieces of evidence and manipulated others. Griff would come off as the martyr—a falsely accused, grief-stricken husband, dragged from the graveside of his beloved wife by an overzealous cop. It was a think-outside-the-box approach, and Griff liked it. They spent the rest of the visit going over the details of Kate's affair, and the confrontation at the motel, so Walters's investigator could start collecting evidence to back up Griff's version of events.

"The blood on the shirt that this cop made such a stink about, you're saying that's your own blood? From when your wife's boyfriend slugged you?" Walters asked, scribbling notes.

"Yes."

"Oh, that's good, that's *very* good. And you left your wife alive, in the love nest with the other man?"

"At the motel, yes."

"I love it. She's pressuring him to leave his wife and kids. He doesn't want to do it. And *he's* the last one who saw her alive, not you."

"And that's not all. I don't know if this helps or hurts us, but you should know. It's my belief that Kate was pregnant with Saxman's baby."

Walters raised his eyebrows. "Really."

"Yes. Now I have no proof of that. She never told me directly. But I lived in the same house as her, and I'm fairly certain."

"A rich doctor with a wife and three kids at home. A pregnant mistress who's starting to make demands. It's classic. One thing, though. This was Thursday night, you say?"

"Uh-huh."

Walters paused, a thoughtful look on his face. "But she filed for divorce Friday morning."

"Yes."

"So presumably she got out of the motel in one piece and made it to the courthouse. That's a wrinkle, but we can finesse it."

"A wrinkle in what? Where are you going with this?"

"The fastest way to convince the world you're innocent is to make somebody else look guilty," Walters said. "This doctor is gonna be our alternative suspect. We hold a press conference, and divert attention onto him."

Griff frowned. "But what if *he's* innocent?"

"What do you care? He screwed your wife, punched you in the face so you bled all over your shirt, made you look guilty when you're not, and now you're rotting in a jail cell and he's walking around free. This is your chance to fight back, my friend."

"It would serve him right," Griff said.

"There you go, that's the attitude."

"Is my father-in-law on board with this plan? He says he wants to end the media circus, and this strategy will only make the story bigger."

"Keniston hired me to clear your name, and I have to do that the best way I know how. The press'll fall all over themselves crucifying this other guy. Trust me, it's the way to go."

Griff nodded. "All right, I'm in."

"This will take a few days to pull together. I'm going to agree to postpone your bail hearing so you don't have to go to court. It's more important to negotiate with the prosecutor and persuade her not to file charges. But you'll have to spend a few nights in jail."

"It's worth it if it means I don't get charged with murdering my wife."

Walters smiled reassuringly. "That's the plan, my friend, and I think we can pull it off."

They shook hands, and Griff was escorted back to his cell. He felt euphoric for a good five minutes or so after the meeting ended at the thought of getting out of jail, and of taking that smug asshole Owen Rizzo down a notch. He was elated, as well, that his father-in-law believed in him enough to pay the freight for someone like Leonard Walters. But then Griff remembered that Kate was dead, and the good feeling began to fade. He thought about the fact that Kate's body had been lowered into the cold, hard ground without him there to say a last good-bye. She was under there now, as she would always be, with six feet of dirt between them. Griff lay down on his bunk and stared at the ceiling, too miserable to move.

32

Keisha barged into Owen's office and told him to pull up CNN on his computer.

"Is it about the kid?" he asked.

The lead story on the front page of the *Register* had Owen's stomach in knots. The star forward of the high school soccer team had been clipped by a TV truck yesterday. The kid would be fine, but he had a fractured tibia and would be out for the season, just as the playoffs were starting.

"No, it's about Rothenberg, about the murder. You need to see this," Keisha said.

Owen went to CNN, turning the monitor so Keisha could see. They were livestreaming a press conference straight from the steps of the Belle County Courthouse. Leonard Walters, the big-shot lawyer from New York, was speaking to the press about the Rothenberg case.

"I know that guy," Rizzo said. "He represented the kingpin on my biggest drug cartel case. What's he doing in *this* town?"

"You're not gonna like it, Chief."

Leonard Walters sported the standard lawyer's winter uniform of dark wool overcoat with a sober gray scarf tucked under the collar. It made an impressive contrast to his snow-white hair as he spoke into a bank of microphones.

They had come into it in midsentence.

"—pregnant with another man's child. Ask Chief Rizzo whether the autopsy found evidence of that! What are the police hiding? Naturally when Mr. Rothenberg found out about his wife's affair, he became extremely angry, but he did not take his anger out on his defenseless, pregnant wife. No, he went after her seducer, a married man, a father of three, a doctor at the hospital in this very town, by the name of Ethan Saxman. The two of them got into a fistfight at the Pinetree Inn on Thursday night. Mr. Rothenberg was merely defending his wife's honor. The gentleman standing beside me is the night manager at the Pinetree Inn, Mr. Rajit Singh. He was an eyewitness to that fight, and will speak to you momentarily to corroborate everything Mr. Rothenberg says. He'll tell you Mr. Rothenberg was bleeding from a cut on his lip—which explains the blood on his Brooks Brothers shirt. He'll also tell you that when Mr. Rothenberg left the premises, *Mrs.* Rothenberg was safe and sound, left alone in this other man's company. I discovered this evidence with one phone call. Why didn't Chief Rizzo find it? Or did he, and decided not to tell you because it's bad for his case? Ask the chief whether a DNA test was already conducted on the bloody shirt. It was, but he won't tell you the results, because they undermine his attempt to frame an innocent man."

Keisha grabbed the mouse and clicked pause. "Is that true, Chief? It's Rothenberg's own blood on the shirt?"

"So what? Killing someone is a violent business. Rothenberg could've hurt himself going after his wife."

"If you knew it was his blood and not hers, why didn't you tell me that?"

"It doesn't make him innocent."

"You've been saying she was pregnant, but did you know it was this other guy's baby?"

"We don't know that yet. The ME sent samples to the FBI lab for fetal DNA testing, but it takes weeks to get the results."

"What if it is, though?"

"Why is that a problem for the case? If Rothenberg's wife was pregnant by another man, his motive to kill her was even stronger."

"But you knew Dr. Saxman was in the picture, and you didn't say anything to anybody?"

"He shows up in her phone records, that's all I know," Rizzo said, with a defensive shrug.

"How much were they calling each other? Enough to know he wasn't treating her bunions?"

"Look, I haven't even gotten all the phone records I subpoenaed yet, all right? I didn't know anything specific. And what's your point, anyway?" Owen asked.

"My point is, there's another viable suspect here, one we should've been investigating all along."

"Keisha, do you know what the leading cause of death for pregnant women is in the United States? It's homicide by husbands and boyfriends. I kid you not. Go look it up."

"Yeah, but Saxman *was* her boyfriend, so why are you fixated on the husband? Hold on a second. *Saxman*. That name's ringing a bell."

"We interviewed his wife. He's married to the yoga teacher," Rizzo said.

"Not because of that. Wait here."

Keisha got up and ran out of the room.

"*Shit*," Owen muttered, and kicked his desk.

If he lost Keisha, if she went over to the other side and started working against him, that would make his life harder. But it wouldn't change Owen's mind. He was sorry to learn that Kate had become involved with this other man, but he wasn't surprised. Her marriage had been miserable. Owen remembered the rage in Rothenberg's face as he pounded on the plate-glass window the night of the storm. Rothenberg was the classic jealous husband, willing to murder his wife rather than let her go. He killed her, Owen knew it in his gut. If Keisha couldn't see it, he'd work the case on his own.

Keisha was back, with a pink message slip in her hand. "Chief, we had a call to the tip line yesterday on this Dr. Saxman. This is no coincidence."

"What does it say?"

"The caller was a female, chose to remain anonymous, and was using caller ID block," Keisha said, reading from the slip of paper. "She advised us to search a vehicle belonging to a Dr. Ethan Saxman, and we'd find evidence of the murder. She gave the make and plate number of the car. We've had hundreds of calls to the tip line, and haven't had time to follow this one up yet. Do you want me to get started working on a warrant?"

"You're accusing *me* of jumping to conclusions, yet you're ready to go after the doctor just because Rothenberg's lawyer says so. That tip could've been called in by Leonard Walters' secretary, for all we know."

"I'm simply suggesting that it's our job to investigate all leads," Keisha said, drawing herself up huffily.

"Maybe you haven't noticed, but with our limited resources, we don't have that luxury."

"Don't we owe it to the town to try?" Keisha asked.

"This town wouldn't know a murder investigation if it jumped up and bit it in the ass. We owe the victim justice. That's what we owe. The town has been nothing but an obstacle to achieving that. Did you know Rob Womack is passing information to the mayor behind my back?"

Keisha shook her head. "Last time I checked, Chief, the mayor was on our team."

"Come on, Keisha. Tell me you don't see it. These people are conspiring against me. They'd rather see me lose my job than catch her killer."

"Small towns are rough. You have to go that extra mile before people accept you. And no offense, Chief, but you've made some decisions that rubbed people the wrong way."

"They can't stomach an outsider telling them how to run things, that's the problem."

"Yeah, well you could make more of an effort to get along. I read the paper this morning. People are pissed about the traffic accident, and they're starting to question the investigation. Why not make a show of good faith? Tell them you're reassessing your case and looking at other suspects."

"My case is fine, thank you very much," Owen said, his mouth setting in a grim line.

The nerve of this kid, after he got her the job. Did she have some kind of problem with him? She'd complained about how he asked her to take the notes in the interviews. Was it that? He was only trying to train her. Kids these days, they wanted to run the show from day one, whether they were ready or not.

"What do you have to lose, Chief? Bring Rothenberg and his lawyer in for an interview. Ask them to provide us with a rundown on all the evidence that they claim exonerates him. Then we check it out and see if he's telling the truth. Meantime, I'll look into this doctor, and his relationship to the victim. I'll get a warrant on the car. I know it seems far-fetched, but it does happen sometimes that you get the wrong guy. Maybe we rushed to judgment on this one."

"Yeah? And what do you think happens if I'm wrong?"

"If we're wrong, we need to say so," she said.

"And then the mob screams for my head." Owen tossed the newspaper across the desk at her. "You saw this crap. I'm trying to run a murder investigation, and I'm getting second-guessed because of some goddamn soccer championship. That's what I'm dealing with here. I have to stand up to it. The second I show weakness, I'm done. And if I'm done, you'd better watch your back, because without me here to protect you, you're next."

Keisha shrugged, and it could have meant one of two things. A, justice must be served no matter the negative repercussions for our own careers. Or B, you're the one with the problem, not me, so why should I give a shit? Owen tended to think it was the latter. So much for loyalty, and this freaking job. All he wanted was to do right by Kate Eastman. If he cut a corner here or there, he did it in the interests of justice. But nobody seemed to appreciate that. If they didn't value his efforts, then maybe they didn't deserve his service. He wished he could go back to his old job, with real cases and real cops to work them, but it had been filled, and besides, he had to think of the kids. He had another option if things here became untenable. His cousin in Wisconsin was CFO of a big company that made the fluorescent lights that were used in department stores. They were looking for a new chief of security. It paid significantly more than Owen was making as chief of police, and his cousin had kids his own kids' age. Wisconsin was cold in the winter, but no colder than this hellhole.

The only thing holding him back from quitting was the desire to solve Kate's murder and put her smug psychopath of a husband in jail for good. Unfortunately, that was proving to be a harder task than he'd anticipated, and he was starting to think it might not happen. He was confident he could make the case against Rothenberg eventually, if given sufficient time and resources. But that was the problem. The resources were sadly lacking. And now, with the kid getting hit by the van, Owen felt the town turning against him, and his time running out. Maybe this case was destined to be his white whale. All the best cops had them, if they'd been on the job long enough. Those cases where you knew in your heart who did it, but for whatever reason, you couldn't prove it. The ones that got away, they haunted you forever. Would Kate turn out to be that for him?

33

The front doorbell rang around five o'clock, as Aubrey was putting away the groceries from Whole Foods. She had a load of laundry in the dryer. The kids were just home from sports, settling into homework. Ethan was back early from the hospital, as he'd been every night since Kate died. He was upstairs now, crying in the shower.

Lilly, sitting at the kitchen island with her algebra book, looked up in surprise at the sound of the bell. "Who's *that*?"

In Belle River, only strangers used the front door. Family, friends, and neighbors came in through the mudroom or the garage, shouting hello without bothering to knock. This must be something official. Aubrey hoped it was the event she'd been waiting for. She felt excited and sick at the same time, like at the cabin, when Logan learned the truth about his dad. Nothing wrong with seeing a person for who they really are. But it was still hard, watching your kids grow up and face the harsh reality.

"I don't know, honey," Aubrey said. "Why don't you go see?"

Lilly came back a moment later, her face white with worry. "It's a lady from the police. What should we do?"

"Well, if she's from the police, we'd better let her in," Aubrey said.

And so the final piece of the puzzle fell into place. Aubrey had been waiting for this moment for a very long time. Ethan's comeuppance. She never thought she could pull it off, but she did. She shouldn't have doubted herself. She wasn't the naïve fool they took her for. She was a magna cum laude graduate of Carlisle (would've been a summa if not for freshman spring) whose perseverance had paid off.

After she found out about Ethan and Kate, Aubrey spent months paralyzed with grief and rage. She'd lie awake at night, sometimes with Ethan beside her, sometimes alone, thinking about the two of them together, and wishing them dead. No matter where she was or what she was doing during the day—teaching a yoga class, chatting with the other moms as she waited for Logan to finish soccer practice, making lentil soup, braiding Viv's hair—in the back of her mind, Aubrey was fantasizing about killing her husband and his mistress (she no longer thought of Kate by her name). Their deaths were always grisly and painful, whether she did it with a gun or a knife, or poison, or ran them down with a car. She visualized the looks on their faces in the moment they realized they were going to die. She played over and over in her head the words she would say to make them understand that she had won and they had lost. It was all she thought about.

Aubrey thought constantly about killing them, but she didn't act, because she was afraid of getting caught. Not on her own account, but for her kids. She couldn't leave her children alone in the world, with the double stigma of a dead cheater father and a mother who was a murderer. People would talk behind their backs. There would be no more playdates, no more birthday-party invitations, no mom who earned brownie points by serving as room parent or chairing the middle school dance committee. Aubrey had grown up without any of those things, and she knew how much it hurt. She wouldn't do that to her kids. Leave them to be raised by Ethan's snooty parents, who would badmouth Aubrey and turn them against her? Never. The punishment for Kate and Ethan had to look like an accident, so Aubrey could escape unscathed and live happily ever after with her children (and, if things went how she hoped, with Griff, who would make a caring stepdad).

But an accident seemed so complicated to arrange. Aubrey thought about it for hours on end and got nowhere. She was not technically inclined. The CSI stuff was sure to trip her up. Any plan she devised would end up overlooking some key detail—fibers or hairs or a computer search on how to dismember a body that she forgot to erase. Eventually she decided that her best option was to get somebody else to do the dirty work. If Aubrey didn't actually commit the murder herself, they couldn't trace it back to her. But she was a housewife, a mother and a yoga instructor, not a hardened criminal. She didn't know how to hire a hit man. You couldn't just go advertising on Craigslist, could you? It seemed like too big a risk, so she did nothing, except to obsess and get increasingly mad at herself.

One night, after the kids were in bed, when Ethan was out, and Aubrey was drinking tea and feeling alone, she took a frayed copy of the *Tao Te Ching* that she'd owned since grad school down from the shelf in the living room. The book fell open to a chapter she'd read many times, though not in years. It was a chapter on self-control and self-mastery, and challenged the reader to think about the following question: *Can you remain unmoving until the right action arises on its own?* That was it, Aubrey realized: the question was the answer. Aubrey needed to wait, to stay positive, and trust herself, and the solution would eventually become clear.

And so it did. On a chill, rainy Wednesday afternoon, a couple of days before Kate met her end in the Belle River, Aubrey happened to see Tim Healy duck into Shecky's Burger Shack. Something furtive in Tim's manner caught her eye. Shecky's was such a Carlisle hangout that an image popped into her mind of Tim carrying on with some college babe. She dismissed it out of hand. The idea of Tim Healy with some nineteen-year-old was ludicrous. He'd always struck her as loyal as a dog. But then she thought, hmm, you never know. And if it was true, well, wouldn't that serve Jenny right.

Ever since Aubrey learned that Jenny had kept silent about the affair, she'd been rethinking their friendship. Years earlier, when Jenny moved back to Belle River from New York, Aubrey welcomed her with open arms. Aubrey was a young mother, a doctor's wife, making her life in Belle River. Jenny had grown up and gone to college in town, but she'd never been an adult there. From the beginning, Aubrey invited Jenny to everything—dinner parties, yoga class, the annual benefit at the hospital. Once Jenny and Tim got married and started a family, Aubrey invited Jenny to join her playgroup, her babysitting co-op, her girls'-night-out group, and recommended her to the director of the top preschool in town, which resulted in T.J. getting accepted in a very competitive admissions climate (and Reed, too, since siblings got in automatically).

Aubrey wouldn't say Jenny was ungrateful for her help, exactly. But neither did Jenny acknowledge that Aubrey was now her equal. Jenny had looked down on Aubrey since the day they met, in Whipple twenty years earlier, when Aubrey walked in with her ratty clothes, her enthusiasm, and her naïveté, and smacked into the wall of Jenny's condescension. Aubrey had come a million miles since freshman year. She'd done coursework toward her master's (though admittedly never finished), married a doctor, bought a big house, started a successful yoga studio whose clients worshipped the ground she walked on, and had three amazing children. But as far as Jenny was concerned, nothing had changed. It took that awful Labor Day party to show Aubrey where she really stood with Jenny. The fact was, Jenny still looked down on her, still took their friendship for granted, and would trample on Aubrey's happiness in order to preserve her own.

If Tim Healy was doing something nefarious, Aubrey wanted to know. Tim hadn't spotted her. Aubrey waited for a couple of minutes before following him in, so it would look like a coincidence.

The inside of Shecky's hadn't changed in decades. It still had the long counter with the stools that turned, and the stainless-steel backsplash with the pies rotating in glass cases. The smell of the place—a combination of overly sweet pie, burnt grease, and undergraduate sweat—never failed to bring back memories of freshman year, when she'd spent so much time here. The all-nighters before exams, the plates of home fries after a frat party to ward off a hangover. And of course, the day that Lucas Arsenault died. None of them had come to Shecky's much after that.

The place was packed at three o'clock on a Wednesday afternoon with Carlisle kids laughing it up. *Go ahead, be happy while it lasts, you'll learn the hard way,* she thought. Tim sat at the counter, next to a girl in skinny jeans with a long ponytail who was giggling and sipping a soda. As Aubrey watched, the waitress placed two vanilla milkshakes on the counter in front of them. Well, well. Tim Healy, buying a young girl a milkshake, who'd've thought. Men were beasts.

The stool on Tim's other side was empty. Aubrey slipped into it.

"Hey, Tim. Fancy meeting you here," she said.

"Aubrey. Hi."

She wished she had her phone out to capture the look on his face. He literally blushed. Caught in the act for sure.

"Is this your friend?" she asked, nodding toward Miss Ponytail.

Tim looked confused. "What?"

Aubrey realized that the girl with the ponytail was actually talking to the guy on her other side, who looked about eighteen and wore a Carlisle Rugby T-shirt.

"Um, I was wondering why you have two milkshakes," Aubrey said.

"It's something I like to do on Lucas's birthday," he said sheepishly. "Years ago, when I used to work here, before I had a car of my own, Lucas would pick me up at the end of my shift and give me a ride home. I'd always spot him a vanilla milkshake for the trouble. It was kind of a ritual for us. So every year on his birthday, I order two and I drink one. The other is for his memory."

"Today is your cousin Lucas's birthday?" she asked.

"He would've been forty," Tim said. "I can't wrap my head around that. To me, he's forever young, like the day he died. It was right here, you know, right at this counter that I talked to him last. From what I remember, anyway. I miss him every day."

Tim stared across at his reflection in the backsplash, and Aubrey had the distinct impression that he was visualizing Lucas sitting beside him. And there it was, the moment of insight she'd been waiting for: Tim Healy was hung up on his dead cousin. He'd never recovered from Lucas's death. The night at the bridge was real to him still, always playing in the background the way Ethan and Kate's affair did for her. Aubrey realized in that moment that Tim wanted Kate dead as much as she did. Or, if he didn't, it was only because he didn't know the truth about Lucas's death, and she could fix that. Tim was the sort of person who might actually do something about it, too. He had anger-management issues. Jenny blamed it on the severe concussion he'd suffered years ago trying to save Lucas's life, and swore he was gentle as a lamb with her and the boys. That was probably a lie. There had been rumors of incidents over the years—a fistfight on a jobsite, a confrontation over a parking space at the Walmart outside town where a security guard had to intervene. Tim had actually been ordered to court-mandated counseling over that one. The anger was there. All Aubrey had to do was figure out how to channel it, and maybe she could finally get her revenge without taking the risk.

She glanced around the crowded room. The place was jammed to the gills, the volume deafening. Nobody would overhear what she was about to say. She leaned toward Tim.

"I remember Lucas, too. How could I forget? I was there that night. I witnessed his death. I've always felt that justice was never done."

Tim's eyes flew to her face. "What do you mean?" he asked, and she saw him hold his breath as he waited for her to answer. She had him now.

"Hasn't Jenny told you the truth?" Aubrey asked innocently, remembering very well Jenny's confession that she hadn't.

"The *truth*?"

She lowered her voice an octave. "Didn't she tell you that Kate pushed Lucas off the bridge? That we both saw it, and lied about it to the police because Mr. Eastman pressured us to?"

"*No.*" He went limp, leaning heavily against the counter. "That's what I always suspected, but Jenny swore he jumped. So did you, Aubrey. You're telling me you've both been lying all these years?"

She touched his arm. "Oh, Tim, I'm sorry. I never would've said anything, except I thought you knew. You were standing right next to me that night. You saw everything."

"The concussion wiped out my memory. You knew that."

"Somehow I thought you got it back."

"No. I can't remember a thing after Jenny and I left the parking lot. It's like the rest of that night never happened."

"And your wife didn't set you straight? But what am I saying, Jenny's not the bad guy here. *Kate* is. Don't get me started on Kate Eastman."

"What did she do, Aubrey? Please, I'm begging you. Tell me," he said.

"Well, to put it plainly, when Lucas tried to break up with her, she pushed him off the bridge," Aubrey said.

"I knew it. I always knew in my heart that it was her. That *bitch*," Tim said, then caught himself. "I'm sorry."

"Don't apologize. You have a right to be angry. If Lucas was my cousin, I swear, I'd kill Kate for what she did."

"Tell me exactly how it happened," Tim said, clenching and unclenching his fists. The rage gathering on his face was just what she hoped for.

"Lucas told Kate it was over, and she started screaming like a banshee, and pounding him with her fists. He was walking backwards to get away from her, and she pushed him right through that gap in the bridge. Trust me, it was no accident. She knew the hole was there. Jenny and I were in complete shock. I think that must be why, when Mr. Eastman showed up, he could manipulate us so easily. We were both traumatized. I still am, to this day. I bet Jenny is, too, and that's why she could never bring herself to talk to you about it. But Kate? Didn't bat an eyelash. I've never once heard her say she's sorry. You'd think she'd feel at least a little guilty. But no. She kills a man, and flies off to Europe like she doesn't have a care in the world. Life is sweet when Daddy's there to clean up the mess."

"It's so unfair," Tim said. "He's dead and she got away with it. Not only got away with it, but lived like a queen off Griff Rothenberg's money."

"Oh, Kate's living it up to this day on other people's money. Think about it. Living in Daddy's house. Never worked a day in her life. You should really confront her. Tell her you know what she did. How you feel about it. What you think of her. It won't bring Lucas back, but at least you'll be calling her on her bullshit. Somebody ought to."

"She'd never agree to it," Tim said. "Kate knows I hate her guts. She'd never sit down with me to discuss this."

Aubrey nodded. "I hear you. Kate is very good at avoiding unpleasantness. If you want, I could act as a go-between and see if I can arrange a meeting."

"You'd do that?" Tim asked.

"Yes, but on one condition. That you don't tell Jenny. I had no idea she never told you, or I wouldn't've opened my mouth. If you confront her now, she'll figure out it came from me, and that could ruin our friendship."

"All right, if you insist. I won't say anything to Jenny."

Lying awake that night thinking about logistics, Aubrey had a brainstorm. Her biggest worry was that Tim Healy didn't have the balls to commit actual murder. Aubrey could imagine a scenario where she got the two of them together, and they traded a few choice words and agreed never to cross each other's paths again. She wasn't going to all this trouble to arrange a polite spat. The idea was, get Tim worked up into such a rage that he actually killed Kate. That might require an extra push, a bit of stage management to trigger his temper. If Aubrey could arrange the meeting to happen at the old railroad bridge, the very place where his beloved cousin died, Tim would be primed for violence. Getting them to the bridge was key. If anybody found out she arranged the meeting, Aubrey would say she was trying to help two old friends work out their differences. Nobody would fault her for that.

On Thursday, Aubrey dialed Kate's cell repeatedly to try to set up the meeting, but got no answer. When Aubrey couldn't get Ethan on the phone either, and when he didn't come home for dinner Thursday night, she knew that the two of them were together doing their filthy business.

Aubrey fed the kids and cleaned up dinner. She kicked Ethan's nasty cat out of the house for the night. She watched *Friends* on Netflix with Lilly, and pretended to laugh whenever the laugh track came on. But by the time all three kids were in bed, Aubrey still hadn't heard back. Was Kate going to avoid her forever, escape punishment by the simple expedient of not answering the phone? It was intolerable. Aubrey sat at the kitchen island and, instead of drinking her usual herbal tea before bed, polished off an entire bottle of sauvignon blanc. *See what you're doing to me*, she thought, *drinking alone, which I never do!* They were ruining her life. Around two o'clock, the bottle empty, Aubrey dialed Kate's phone one last time, and got voicemail. But this time, she left a message.

"I can't believe you won't pick up my calls," she said, through wine-sodden tears. "I always loved you, Kate. You were my idol. I know you're sleeping with my husband. You're probably with him right now. You never cared about me, or my kids. We're nothing to you. You don't have the guts to face me, do you? You're a coward. I want to die," Aubrey said, and hung up.

She threw the phone down on the counter, certain she'd just torpedoed her own brilliant plan. Kate would never call back now. She poured the dregs of the bottle into her glass and let the tears flow. It was three before she dragged herself to bed.

At 7 A.M., the jangle of a ring tone pulled her to consciousness. She grabbed her phone from the bedside table and was shocked to see Kate's number. Wouldn't you know it, that self-pitying message did the trick. Kate loved Aubrey when she was down.

"Hello?"

"It's Kate."

Aubrey looked at the clock. She was half an hour late getting up, her head was throbbing, and her eyes burned. "It's seven in the morning," she muttered.

"I know, I just—I'm calling to say you don't need to worry. Ethan and I ended it. Just a little while ago. It's over, for real."

Aubrey remained silent, trying to breathe, the angry pounding of her own heart reverberating in her ears. If Kate thought she could fix things by admitting she'd spent the entire night with Aubrey's husband and then claiming they'd ended the months-long affair in the light of the morning, she was stupider than she looked. There was no fixing this. The betrayal was too big.

"Aubrey, are you there?" Kate asked.

"Yes."

"I know what I did was wrong, but you have to understand, I've been in a really weird place. Griff's dad going to jail turned my life upside down. I see now that my own unhappiness made me act selfishly. I need to take care of *me*—get out of Belle River, move on from Griff, find work I care about. If I can do that, I'll stop messing up, and stop hurting my friends. I'm sorry for what I did, Aubrey, I really am."

Aubrey remained silent. Kate paused. "Aubrey?"

"Now is not a good time to talk. We need to meet in person."

"What? Why?"

"So you can apologize to my face. You owe me that much," Aubrey said.

"I already said I'm sorry. Is that really necessary?"

"Yes, Kate, it *is* necessary. Let's meet tonight, before the dinner," Aubrey said.

"The dinner, right. Ugh, I may not go to that. Things with Griff have gotten really bad. He showed up—oh, you don't want to know. Anyway, I'm meeting my lawyer and filing for divorce this morning. There's some money that—well, that's beside the point. Anyway, I was thinking of leaving town for a couple of days, to give Griff a chance to clear out of the house. I'm not in the mood for celebrating."

"We plan a party for you, and arrange our schedules to be there, and you decide to ditch us at the last minute. Really, Kate?"

If Aubrey's plan worked, Kate would be dead by dinnertime, but Aubrey couldn't resist needling her.

"Won't it be awkward?" Kate said. "Given the circumstances, I mean."

"That's why I want to meet first, to clear the air. Just you and me, without Jenny," Aubrey said.

Kate sighed. "If that's what you want, fine. Tell me where."

"I'll text you the address for your GPS," Aubrey said. Kate was an idiot with directions, and followed her nav blindly. She would drive right to the boat-launch lot and still not have a clue where she was.

Aubrey got the kids off to school and went to the yoga studio to take care of some paperwork. She called Tim from the phone on the receptionist's desk to let him know the meeting was on, and where. Anybody coming into the studio had access to that phone. Using it would give Aubrey plausible deniability about her role in the meeting if the cops ever started asking questions. (It turned out she'd actually learned something from her months of researching how to commit murder.)

Driving down River Road that evening, as the light faded from the November sky, Aubrey felt calm and clearheaded. Her hangover was gone, her pulse was normal, and her palms were dry. The rain had just started, and the headlights illuminated the raindrops so they looked like diamonds falling. The National Weather Service said it would rain all night, which would help with washing away tire tracks and footprints and such. Her assistant Mikayla was picking up the girls from sports and babysitting till Aubrey got home. Logan was going to Jaden's house for dinner, and getting a ride home from Jaden's dad. She'd figured out which item would be most useful to frame her husband for his mistress's death, and she had a plan for getting it. She wore gloves, which did not look out of place on this chilly night, so no fingerprints. Aubrey had thought of everything.

Ten minutes later, Aubrey and Tim were sitting together in Aubrey's car when Kate pulled into the deserted lot. Aubrey flashed her lights, and Kate parked nearby and got out of the car. Now came the tricky part.

"Wait here," Aubrey said to Tim. "There's something I need to tell Kate first. Then I'll wave to you, and you get out and escort her to the bridge. She's going to confess everything, and say she's sorry. She wants to do it there."

"All right. Thank you for arranging this, Aubrey. It's very important to me."

"You're welcome."

Aubrey got out, noting with disapproval that Kate wore a dress and cute flats, with some sort of silky evening coat on top. How inappropriate to the occasion. Then she remembered that Kate still thought they were going to dinner afterward. Hahaha, nope. Aubrey had already canceled the reservation, and told Jenny that Kate was sick. *No birthday dinner for you.*

"Why are we meeting here?" Kate said. "It's starting to rain, and it's dark."

"Don't worry. It'll be quick."

"Who's that in the car? Is it Ethan?" Kate said, and the eagerness in her voice was telling. Ethan was the one who'd ended it, then. Served Kate right. But Aubrey sensed an opportunity, a way to make sure that Kate would follow Tim to the bridge without balking.

"Ethan needs to talk to you, Kate," Aubrey said. "He's right down that path." She pointed to the trailhead.

"Down the path? Why?"

"He wants to speak to you privately about some arrangements. He wouldn't explain it to me."

Kate nodded. "I understand. There's . . . a complication. We left things up in the air." She paused. "You're okay with this, with me and Ethan talking?"

"Not really, but I don't have much choice, do I? He insists. Do me a favor, though. My phone is dying, and I need to call the kids. Can I borrow your phone?" Aubrey asked.

"Sure." Kate rummaged in her handbag.

"Give me the bag, I'll find the phone. It'll be waiting right here when you get back. You'd better hurry. Tim will show you where Ethan is."

Aubrey signaled to Tim, who got out of her car.

"Tim? What's *he* doing here?"

"Oh, he happened to be here, something to do with the crew team, I think. The path is confusing, so he'll help you find Ethan. I probably shouldn't go with you."

"No."

"Just follow Tim."

"All right," Kate said, frowning, as she turned toward Tim.

It's amazing what people will fall for when they underestimate you. Kate thought Aubrey was too stupid and spineless to stick up for herself. Aubrey was a pathetic fly buzzing around Kate's brilliance. It would never in a million years occur to Kate that Aubrey could outsmart her.

Aubrey got back into her nice, warm car, and watched Kate march off to her death. It wasn't until the day the police came to the yoga studio to interview her that Aubrey discovered Kate had been pregnant that night, with Ethan's baby. That must have been the "complication" she so delicately referred to. Aubrey had to admit, the thought of the innocent baby made her sad. But with Kate for a mother and Ethan for a father, the poor thing was better off dead.

That part of the plan—the killing-Kate part—went off without a hitch. It was a shame that Aubrey hadn't been able to figure out a way to get Tim to kill Ethan, too, but of course, he had no motive to do that. She had to settle for framing Ethan for his girlfriend's murder. That's where the anonymous call to the tip line came in, and why a detective now stood at the front door, presumably with a search warrant in hand for Ethan's car. Aubrey would get *almost* everything she wanted—Kate dead, full custody of the kids, the house, and all the money. Ethan wasn't dead, but he was about to go to jail for the rest of his life, and that would be satisfying. She'd be sure to send him a Christmas card every year—Aubrey and the kids in matching outfits, with Griff smiling in Ethan's place. That would feel very good.

Aubrey kissed the top of Lilly's head. "Finish your homework, honey. I'll go talk to the lady."

She opened the front door to find the young detective who'd interviewed her at the yoga studio, along with an older officer she didn't recognize.

"Detective Charles," Aubrey said. "What a surprise. Can I help you?"

"Ma'am, apologies if I'm interrupting dinner. My colleague and I have a warrant to search your husband's car in relation to the death of Katherine Eastman."

"Oh, my," Aubrey said, her hand shooting to her throat in feigned shock. "Well, I guess you'd better come in."

34

People are gonna think we're having an affair," Robbie said, as he got into Jenny's minivan, making the seat dip with his muscular bulk.

It was nearly seven o'clock, and the town parking garage was empty and echoing. Jenny had waited around until everyone left, because Robbie made a big deal about keeping their meeting secret. He'd shown up to the garage in plain clothes, in the family car instead of his cruiser, when he'd always come to her office before, in broad daylight and in uniform. She found it odd.

Jenny gave him side-eye in the dim light. "The spy stuff was your idea."

"Kidding, kidding," Robbie said, tapping her on the arm good-naturedly enough that she relaxed. "How're the kids?"

"Good. T.J.'s excited for basketball. Reed's got the robotics tournament next week. Yours?"

"Keeping us on our toes," Robbie said. "Maddie's running for seventh-grade president."

"I heard. That's wonderful. I told Val, I'm happy to help map out the campaign strategy."

"Oh, that'll be a load off her mind. Posters and speeches and stuff are not Val's thing. Thank you."

"My pleasure." Jenny paused. "So you said you needed to talk in person, that what you had was too sensitive for the telephone. This is about Chief Rizzo, I assume?"

Robbie's face took on a pained expression. "Sort of. It's about the Rothenberg case more generally, but—yeah. All right. Let's start with Rizzo. Jenny, I need to know. Are you making any progress in moving him out of the chief's job?"

"Hard to say. Jake Goodwin getting hit by that TV truck has some folks on the town council questioning Rizzo's priorities. But is it enough to get him voted out? Probably not without real proof of misconduct. Have you found anything we can use?" Jenny asked.

"It's possible that Rizzo raided the overtime fund to pay for his outside-expert reports," Robbie said.

"It's possible, or he did?"

"I have a strong suspicion, but I can't prove it yet. I don't have the password to the accounts," Robbie said.

"Who does?"

"Pam Grimaldi used to. Now it's just Rizzo and his personal secretary, and she's loyal to him."

"Well, if we could prove Rizzo used overtime funds to pay for outside experts, and that's why he didn't have the money for traffic enforcement the day of Kate Eastman's funeral, then yes, I could go to the council with that. People are upset enough about the impact on the soccer season that it could turn the tide. But if we can't prove that? Do you have anything else?"

"I may be able to document problems with his handling of the Eastman case. Detective Charles came to me with concerns that Rizzo is suppressing evidence, just like that lawyer said in the press conference. Rizzo knew that it was Rothenberg's own blood on the shirt, and he kept it quiet because it didn't jibe with his theory of the case. He also knew based on phone records that the victim was having an affair with Dr. Saxman, but he did nothing about it."

"A lot of people knew about that affair, Robbie. *I* knew, and I didn't call the police."

"You're not the one trying to lock up the victim's husband for murder and throw away the key, are you?"

"True," Jenny said.

"Also, they got a call to the tip line days ago saying that evidence of the murder was hidden in Saxman's car. Keisha wanted to get a warrant to follow up on that tip, and Rizzo's been dragging his feet. She had to threaten to go over his head to *you* to get him to agree."

"What evidence is in Ethan's car?" Jenny asked, shocked.

"We don't know yet. Because of the delay, they only got the warrant this afternoon."

"Jesus," Jenny whispered, going pale in the half-light.

Jenny had never believed that Griff would hurt Kate. But Ethan? That seemed more plausible given that the man was a known liar and cheat. How horrible for Aubrey if it was true, and for their children. And how dangerous for Jenny. Aubrey was unstable enough already. If things got worse for her, it was impossible to say how she might react, what she might say about Kate and their shared past, or to whom.

"If I was running the department," Robbie said, "I would have searched that car the minute the tip came in, and maybe we'd have a different guy locked up by now. It's dereliction of duty on Rizzo's part if you ask me."

"This case is such a minefield, Robbie. I don't know what the answer is, but I'm not convinced that going after Dr. Saxman is a good idea, or even that it's the right moment to get Rizzo fired."

"Indecisiveness doesn't suit you, Jenny," Robbie said, an edge to his voice.

"What's that supposed to mean?"

"You need to make up your mind. I didn't want to have to do this, but you're leaving me no choice. Wait here, I have to show you something."

Robbie got out and walked over to his own car, his footsteps echoing eerily in the empty garage. He came back carrying a bulky manila envelope, and placed it on the console between them. Something in his expression made her nervous.

"What's in it?" Jenny asked.

"Open it and see," he said.

Jenny turned on the task light. She opened the bulky envelope, reached in, and pulled out a second envelope, this one clear plastic, sealed with evidence tape. The label on it said that the item had been recovered by Officer Robert Womack at 9:30 P.M. the night before at a location described as "fence near bridge over Belle River, approx. 1 mi from River Road boat-launch parking lot." Inside the plastic envelope was Tim's favorite cap—the ratty, old Healy Construction cap that Jenny had been trying to get him to throw away for years. She turned the envelope over and examined the inside of the cap through the plastic to make sure. The initials "T.J.H." were written on the label in faded permanent marker, right where she knew they would be.

"Why do you have Tim's hat?"

"Because I found it, in a place it shouldn't have been," Robbie said.

"This says you found it at the bridge. Are you trying to imply something from this?" Jenny asked. She was beginning to feel nauseous, because the implication was clear.

"From the beginning I thought the victim probably went into the river from the bridge, not from the boat launch like Rizzo was saying. So I raised the idea with him, and he laughed me out of the room, which naturally pissed me off. I decided to prove him wrong. It was an ego thing on my part, frankly. Yesterday, on my own time, I went out to the bridge for a look-see. And I found Tim's hat hooked on the fence, where you'd push it down to climb over. The ground had been disturbed there pretty recently."

"I'm not sure where you're going with this, Robbie," Jenny said, though of course she knew, and it terrified her.

"When I first heard about this case—when I heard who the victim was, and how the body was found in the river—naturally I thought about Lucas Arsenault's death and how the Arsenault family always blamed Kate. Look, Jen, I love Tim, and I can't believe he would hurt anybody. I'm sure there's some other explanation. But Tim had a motive. We both know he has anger-management issues. And this cap proves he was there recently. I'm not saying I think he did it. I'm just saying that somebody like Rizzo—who we know is capable of accusing someone on thin evidence, who has issues with you personally because he doesn't like being told what to do—well, that's not the guy you want in charge of the police department at a moment like this."

"The fact that you found this cap at the bridge—if that's even *true*—means nothing," Jenny began, her voice shaking. "Tim could have been there for a million reasons. It was just Lucas's birthday, and Tim is sentimental. He was probably there to throw flowers in the water or something. If you're implying Tim had anything to do with Kate's death—"

"No."

"—then you can get out of my car right now."

Robbie held up his hands. "Calm down. I said, I'm not implying that."

"It sure sounds like you are. We both know you want the chief's job, Robbie. And we both know this little stunt is intended to blackmail me into helping you get it."

"Blackmail? Never. I'm trying to help out an old friend. And just so you know, I'm not making this up, Jenny. I have pictures of the cap stuck on the fence where I found it. I can show you on my phone."

"Maybe you planted it there before you took the pictures. Maybe you didn't. Either way, it means nothing. Tim has a defense a mile wide, and besides, he has an alibi for the time when Kate went missing."

He did, since Jenny would say he was with her, even though that was not true.

"I'm sure he has an alibi," Robbie said. "But the last thing you want is for Tim to be put in the position of getting arrested and having to defend himself. That would be a nightmare for you and your family. It would be much better if this piece of evidence never sees the light of day. And for that, yes, you need my help. You need me to go against procedure and suppress evidence, which is not something I take lightly. I'd consider doing it for the good of this town, but then I would need you to put the town first as well, and move against Rizzo even if the timing doesn't seem convenient right now."

They were at an impasse. Jenny couldn't predict what Robbie would do if she said no. She had no choice but to give him what he wanted, or else he could make big trouble for Tim. But Jenny would make damn sure that she and her family were fully protected in return.

"I want to be clear where you stand, Rob. You agree that Tim had *nothing* to do with Kate Eastman's death," Jenny said.

"Of course. No argument with that."

"All right," Jenny said with a sigh. "Here's what I propose. I will do everything in my power starting first thing tomorrow morning to get Owen Rizzo fired and make you chief of police. I won't stop till I succeed, even if it means getting the college involved to pressure the town council. But I want a few things in return. I want that hat back right now. I want the pictures of it deleted from your phone. And I want us to agree that we stop this witch hunt pronto. Kate Eastman killed herself, period. Griff Rothenberg needs to be released. Unless they find a murder weapon in Ethan Saxman's car, which I highly doubt, we should leave him out of this, too, and not risk another failed investigation. Kate's death was a suicide. The sooner we can get the ME to rule it one, the better for this town, and for everyone involved."

"Agreed."

"Good. Now, hand me your phone so I can delete those pictures."

Robbie took out his phone and scrolled through his photos. He handed the phone to Jenny, and her heart sank. The hat, stuck on the dilapidated fence, looked so natural, and so incriminating. She could imagine exactly how the wind took it off Tim's head and deposited it there. Pictures could be doctored, yes, but these looked genuine, and with a sick feeling in her stomach, Jenny faced the possibility that her husband had murdered her old friend. She deleted the photos, and gave the phone back. Then she took the plastic evidence envelope with the hat inside, and shoved it into her handbag.

"I hope this unfortunate piece of business won't impact our friendship," Robbie said, "since I plan on us working together for many years to come."

"I'll get over it. I appreciate you coming to me first, so that we could work out a satisfactory arrangement."

"Friends?" he asked, extending his hand.

"Friends," she said, shaking it.

"Have a good night," Robbie said, and got out of the minivan.

Jenny watched him walk back to his car and drive away. Once he was gone, she took the sealed plastic evidence envelope from her handbag and, using the sharp tip of a pen, ripped it open savagely. She held the cap to her face, and breathed in her husband's scent. Jenny had known Tim Healy her whole life. She'd been married to him for sixteen years. She knew that Tim had never been the same after suffering a head injury on that awful night. He was unpredictable at times, even angry, but she never would have thought him capable of hurting Kate. Jenny knew Tim's face better than she knew her own. She knew when he'd had a tough day at work, when he was sad, when a migraine was coming on (he'd suffered from them ever since that night), and when he was feeling especially in love with her or the kids. She knew what he did all day, whom he saw, where he went—or so she thought. But people could fool you pretty easily, even people you loved. All they had to do was lie, or choose not to tell the whole truth. Jenny should know. She'd lied to Tim for years about Lucas's death, though maybe what she'd learned tonight was that she hadn't gotten away with it.

It was nearly nine by the time she got home. The kids were upstairs getting ready for bed. A scrawled note on the kitchen table in Tim's messy handwriting said "pizza in oven." Suddenly she was starving. She grabbed the foil-covered packet out of the oven with her bare hand, and stood at the stove, wolfing down a slice, as Tim walked in.

"Hey, babe," he said. "How'd your meeting go?"

Jenny wiped her mouth with a napkin. For the first time since last Friday, Tim sounded relaxed, normal, like his old self. Things between them were just beginning to feel right again. Jenny didn't want to risk that, and yet she couldn't ignore the terrible suspicion in her heart. She had to know.

"My meeting was . . . strange," she said.

"Strange, how?"

She walked over to the table, and pulled his cap out of her handbag.

"Robbie Womack gave me this. He found it at the old railroad bridge, stuck on the fence where the No Trespassing sign is."

Jenny collapsed into the chair as if she'd used her last ounce of energy showing him the hat. Tim came and sat down across from her. He picked it up and looked at it like the hat was a puzzle he was trying to solve.

"What did Robbie say?" Tim asked finally.

"That he wouldn't tell anyone. That he understood the cap being there didn't mean anything."

Tim nodded. "That's good."

She took his hand and looked into his eyes. "What *does* it mean, Tim?"

He took a deep breath. "I've been working up my courage to tell you this, but it's hard."

"Go on."

"Last week, I ran into Aubrey at Shecky's."

"*Aubrey*?"

He nodded. "It was Lucas's birthday that day. Aubrey walked in, we got to talking, and at one point she asked if I knew the truth about Lucas's death. And then she told me. She told me the thing you've been keeping from me for twenty-two years, Jen. That Kate killed him, deliberately."

Jenny looked down at the table. Tears gathered in her eyes. "It's true," she whispered. "I lied. I guess you know that now. I'm so, so sorry, Tim. And I want us to talk about that. But first I have to ask. What happened after Aubrey told you this?"

"Aubrey said that she could get Kate to apologize. I should meet them at the parking lot near the old railroad bridge. I thought finally, after all these years, Kate's coming clean."

That goddamned Aubrey. This was all her doing. Aubrey had been looking to get back at Kate and Jenny both. A wave of pity for her poor husband swept over Jenny. Tim was no match for Aubrey, or for any one of the three of them. Tim was an innocent compared to them, a lamb among wolves. She should have protected him better.

"Why didn't you tell me?" Jenny said. "I would have said not to go. Aubrey can't be trusted. She set you up."

"No, Aubrey's the one who told me the truth," Tim said. "The only one who did. And she tried to arrange for me to hear it from Kate directly. You know how much that meant to me? I didn't tell you because she asked me not to, and because I didn't trust you not to interfere. I didn't *trust* you, Jen. My own wife."

"I understand," Jenny said. "And I deserve that. But in my defense, I was so young when this happened. They pressured me to lie. I should have told you the truth years ago, but I'd been lying for so long, I didn't know how to stop. I was afraid of what it would do to our marriage. I wanted to protect you. Can you understand that?"

"I can try. You're still my wife. I still love you. That hasn't changed."

Jenny nodded miserably, tears spilling from her eyes. "I love you, too. No matter what happened last Friday, I love you, Tim."

And she did. She loved the things about him that any woman would love in a man. That he was strong and handsome. That he was a good father, and could fix anything—the house, their cars, her phone when it broke. That his eyes lit up when she walked into a room. That he'd been there for her when her father died. That he grilled a mean steak and did the dishes. All of it.

"I didn't want it to happen," Tim said. "I went to the parking lot like Aubrey said, and—"

"Stop," she said, and put her fingers to Tim's lips. "It's better if I don't know the details."

"Let me talk. I don't want secrets between us anymore."

"All right, I understand. If that's how you feel, go ahead."

"Aubrey told me to park off the road, where nobody could see my truck, and to get into *her* car to wait for Kate. That seemed strange to me. I probably should've known then that something was fishy, but I was so focused on what Kate would say. When she showed up, she was shocked to see me. She thought she was meeting Aubrey alone, but Aubrey drove off and left us together. Kate didn't want to talk. I kept pushing her toward the bridge because I wanted to confront her about Lucas. I was desperate to get the truth, and I got carried away, Jenny. I said things to Kate, terrible things. I made her jump," he said, tears streaming down his face.

"Kate jumped?"

"Yes, of course. I would never—did you think I *pushed* her?"

"No, of course I didn't think that," Jenny assured him, but inside, she was deeply relieved, because she hadn't been sure.

"So you told her to jump, and she just did it?" she asked.

"I told her I knew that she pushed Lucas off the bridge. She tried to make excuses, like she just got carried away. I wasn't having that. I told her she was despicable, and a coward for not taking responsibility for her actions. Jenny, I said she deserved to die, and she should jump and do everybody a favor."

"And then she did?"

"Not right that second. She was standing there staring at the water, and I walked away. But obviously she listened in the end."

"So you didn't *see* her jump?"

"No, but obviously she did it. It was my fault. If you'd been there, you'd understand. I talked her into it."

"Tim, Kate's been suicidal ever since I've known her. Her life was a mess. Divorce, an affair, she was broke. This wasn't about you. It wasn't even about Lucas. Kate killed herself for other reasons."

"I read in the paper that she was pregnant. I never knew that. It's eating me up inside."

"How would you know? You couldn't have known, babe."

"I'm so sorry."

"But it wasn't your fault," Jenny insisted. "You didn't push her off the bridge. You didn't even see her jump. You left her there alive. What she chose to do after that was her own decision. She could have stood there for another hour thinking about all sorts of things. For all we know, she could've fallen in by accident. You have to stop being so hard on yourself."

"I don't know if I can."

He collapsed into her arms, and she held him, stroking his hair. They cried together for a while. Jenny cried for Kate, her dazzling friend, whose flaws were fatal in the end. But most of all she cried for Tim, her husband, whose act of bravery as a young man had left him damaged. Whether he caused Kate's death or not, he would carry the guilt forever.

Jenny looked around her kitchen, that she loved so much, and into the den, where Tim had made a fire in the fireplace, as he often did on cold nights. Such a cozy scene, smelling of woodsmoke and pizza and home, with the sound of the kids' footsteps on the ceiling above. Neither Jenny nor Tim could bring Kate back. There was no reason to tear down the life they'd built together because of guilt for something that wasn't even clearly Tim's fault. They had too much to lose, and nothing to gain. The best thing was to clean up the loose ends, and move on.

Jenny grabbed the cap, and walked over to the fireplace in the next room, where the embers burned low and red-hot. She moved the fireplace screen aside and laid the hat on top, jabbing it with the iron poker until it caught and flared up. Tim came to stand beside her.

"I'm sorry," she said. "I know you loved that cap."

He put his arm around her and held her tightly as they watched it burn. "Doesn't matter," he said. "What matters is us. This family."

When the hat was reduced to ashes, Tim carefully replaced the fireplace screen so embers wouldn't singe the carpet. Jenny took his hand, and they walked up the stairs together to tell the kids it was time for bed.

35

Griff was released with no fanfare, in sharp contrast to the manner in which he'd been arrested. He signed a few forms. His clothing and wallet were returned to him, but not his phone, which had been sent off to some forensics lab for analysis and, now that his charges had been dropped, would supposedly be returned by mail. (The delay upset him; the phone contained all his recent pictures of Kate, and he wanted to be able to look at her.) A corrections officer flipped a switch, and the metal gate of the county jail opened with a harsh clang. Griff trudged out into the cold morning, where ugly snow flurries swirled under a glowering sky. The parking lot was nearly empty. There were no reporters, no TV trucks, no flashbulbs. The image of Griff being handcuffed while spread-eagled against a police cruiser had been beamed to screens around the world, but the press wasn't interested in documenting his innocence.

He turned around and looked back at the jail, an ugly modern building made of brownish brick. What a relief to be out of that shithole. As Griff checked his wallet to see if he had enough cash for a taxi, a nondescript sedan pulled into the parking lot and rolled up to him. The driver leaned over to open the passenger door. He was pudgy and jovial-looking, with a scruffy beard.

"Mr. Rothenberg?"

"Yes?"

"Leonard Walters sent me. I'm your ride. Hop in."

Griff thought twice about getting into the car with a stranger, but what the hell. It was cold out and warm inside, and if this guy turned out to be a serial killer, it wouldn't much matter. Griff had nothing to lose anymore, and nothing to protect.

"Randall Falk," the driver said, handing Griff a business card.

Griff glanced at it as he settled into the passenger seat. "You're a private investigator."

"Yessir. Local. Working on contract for Mr. Walters. I'm the one who worked on corroborating your story. Where can I take you?"

"I don't know. Shouldn't I talk to Walters? Why didn't he come himself?"

"Oh, Mr. Walters is in Arizona by now. Big case. A mom shot and killed a chaperone at a school dance for saying her daughter's outfit was slutty. It's getting a lot of press."

"I see."

"No worries, though. The bill for his services was sent directly to your father-in-law. You're free and clear."

"Just like that?"

"Well, I'm not saying it wasn't a shitload of work. I spent days tracking down leads to prove your wife was alive when you left her. I got the manager from the Pinetree Inn. People from the bar you went to that night. Your cabdriver. A next-door neighbor who's an insomniac who saw you come home at three o'clock in the morning. The whole nine yards. Mr. Walters presented the evidence to the county attorney and the acting chief of police late yesterday, and that's how come you're out."

"I see. Thank you."

"It's what I get paid for. Uh, so where to?"

Griff gave the address to the house on Faculty Row, not because he wanted to go there, but because there was nowhere else to go.

"Wait a minute, you said *acting* chief of police?" Griff asked, as they headed for the highway.

"Yessir. Owen Rizzo was relieved of duty. The new guy is Robert Womack, been on the force here for some time. Unimaginative as heck, but a decent enough cop. I don't expect you'll be hearing from him though."

"Why not?"

"Oh, they'll focus on the doctor now. They're done with you. You have Mr. Walters to thank for that. He made sure the case imploded in full view of the press. The cops couldn't come back to you now if they wanted to. Not even if they found new evidence."

Griff gave him a dubious look. "What type of new evidence are you talking about? You think I did it?"

"I can't say with certainty what happened to your wife. I know she was alive when you left the Pinetree Inn, but based on the autopsy report, that was twelve to eighteen hours before she died. They're focusing on this doctor fellow now, but your wife was seen alone at the courthouse after she left *him* at the Pinetree Inn on Friday morning. Where she went after that is anybody's guess. Nobody's paying me to look into it anymore, so it's not my problem."

It dawned on Griff that for the rest of his life, people would wonder if he had murdered his wife. At least, they would in Belle River. Outside the car window, the road was gray with grit and salt, and the trees that stretched to the horizon on either side were bare. Kate had hated it here, but Griff never had. He loved Carlisle too much to hate its hometown. But now all he wanted was to go far away, and never lay eyes on this place again.

"That's not to suggest you did it," Falk said. "I was not implying that."

"Uh-huh. Thanks."

"Who do *you* think did it? Was it the doctor?" Randall Falk asked.

"I wouldn't know," Griff said, and shut his mouth tight. He didn't want to talk about Kate's death to anybody, let alone to this idiot, who was starting to annoy the crap out of him.

"They found her pocketbook in his car," Falk said. "To me, that's pretty compelling. He could say she left it in his car the night before, when they met up at the inn. But that's not possible, because she would've needed the pocketbook Friday morning at the courthouse. So it stands to reason she met up with the doctor again later, on the night she died."

"I thought you said you don't know who killed her."

"I said I wasn't certain, and I'm not. But Saxman had opportunity, and he had a motive. The guy has a career and three kids to protect. If she was pressuring him to leave his wife, or threatening to reveal the affair, he might've killed her to stop her from doing that."

They pulled up to the house just in time, because Griff was getting ready to punch the guy out for talking about Kate like that.

"Here we are, safe and sound. My mission is complete," Falk said.

"Thanks." Griff handed back the business card, but Falk waved it away.

"Oh, no, keep it. Give me a call if you get curious about your wife's demise. I'd be willing to offer a reduced rate."

Griff nodded curtly and ran into the house to get away from that guy. Inside, it was dark and airless, and smelled of beer and of Kate's perfume. Thoughts of her overwhelmed him. He stumbled to the living room without turning on the lights, and collapsed on the couch in a ball, pulling a blanket over his head. A draft rattled the blinds, reminding him of the day that he looked out to see Chief Rizzo and the detective ringing the doorbell, coming to tell him she was dead.

He'd finally remembered where he'd seen Rizzo before. It was at Henry's Bistro with Kate, on a night Griff had gone out looking for her in the middle of a storm. Figures he'd be trying to make sure she was safe, while she was busy getting it on with some stranger in a bar. Rizzo was just her type, dark and intense-looking, and she never could keep her panties on. But that was ancient history now. Griff was beginning to feel like he'd lived for a long time, that he'd seen and done everything, and that nothing had turned out right. He didn't know what to do next, so he watched the shadows move across the room, and once it was dark, he slept.

Somebody pounded on the door. Griff sat up and peeked through the blinds. It was Jenny. Strangely, he was happy to see her, or if not happy to see Jenny in particular, then at least relieved to see another human being.

He opened the door.

"Hey," she said, rubbing her hands together and stamping her feet against the cold. "Sorry to drop by out of the blue like this, but Keniston's been calling and calling. He said you're not answering your phone."

"They confiscated it."

"Oh, no. I'm sorry. Let me look into getting that back for you."

"Yes, thank you. They said they would mail it, but if it's possible, I'd like to get it right away. It had pictures of Kate on it, and I want them."

Pity leapt into Jenny's eyes. So she thought Kate didn't deserve his grief. Who the hell was she to decide that? Griff started to close the door.

"Hey," Jenny said, putting her hand on the door to stop him. "I know this is a difficult time, but I need you to come with me. Keniston went into the hospital last night, and he wants to see you. He's at Carlisle General. Griff, he stood behind you, paid for your defense. I know it's hard, but you should go."

"Of course," Griff said, nodding. "Let me get my coat."

Twenty minutes later, they stood outside Keniston's hospital room, talking to Benji Eastman.

"He's developed a heart arrhythmia," Benji said. "They think it was brought on by stress and the chemo. He's pretty weak, but he wanted to see you before—well, just in case anything should happen to him."

"I'm glad to be here," Griff said. "I'm grateful to him for taking my side in this mess, and I want to thank him in person. I'm grateful to you too, bro."

"I never believed for a second that you could hurt Kate. None of us did. Dad wants to talk to you and Jenny about the case. If it's all right, I'm gonna duck out, go grab some coffee."

"Sure thing. Take care, man."

They shook hands, and clasped each other on the back warmly. Griff had always liked Kate's half brothers. With Griff's father in prison and his mother not in his life, Kate's family had been his only family for a while now. He was going to miss them.

In the room, Keniston lay barely breathing under the flimsy hospital blanket, hooked up to tubes. Griff couldn't believe such a fierce lion of a man could be brought low like this.

"Feels like just a minute ago that he was in his prime, and now look," Griff whispered.

Keniston opened his eyes. "I'm not dead yet," he croaked. "And I can hear you."

The three of them laughed. Keniston's laughter turned to choking.

"Water," he said.

A Styrofoam cup with a straw sat on a wheeled table beside the bed. Jenny held the cup for him, and he drank.

"Better," he said, and cleared his throat, gazing at Griff with a look akin to wonder. "I'm amazed to see you out of prison, son. I wasn't sure we could pull it off."

Tears sprang to Griff's eyes. "I'd still be in that damn cell if not for you. I can't thank you enough for what you did for me, Keniston."

"You *should* thank me. Jenny here was no help," Keniston said, in a joking tone.

Jenny flushed bright red. "What are you talking about? I replaced the chief of police to get him off Griff's back. That wasn't easy."

Keniston raised a bony hand, then let it drop back down to the blanket wearily. He cleared his throat again. "I was teasing. But I do have something serious to discuss. I'm concerned this new fellow is making the same mistakes. I want this ended. I don't want some big investigation into this doctor that Kate was mixed up with. From what I understood, Walters conjured up the evidence against this fellow, to divert attention and get Griff out. I don't want some new unjustified arrest on my conscience."

"I understand," Jenny said, "and I agree completely."

"But Walters didn't make up evidence," Griff said. "What he said was true. Saxman's the last person we know saw Kate alive. And now they found Kate's handbag in his car. We can't just let that go. The police should investigate."

"Kate leaving her bag in his car doesn't prove he killed her," Keniston said.

"Keniston's right," Jenny said. "We don't want to make the same mistake Rizzo did. We're hoping to rule Ethan Saxman out as a suspect and announce that to the press in the next day or two. I'm sure you both know there's been another option on the table all along."

"Suicide," Keniston said.

"Exactly," Jenny said. "Rizzo decided Kate was murdered based on an expert's opinion about the nature of her skull fracture and the absence of water in her lungs. We brought in a different expert, and no surprise, he has a different opinion. He believes Kate's injuries were sustained when she fell, or jumped, from the railroad bridge. So unless new evidence comes to light, it's likely the coroner will rule Kate's death a suicide, and we'll close the case."

"And Saxman just skates away?" Griff said.

Griff didn't believe Saxman killed his wife. Not directly. But if he'd never seduced her, never turned her away from Griff, then Kate would be alive right now. Saxman ought to pay for that.

"He'll suffer, don't worry," Jenny said. "He's going to lose his job because of the negative publicity, and Aubrey will divorce him for sure after this."

"It's not enough," Griff said, and hung his head.

They all fell silent. After a moment, Keniston lifted his hand, which appeared to take great effort. Carefully, so as not to dislodge any tubes, Griff took Keniston's hand in his own.

"Griffin," he said. "Isn't it Kate you should be angry at?"

"I can't. I never could be angry with her," Griff said.

"That's what I was afraid of. I feel responsible," his father-in-law said, and his eyes were watering. Griff had never seen the old man cry in all the years he'd known him, not even at the funerals of his own wife and daughter. He was shocked to see it now.

"Responsible for what?" Griff asked.

"For the fact that you married my daughter. I sent you to her because I couldn't handle her anymore. I did that knowing full well how she crushes the people who love her. And now she's crushed you. It's my fault."

"It's all right. I chose my life. I chose *her.*"

"It's not all right. I'm going to make it up to you," Keniston said.

Griff and Jenny exchanged glances over Keniston's head. Jenny was probably thinking the same thing he was—that Keniston didn't have enough time left to make anything up to anybody.

"I spoke with my lawyer. You won't have any problems about the money."

He closed his eyes, and seemed to fall into a deep sleep. Griff and Jenny waited for a while longer, but then decided they should probably let him rest. They both had tears in their eyes as they left the hospital room, because they knew it was the last time they'd see him.

As Jenny drove down the hill from the hospital, Griff took a deep breath and looked out over the town nestled in the valley below. He could see the lights of College Street, and the beacon on top of the Ogden Library tower. Carlisle was perfect from up here, and yet it was spoiled, because he couldn't look at it without thinking of Kate. But then, every place in the world made him think of Kate. No place was untouched. He thought of her in New York, as she'd stood glowing in the light at the middle school dance. He thought of her in Paris, thin and haunted in the tabac, as he begged her to come away with him. He thought of her on their boat with her golden hair rippling in the breeze, or on a sunny piazza in Italy, a drink in hand, laughing her throaty laugh. He could go to the ends of the earth and never find a place that didn't remind him of her.

"I want my phone," he said to Jenny. "I need those pictures."

She shook her head. "Griff."

"Just stop, all right. If you're going to tell me to get over her, I can't, and I don't want to hear it."

"I wouldn't presume to tell you that," Jenny said, her hands on the wheel.

She looked over at him, and in the light from the streetlamp, he saw the sympathy in her eyes.

"None of us will get over Kate," she said. "Aubrey and I loved her, too. I remember Kate at a burger feed on the Quad, the first day of freshman year. She was laughing and twirling around, with all the boys staring at her, and I thought, I've never seen a person so full of life. Those were the glory days, though, right? We were so young, so impressionable. I feel like we just fell into each other's arms, best friends at first sight. We didn't stop to think that we might be bad for each other. I'm not saying anything against Kate. Just that it was a bad combination, in hindsight. She was bad for you, too. You just don't see it yet."

"Of course I see it, but I still love her," Griff said defiantly.

"So do I. But we have to go on, Griff. *You* have to go on. What other choice is there?"

36

Two Years Later

It was Christmastime, and Griff and his first mate were taking the day off from their usual routine of fishing charters and snorkeling excursions. He'd met the first mate in a bar in Charlotte Amalie a few months back. She was an Australian girl by the name of Gemma who was traveling the world, paying her way by crewing on boats. Gemma knew how to sail and guide and run a charter website. The two of them worked well together, so well that she'd recently migrated from sleeping on the leather banquette in the lounge to sleeping in the stateroom with him. It was a relief to be with someone uncomplicated, who was content to put in a hard day's work on the water, fall asleep to the rhythm of the waves, and not say much. If Gemma knew anything about Griff's past, she never mentioned it.

The weather was perfect—eighty degrees, sun glittering on an aqua-blue sea, balmy breeze. They anchored in a sheltered cove off Anegada. There was a spot there that he wanted to show her, a mile-long stretch of sugar-white beach with sublime waves, completely deserted. They got out a couple of stand-up paddleboards, jumped off the back of the boat, climbed on the boards, and raced to shore. Griff got tossed off his board in the heavy surf, and emerged from the waves laughing and sputtering to find Gemma already on the shore.

"Hah, I beat you," she said, shaking water from her short blond hair.

She was strong and tan, with a beautiful smile. Griff kissed her, and she tasted of the ocean.

Gemma had brought along a beach blanket in her waterproof pack. They tried to spread it on the sand, but the wind kept taking it.

"Hold on, I'll get some rocks," he said, and headed down the beach a ways, toward a tidal pool that looked promising.

Griff leaned over and picked up a rock. The feel of it—rough, heavy, wet—made his vision go dark. He was standing on the bridge, on that rainy night, staring down at another rock in his hands. He'd never meant to hurt Kate. He'd followed the phantom copies of her texts, followed her to the bridge, meaning only to help. To be her champion. To win her back. When Griff overheard Tim Healy threaten her, he picked up the rock to defend her. But Tim ran off before Griff could intercede. Kate was alone on the bridge, sobbing, kneeling at the edge of a chasm, staring into the roiling water below. He went to comfort her; that was all. At the sound of his footsteps, she looked up with desolate eyes. But when she saw who it was, her expression changed—to rage, to disgust.

"*You!*" she yelled. "Are you too stupid to understand we're done? Stay away from me, Griff. Get out of my life!"

He never meant to hurt her. But those words. The way she turned on him. The hate in her eyes. Griff lifted the rock in his two hands, and brought it down with all his might on the crown of Kate's head. For a second, she looked surprised. Then she crumpled sideways and plunged into the river.

Griff heard Gemma call his name. He blinked hard, turned around, and started walking back toward his new life. With every step he took down the white-sand beach, he pushed Kate's memory further into the past, where it belonged.

Griff and Gemma spread the blanket on the sand and anchored it with the rocks he'd gathered. He breathed in the salt-scented air and let the

Caribbean sun warm his face. By the time they settled onto the blanket, he felt all right. Better than all right. He felt good.

"Hey, I've got a surprise for you," Gemma said.

She pulled a towel-wrapped bundle from her pack, unrolling it to reveal a plate of shrimp sandwiches and two splits of champagne.

"Our Christmas feast. Do you like it?" Gemma asked.

"I love it," Griff said, and laughed like a free man. Which he was.

Acknowledgments

This book would not exist without the inspiration and guidance I received from two of the greatest women in publishing—Meg Ruley, my stalwart agent and friend who always believed in my writing and knew better than I did that I had more books in me, and Jennifer Enderlin, brilliant editor, publishing maven, and true collaborator. This book is Jen's baby as much as mine. Thanks also to the many talented people at Jane Rotrosen Agency and St. Martin's Press who have helped along the way, especially Jessica Errera, Rebecca Sherer, Caitlin Dareff, Lisa Senz, Brant Janeway, Jessica Preeg, Erica Martirano, and Jordan Hanley.

I was a nomad while writing this book, and worked on it in a number of places. Special thanks to the staff at the Howe Library in Hanover, New Hampshire, which is a welcoming place to write as well as an incredible community library. And to the people at the Four Seasons in Miami, where I wrote the final chapters at a desk with a fabulous view of Biscayne Bay—if only all my writing days could be like those.

And thanks to my husband and kids, who support and inspire me always.

Turn the page for a sneak peek at
Michele Campbell's next novel

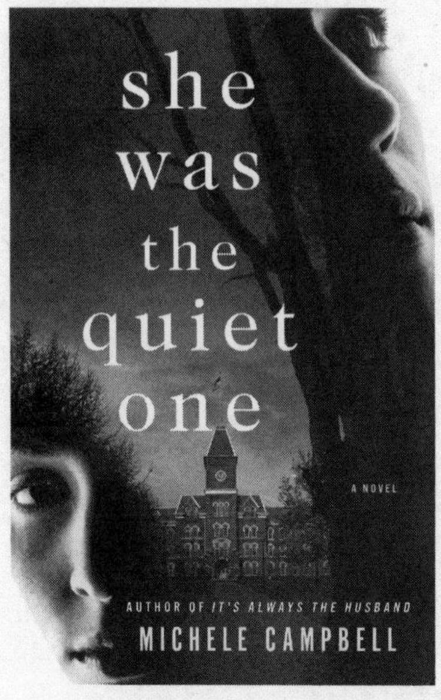

Available July 2018

1

February

They locked her in the infirmary, and took away her phone, and anything she might use to harm herself—or someone else. The school didn't tout this in its glossy brochures, but that's how it handled kids suspected of breaking the rules. Lock them in the infirmary, isolate them, interrogate them until they cracked. Usually you got locked up for cheating on a test, or smoking weed in the woods. In the worst-case scenario, hazing. Not murder.

She lay on the narrow bed and stared at the ceiling. They'd given her sedatives at first, and then something for the pain. But her head still pounded, and her mind was restless and foggy all at once. A large lump protruded from the back of her skull. She explored it with her fingers, trying to remember what had caused it. At the edge of her consciousness, something terrible stirred, and she pushed it away. If she turned off the light, she would see it, that thing at the edge of the lake.

That thing. Her sister. Her twin.

All across campus on this cold, dead night, silence reigned. She was being accused of a terrible crime, and there was nobody to speak in her defense. They'd called her grandmother to come defend her. But her grandmother believed she was guilty. Even her closest friends suspected her, and she had to admit, they had reason to. She and her sister had been close once, but this awful school had changed that. They'd come to doubt each other, to talk behind each other's backs, rat on each other for crimes large and small, steal from one another. Mere days earlier, they'd gotten into a physical fight so intense that the girl who interceded wound up with a black eye. That girl hadn't told—*yet*. But she would now.

It wasn't fair. Just because they'd had a fight didn't mean she would kill her sister. How could she? Her sister was the only family she had left. Everybody else had died, or abandoned her. Why would she hurt her only family, her only friend? But every time she closed her eyes, she saw the blood on her hands, the stab wounds, the long hair fanned out. Her sister's face, white and still in the moonlight. She was there when it happened. Why? It couldn't be because she was the killer. That wasn't true. She was innocent. She knew it in her heart.

But nobody believed her.

2

The September Before

Sarah Donovan was a bundle of nerves as she fed her kids a rushed breakfast of instant oatmeal and apple juice. Four-year-old Harper and two-year-old Scottie were still in their pajamas, their good clothes hidden away among half-unpacked boxes. Today was opening day at Odell Academy, the prestigious old boarding school in New Hampshire, and Sarah and her husband, Heath, had just been appointed the dorm heads of Moreland Hall. They'd been laboring in the trenches as teachers for the past five years, and this new job was a vote of confidence, a step up into the school's administration. It came with a raise and faculty housing and the promise of more to come. Sarah ought to be thrilled. Heath certainly was. Yet she couldn't shake a sneaking feeling of dread.

"Hurry up, sweetie, two more bites," Sarah said to Scottie, who sat in his high chair playing with his food, a solemn expression on his funny little face. Scottie was like Sarah—quiet, observant, a worrier, with a lot going on behind his eyes—whereas Harper was an open book. She met life head on, ready to dominate it, just like her dad.

"If you're done, Harps, go brush your teeth."

"Mommy, I'm gonna wear my party dress," Harper announced as she climbed down from her booster seat. She was beautiful, and she knew it, with big blue eyes and wild mane of curls, and she loved to dress up and show off.

"You have to find it first. Look in the box next to your bed."

Harper ran off, and Sarah glanced at the clock. They had half an hour till the students and their families began to arrive. Sarah had spent the afternoon yesterday preparing for the welcome reception, and as far as refreshments and party supplies were concerned, she was all set. Five large boxes from Dunkin' Donuts sat on the kitchen counter, along with multiple half-gallons of apple cider and lemonade, napkins and paper plates, party decorations and name tags. All that remained was to move everything to the common room and plaster a smile on her face. So why was she so nervous?

Maybe because the stakes were so high. Heath and Sarah had been brought in to clean up Moreland Hall's unsavory reputation, and the task was daunting. Bad behavior happened all over Odell's campus, but it happened most often in Moreland. Sarah thought it must have something to do with the fact that a disproportionate share of Moreland girls came from old Odell families. (Moreland had been the first dorm at Odell to house girls when the school went coed fifty years before, and alumni kids often requested to live in the same dorms their parents had.) Sarah had nothing against legacy students per se. She was one herself, having graduated from Odell following in the footsteps of her mother, her father, aunts and uncles, a motley array of cousins. But she couldn't deny that some legacy kids were spoiled rotten, and Moreland legacies notorious among them.

At the end of the last school year, two Moreland seniors made national news when they got arrested for selling drugs. The ensuing scandal dirtied Odell Academy's reputation enough that the board of trustees ordered the headmaster to fix the problem, once and for all. The previous dorm head was a French teacher from Montreal, a single guy, who smoked two packs of cigarettes a day—hardly the image the school was looking for. He got demoted, and Heath and Sarah brought in to replace him. A wholesome young couple with two adorable little kids to set a proper example. That was the plan, at least. But there was a problem. Neither Sarah nor Heath had a counseling background. They knew nothing about running a dorm, or providing guidance to messed-up girls. Sarah had spent her Odell years hiding from girls like that, and—to be honest—Heath had spent his chasing them. That was all in the past of course. The distant past. But it worried her.

When Sarah raised her concerns, and Heath soothed them away and convinced her that this new job was their golden opportunity. How could they say no? Heath had big plans. He wanted to advance through the ranks and become headmaster one day. The dorm-head position was his stepping-stone. He didn't have to tell her how much he wanted it, or remind her how desperately he needed a win. She knew that, too well. Teaching high school English was not the life Heath wanted. There had been another life, but it crashed and burned, and they'd barely survived. With this new challenge, Heath was finally happy again. She couldn't stand in his way.

And he *was* happy. He strode into the kitchen now looking like a million bucks, decked out in a blue blazer and a new tie, with a huge smile on his handsome face.

"Ready, babe?" he said, coming over and planting a kiss on Sarah's lips.

"Just about. You look happy," she said, lifting Scottie down from his high chair.

"You bet. I've got my speech memorized. I've got my new tie on for luck—the one you got me for my birthday. How do I look?"

"Gorgeous," she said.

It was true. The first time Sarah had laid eyes on Heath was here at Odell, fifteen years ago, when he showed up as a new transfer student their junior year. He was the most beautiful thing she'd ever seen, and despite the ups and downs, that hadn't changed.

Heath checked his watch, frowning. "It's after nine. You'd better get dressed."

Sarah had thought she *was* dressed. She'd brushed her hair this morning, and put on a skirt, a sweater, and her favorite clogs, like she usually did on days when she had to teach class. But looking at Heath in his finery, she realized that her basic routine wouldn't cut it in the new job. She'd have to try harder. That wasn't comfortable, any more than it had felt natural earlier this week to give up their cozy condo in town and move into this faculty apartment. Moreland Hall was gorgeous, like something out of a fairy tale. Ivy-covered brick and stone, Gothic arches, ancient windows with panes of wavy glass. The apartment had a working fireplace, crown moldings, hardwood floors. But it didn't feel like home. How could it? It didn't belong to them; even the furniture wasn't theirs. Not to mention that the kitchen window looked directly onto the Quad. Anybody could look in and see her business. Life in a fishbowl. She hoped she could get used to it.

"Harper's getting dressed," Sarah said. "I'll take care of Scottie. Can you move the refreshments to the common room and start setting up?"

"Sure thing. And, babe, don't be afraid to do it up, okay? You look hot in fancy duds."

Heath grinned and winked at her, but Sarah couldn't help completing the thought in her mind. *Unlike the rest of the time, when you look like you just rolled out of bed.* But Heath hadn't said that, and didn't think it. That was Sarah's insecurity speaking.

It took fifteen minutes to clean Scottie up, coax him out of his pajamas and into some semblance of decent clothes. Five more minutes were spent swapping out Harper's Elsa costume (which was what she'd meant by party dress) for an actual dress. That left Sarah ten minutes to dress herself. She dug through boxes, but couldn't find her good fall clothes. She ended up throwing on a flowery sundress because it was the only pretty thing she could lay hands on, but topping it with a woolly cardigan against the September breeze. Not her most polished look, but it would have to do. She swiped on some bright lipstick, gathered the kids and the dog, and set out for the common room.

They were only a few minutes late, but when she got there, the room was empty, the tables and chairs were missing, and Heath was nowhere to be seen. She had a minor heart attack, until she caught the sound of Heath's rich laugh floating in through the open window, and looked out onto the Quad. Her husband stood on the lush, green lawn, surrounded by the missing furniture, and a gaggle of leggy, giggling girls.

"Hey, what are you doing out there?" Sarah called, laughter in her voice as she stuck her head out the window. With Heath, you could always expect the unexpected.

He turned, flashing a movie-star grin.

"Here's my lovely wife now. Girls, may I introduce your new co–dorm head, the amazing and brilliant Mrs. Sarah Donovan. Babe, come on out. It's a beautiful day, I thought, why not party on the Quad?"

Party on the Quad? Girls whooped and high-fived at that. Did Heath understand who he was dealing with? Sarah had some of these girls in her math classes in years past. They were the worst offenders, the delinquents, the old-school Moreland girls, accustomed to bad behavior and few repercussions. She'd have to sit Heath down and have a talk about setting an example.

Sarah led her children and the dog down the hall and out the front door of Moreland Hall. They stepped into the sunshine of the perfect September day. Harper ran to her daddy, who hoisted her up onto his hip. Max, their German-Shepherd mix, ran circles on the lawn, as Scottie chased after him, squealing. Music filtered out from a dorm room farther down the Quad. And those Moreland girls—the same ones who surfed the Web in her classroom and snarked behind her back—made a fuss over her, and said how much they liked her dress. She didn't buy the phony admiration. As they circled around her, long-legged and beautifully groomed, drawling away in their jaded voices, Sarah felt like they might eat her alive.